THE WISDOM OF PERVERSITY

Also by RAFAEL YGLESIAS

A Happy Marriage

Dr. Neruda's Cure for Evil

Fearless

The Murderer Next Door

Only Children

Hot Properties

The Game Player

The Work Is Innocent

Hide, Fox, and All After

The Wisdom of Perversity

A NOVEL BY

Rafael Yglesias

ALGONQUIN BOOKS OF CHAPEL HILL 2015

Published by
Algonquin Books of Chapel Hill
Post Office Box 2225
Chapel Hill, North Carolina 27515-2225

a division of
Workman Publishing
225 Varick Street
New York, New York 10014

Printed in the United States of America.
Published simultaneously in Canada by Thomas Allen & Son Limited.

LIBRARY OF CONGRESS CATALOGING-IN-PUBLICATION DATA
Yglesias, Rafael, [date]
The wisdom of perversity : a novel / by Rafael Yglesias.—First edition.
pages ; cm
ISBN 978-1-61620-384-9 (hardcover)
1. Child sexual abuse—Fiction. 2. Life change events—Fiction.
3. Friendship—Fiction. I. Title.
PS3575.G53W57 2015
813'.54—dc23 2014031971

10 9 8 7 6 5 4 3 2 1
First Edition

For Donna, who understands and heals

THE WISDOM OF PERVERSITY

No Thanks

—— November 2007 ——

BY NIGHTFALL ON Thanksgiving, Brian Moran was alone.

He had disposed of family obligations. At the Gotham Bar and Grill restaurant, he had treated his father to a midafternoon feast of squab and foie gras terrine, heirloom turkey with duck confit, sour-cherry stuffing, and potato puree cranberry compote. Dad had made fun of him for ordering butternut squash soup, no cream, as a starter and Greenmarket vegetables for his main course. When he passed on dessert, the old man pretended not to understand why spiced pumpkin cheesecake didn't qualify as vegan.

While walking home, he had called his late mother's sister in Santa Monica and promised Aunt Helen that he would see her when next he was summoned to LA, explaining for the one-millionth time that although he worked in the movie business he was hardly ever on the Left Coast.

Once safely alone in his apartment, following the advice of his shrink, he supplemented his daily dose of libido suppressor with a soupçon of Xanax, half a milligram, to help him endure this night of national gratitude.

Once the sun set on a family holiday, like a vampire Brian yearned to satisfy his appetite.

Logistically it was hard to be bad on Thanksgiving. Depraved young women had their own dull families to attend to. Having the urge at all was discouraging. Still, he had reason to congratulate himself. He had been a good boy for almost a year. Six months since he had even felt tempted. The pills had worked. Until tonight. Would they work again tomorrow? Would they avail throughout the holiday season? Something about Christmas decorations inspired delinquency.

What he craved was excitement. Instead he turned on the sedative of his fellow Americans—television.

First CNN. Unfortunately there were no genuine tragedies to take his mind off his own slow-moving pathos. No ex–football star cutting his wife's throat. No twin towers pancaking. No ostracized teenager assassinating his entire class.

Then MSNBC. The experts were very excited the election was only a year away. But they conceded there was little suspense about the primaries: it would be politically correct Hillary versus someone boring like Romney. Couldn't even hope for Edwards against McCain—Eros versus Thanatos. He despaired of the republic. Despite the disastrous Bush years, the Democrats would find a way to lose in '08.

How about a movie? He tuned to HBO.

That was when his luck truly ran out.

They had scheduled a film directed by Jeff Mark, made a mere fifteen years ago but already a holiday classic: *Home for Chanukah.* He had to give the schmuck credit: Jeffrey had made a Jewish holiday as American as apple pie.

He shut off the boob tube and moved to his computer to check on e-mails. He was tempted to rely on the Internet for a secondhand version of what he pined for. Sadly, his therapist had declared porno also to be taboo, a gateway to misbehaving in the flesh.

He reread the opening chapters of his favorite novel, *Great Expectations.* Dickens was always a comfort, a man who understood childhood was the ideal soft metal for the permanent engravings of evil.

Drowsy from the pills, he went early to bed. Prone in the dark, the miserable facts were clear: *My friendships are a sham, my only pleasure forbidden, my salvation to never, ever be myself.* Brian Moran did not give thanks. He decided that tomorrow he would stop taking his medication.

Five Seconds of Grace

— March 1966 —

BRIAN MORAN USED to be a shiny-cheeked boy of enthusiasms, imbued with inexhaustible energy to pursue them and a generous impulse to share their delights with his nearest and dearest. In turn, he was profoundly grateful to anyone who provided a new excitement.

In 1966, Brian was especially thankful for an invitation from his best friend, Jeffrey Mark. Jeff had asked Brian to accompany him on a visit to his cousin Richard Klein, who worked for NBC in Rockefeller Center. The forty-two-year-old Klein was a vice president of marketing, able to promise the two boys a private tour of the television and radio studios.

Klein met them in the lobby, introduced them to Joe the security guard, and rode with them up to the eigth floor. There a reception area was shielded by a glass wall whose transparency was interrupted by three huge letters—NBC—the *N* bright yellow, the *B* sky blue, the *C* bloodred. Behind it was a receptionist wearing a single earphone and talking into a tiny mike suspended in front of her lips—had this been the extent of the tour Brian would have returned home deeply impressed. Klein then led them down a staircase, through double metal doors emblazoned with a warning—NBC PERSONNEL ONLY—into a bare concrete hallway.

Klein ignored Jeff's repeated honks, "Where we going?" while they passed through a series of double doors below confounding signs—NO ACCESS; TALENT ONLY—finally crashing through a single door with an unilluminated red lightbulb suspended above the warning: DO NOT ENTER WHEN RED LIGHT IS ON. Klein held the forbidden door open for them to pass through. When they did, they discovered they were backstage in a television studio, facing a jumble of props. A swami's headdress, used in one of Johnny Carson's recurrent comedic pieces, immediately caught Brian's eye. "It's *The Tonight Show,*" he said, thrilled.

"Enjoy. I'll be back soon," said Klein, stepping back, letting go of the soundproofed door. It whooshed shut.

"This way, boys," someone called. They turned, amazed to see the rainbow-colored curtain of *The Tonight Show* being parted for them by a teenager with tight blond curls. He was wearing the uniform of an NBC page: red blazer with gold buttons, starched white shirt, navy blue tie, and neatly pressed gray trousers.

"Hi, Brian," said Sam the page as he passed through, lifting Brian's eyes into a grin of brilliant teeth. He had met this smiling teenager only once before, six days ago last Sunday, at the same time he had been introduced to Richard Klein. Brian had climbed the two flights from his apartment to Jeff's earlier that morning, his usual routine on a weekend. They were three hours into a marathon game of Monopoly when the NBC executive and the page poked their heads into Jeff's bedroom to say hello. Jeff presented Richard as "my famous cousin, the vice president of NBC."

"Famous," Klein repeated and chuckled. "I'm *a* vice president, not *the.*" He went on to introduce Sam as "my Little Brother."

After they left, Jeff had explained, "Sam's a Jewish orphan. Cousin Richard is his Big Brother. You know, like in those dumb public-service ads. But that's for Catholic boys. This is the same, only it's for Jewish kids who don't have fathers." Brian had asked what had happened to Sam's father. Jeff shrugged. Then he said, "For a Jew, Sam's very blond." Brian knew immediately Jeff had borrowed that observation from his mother,

Harriet. Whenever Jeff quoted her, he did an unconscious imitation of her voice, his nasal whine deepening to produce the rasp of her sarcasm. Harriet's singling out Sam's blondness for comment meant there was something about it worth mocking or criticizing, since she talked about others solely to belittle or excoriate. At the time, Brian had enjoyed puzzling over what was wrong with Sam's blondness. He liked mysteries because they promised solutions. The worst frustration of being a child—and sometimes it seemed to him childhood consisted entirely of frustration—was the profound mystery of grownup behavior.

But no mystery could distract from the awe he felt as he entered the studio stage and took the very steps that Johnny Carson walked five nights a week. Brian's entrance, of course, came unheralded. He was not greeted by the bellowing welcome of Ed McMahon, announcer and commercial pitchman, or the brassy flourishes of Skitch Henderson conducting *The Tonight Show* band, or cheered by a revved-up audience of out-of-towners. Although no one was there to see him, Brian looked down shyly, partly overcome by the expanse of empty seats pitched at him and partly to make sure that it was really his Hush Puppies striding onto hallowed ground. While staring at the stage floor, he noticed four small pieces of yellow tape laid down at unrelated angles. He knew from his father they must be Johnny's "marks" indicating where he should stand while delivering his opening monologue. Before he gave up acting full-time to take a teaching job at a specialty public high school for the performing arts, Brian's father, Danny Moran, had a lucrative one year stint as a philandering husband on the soap opera *General Hospital*. As a result, he never tired of explaining to his curious son how things were done on television.

"Wow," Jeff said as he arrived beside Brian. "Look." He pointed to the right.

Brian followed his friend's finger to a banal arrangement of furniture Brian thought of as a fabled kingdom. In true scale and color he saw what he had previously known only as pixels: Johnny's desk, an upholstered club chair for Johnny's guest, and a couch onto which the interviewees shifted after Johnny dismissed them.

"This is boss." Jeff ambled over to the green-carpeted area of the set. He climbed up a step that raised it a level above the surrounding stage floor. He scaled this height casually, as if he belonged. *But Jeff doesn't belong, Brian thought. No eight-year-old boy has the right to mount Johnny's set.*

Nevertheless Jeff invaded the sacred place with his awkward walk, fearlessly rambling about Johnny's desk, Johnny's swivel chair, and four potted plants arranged in front of a backdrop of a painted-on Manhattan skyline.

"Hey!" Sam shouted, waving at Jeff to get off.

"This is so boss." Jeff settled into the upholstered guest chair, nicknamed "the hot seat" by a giggling actress Brian and Jeff had seen on one of the thrilling nonschool nights they had been allowed to stay up well past Johnny's monologue.

Panicked now, Sam let go of the rainbow curtain and skimmed on the polished sea in his loafers to Johnny's island, stopping short of making landfall himself. "Jesus! Get up. Don't sit there."

"Why not?" Jeff complained in his most nasal, mewling infant tone.

"You're not allowed. Get up!"

Jeff honked at Brian. "Hey, Bri. Come over here. Sit in Johnny's chair. You be Johnny. I'll be the guest."

"No," Sam shouted. He pirouetted at Brian, red blazer twirling like an ice skater's skirt and ordered, "Stay there!"

Brian obeyed.

"Don't be a jerk," Jeff said to Sam. "No one's here."

Sam became a siren of panic: "Get up! Now! Right now!"

"Why?" Jeff complained. "You haven't given me a reason." It was Jeff's particular gift, which would serve him well throughout his life, to be able to challenge the limits people wanted to impose, and seemed particularly eager to impose on him, without provoking rancor. He had called Sam a jerk, ignored his warning, disobeyed his order, and now demanded an explanation, which Brian thought ought to have earned him a blow on the head or at least forcible ejection from the hot seat, both of which broad-shouldered Sam could easily accomplish. Instead the page's knees buckled, palms flush in prayer. He pleaded, "Please . . . before somebody sees. Please get up."

"Don't be such a scaredy-cat," Jeff said, dismissing him with the back of his hand. "Cousin Richard said we were allowed."

As far as Brian knew, Klein had said nothing about what they were permitted to do. Sam, however, was desperate to believe: "Dick really said you could sit on the set?"

Jeff nodded confidently, a quiet assertion that convinced Brian his best friend must be lying: if he really had permission he would have shouted it.

Sam buttoned his blazer, straightened his tie. "Okay," he conceded. "But if somebody comes in, you'd better get up. Dick's not the president of NBC."

"Come on, Bri!" Jeff called. "Get in Johnny's chair and interview me."

Brian nevertheless checked with Sam for permission. The page nodded in resignation. "I'll watch the door. Just don't touch anything." He punched the curtain to make an opening and disappeared behind its quivering colors.

"Hurry up!" Jeff ordered. "You pretend to be Carson. I'll pretend I'm Don Rickles. 'Get over here, you hockey puck! What am I, chopped liver?'" Jeff paused in his imitation of the rude comic to gag with laughter and self-applause. Rickles's insults were delightful to Jeff and Brian because they sounded obscene even when they weren't. Was "puck" really "fuck"? "Hockey puck" really "stupid fuck"? They couldn't be sure. Why would Carson tolerate, even in jest, being called a stupid fuck? Yet it required no imaginative leap to assume obscenities from the hideous Rickles. He was a gargoyle: nearly bald bullet head, squashed peasant nose, tiny vicious eyes of a foraging rodent. Certainly that was the thrill of Rickles as a guest. While spitting invectives, he swiveled his no-neck fleshy head from Johnny to Ed, occasionally including the audience as his target, who seemed to adore him anyway. Most tantalizing of all to the boys, Rickles perpetually flirted with the ultimate taboo—saying a swear word on television.

"Look at this," Jeff said, back in character as Rickles, mocking Brian for standing indecisively beside Johnny's chair. "Look at the goy trying to sit. What's the matter? Scared the Jew left germs? What a hockey puck!" Jeff doubled over, choked with laughter of self-appreciation.

Accepting Jeff's casting, Brian sat in Johnny's chair, imitated the master's long-suffering smile, and delivered a Carson put-down: "It's always a joy, a real thrill, when they let you out for the week, Don. What are Sunnydale's hours these days?"

Jeff stopped laughing. "That's wrong," he scolded. "That's not what Johnny would say."

Normally Brian would have been stung by this criticism, but he was overcome by the bliss of floating on Johnny's chair. Although he had released his full weight on it, Brian hadn't sunk at all. He was borne aloft, a king on a throne. And there was more treasure for Brian to discover while seated behind Johnny's desk: he spied a shelf, built where normally there would be a drawer, shielded from the prying eyes of the camera and studio audience.

Meanwhile Jeff was correcting him. "Right? How do they know Sunnydale is a nuthouse unless you say it? You have to say 'What are the funny farm's hours these days?'"

Brian pointed at Johnny's desk, widening his eyes, an urgent pantomime of alarm. Here was the proof eight-year-old boys shouldn't be allowed on Johnny's set: he had uncovered a whopping grown-up secret, the hiding place of a star.

"What?" Jeff said. He didn't rise from the hot seat and come around to see for himself. "What are you pointing to?"

"Hurry up and look," Brian whispered.

"What is it!" Jeff jumped up and stepped away from the desk, distancing himself from whatever grisly object Brian had found.

Brian insisted: "Just look."

Jeff asked plaintively, "Is it a spider?" He had a squealing fear of spiders, odd for a New York City boy. Although cockroaches were plentiful, spiders were almost unknown.

"No!" Brian shouted. "Look!"

"Jesus, lower your voice," Jeff complained. He lurched forward, then hesitated by the corner of Johnny's desk. "You sure it's not a spider?"

"It's a secret shelf," Brian resorted to a stage whisper. "Look." Brian pushed his chair away to make room.

Jeff kneeled, peering into the hiding place. Brian leaned in. Together they inspected its shadows. They discovered two precious items: a coffee mug and a glass ashtray. Jeff reached into the darkness—"No," Brian objected—and drew a royal blue cup into the light. "Put it back," Brian pleaded.

Jeff dipped his nose into its cylinder and sniffed.

"Put it back," Brian repeated.

"Here," Jeff thrust it at him. "Smells funny." Brian reluctantly accepted the mug. Jeff took out the ashtray. "He smokes?" he asked the empty seats. "I've never seen him smoke." He bumped Brian's shoulder. "You ever see him smoke?"

Holding Johnny's mug had entranced Brian. He understood this was trespass, sitting in Johnny's chair, fingers curled about Johnny's cup, and yet he felt at home. Briefly the child Brian had an hors d'oeuvre of the paradox that would become the main course of his adult life: how could he feel at once so comfortable and so out of place?

"I've never seen him smoke," Jeff declared. He returned to the hot seat, cradled the heavy glass ashtray between his legs, and stared pensively at a prism of colors dancing across its surface. "He can't use this. We'd see the smoke." He sat up, inspired. "What's that smell of?" Jeff nodded at Johnny's mug.

Brian put the mug down. He gripped the desk's edge, braced as if the odor might blast him, then bent over the cup's empty well. He paused to glance at Jeff and wink mischievously (as Johnny would, to involve his audience) before taking an elaborate whiff. "Milk?" Brian joked.

"Cut it out! Is it booze?"

Brian didn't think he had ever heard Jeff, or anyone in real life, say "booze." It was the kind of word Jimmy Olsen might say on *Superman*, or a gangster on *The Untouchables*. Jeff was right, though—must be booze. Otherwise, why hide the cup? Brian cleared the air several times with his hands and gradually lowered his nostrils over the mug. Brian inhaled noisily, nodded in solemn deliberation, and delivered another punch line: "Yoo-hoo?"

"Cut it out," Jeff said. "Smell it." Jeff folded over until his head rested on his knees. "This is serious! We have to figure it out!"

Perhaps this was why they had become best friends: no matter how shallow, unreflective, and thoughtless Jeff could be about the great issues (for example, whether Roger Maris had broken Ruth's single-season home-run record fair and square), Jeff had an insistent desire to unscrew the back panel of the adult world and inspect its works. They had that in common: an impatient, humorless need to know. Jeff was right to scold him. Brian knew he should take this question seriously. Brian dipped his nose below the mug's lip, shutting his eyes to concentrate.

He smelled . . . soap.

"Brian," Jeff called.

To maintain peak concentration, he kept his eyes shut. "It doesn't smell of any booze. It smells like they washed it."

"Brian," Jeff said urgently.

"Brian!" came a different voice, an authoritative bass belonging to Richard Klein, NBC vice president. "Put Johnny's mug down!"

Brian's heart exploded. That was the sensation: a terrible thump in his chest, followed by a ghastly feeling that all of his blood was leaking into his Hush Puppies. He shoved himself clear of the desk. Johnny's mug spun from the force of his release, its base emitting ominous notes.

Jeff jumped out of the hot seat and with flailing arms leapt off the carpeted island onto the black sea, a terrified passenger abandoning ship. In a flash, Jeff managed to appear to have had nothing to do with the violation of Johnny's set, while Brian was caught red-handed in the sacred chair, Johnny's royal blue mug spinning on the desk.

"Brian, get the fuck out of Johnny's chair!" Richard Klein bellowed, red-faced.

Other than his important job title, Brian knew little about Klein. When Klein and Sam had popped into Jeff's room last Sunday to say hello, he had impressed Brian, in dress and speech, as quite different from Jeff's slovenly dad or Brian's garrulous father. Klein wore a gray pin-striped suit enlivened by a maroon tie and he smelled of Old Spice, an aftershave familiar to Brian because his father doused himself with it on very special occasions, like when he took Mom out for her birthday. It usually tickled his nose. At one point Klein had leaned close to Brian to peer at the Monopoly board. One whiff of him had provoked Brian into a series of violent ah-choos. "You're allergic to adults," Klein had joked, patting Brian's helmet of very straight black hair. Richard Klein had also impressed him with the self-confident way he smiled indulgently at the awed questions Brian had asked about his glamorous job. He had also made clever fun of Harriet's hypochondria. Jeff's mother spent most of her waking hours in bed with a heating pad that she shifted restlessly, always with a groan and a sigh, the location of her complaint moving from lumbar to forehead to kneecap, a general invalidism that prevented her from cleaning, shopping, or cooking. "Have to get back to your mother's hospital bed," he had kidded as he left. He seemed a master of self-control, nothing like the easily upset adults of Brian's experience. So this new side of Klein, red-faced, spewing obscenities, made it clear to Brian that he was in big, big trouble.

Brian's essential shyness, his reflexive reluctance to announce his desires, to demand his due, was trumped by a keen sense of what is just and what is unjust, in particular when someone attempted to apply justice to him. He got to his feet and declared the truth, "It was Jeff's idea!" Unfortunately for his righteous cause, the energy of his rising out of Johnny's magic chair caused it to recoil rapidly and whack hard into the base of a tall potted fern.

The large planter wobbled violently. They all watched as the wobbling worsened, tipping more and more precariously, until it seemed inevitable that a collapse onto the painted Manhattan skyline would result. Brian glanced at Klein and Sam. Both were paralyzed with horror. Brian saw the future with oracular clarity: a toppled fern destroying the set would transform embarrassment into disaster.

He leapt at the potted plant without regard to his body's preservation. His chin smacked painfully into the brick-colored pot, but he remained fixed on his goal, flinging his arms around the moist planter. Its circumference was too great for him to encompass and too heavy for him to prevent from tipping over—except by pulling it onto himself. The ceramic planter fell against his neck and shoulder; wet soil spilled down the collar of his one and only white dress shirt, especially ironed by his mother for today's grand occasion.

"Help," he groaned, squeezed by the planter's weight. He had forestalled the destruction of the set, but the fern was still in jeopardy and so was Brian. The pot continued to slide farther onto him, dirt spilling at a faster rate.

Sam righted the planter. Brian rolled onto his back and sighed. Only then did he feel the ooze of slimy soil settling into the canal of his spine, sliding toward an embarrassing crack in his bedrock.

"Get up!" Klein yanked him to his feet. "Jesus Christ, look what you did!"

Brian reached around with his left hand, halting the descent of the damp soil at the small of his back, aware his clean shirt must be ruined. "I know," a miserable Brian conceded.

Klein pointed at the green carpet. "You stained Johnny's rug."

Now Brian saw his saturated shirt had left a brown smudge. Horrified, he dropped to his knees, trying to soak up the moist residue with the palms of his hands, mumbling, "I'm sorry, I'm sorry . . ."

"Cut that out. You're making it worse." Klein tugged him off the set onto the bare stage. He let go to fish out a silver money clip from his pocket, peel off a twenty-dollar bill—a wonderfully large sum to Brian—and handed it to Sam. "Go to building services. Ask for Fred. Give him this to clean it up. Pronto. Before Props sees it." He leaned close to Sam. "Don't say the boys were in here. Got it? Say you knocked it over. I'll protect you. Understood?"

Sam nodded solemnly.

Klein said, "Move it," to Jeff and retook Brian's hand to pull him clear of the scene. Fast. The rainbow curtain and the shadows of backstage went by in a blur of shame. They burst through the metal door into the fluorescent hallway, decorated by warnings that now seemed to have been well thought out. A mortified Brian concurred wholeheartedly with the wisdom of the signs—AUTHORIZED ENTRY ONLY; NBC EMPLOYEES ONLY—and especially with that vaguest yet most profound distinction of all—TALENT ONLY. Brian agreed he should have been kept out.

Richard turned a corner into what looked to Brian like a submarine: a narrow, windowless gunmetal hall lined with doors, each fitted with a glass porthole. He hopped on tippy toe to peek into them as they rushed past the rooms. He was able to see only a blur of sleek electronic equipment.

"Hey, Dick," a fat man in a T-shirt called from the open door of a room they whooshed by. "Who you got with you? New VPs of programming?" His laughter followed them around a corner.

Jeff stopped dead in his tracks.

Klein poked him in the back. "Keep moving."

"What's that?" Jeff barked.

Brian looked at what his best friend had spotted. Behind a plate-glass wall there was a nearly empty white room: no chairs or desk, only a single machine rising from the floor, like Manhattan bedrock erupting through the building.

"That's Grace," Richard said. He put the flat of his right palm on Jeff's skull and urged him forward. "Keep moving."

Jeff allowed his head to flop forward, but the rest of his body did not move. His head snapped back. "What's Grace?"

"Keep moving and I'll tell you." Klein pushed Jeff's skull again.

Jeff planted his feet. "What's it do?"

Brian moved beside Jeff to study this marvel. Tiny yellow, red, and white lights flashed throughout the breadth of the mechanism; switches flipped up and down, recording tape snaked through heads—a miniature world of ceaseless activity.

"Grace is on all the time. She checks every word spoken live over the air. Now move it." With a stiffened index finger he poked Jeff hard in the back.

Jeff stumbled forward two steps, then dug in his heels. "Checks for what?"

"I'll tell you later." Klein poked him again, even harder. "Move it."

Jeff did a one eighty, asking as he turned, "Checks what?" He braked by splaying his feet, wedging them against the wall as he faced Klein.

"To catch curse words," Klein snapped. "All words go through Grace. There's a five-second delay between what someone says in the studios and its going out over the air. Grace can recognize in five seconds whether someone has said a bad word. If they have, she covers it with a noise. We call it a 'bleep.'"

"Wow," Brian whispered, gazing at the marvel with loving admiration.

"What curse words?" Jeff persisted.

Richard snapped, "Don't be a wisenheimer, Jeff. Keep moving."

"Which ones? *All* the bad words?"

"Okay, you want to hear me say bad words. Fine. Move your ass, and when I get to my office I'll tell you all the naughty words that Grace knows."

Jeff grinned, turned on his heels smartly, and they were on the move again. Brian was sorry to leave Grace and sorrier still, thinking of the moist soil welled in the small of his back, that he couldn't bleep his own mistakes.

Klein led them down a flight of metal stairs, feet clattering, onto a featureless landing beneath painted red letters: 8TH FLOOR. There they passed into yet another universe, this a hushed world of gray carpet and tall oak doors, all shut. Richard steered for one that was discreetly labeled MEN in raised black letters. He pushed it open, propelled Brian ahead of him into a bathroom designed for one, and called back to Jeff, "Wait right here. Don't move. Got that?" Klein followed Brian into the men's room and shut the door. Jeff heard it lock.

Standing alone in the hallway it made Jeff very nervous how long Brian and Richard were inside the men's room. He hopped from one foot to the other to calm himself, a lucky choice since a secretary who passed didn't ask why he was waiting outside the bathroom. "Someone in there?" she announced her assumption as she walked by. He put his thumb into his mouth to comfort himself.

And for Brian, his time in the men's room with Richard Klein lasted far longer than the quarter hour that actually elapsed. No matter how many years passed, those minutes remained ineluctable to Brian's heart and mind. No matter how often he tried, with this drug or that therapy, with whatever philosophy of understanding, spiritual or vulgar, for Brian their time together lasted forever.

At first, standing in the cramped space between sink and toilet, comforted by the familiar cloud of Old Spice emanating from the adult male, the world he knew remained. He was a boy, a messy, embarrassed boy, and Klein was a powerful, protective grown-up. The task of cleaning himself was all that mattered, and Klein's help was welcome.

Klein gathered the back of Brian's shirt around the lump of muddy soil to prevent it from spilling. He told Brian to take it off. Eager to rectify all his mistakes, Brian hurried, fumbling with the buttons, then sliding his arms free.

Klein dumped the soil into the toilet. He turned on the cold water, ran it over the muddy stain, finally lifting the shirt up to the mirror's lights for examination. He sighed. "You need a new shirt."

Brian thought of his mother's profound distress at anything that had been spoiled, especially something expensive. Klein caressed the boy's worried cheek. "I'll buy you a new one." He turned Brian around to peer at his nude back, smeared by soil. "Let's get you clean." Klein tugged at the roll of toilet paper until he had a wad. He moistened it and wiped the base of Brian's spine. The wet paper felt cold. Brian arched forward, grabbing the slippery edge of the sink. "You're ticklish, aren't you?" Klein whispered in his ear.

Brian nodded. He looked at himself in the mirror and that was all he saw—Brian waiting to be clean. Klein's husky voice whispered, "Let's check your underpants."

Puzzled, Brian looked for Klein in the glass, but he was out of range. Then he felt the adult's hot fingers touch bare skin, infiltrating under the elastic band of his Jockeys, and the boy in the mirror was gone.

No Smoking

— February 2008 —

JULIE WATCHED HER husband bend a stick of spearmint Trident to fit into the greedy cavity of his mouth. There it joined a sickly green wad that had been expanding for the past hour with regular additions while Gary alternated furious chewing with sips of his morning coffee. The combination of Zabar's house blend and spearmint must be disgusting, she thought; probably caffeine was intensifying his longing for a cigarette. Why didn't he take her advice and switch to chamomile tea? Both knees were pumping with anxious energy, shaking the table and making his inflated stomach undulate like a water bed. Gross. And she was gross to think her husband gross. How dare she feel revulsion for the man she loved?

The sound track of his gum smacking intensified the anxiety she felt listening to Gary's interrogation of their fifteen-year-old son Zack. The grown-up sounded like a manic adolescent himself, "Smack, smack—so, Zack—smack, smack—are you going to run for Student—smack, smack—Council?" How was Gary going to remain smoke-free until today's acupuncture treatment? She saw him take a morning dose of Wellbutrin; he was practically crawling out of his skin anyway. Imagine what he would be like without medication!

And what was that smell? If Gary hadn't had a cigarette for three weeks, what was that musty odor hovering over the table? No one at last night's dinner smoked. No one they knew still smoked. It was the peer pressure of all middle-class white males becoming nonsmokers that had finally provoked the morbidly competitive Gary into quitting. But had he? Was he perverse enough to try to fool her? She hadn't bugged him about his smoking, loathsome though she found the habit, and in spite of her distress at the thought of Zack's losing his father, especially while they were so intensely irritated by each other. Maybe that was the explanation: Gary was hiding his failure from his disappointing son?

She sniffed him discreetly while she cleared his empty plate. The dish was squeaky clean of its tower of pancakes and fan of bacon, as if it had been run through the dishwasher on the Pot Scrubber setting. Had Gary lapped it like a dog?

She saw with painful clarity how her husband must appear to their teenage son, a masticating hog spewing hostile questions: "Why aren't you joining the school paper? Why aren't you on the debate team? Why aren't you running for class president?" *Why are you less than I was at your age?*

Her boy was lovely: thick chestnut hair, soulful hazel eyes, pink lips that had never tasted corruption. And his heart was pure. She had ample proof, from how as a toddler he had shared toys in the cutthroat sandboxes of Riverside Park to the continuing inclusion into his set (the cool high school kids) of nerdy boys like Richard Bernstein, and overweight but smart girls like Hilary Gordon. How dare Gary feel unsatisfied because Zack's PSAT score fell short of the ninety-ninth percentile? So what if he got B's, not A's? Her boy was goodness personified.

Zack interrupted his father's barrage. "So what's next week's column, Dad?" That was a low blow from her angel. Zack knew next week's column was always the rub, the Sisyphus deadline. No sooner had Gary met Friday's demand for eight hundred words on the legal issue of the week than anxiety over the next topic roiled his sleep. "I'm a lawyer, not a writer," he complained as each deadline approached, forgetting that before O. J.

Simpson's trial had triggered a craze in the media to cover lurid criminal trials Gary had maintained all good lawyers were skillful writers. "The great American novel is probably a brief on file in the federal courthouse" was the lead of his debut column in *Manhattan Mag,* and it became the quotidian quote cited on *American Justice,* the cable TV show that had Gary under contract to appear regularly as a legal expert. But his celebrity was accompanied by a punishment: tense waits in the no-smoking greenroom. Before he quit, Gary confessed to her he'd broken that law, sometimes sneaking a cigarette in the bathroom, locked in a stall, exhaling at the bowl as if the smoke could be flushed away. So if he had slipped again, why wouldn't he confess it to her? She had never scolded him, especially not for his sloppy personal habits.

Zack smirked at his father's panicked stare. "Well, Dad?" he said, tone prodding. "No ideas yet? How about a new angle on JonBenét? People never get tired of that case, right?"

Gary smacked and popped his gum, twitching legs rumbling the table while his eyes roved, on the lookout for another stack of pancakes. "That's true," he answered. "But I'll probably write about something new. Maybe this." He tapped a color photograph on the front page of the *Times:* a balding middle-aged man being led away in handcuffs down the broad steps of an office building. Beside it were three black-and-white 1980s vintage yearbook photos: two were of light-skinned black preteens; the other a gap-toothed white kid with a slicked up tower of blond hair. "Maybe this Huck Finn Days case."

"That's about sex, isn't it? Weren't those boys fucked up the ass?"

"Zack!" Julie reproved him.

"What, Mom? They claim they were raped, right?"

Gary thumped the table. "No! That is, we don't know. Thanks to the tabloids and the web, this case has been hopelessly distorted. It's gone viral that two of the boys were sodomized. But in fact we don't know what the accusers said beyond the umbrella term 'molested.' And since it all happened more than ten years ago, there's no forensics." Gary chewed thoughtfully before elaborating. "According to my source in the DA's office, these are pretty questionable witnesses. Two are addicts; the other has been hospitalized for depression. You know with these cases there's always the danger of a *Children's Hour* scenario, a possible witch hunt."

"So the issue isn't little boys getting screwed, it's overzealous prosecution?" Zack made a contemptuous buzz with his lips. "That's a little boring. Isn't sodomy hotter than perjury?"

"Zack, please," Julie said.

"What?" Zack pretended not to know why she had complained.

"Exactly, sodomy is hotter," his father said, pleased Zack was taking him on—much better than indifference. "But the luridness is what makes these accusations so dangerous. Huck Finn was a terrific charity for underprivileged kids, everybody agrees it's great, and it's about to be shut down because of Internet chatter. It's trial by blog." Gary clapped. "That's it! That's my lead."

"Oh no," Zack bowed his head, clutched and tugged hard at the drapery of his locks. "Don't fall for that bullshit," he moaned.

"What bullshit?"

"That the Internet has changed everything," Zack said, sneered.

"Honey, stop pulling on your hair." Julie reached to stop him. Zack ducked away but at least sat up straight and stopped tearing at his hair.

"Of course it's changed things." Gary goggled at his son. "Don't you, of all people, think that blogs, Facebook, YouTube, this new thing Twitter, has transformed how we get information?"

"It's *changed* how we get information," said the teenager. "It hasn't transformed anything."

"You're wrong," his father declared. "One way it's transformed legal cases is that the alleged molester, Sam Rydel, and his defense team are too focused on PR. They keep trying to debunk these bloggers, which makes their accusations go viral, when they should just shut up. Force the prosecution to prove its case."

"But doesn't this Rydel guy have a big reputation to defend? He's a big honcho at Huck Finn and he owns some kind of university . . ."

"Not a real university." Gary's voice was steeped in the contempt he felt whenever anyone got a fact wrong, his dismissive tone implying they would never recover their credibility with him. "It's a so-called broadcasting academy, claiming to teach technical jobs in TV and radio. Their students are poor, mostly minorities, who are set up with federal school loans to pay for these basically worthless degrees."

"How do you know they're worthless?" Zack said. "'Cause it isn't Harvard?"

"No. I know because I check my facts before I make an assertion. Less than ten percent of the academy's graduates get jobs in radio or TV, and they're saddled with loans that either they or we—the taxpayers—end up paying. This semi-scam has made Sam Rydel a fortune. He's worth something like thirty million. That's the real scandal. But nobody's covering that. Instead the media is obsessed with whether or not Rydel had sex with boys. Anyway, my point is that although Rydel has a perfect right to answer the bloggers, don't misunderstand me on that score—"

"Score?" Zack interrupted. He winked at his mother. "Who's keeping score? Oh, it's you, right, Dad? You're the scorekeeper in chief."

Zack was pressing his luck, Julie thought, though she was sympathetic to his plight. Something ought to be done to silence Gary's nagging of Zack because the son didn't share his father's strengths (or his weaknesses, she might one day be forced to point out) and wasn't interested in winning the same battles (or suffering the same defeats, she might one day need to remind her husband). Still, she felt he was pressing his luck. To pacify Zack, she patted his forearm.

"Okay, smart-ass." Gary tilted back in his chair, chewing double-time. "You asked about my next column. Why ask if you don't give a fuck about the answer?"

"Gary, please . . ." Julie said.

"What? He can make fun of me and my work and I've got to fucking like it?"

"Your language. We shouldn't be cursing each other over breakfast."

Gary stood up. His shirt was a size too small. His breasts appeared to be almost as large as hers, at least a B cup. She looked away. "He's fifteen! You think he doesn't know them?" Gary spat them at Zack: "Shit. Fuck. Cock. Cunt. Asshole. Motherfucker. Anything you haven't heard before?"

Zack's grin became a wince. "No."

"Then we're clear on that *score*! Thanks for breakfast," he tossed at Julie, storming off in the direction of his study.

Her son lowered his head, hair shading pain. "Zack," she called into the cave of his unhappiness. Her boy meant well. Sure, he had provoked Gary, but look at him blinking back humiliation, full of regret. "Zack, you know what? You know what the problem is?"

"What?" he mumbled.

"Your father is very proud of you. That's the problem."

Zack straightened, pushing back his hair, exposing a high brow as impressive as his father's. Big Brain, she had nicknamed the skinny twenty-four-year-old Gary when they first met, for his shining forehead and the intensity of his debating skills. Zack didn't have his father's energy. He was dreamy and contemplative. *Like me*. "What are you talking about, Mom?"

"That's why he's so hard on you. He's as proud of you as he is of himself so he isn't careful about your feelings—because he thinks they're his feelings." She wasn't sure she had made sense. "Do you know what I mean?"

"Yeah, you mean he doesn't have any idea who I am." Zack noisily shoved his chair away from the table, the legs gouging her sanded, stained oak floorboards. She didn't waste a complaint; the battle to maintain her floor's purity had been lost a decade ago. When declaiming to dinner guests Gary liked to tip back in his chair, each oration leaving its scar in wood. Julie had tried to protect it by putting a rug under the table, but after a week she had to remove it. During a dinner party to impress new contacts in the world of talk television, Gary had leaned back to make a point in grand style about the three knocks Kato Kaelin heard on his air-conditioner; his chair legs slid on the rug and Gary toppled backward onto his ass. Luckily, although his head whacked hard on the floor, he came away with no worse than a small lump. The amazing part was that Gary resumed his oration case while being helped off the floor, passively lifted like a statue in the fallen chair, all the while not missing a beat. "Your husband has amazing concentration," the CNN legal reporter commented to Julie. Julie was thinking, *He's become a monster.*

"Zack—" she tried to delay her son.

"I've got rehearsal," he said, meaning Trinity High School's production of *Romeo and Juliet;* much to her delight he had landed the part of Romeo, a compliment to him, since he wasn't a senior and leads were supposed to be reserved for them. (Gary hadn't approved. "With your grades? Taking all that time away from studying? That smart? I mean, you're not going to be the next George Clooney.") Zack left for his bedroom, presumably to fetch his school backpack. She was alone with the breakfast plates. She had cooked and now before going to her job she was supposed to clean up. Yeah, she sure was living in a feminist paradise.

She gathered silverware and plates, put them in the sink, returning to fetch coffee mugs, butter dish, maple syrup jar. It was an effort to leave the kitchen a mess even briefly, but doing nothing to clean up the quarrel between father and son was even more unbearable. Teeth clenched, she forced herself to not immediately load the dishwasher. She couldn't allow yet another ugly outburst to pass without comment.

Julie's determination hiccupped as she reached the shut door to Gary's study. Here her prized floorboards were striped with white gouges from Zack's preteen love affair with roller blades. Gary had managed to belittle that interest and eventually discourage it through shaming and indifference, rarely indulging Zack with excursions to Riverside Park and only then with sufficient grumpiness and belittling observations to forestall new requests. *I love my family,* Julie chanted silently for courage. *I love my men and I want them to love each other.*

She knocked.

"What!" Gary barked.

She stepped into his lair. Gary was in an unusual pose, perched on the windowsill, staring out at the restless Hudson River. No cigarette smell, but he had the window open as far as it could go. The February air was raw; goose bumps tickled her bare arms. She longed to return to the kitchen, to the satisfaction of cleaning.

"What?" Gary demanded, still facing away. Julie shut the door behind her to be certain Zack wouldn't overhear. "What. Is. It." Gary telegraphed irritation, continuing to give her his back.

Her throat constricted. She was frightened to ask her husband to show their child love. "I'm scared." It was the whole truth.

Gary immediately shut the window. He hurried over to her, wearing a worried frown and a searching gaze. "What is it, sweetie?" Abruptly he was a loving puppy, placing both paws on her shoulders, facing her nose to nose with affectionate curiosity. He had been patient and sweet like that when her mother died soon after they had begun dating, holding her week after week while she cried and moped and never really explained her grief, never confessed to Gary that losing her mother felt as if all hope of improving herself was also gone.

"I'm . . . I'm worried . . ." she stammered her way into what she wanted to say, "about Zack."

"So am I." Gary puffed up, ready to speechify.

She raised a hand to stop him. "I mean: I'm worried about *you* and Zack."

"Oh." He rolled his eyes. "You're worried about *me* and Zack." He turned away to fetch a stick of Trident from a towering stack on his desk. That reawakened her suspicion he had been cheating. Why else would he be sitting at an open window in winter, contemplating a view he'd seen daily for nineteen years? It wasn't plausible that the anxious, efficient Gary would be meditative. As if to prove that point, he restlessly pulled a wrapper off the gum, fed a stick to his maw, and chewed, glaring at her defiantly.

"Honey," she said, anxious to calm him, "I'm not criticizing you. I don't think you realize how much you mean to Zack. He worships you." The instant she spoke that overwrought sentence she regretted it. The hyperbole was obvious and would offend.

"Really?" Gary's jaw ceased working angrily, his face relaxing into delight.

Forward, then, into shameless flattery: "Of course. You're brilliant and so successful. Think how hard it must be to have a father like you. How can he ever hope to be your equal?"

Gary was mesmerized by her bait—for a split second. Then he frowned. "No. He's like every teenage son in the history of the world. He thinks his father is an asshole. And you know what? He's right. For wasting my time trying to get him to like me, I'm a gigantic asshole."

"He doesn't think you're an asshole. He's intimidated by you," Julie argued, although she was relieved Gary hadn't been fooled. "You're perfect and he's not—"

"I'm not perfect," Gary snapped, and winced at having to make this concession.

"To him you're perfect. Everything he has trouble with, you do perfectly." She meant that. Gary's facility with language, formidable debating skills, and the blunt confident way he presented himself to the world must loom as unassailable mountains to Zack.

Gary's mouth twisted skeptically, but he nodded.

She pressed her advantage. "And every time you criticize him it makes Zack feel he'll never measure up."

"What are you talking about? I have to criticize him."

"Why?" Julie shot back.

He goggled at her. "Why!"

"Why?" she insisted.

Gary sneered. "Because you won't."

She decided to ignore that provocation. In his work it was routine for Gary to react to any dispute with attack. "His teachers criticize him. His friends criticize him. The world is ready to find fault night and day. He doesn't need more of it from us."

"What do you want from me?" Gary's angry front abruptly collapsed. His nose and mouth scrunched together and he moaned piteously, "What do you want from me? I can't watch every fucking word I say! This is my home." Tears welled. Tears! When had she last seen tears in her husband's eyes? "This is my family. Can't I relax with my own family?" He turned away to lean on his desk, a hand inadvertently toppling the stack of gum. "I can't take this," he whispered. "I'm falling apart."

Moved by his confession of turmoil, she put a hand on his bowed back. This part of him rippled with muscles. They were formed in his youth, lugging a backpack laden with thick, sharp-edged tomes up and down Cathedral Parkway to Columbia Law School. She pitied him and whispered, "Of course you can be yourself with Zack."

Voice warbling, he mumbled, "I can't."

"Sure you can," she soothed. She felt tenderness for him, reminded that behind the pomp of his debates lurked an easily discouraged boy. Gary's desire to succeed in his dealings with Zack was so profound he dreaded failure as a father with the same intensity he feared losing a case.

"I can't quit smoking like this," he whined. "I just can't." He collapsed in his swivel chair. Its cushion gasped. "How can I quit with this Sturm und Drang going on all the time? I've talked about it with my smoking coach. He says until I'm past the first six months I have to reduce stress. So I'm not gonna get involved anymore. I'll just tell Zack everything he does is brilliant. Okay? He won't feel criticized and I won't smoke. That satisfy you?"

Long ago Julie had accepted the truth about her husband's character, that it took a massive effort for Gary to think about anyone but himself; nevertheless she was shocked to rediscover his self-centeredness. It was unforgivable. *This man is too selfish to love.* "Yes." She hissed the word. "That'll satisfy me." She slammed the door on her way out.

Back in the kitchen she put on yellow rubber gloves, jerked the dishwasher open, turned the hot water on full blast, rinsing and scrubbing the breakfast residue off the plates before loading them. Gary often mocked her for that meticulousness, saying, "You're washing the dishes twice," but it really was harder to get off encrusted food after the dishwasher failed to live up to its name. She was attacking the frying pan with Bar Keepers Friend when she heard Zack's heavy tread in his black rubber-soled shoes. "Bye, Mom," he called from the hall as he tramped out of the apartment.

She wouldn't see him for hours. What was their last exchange? Something angry. Not their true feelings for each other. She pulled off the soapy gloves and dumped them in the sink, then hurried to the foyer, arriving as the front door banged shut. She pursued him into the building's hallway, catching him at the elevator.

Zack was alarmed by her approach. "What is it, Mom?" he asked as she embraced him, her right hand clutching his thick, abundant hair.

"Have a good rehearsal," she whispered into his ear, then stepped back with a flourishing release of her long arms, an admirable willingness, she felt, to share her treasure with the world.

Zack, flustered, nodded. "Sure, Mom. Thanks." The elevator arrived. He stepped in gratefully.

"I love you," she called.

"Love you," he mumbled, eyes down. "Bye." He jabbed the Close Door button.

In the kitchen, beyond the range of Gary's arrows, she finished scrubbing the All-Clad, cheered by the task's righteousness. She dried the silver pan to gleaming, returned it to the cabinet, used the dish towel to wipe down the stainless-steel sink, pleased by the way the morning sun shimmered on its surface. She draped the washcloth over the faucet to dry, used a broom to sweep up the five crumbs she spied on the black-and-white tile floor. The kitchen was spotless, the dishwasher purring. She moistened a paper towel and left to wipe the dining room table. It was when she lifted the newspaper that she first saw the photograph of the man accused in the Huck Finn Days sex abuse case.

They still subscribed to the paper version of the *New York Times* although only Julie read it. Gary compulsively checked the news every five minutes on his iPhone or MacBook, had read everything he cared about at least twelve hours before the printed version arrived. Zack never read what Julie thought of as the "real paper" and laughed at her for, as he put it, "always being a day late." Still, in the vain hope they might someday rejoin her in the pleasures of reading the news over breakfast, she brought in the paper every morning and became accustomed to only her interests being ruffled: the Science, Arts, Style, and Home sections. The untouched A section would survive for an unloved twenty-fours on the coffee table until it met its fate in the recycling bin the next day. As she picked up this morning's *Times* she took a second look at the face on the front page. That was when she recognized him.

The evaluating eyes were unmistakable. Sam the NBC page's tight blond curls were gone, replaced by a bald peak and a closely cut, almost shaved laurel of gray hair but seeing those heartless eyes up-close, the settled middle-aged face began to resemble the teenager's handsome angular features, and finally the name, Sam Rydel, at last resonated. This past week, when Gary talked about the case, she idly thought it reminded her of a character in a novel, not someone from her past. But Sam was definitely his first name, and although she wouldn't have been able to come up with it on her own, now that she saw it in print she remembered that Sam the page's last name was Rydel. *It's him.* Incredible. There he was, all grown up, doing to disadvantaged boys what had been . . .

But she didn't know for certain. And she respected Gary's principle: you must be sure of your facts. A few times, all of them before she started taking Zoloft, she had lived to regret getting herself riled up that a teacher or camp counselor was too fond of her beautiful Zack.

Sam the NBC page might have grown up to become a pedophile, though. Isn't that what happens to some men who were molested as boys? And Klein must have molested Sam. More than molested. He had lived with him, didn't he? Sam was his ward, right? She couldn't remember. She had been a child and, anyway, didn't like to think about it. But Klein had certainly exposed Sam to his molestations of children, and now Sam was doing the same to these poor boys who had no fathers, boys just like him. And what about Cousin Jeff? And his best friend, the dark-haired Brian, who was famous too? And why were they all so goddamn famous? Even this Sam had done well. Worth thirty million, Gary had said. Was everyone who was famous really a creep?

You're being hysterical, she lectured herself. Damning adults she knew nothing about. Cousin Jeff had been a stranger for over thirty years, since their fathers had quarreled about money. She had wondered about his glamorous life, and Brian's too, when she noticed his name in an ad for a play or a movie. Klein and Sam she had happily heard nothing about since her father mentioned, years and years ago, that Klein had been fired from NBC and had started some kind of business, but she had acted as if that was of no interest to her so she never heard details of what he was going to do. Her father died a few years later and he was the only one who ever mentioned Klein. Klein must be a hundred by now. How old was he back then? Must be dead. While still a teenager, she had often wondered about Sam's fate with Klein. Sam was an orphan, she remembered that, or at least he had no father, at the time a circumstance she had encountered only in books.

She decided her eyesight was too blurry to trust at arm's length. She moved the photograph up to her nose, Rydel filling her vision while he was led away in handcuffs out of his Broadcasting Academy. A scam or a fraud or something, Gary had said about it.

Yes, she knew this Sam Rydel. This was the unpleasantness she had wanted to forget ever happened, the neighborhood of evil she always detoured, taking the longer duller route. This was the dark alley she had once stumbled into and, in the half consciousness of falling sleep, had mistaken as real.

Okay, it was real. It had happened. She knew that. Who was she kidding? She had never doubted its reality, not for a single solitary moment.

Yes, she needed to put away things neatly in drawers, the mess out of sight. Okay, she was "obsessive compulsive," as the pill-pushing psychiatrist had diagnosed her. Still, she didn't understand how it was possible that glimpses of this notorious Sam Rydel on television during the previous week hadn't jogged recognition. Why was it so clear to her all of a sudden that this photograph of a chubby middle-aged man was the lean blond boy in her evil fairy tale, a handsome prince who had turned into a toad?

Nevertheless she *was* sure. Those were the hungry and cold eyes that had watched her timidity and her shame. She squeezed her legs together, clenched her hands into fists, crinkling the *Times* so Sam's face wobbled and creased, but she didn't crush his baleful eyes. They saw her still. "No," she said aloud. She shook her head and insisted to the newspaper: "No."

She leapt from the chair as if Klein's greedy fingers were climbing her thigh. She hurried to the kitchen's service door and tossed the evil eyes into the paper-recycling bin. Heart pounding, she returned to her spotless kitchen. "So what?" she said aloud. No answer except the hiss and groan of the radiator and a steady drip of the dish towel drying into the sink. She squeezed it hard, moved the damp cloth into a sunny spot on the counter. *What difference should it make to her that Sam had become a pedophile because of Klein?* Klein was the man who had ruined her and he was dead. And what had been done to her, what did it amount to, after all? Everywhere, all over the world there were millions of kids who had truly suffered: Mengele's experiments on children at Auschwitz; boys and girls used as sex slaves in Thailand; child soldiers forced to kill in Sierra Leone. The list of ghastly crimes was endless, itself too painful to contemplate. *Don't be a baby. What happened to you was almost nothing. It was nothing. It was less than nothing.*

Maybe I'm wrong and he's not the same Sam, she decided. She walked into the maid's room, which they had converted into a pantry with a small desk area for her use. She opened her old iBook, a computer Gary and Zack laughed at and that increasingly was threatened with uselessness thanks to how goddamn slow it was becoming, repeatedly stalling like an old car. She launched Safari. She kept her hands folded in her lap while it loaded the *Times'* home page . . .

There. The featured story was about Sam Rydel: four accusations from poor boys, now grown men, saying they had been molested. In a slide show! Why the hell was the *Times* doing a slide show of this disgusting story, like it was a Fashion Week runway? She tapped her trackpad to freeze it on Sam Rydel. Instead a different face appeared.

She shrieked and jerked hard against the back of her chair to get away. She almost tipped over. She gripped the sides to steady herself. She stared at the appalling image. Time had transformed the jolly, rounded features and the confident smile. The once plump cheeks were sunken, wrinkled, and drawn, his now downturned mouth strained to form a grin, filled with dentures that looked too big and too white. And the full head of hair, whose color, incredibly, she couldn't remember, was gone, exposing a frail spotted skull. But even without the help of the *Times'* caption—"Richard Klein, Founder of the American Broadcasting Academy"—she recognized the true villain of her past. In two clicks of her mouse, she discovered he wasn't dead. He was eighty-four, retired and reported to be ill, but she learned that in 1983 he had founded both the school and Huck Finn Days, had hired Sam Rydel, and eventually left him in charge of both academy and charity. The final astonishing, most chilling fact she discovered was the absence of a fact: There were no child molestation accusations against Klein. Not even a hint of one.

She flipped the iBook shut. *Cleansing breath.* She felt better as she exhaled slowly. *And now it's time to clean.*

She started with Zack's room. He was supposed to make his bed but rarely did and the thought of unmade beds, no matter how far from her sight, nagged as dangerously careless, as if she had left the back door unlocked. She found his sheets in a tangle, the navy blue quilt in a lump on the floor, pillows propped against open closet doors (thrown in anger?) dirty clothes half in, half out of the hamper, along with two clean pairs of chinos that had fallen off their hangers. She spread the pale blue sheet over the mattress, averting her eyes from two white stains, tucking in only the bottom, knowing Zack didn't like the sides to be battened down. She collected the comforter, finished making his bed and straightened his closet. Her mind had emptied. Shafts of sunlight glistened on the windows of the building opposite. A weak winter sun had fought through a cold gray sky. Maybe on the way home from work she'd stop at Bed Bath & Beyond and pick out new bedding. Zack ought to have pristine sheets.

She bent over to pick up her son's discarded denim jacket, worn yesterday to school but dropped in favor of a warmer goose down this morning. Maneuvering the sleeves onto the hanger brought the fabric near her nostrils.

She smelled cigarettes.

For a moment, she held the disgusting odor flush, shocked into paralysis at the true criminal revealed. Here was the source of the forbidden vice drifting through the apartment all morning.

This last blow was too much. She backed up to Zack's made bed and sagged on it, as near to fainting as she had ever come in her life. She sniffed the jacket's collar and sleeves to check her first impression. The burnt, sour smell was unmistakable. She patted the pockets. Something crinkled. She fished out a flattened pack of Camel Lights in the right pocket. Zack was smoking Lights. He was willing to brave cancer but not too boldly. How hilarious. How pathetic.

My God, she realized with a fresh jolt of dismay, he had smoked an entire pack! Her baby, only fifteen years alive on the face of the earth, lungs pink and vulnerable as a newborn's, and clouds of this poison had gone into him. She clutched the pack to crush it vengefully but then instinctively caught herself—an ancient precaution—when she felt a single cigarette still resident, nearly flat, cowering in the corner.

She tore the pack open and removed the malefactor. She hadn't held a cigarette in her hands in a decade. A tiny camel printed above the filter looked surprisingly elegant. She didn't remember the logo from her days as a smoker, didn't recall so distinguished an object impressed on the delicate paper.

Zack was ruined. The fact was a kick in the stomach. He was just another enthusiastic participant in the spoiled world. Keeping him innocent had been a fool's wish. Sooner or later everyone is defeated by their desires. Gary cared more about being a celebrity on television than loving his child, and Zack's lungs would be filled with the soot of his resentment. She was helpless to prevent them from sullying their once pure love. She remembered the amazed delight on Gary's face when she coaxed him to hold his newborn son. And Zack had lain happily and peacefully in his daddy's arms. Now they loathed each other.

In her sore muscles and aching bones Julie felt the countless hours of dreary errands she had performed energetically out of her longing to make a nurturing world for Zack. That goal had sustained her through the tedium of motherhood. She was a fool. She was a fifty-three-year-old fool.

She checked all of the denim jacket's pockets. She might as well know the worst. No other vices were discovered. No joints, no pornography, no Saturday Night Specials. Not even matches. He must have used up all the matches lighting nineteen cigarettes.

Needing a match was what gave her the will to stand up and get out. She called to the shut door of Gary's study that she was leaving early for work. Instead she went to Riverside Park, to the company of bare trees and frozen ground. There, despite dizziness and a wave of nausea, she enjoyed a lonely splendor while she smoked the last cigarette in her son's forgotten pack.

Birthday Present

— April 1966 —

"COME ON, TELL me. What did you get?" Brian demanded of his best friend. Jeff had telephoned to brag about the birthday present he had received for turning nine, given to him two days early so he could enjoy it over the weekend.

"Guess."

"I did guess!" Brian twisted the kitchen telephone's long white cord tight around the knuckle of his index finger, watching the engorged tip turn crimson. "I give up. Okay? I give up."

"A tape recorder. A portable tape recorder!" Jeff's perpetual whine, when excited by pleasure, added a squeak. "An *RCA*," he emphasized.

"Is RCA the best?" Brian took the hint.

"Definitely. Cousin Richard says RCA is the best electronics company in the world."

Brian unwound the phone cord, watching his fingertip pale to a normal hue. The mention of Jeff's cousin took him away from the pleasure of anticipating how he was going to enjoy his friend's new toy. It took him away from a bright world he understood and transported him into a darkened room whose shadows he could not describe.

Getting no reaction, Jeff added, "NBC uses all their stuff."

"What do you mean?" Brian asked to cover the confusion brought on by a vivid memory of Richard Klein's fingers insinuating under the elastic of his Jockeys until he could caress each of his butt cheeks. "All dry. Let me check if anything spilled down your front," he had said as his warm hand slid around and touched him where, as far as he knew, no one else had ever touched. Brian had said nothing to Jeff about those fifteen minutes in the bathroom. He had said nothing to anyone. It was the first profound secret of his life.

"What do you think I mean? I mean all the NBC radio equipment and all their cameras and things for television and stuff are made by RCA."

"Wow," Brian said, refocused on the fun of Jeff's good fortune. "So what does it do?"

"What does it do? It records and then it plays back, you know, what you record."

"So what are you gonna record?"

"Come on up. We'll make a radio play."

"A what?"

"A radio play. Like *The Shadow* or something."

Brian whipped the knotted phone cord against the kitchen wall. "I've never listened to a radio show. And who cares about radio? Why don't we do a television show?"

Jeff buzzed contemptuously. "Can't do a television show with a tape recorder, dummy. Come up. We'll make a radio play. Just like a play, only on radio."

"It's portable, right? The tape recorder's portable?"

"So . . . ?"

"Why don't you come downstairs?" Jeff lived on the fourth, and top, floor of their sixteen unit apartment building in Queens, Brian on the second. This allowed them unsupervised movement to each other's apartments, although ninety-nine percent of the time Jeff insisted Brian come up to him.

"My mom wants me to stay home."

"Why?"

"She loves me so much." Jeff slowed his whine to a moan. The drawl hurt Brian's ears. He moved the receiver away. Wisely, because Jeff's voice went up in volume and pitch as he added sarcastically, "She loves me sooo much. She loves me more than any mommy on the planet."

"What planet?" Brian asked, willing to play the straight man.

"The planet Cuckoo. Come on. Ask your mom."

"Mom!" Brian shouted. No response.

"What did she say?" Jeff asked, then prompted, "Tell her it's my birthday."

"It's not your birthday."

"I got my present today. We're celebrating it today."

"Wait up," Brian said, and he let go of the phone. It dangled on the long cord like a hanged man, receiver thudding against the wall. He walked past the living room where his mother sometimes did her reading for work. All quiet and clean in there. She must be making beds or something.

He entered the hallway to the bedrooms. Behind his parents' shut door he heard his father Danny energetically rehearsing lines. It was Saturday. Tomorrow he was going to be doing a reading of a new play by someone Danny knew, not a friend exactly, but someone he called a friend, as it was explained to Brian by his mother. His father wasn't being paid. Readings were something you did as a favor, but it might, as his dad put it, "do me some good," because other important theater people would be there, see him, maybe think of him for other things, and also if this play found a "backer," then he might end up in the cast. It was a little confusing because his father was teaching full-time so he couldn't be in plays except during the summer, and no one could know in advance when a play might go on. When he asked his mother to explain this contradiction, she said, "It makes your father happy to do readings." In any case, Brian understood that his father was busy and not to be interrupted.

He found his mother, Rose, seated on his neatly made bed, reading his illustrated edition of *The Adventures of Tom Sawyer* with a broad smile. "Mom?" he asked tentatively.

"It's marvelous," she announced, as if the discovery had occurred that very moment. "I forgot how marvelous. Of course, it's a children's book, but still. So charming and funny and truthful." She laughed again. Rose was a solemn woman when alone with her thoughts, but that seemed to make her all the more appreciative of anyone who could bring her out of the shadows. Brian often acted the clown for the pleasure of watching her light up. "You've read it, right?" she asked. Brian nodded. She closed the cover, running her hand lovingly over the raised letters of the title. "It's so funny," she said wistfully.

"Mom, can I go to Jeff's?"

"Isn't it too early?" Rose asked, her way of disapproving. When the boys were toddlers, the mothers used to talk together for hours at the Fresh Meadow's playground. Those frequent contacts had declined and nearly ceased once the boys were able to play independently. A few months ago, Jeff's mother, Harriet, had asked Brian why Rose never called her. He reluctantly asked his mother for an explanation. Rose said Harriet's mean remarks about friends they had in common were "ugly to listen to," and added, "I'm sure she's saying terrible things about me behind my back." Her answer made sense, but he could hardly pass it on to Harriet.

"They're up. Jeff's dad is already at work."

"Right, he opens the store on Saturdays, I forgot." She studied Brian as if he were hiding something from her.

"Mom?" he prompted.

"What are you boys up to today? No mischief, I hope."

"Nothing. Just playing Monopoly." He didn't want to mention the tape recorder. You never knew how a grown-up might react to such a thing. At the very least she would be curious about the machine and he'd get stuck explaining something he'd never seen.

Rose continued to peer at him. She was prone to suspicions, although her guesses at wrongdoing were remarkably off target. "Why don't you wait an hour? It's only eight thirty."

Only eight thirty? Brian had been up since six, suffering through *Modern Farmer* and *Sunrise Semester* until the relief of *The Rocky & Bullwinkle Show.* Mr. Peabody was especially funny this morning. But that was an hour ago. Practically the whole day was gone. "Harriet's up and Jeff's on the phone right now. Okay? Can I go?"

"Why don't you invite him here? I'll make you boys French toast."

"He can't. Okay? Can I go?"

"Why can't he come down?"

Brian leaned his head against the wall and groaned. "Mom," he complained.

"Just tell me why he can't come down."

"Jeff needs me to help him with something."

"Help him with what?"

Brian stared at the embossed gold letters on the cover of the book in her lap, calculating whether it might help to mention the tape recorder. He could omit that it was portable so going upstairs would seem unavoidable. A better idea struck: "Jeff's doing a really great thing today, Mom, and he says if I hurry he'll let me help him."

She squinted skeptically. "Help with what?"

"He's gonna allow me to paint his fence white," Brian said, making a dopey face.

She frowned while figuring out his joke. Finally her downturned mouth lifted. "I can't believe you got me to fall for that," she said, laughing.

He pressed: "His mom wants him to stay home today. 'Cause it's almost his birthday or something like that. He's on the phone. Can I go?"

Still chuckling, she nodded.

Jeff was waiting for him at his front door, proudly cradling the tape recorder in his arms. It was the size of a large spiral notebook, housed in beige plastic, a row of shiny black buttons below two translucent reels.

As soon as the door shut behind them, Harriet's voice carried down the long hall from her bedroom, demanding, "Jeff? Is that Brian?"

Jeff ignored his mother's question. He pointed at the full reel of tape on the left side. "It'll record an hour on Long Play."

"What's Long Play?"

"I'll show you," Jeff said, and he walked down the hall toward the bedrooms.

"Jeffrey? Who is it?" Harriet called. Jeff continued to ignore her, carrying the tape recorder before him, power cord trailing in his wake. Brian picked up the plug to prevent it from being damaged by bumping on the floor, and that's how they appeared to Harriet when Jeff paused outside her room, friends tethered like mountain climbers. "Hi, Brian," Harriet said as faintly as if she were about to expire. She lay above the covers of her bed wearing a pale pink slip, a heating pad on her meaty right arm and shoulder, her torso and left leg under a red and black knit afghan, the right leg and its varicose veins exposed. This pose was unvarying, except for the location of afghan and heating pad. They were shifted daily, according to new and recurring maladies.

It felt to Brian as if he had never seen Harriet on her feet for longer than a few seconds. She worked for New York City's Parks Department, not implausibly as a ranger but as a safety inspector, a job suited to her critical nature. She reviewed the equipment and condition of the more than one hundred playgrounds in Queens. When exactly she rose from her bed and went outside to check on them was a mystery to Brian. Sometimes she wasn't in the apartment, so she was up and about somewhere, but those occasions were unusual. While Harriet was at home, Brian occasionally caught her moving a few steps from the bed to fetch an errant section of the Sunday *Times,* but no greater a jaunt than a few feet. If Brian stayed for supper they ate in Jeff's room, usually TV dinners they prepared themselves. Sometimes they ordered pizza and Harriet ate her slices in bed off a tray. When Harriet's physical complaints migrated to her stomach they went out with Saul, Jeff's father, to Zolly's Deli for franks and a knish.

But under no circumstances could he remember eating a meal with Jeff's mother in their dining room. Of course, Brian knew there were occasions when Harriet left her bedroom. While on his way to the bathroom in the hall he'd sometimes notice it was empty and later discover she was back under her cherished red and black blanket sipping chamomile tea, but her arrivals and departures always escaped his scrutiny.

"Why are you carrying your present around?" Harriet asked. "You'll drop and break it."

"It's portable, Mom. I'm portabling it to my room." Jeff walked out of his mother's line of vision.

"Bri, how is your mother?" Harriet asked Brian, still a visible target.

"Fine." From the hallway's shadows Jeff motioned for him to keep moving.

"I haven't seen or talked to her in so long. Did she get a job? Is that why?"

Jeff tugged the electric cord taut, to urge Brian away from his mother's interrogation. Brian didn't dare go without her permission. Harriet intimidated him: the raspy voice, her ill temper, her invalidism, and especially the fact that she worked for the City of New York made her seem capable of terrible vindictiveness, although exactly what harm she might inflict remained fuzzy. "Yes, she's working," Brian said, puzzled that Harriet was asking this question for the fourth time since his mother started her new job six months ago and that each time Harriet behaved as if she had never heard him explain it before.

"Where is she working?"

"*Time* magazine."

Jeff jerked the electric cord. The plug flew out of Brian's hand and smacked into Jeff's concave chest. He doubled over, sagging to his knees melodramatically, pretending a mortal wound. Brian moved partway out of the doorframe to enjoy the performance, but Harriet apprehended him, demanding in an astonished voice, "What does she do for *Time* magazine, for God's sake."

"She's an assistant editor," Brian said. He added tentatively, "I think I told you about it."

"Brian has to come and play now, Mom," Jeff called, careful to keep himself out of her line of vision.

"Don't be fresh with me!" Harriet snapped. Jeff gave up, head down, walking ahead to his room. "What did you say, Brian?" She waited with a frown.

He decided against repeating that he had already told her all this. "Mom works for the books editor . . . ?" Brian said so plaintively it came out as a question.

"Oh, she's a secretary," Harriet said, as if that were a great relief from the terrible confusion Brian had created.

Brian considered whether he could just say yes and run into Jeff's room. Harriet would never get out of the bed to pursue him. He hoped. The specter of being chased by Harriet in her pink slip on blue and black varicose legs was dreadful. He remained anchored to the doorsill and said, as he had the other times, "I think she's his assistant, you know helps him read the books they might review, but I don't know, maybe I'm wrong."

Harriet grunted. "You don't know. Of course you don't. What do you care what your mother does. As long as she cleans up after you, right?"

"Yeah." Brian was glad to accept the insult if it allowed him to escape.

"I'll call her," Harriet said, as she had promised the other four times they had this conversation. "I owe her a call anyway. Did she take the job because your father isn't getting any parts?"

This too had been asked before and answered as he did now: "Dad has a job teaching theater at the High School of Performing Arts."

"Ah." Harriet nodded wisely. "Well, he gave acting a try. That's all any of us can do, right? Try to do what we love. Even if we fail."

Brian nodded and waited.

"Go on," Harriet said. She adjusted her blanket to cover her feet, heels and big toes blackened with dirt. She definitely walked sometimes, Brian noted. "Hurry up," she said as if he had been dawdling. "Jeff is dying to show off his birthday present."

When Brian arrived at the sanctuary of his friend's room something shiny flashed at him. He screeched and jumped away.

"It's a mike." Jeff displayed a narrow silver tube connected by a long black cord to the tape recorder. He explained how the machine worked, that one of the black buttons controlled whether the tape played for a half hour or one hour (the difference being a loss of recording quality for the longer time) and finished with a lecture on the delicacy of how to properly thread the narrow shiny tape through the spools and recording heads. He did not allow Brian to touch it. Jeff was jealous of the pleasures of his toy and who could blame him? It was better than the best of toys because it wasn't a toy at all. This was an object from the grown-up world, hurled down to their lesser realm by a beneficent god.

Brian soon learned that the gift giver was not Jeff's parents, as first he had been led to believe. While Jeff finished threading the reels, he said, "You know what's great?"

"What?" Brian's eyes were fixed on the fascinating tape, one side gleaming, the other dull. Jeff had explained the shiny side had to face the recording head.

"No kid in the world has a machine like this," Jeff said. "In fact, nobody in the whole world has one. You know why?"

"Why?" Brian dutifully asked.

"Because it's a sample. RCA gave one to all the NBC executives. My cousin gave it to my parents to give to me. RCA's not even putting it on the market until Christmas. So nobody has it. Nobody in the world has it."

"You mean, your parents got this from . . ." Brian caught himself from saying Richard's name. He hadn't said it since visiting NBC. In the meantime, Jeff had talked about Klein a lot, quoting Cousin Richard's gossip about *The Tonight Show* and laughing about Brian's having knocked over the plant. Brian had limited his responses to grunts. Vaguely Brian felt it was a kind of confession to say Klein's name, the first step to telling what had happened in the bathroom. And how could he do that? He had no words to explain the experience and he didn't want to try to describe his penis's amazing reaction to the spiderweb caress of Richard's fingers.

Without a vocabulary, he was silenced, even with the friend who knew everything about him.

"Yeah, from Cousin Richard," Jeff said. "He got it for free and gave it to my parents to give to me for my birthday." He pressed the Play and Record buttons simultaneously, picked up the mike, and shoved it under Brian's nose. "Say something."

"Something," Brian said. He pointed to the two depressed buttons. "Why did you press both buttons?"

"You have to press *both* Play and Record to record."

"Why?"

"So you don't accidentally press Record. Because Record tapes over things, you don't want to accidentally start recording."

"Oh . . ." Brian said as understanding came to him (from his logical mind, not Jeff's foggy explanation) that having to press both buttons made an accidental erasure less likely since all other functions could be accomplished by pressing one button. He became lost in fascination at this procedural brilliancy of the RCA Corporation.

"Speak!" Jeff insisted. He bobbed the mike for emphasis. It bumped Brian's nose.

"Ow," Brian complained, then sneezed with sudden violence onto the fine mesh of the microphone's head.

Jeff jerked it away. "Jesus!" he complained. "That's disgusting." He hit the Stop button. The Record and Play buttons popped up and the reels stopped. "Go get a tissue."

"I don't have to blow my nose," Brian said.

"To wipe off the mike," Jeff said. "Jesus, you're disgusting."

"You're the one who stuck it up my nose."

Jeff angrily unplugged the mike from the machine and stood up. "I'm going to wash it off."

"Wash it?" Brian said, appalled by this reckless plan. Jeff hurried out with the cord trailing between his legs and vanished around the corner. Brian followed. When he caught up, he found Jeff at the edge of Harriet's bedroom doorway, crouched against the wall in a pose Brian immediately recognized as Vic Morrow, the star of the television show *Combat!*, positioned behind a ruined wall of a war-torn French village, calculating how he could take out the Nazi machine gun. Brian took his cue, hunkering behind Jeff, and whispering in his ear, "Want me to take the point, Sarge?"

Jeff answered with the growling urgency of *Combat!*'s star. "Get the tape machine."

"What?" Brian asked.

"Kraut's on the move," he said. He stood up, stepping boldly into the doorway, exposing his presence. He was not ripped apart by machine-gun fire. Jeff continued on in all the way, checking to make sure his mother's bedroom was empty, and turned back to Brian. "Must be chowing down. Get the machine, Corporal. On the double."

Brian didn't know why Jeff wanted the tape recorder, but at least the madness of washing the mike had passed. He hurried to Jeff's room and grabbed the machine. He cradled it tenderly while carrying the marvel to Harriet's bedroom. Entering, he was shocked to discover Jeff's head and torso under her bed, legs and feet sticking out.

Brian whispered, "Jeff, what the hell are you doing!"

"Bring it here," came the urgent reply.

Brian's knelt beside the box-spring mattress, uneasy to be so near the subterranean gloom under Harriet's bed. Jeff's face appeared from the shadows, demanding, "Give me the plug."

"What are you doing?" Brian repeated, although he knew and was already complying.

Jeff made a failed effort to lend a snooty British accent to his nasal whine: "Surveillance, James."

Brian did his best to sound as sly as Sean Connery. "Well, Q, let's hope this little toy of yours doesn't blow up in our faces."

"Hurry up! Give it," Jeff said, abruptly dropping out of character. Brian handed him the plug and waited, the tape machine in his lap. Jeff complained. "You have to get under here."

This demand was full of dread for Brian: first, the prospect of crawling under Harriet's bed, and second, the danger of both of them being deaf and blind to her return. But to waste time by protesting seemed just as dangerous. He put the recorder on the floor and crawled in on his belly, pushing the machine ahead of him into the dusty, claustrophobic space, feeling doomed, as if he were entering a mummy's tomb in a horror movie.

"I'm trying to find the outlet to plug it in," Jeff said as he propelled himself deeper into the shadows.

Something touched Brian. A furtive creature brushed his cheek and nibbled at it gently. He screamed. Jeff panicked, forgetting he was under a bed, and tried to stand. His head whacked into a metal spring. "Ow!" he complained while Brian retreated from the animal chewing on his face, abandoning the tape recorder, pushing himself backward with enough force to clear the frame with a single shove. His withdrawal allowed him to see what had taken a bite out of his cheek. It was a balled-up woman's stocking. Brian touched his cheek. No blood. "What is it!" Jeff was shouting. "What the fuck is it?"

"Nothing," Brian admitted glumly.

"Nothing! Is my mother coming?" he demanded.

Brian stuck his head out into the hallway. Something strange was on his face. He wiped at it, his palm coming away with a thick layer of dust. It was filthy under Harriet's bed, and something about how dirty it was convinced him that if they were caught putting the recorder under her bed Jeff would be forgiven, but he would not.

Heart pounding, Brian whispered frantically at the soles of Jeff's Keds, "Hurry up!"

"I've plugged it in," Jeff's muffled voice replied. "But I can't see the buttons to start it recording."

Desperate to get the dreadful enterprise over with, Brian dropped on all fours and slid on his belly under the bed. He found the tape recorder with blind fingers, and from memory located the Play and Record buttons. He pressed them simultaneously. They locked in place. The soft whirring movement of the reels confirmed his success. "Let's go!" he whispered to Jeff. They banged heads shimmying out from under the mattress and banged shoulders going through his mother's bedroom door.

When they arrived breathless in Jeff's room, Brian laughed at Jeff. "Look at you." Brian took hold of Jeff's shoulders, planting him in front of an oval mirror attached to his dresser. His kinky hair was gray with dust.

"Oh yeah?" Jeff honked, turning Brian to show him the right leg of his Levi's, a wide stripe of dust running from thigh to cuff. The boys studied their twin dirtied images in the mirror with pleasure, Jeff's hand perched on Brian's shoulder, Brian's arm resting on Jeff's.

"Jeff!" Harriet howled from her room.

They jumped at the shock, holding onto each other, not moving.

"Jeff!" she repeated sharply.

"What?" he shouted back. "We're playing."

"Get in here. Right now." Harriet's demanding a face-to-face implied she'd found the recorder; usually Harriet was satisfied by yelling at them from her bed, using the hallway as a megaphone. Jeff shook his head to rid it of dust. Brian grabbed the loose fringe of Jeff's Fruit of the Loom T-shirt, fluttering it to free the droppings. "Jeff!" she insisted.

"Come with me," he whispered as he walked out. Brian brushed off his Levi's, following without much hope of getting rid of all the evidence. They were doomed. So stupid. Of course she could hear the machine. And it was such an obvious thing to do with a tape recorder! Dumb, dumb, dumb.

Jeff stopped on the sill of his mother's doorway without warning. Brian bumped into him. Jeff shoved him away. "Get off me."

Harriet was settled on her bed, sipping from a steaming mug. The tape recorder wasn't in evidence. "Uncle Hy is bringing your cousins over today to celebrate your birthday. I want you to be nice to them. Especially your cousin Julie. Her mother praises her to the skies, so she expects everyone to make a fuss over her. And Noah is just a hopelessly spoiled brat. But I want you to make an extra effort to play with them. Don't close your door and ignore them." Harriet sipped her tea while she shifted her baleful gaze at Brian. "And Brian, I want you to make sure Jeff is nice to his cousins. You're a polite boy. You wouldn't ignore your cousins. So you make sure Jeff is a good boy."

Brian's throat constricted. That they hadn't been caught intensified his nervousness about what would happen when they were. He nodded. Harriet seemed satisfied and dismissed them.

Back in Jeff's room, they resumed their marathon Monopoly game, doomed never to conclude because they were both allowed a credit line of fifty thousand dollars from the bank. While Jeff easily paid out the fifteen hundred for landing on Brian's hotel on Park Place, Brian asked for information about Jeff's cousins, whom he had never met and rarely heard mentioned. "Julie's eleven. Noah's little, still a baby. They're Uncle Hy's kids. Hy is my dad's brother. He's a dentist."

Brian accepted that as a thorough briefing. He did not ask about the implications of these children's being the offspring of Saul's more successful older brother, Hyram. He didn't know that Harriet despised them for having more money, and since they were richer, she also desperately wanted their good opinion. He didn't know that there was a practical consideration to Harriet's anxiety about how Jeff treated these relations: Saul owed his brother Hy twenty-seven hundred dollars, borrowed a year ago to start Saul's new business, a stationery store near the new Lincoln Center complex in Manhattan. It would never have occurred to Brian that any relation of Saul's was capable of intimidating Harriet because Jeff's father, in appearance and behavior, was the least scary adult Brian knew. Saul resembled a beagle: mournful watering eyes, big snout begging for love, easily cowed when refused, as frightened of Harriet as Brian was, maybe more so. Jeff also bossed his father shamelessly. On the rare Sunday that Saul took the boys to a Mets game (he worked Saturdays and every other Sunday at his store), Jeff honked orders for treats and souvenirs and never failed to get what he wanted out of his dolorous father.

While they alternated paying rents on each other's hotels, Jeff left his door ajar, listening for an opportunity to recover the tape recorder. After a half hour, given Harriet's talent for noiseless jaunts on slippers, Jeff removed his Keds before executing a visual check on her, careful to place his stocking feet along the edges near the wall where the oak floorboards didn't creak.

He returned, reporting that Harriet had stayed put. Half an hour later he tried again. He was gone much longer, and when Jeff reappeared the nervous excitement of surveillance had been replaced by a lowered head and sluggish feet.

"What is it?"

"Shut the door," Jeff ordered.

Brian obeyed. "What's happened?"

"She was on the telephone." Jeff stared through Brian. "Mom was crying," he added.

Brian relaxed. "So what?" Harriet's crying on the phone didn't happen every day, but it did at least once a week.

"She was talking to your mom and crying."

That was a true surprise. "Crying to my mom? What about?"

"I don't know . . ." Jeff mumbled.

"Did you hear what she saying?"

"I think she was saying something . . ." He shook his head.

"What!" Brian poked Jeff's shoulder.

"Something about . . . Somebody's sick."

"Who?"

Jeff didn't answer.

"Who!"

"I don't know! Somebody's got a fatal disease. Cancer." Jeff backed up to his twin bed and sat. He looked down, then up sharply. "Is your mom sick?"

Brian was about to say no, then realized he wasn't sure. True, there was no sign of his mother's being physically ill. But a fatal disease, as he knew from watching *Dr. Kildare,* did not require symptoms. Often terminal patients surfed or sung opera right up until the end, and their last minutes only involved breathing very, very slowly. Dying wasn't like having the flu, where you threw up, sweated a lot, and looked as if all your blood had been removed. The greatest effect of a terminal illness, Brian believed, was on a person's mood. Both his mother's and father's moods shifted often and dramatically. They could both be dying.

Recently they hadn't been around much. His father taught theater during the day in Manhattan and spent most evenings there too, seeing plays with friends in them and doing readings to keep his acting career alive, as he put it. Meanwhile his mother had often gone into Manhattan on weekends to visit her older sister. A few times she had had Brian stay over at Jeff's for dinner while she "helped out" at Aunt Helen's. She told Brian his aunt wasn't feeling well and needed help with her four little children. Brian was an only child, often left alone, and had gotten used to being sent upstairs to Jeff's this past year, although confusingly his mother didn't approve of her own neglect, telling Brian she was "a bad mother for not paying attention to my beautiful boy."

He thought about his mother saying his aunt was not feeling well and he especially thought of how often he would find Mommy sitting alone in her bedroom with red-rimmed eyes. "Maybe it's my mom's sister," he offered. "I think she's sick."

Jeff shook his head. "Sounded like your mom was sick."

"My mom's not sick."

"She's been away a lot," Jeff pointed out.

"Helping my aunt. My aunt is sick."

"Maybe that's a lie."

"It's not a lie!"

"How do know? Have you seen your aunt?" Jeff tugged on Brian's elbow urgently. "It's on the tape. We can find out."

"What?" Brian stalled.

"What my mom said to your mom. It's on the tape."

"Are you sure?" Brian felt like crying. "Are you sure my mom is sick?"

"No. I told you. I couldn't really hear. I was out in the hall and my mom was crying. Who's sick is on the tape. All I know is somebody's sick."

"Maybe it's your mom," Brian said. "Maybe she's sick."

"Of course she's sick. She's always sick," Jeff pointed out. "But she was talking about somebody who's dying." This depressing fact lay in between them like dog doo. A silence ensued, probably the longest silence of their chattering friendship.

The front door bell rang. Its muffled scream broke their paralysis. "That's my cousins," Jeff announced with disgust.

"I'd better go home," Brian said.

"No way! You're staying until we get the tape recorder back."

Harriet hoarsely shouted, "Jeff! Get the door!"

"Come with me to the door," Jeff said.

"Why?" Brian asked.

"Come on!" Jeff stamped his foot.

"Okay." Brian followed his friend dutifully into the hallway as the doorbell screamed again and Harriet yelled again, "Jeff! Answer the door."

"I am! I'm getting it," he shouted as they passed her room. Brian noted Harriet was by now entirely prone on her bed, cherished red and black afghan covering her ruined legs, head propped on an embankment of four pillows. Brian sometimes wondered if Saul was allowed to take one for himself when he went to bed, but then Brian sometimes wondered if Saul ever slept. The unoccupied parts of the queen-size bed were covered in newspapers—that morning's *New York Times,* yesterday's *New York Post* and *New York Herald Tribune.* She was awkwardly gathering them into a puffed-up mass, presumably straightening up. The rest of the room was beyond repair: a mug of chamomile tea and balled-up tissues on the night table, a skirt and blouse draped over the green armchair near the window.

She looked up as Brian peered in. His curiosity about what she might know of his mother's health overcame his usual fear of meeting her gaze. What he saw surprised him. There were the usual semicircles of blackened fatigue and heavy-lidded suspicion, but typical irritation had been replaced by anger. As he walked by, she looked at him as if she wanted him dead. Spooked, he hustled after Jeff.

He caught up as Jeff opened the door to Hy and his two children. He was immediately impressed by eleven-year-old Julie, mostly because she had long raven hair down nearly to her waist, as long as her five-year-old brother Noah's entire body. "What's the story?" Hy said as a greeting to his nephew. "Everybody still in bed? Oh, that's right. Your mother's always in bed." He chuckled. He was a handsomer version of his brother, Saul: same saggy face, but Hy's snout waggled with self-congratulation, head held high and back, like a rearing horse; the thick, wavy brown hair that Saul couldn't control—his lay in three unrelated clumps—on Hy was a leonine mass. And he was the successful brother, proud of his four-bedroom house in Riverdale and busy dental practice on Manhattan's Upper East Side, a man who drove a Lincoln, had a subscription to the philharmonic, and had gone on three vacations to Europe. "Who are you?" Hy demanded of Brian as he stepped in.

"This is my friend," Jeff answered. "Come in," he added to Julie and Noah. Noah had stubbornly insisted on his Yankee cap and jeans; a touch of formality had been added by his mother, a white shirt and navy blue sweater. Julie, in love with ballet, had been talked out of wearing a black leotard and was dressed instead in what her mother hoped was an outfit beyond Harriet's reproach: a gray skirt, a white blouse, a little red sweater unbuttoned at the top and bright red Mary Janes to match her sweater. To Brian, she looked like Christmas. Julie's eyes were almost as black as her hair and they were shaped like almonds. Despite her impressive appearance, Brian felt immediately at ease with her, unusual for him with girls these days, especially older pretty girls—he often suspected they were laughing at him and it was maddening that he didn't know why.

"What's your friend's *name*?" Hy asked.

"I'm Brian Moran," Brian said.

"A nice Jewish boy," Hy joked.

"Hello, Brian. Very nice to meet you," Julie said with a sincere emphasis that made her seem very nice.

"He *is* Jewish, Uncle Hy," Jeff honked. "His mother is Jewish, so he is too."

"Hyram?" Harriet called in her hoarse, demanding voice. "That you? Come and say hello."

Hy turned toward the long narrow hall that led to Harriet. He quailed as if it were a march to the electric chair.

"Hy?" Her volume dropped to a plaintive cry. "You here? I'm dying to see you."

"Hello, Harriet. I'm just here to drop off the kids," he shouted. To Jeff he added in a low voice, "Tell your mother I'll be back with your pop around five."

"Hy? I can't hear you. Is Becky with you?"

"No," he called down the corridor. "Didn't Saul tell you? Becky couldn't come. Her uncle Joe is sick." He took a step backward to the front door and escape, repeating to Jeff, "Tell your mother I'm going to the store to visit with your father and we'll be back—"

Harriet interrupted, "Hy, did you say Becky's sick? Is she all right?"

"She's fine. It's her uncle Joe." As he answered, Hy involuntarily reversed course, taking three steps down the fatal hall. "He's sick. He's a widower. She's brought him chicken soup and is going to spend the day with him. She told me to tell you she'll call later and have a good long talk with you. Didn't Saul tell you? I spoke to him about it this morning." There was an ominous silence from the invalid's room—long enough for Hy to feel he had no choice but to inquire, "Harriet, did you hear me?"

"Becky is cooking? Making soup?" came Harriet's faint reply.

"Not cooking," Hy said, exasperated. He took two more strides toward his sister-in-law's room, then stopped abruptly as he realized he was three feet from entering her lair. As if he were about to catch a train, he talked fast. "Her uncle is sick. She's bringing him chicken soup." Hy wound down abruptly. He sighed. "Doesn't matter. I told Saul. Becky's sorry. She'll call later to say hello and you're gonna see her at Passover. I'm going now to the store to keep Saul company. We'll pick up take-out Chinese for the big birthday dinner." He recited the plan with fond regret, as if he'd already surrendered hope that so well ordered a series of events could occur.

"Oh, I'm so disappointed." Harriet spoke just loudly enough to be heard in a feeble timbre, as if she were fainting away. "I wanted to have a long talk with Becky . . ."

Hy threw up his arms, exasperated. Brian was comforted that a confident adult had as much trouble handling Harriet as he did. Hy pleaded, "Harriet, she'll phone you later, okay? Then you can talk to her to your heart's content." He went limp, head down, arms hanging.

There was another dismal silence. When Harriet broke it, her voice was insistent. "Where is everybody, Hy? Where are Julie and Noah? Bring them in. I want to give them a kiss. And don't you be in such a rush. Believe me, when you get to the store Saul'll be too busy to talk. He's always too busy when I'm there."

Hy surrendered. Accepting his fate, he straightened bravely and waved for his children to follow as he led a doomed march to Harriet's bedroom. All three crowded at the door, reluctant to enter.

"Hello, Harriet," Hy said cheerfully, as if he had just arrived. "Here are the kids. I'd better get going. Saul wanted me to get to the store before lunch." Meanwhile, Jeff pressed up close behind, leaning on his uncle's butt. Feeling the contact, Hy reflexively stepped into the bedroom. Noticing what he'd done, Hy looked around wildly for escape.

Having bagged her game, Harriet ignored him. She extended a hand to Julie. "Jules, honey, you look so pretty. Come here, sweetie. Let me give you a hug. You too, Noah. Come. Give your aunt a kiss. I'm not contagious. It's just my neck and sciatica. They're killing me."

Julie walked up to the bed without hesitation. Brian was impressed. Surely she felt the same revulsion they all did (Noah looked green at the prospect of kissing Harriet) and yet she sailed over to the bed, bent gracefully at the waist as she had been taught in ballet class, and pressed her lips on Harriet's wobbly cheek without reserve.

Jeff tapped Brian's shoulder, nodding in the direction of his room.

They were just outside his mother's doorsill. Their going would be shielded from view. Brian obeyed.

Beating a retreat, they stepped sideways in unison and dashed madly into Jeff's room. There they grinned, holding back laughter as best they could. Brian choked and snorted. Jeff put his hands on his knees and bent over, hissing giggles.

Their joy was short-lived. Harriet shrieked: "Jeff! Brian! Get in here. Right now!" They scrambled back, careful to remain on the hallway side of the doorsill, and presented abashed faces.

"How dare you run away like that? You're being very rude to your cousins." In the silence that followed Harriet's scolding, Julie lowered her eyes, Noah grinned mischievously, and Hy ran his eyes along the ceiling as if inspecting it for leaks. After several intensely painful seconds, she continued, "I have to speak to your uncle privately. Take Julie and Noah into your room and show them what we gave you for your birthday."

Hearing his fate, Hy paled. Noah, gladdened anyway by the punishment of children other than himself, was electrified by hearing news of a present. He shouted in a manic rush, "What did you get? Where is it? Lemme see!"

Brian reacted to this turn of events as if someone had pulverized one of his kidneys. He put a hand on the doorframe to steady himself. How the hell were they going to show off the tape recorder to Julie and Noah while it was under Harriet's bed?

"O . . . kay," Jeff said in a laconic whine. "Come to my room and I'll show you."

"Yay!" Noah pushed past them. Brian stared at Jeff, appalled. Jeff stared back grimly.

"Go on, honey," Harriet urged Julie. "Go and see my Jeffrey's birthday present. I have to talk to your father."

"I can't stay for long" was the last thing Brian heard Hy say as he followed Julie and Noah to Jeff's bedroom.

There Noah scampered in a circle, a dog chasing its tail, chanting, "Where is it? Where is it? Where is it?"

Jeff slammed his door shut. "Shut *up*!"

Noah dropped into a crouch to power a shout: "WHERE IS IT!"

"Noah, if you're quiet, you'll get to see it." Julie cautioned her brother so sweetly Brian was not surprised to see the five-year-old calm down and wait patiently.

Meanwhile Jeff looked at Brian expectantly. *He expects me to get us out of this?* He gave it a try, bribing Noah: "How about we go to the candy store and buy you an egg cream? You like egg cream sodas, right?"

Noah agreed with big up-and-down motions of his head.

"Okay," Jeff clapped. "Let's go."

"FIRST I WANNA SEE YOUR BIRTHDAY PRESENT."

Jeff put a finger on Noah's lips, pleading, "Be quiet! Please!"

Noah downshifted to a loud whisper. "I want to see your present!"

"We can't show it to you," Brian said, hoping to enlist his secrecy by treating him as an equal instead of the dangerous idiot he obviously was. "It's a tape recorder. You know what a tape recorder does, right? It records what people say." Noah nodded solemnly. Brian turned to plead to Julie, "We hid it under Jeff's mom's bed. It's there right now. She doesn't know. It's recording everything she's saying to your dad."

Julie pantomimed her profound shock by covering her mouth with a hand. Noah noted her reaction and grinned. "That's naughty," he announced.

"It's very naughty," Brian confirmed, understanding this was a plus for Noah. "And if we keep it a secret, we get to hear everything they say."

"Everything they don't want us to hear," Jeff added.

"Oh . . . my . . . God." Julie spaced the words.

Noah grinned harder. "That's really naughty."

Jeff whispered, "It's very naughty. So we have to keep it very very secret."

Noah stretched his grin as wide as he could and rapidly moved his eyes from side to side, presumably an indication of the surreptitiousness called for, a display that convinced Brian they shouldn't ask too much of Noah as a covert agent.

But the little boy wasn't the worry now. Brian studied Julie, pretty as a Mouseketeer in her gray skirt and bright red sweater, while her shining black eyes were clouded by an internal audit on the moral question raised by the hidden tape recorder. They were righteous eyes, Brian decided. She was a good girl. Not like him—he had learned that much: he was not a good little boy. He watched her virtuous eyes calculating and feared that out of her goodness she would feel compelled to betray them.

Sex Crimes

—— February 2008 ——

VERONICA STILLMAN'S FAMOUS face, exquisite aquiline features at once delicate and sharply etched, looked up from her plate of asparagus. At her request, they were denuded of Hollandaise sauce. Brian watched her decapitate two, then spear their severed heads. "You eat the tips last," Brian's Irish peasant-stock father had instructed him forty years ago when he took ten-year-old Brian out for a grown-up dinner at a faux elegant French restaurant in Greenwich Village, just the two of them, newly divorced Dad and confused son. "They're the best part, so you leave them for the end." Veronica was Hollywood Royalty. She had been educated, all movie fans knew, at the finest boarding schools in Europe, exiled from home by the multiple divorces and marriages of her movie-star mother and hard-drinking director-father. So Brian watched in surprise while she ate the delicate heads first. He longed to excuse himself and immediately call Danny Moran, now in failing health, to deliver this scandalous news: an expensive international upbringing had somehow resulted in Veronica's being woefully ignorant of proper asparagus consumption.

"Tell me," she began leaning forward, displaying her broad shoulders, bared but for the thin straps of her slinky blouse. She managed to make her question confidential without lowering her voice: "Why do you think Aries Wallinski of all people wants to direct a movie about rape?"

"Excuse me," Brian said, pointing to his mouth, pretending to be chewing on a sourdough roll.

Veronica guillotined another asparagus tip. "I've been trying to get Aries to talk to me about the real reason he wants to direct this movie, but Aries is very sly." Her lips expressed amusement, compassion, and irritation all at once, accomplished with a slight curling that managed to speak volumes on camera, and Brian was as close as a Panaflex to those lips.

"Sly?" Brian was skeptical.

"Don't you think so?" Veronica's mouth closed over a delicate ruffled tip, sliver tines gleaming against her blood red lipstick.

Brian began to daydream about his latest indulgence, the Red Head, wondering if she was available for training this afternoon. "I think of him as mischievous," he said.

Veronica repeated the word as if it were brand new to her: "Mischievous . . ."

"A mischievous five-year-old."

"Really?" She leaned back, eyes wandering away. "I don't think of him as childlike. He doesn't seem anything like a child to me. Not any child I know." She smirked. "Of course, I know he likes children. Especially female children."

Brian was profoundly worried by this unexpected mention of Aries's sexual proclivities. For two months, producer Gregory Lamont had been negotiating Veronica's fee, schedule, script and casting approval, airline tickets for family to visit her while shooting in Paris. Three days ago, Veronica had agreed to sign a contract to start filming in six weeks, pending her approval of a discussion with Aries and the screenwriter, Brian Moran, of a revision of the script. Thus Brian had taken it for granted she had long ago made peace with Aries's past. Her comment mugged that assumption.

She couldn't have only recently learned the facts—they were thirty-one years old: in 1977, Aries had been arrested on a charge of raping a thirteen-year-old fashion model during a photo shoot. He didn't deny having sex with her, taking the indefensible position that it was consensual. Within twenty-four hours of Aries's arrest, the victim and her mother withdrew the accusation that the acts of sodomy and vaginal penetration involved force, but of course the DA pursued the incontestable charge of statutory rape against the then forty-two-year-old Aries, eventually arriving at a plea agreement: Aries admitted guilt to unlawful sex with a minor, was sent to a psychiatric facility for six weeks, receiving treatment for his "sexually aberrant behavior" prior to a sentence the DA and Judge Kaufman promised would not include jail time.

During the legal maneuvering and psychiatric treatment, Aries had become a notorious symbol to right-wingers of all that was ill with America. They didn't view him as a man to be pitied for the multiple misfortunes of his aborted childhood in Nazi-occupied Kraków, or his oppressed youth in Soviet-controlled Poland, or that his pregnant wife and unborn child had been murdered by members of an LA cult; they saw Aries as an unrepentant and enthusiastic member of drug-soaked, sexually indiscriminate, left-wing Hollywood, a depraved man who deserved merciless punishment. After Aries was released from the psychiatric facility, Judge Kaufman soon became irritated that the director's career was not being adversely affected by his crime and was finally incensed by a photo he was shown of Aries apparently partying hard at a nightclub. He abrogated the plea agreement, announcing that he planned to sentence Aries to hard time. Aries fled the United States for Paris, where he had been born and lived until he was five years old. His father had—in one of history's worst family decisions—moved the Wallinskis back to his native Poland mere months before the Nazi invasion. As a French citizen, Aries found permanent sanctuary in France, which bars the extradition of its own no matter the crime. Ever since, Aries had had to live and—more painfully—work in exile from the States, England, and any other nation with an extradition treaty with France.

By 2008, America had grown even less forgiving of Aries's crime. There were plenty of movie people, in particular actresses, who would not countenance working with him. Maybe, during these months of negotiation, Veronica's friends or her agents had been critical of her decision to work with Aries and she was now hesitant to appear in a movie that told the story of a traumatized rape victim's search for justice—no matter how thoroughly on the side of the angels—if it was going to be directed by a convicted rapist.

Brian understood. It was reasonable for Veronica to worry that she could be viewed as not merely politically incorrect (a survivable fault) but politically depraved. Fans would forgive collaborating with a sexual criminal as a likely by-product of working in the movie business, but to help Aries redeem his crime might make his enemies hers. Movie stars fear losing the audience's love above all; to be threatened with even the remote possibility of their hatred was terrifying.

The difficulty for Brian was that Veronica was the sole actress the studio was willing to finance in his arty script—lose her and the movie was dead. Because Aries couldn't come to the United States to meet with her, and Veronica was unwilling to fly to meet with the director without a signed contract, Brian had been drafted to discuss her script concerns before they had a video conference call with Aries to come to a final resolution about what work Brian would do to satisfy her. But apparently Veronica wasn't worried solely about the script. Evidently Brian also needed to reassure her about Aries's sex life.

Racing through these calculations contorted Brian's face. Veronica noticed his distress. She looked apologetic for upsetting him. "I mean," she added gently, "his wife is in her twenties, right?"

"No," Brian said pedantically. "She's thirty-four."

"But she was fifteen when they started up, right?"

"I'm not sure of the dates." Brian had become a hostile witness.

"And of course . . ." Veronica trailed off, demurely dropping her amazing green eyes (as one critic had written, they truly were emeralds) to the beheaded asparagus stalks. "There was the girl he raped," she whispered. She glanced up suddenly as if to catch him off guard. "She was a child."

My God, she's actually testing my moral compass about sex crimes against children. His anxious self, the wary, unhappy boy whom he struggled daily to console, was chased away. Chat was perilous, polite civilities a headache, the brutal diplomacies of the movie business nauseating, but to provide a straightforward statement of his beliefs about this subject into the world of bullshit was a pleasure. "Yes, that's right. The girl Aries raped was thirteen. She was a month shy of her birthday so Aries likes to say she was fourteen. He doesn't understand it's a meaningless distinction. Of course, I'm one of those people who don't see what he did as rape. I see it as child molestation. A meaningless distinction to—"

Veronica interrupted sharply, incredulous: "Child molestation!"

"Yes," Brian was matter of fact. "I don't mean to say it's a lesser crime than rape. But I do think what Aries did was child molestation, not rape. Perhaps to most people that's a meaningless distinction—"

Veronica interrupted again. "What *is* the distinction?"

"Rape is primarily an act of physical invasion; child molestation is primarily an act of emotional invasion. But I don't make this distinction to downplay the heinousness of Aries's crime. On the contrary. In some ways, a thirteen-year-old being drugged and seduced into sex by an adult is worse than being forced. Within limits, of course: severe physical brutality trumps all traumas. I simply mean that *if* there is something worse than having your will overwhelmed by force, then it would be having your desire to please used against you: perverted to serve the will of your enemy." Talking freely in this way Brian was finally able to study Veronica without constraint. She really *was* exquisite. Even more striking in person, which for a movie star, given the aids of makeup, hair, collagen, costume design, and lighting, was unique in his experience. The deep-set emeralds of her eyes, her long, elegant nose, and those fluted lips and strong chin were more dazzling and original that the generic prettiness of TV stars. Precisely because Veronica had some flaws, her looks were never boring. There was a slight bump in her nose, one eye was minutely lower than the other, which lent intelligence to the otherworldly beauty of her face. And those full lips were always slightly parted, ready to be kissed or amused. Brian's eyes trailed down the smooth white column of her neck to her broad shoulders, from the intriguing scoop of her collar to the rise of her breasts. *Of course she excites me. So the fuck what? Doesn't change what you are.*

"I'm not sure I get what you're saying." Veronica furrowed her brow as if irritated, while her eyes brimmed with compassion. This was a complicated look she relied on at some point in every role. It didn't play as a mannerism, a star's lazy signature, but as part of her naturalness, the indelible element of her real self morphing into a new character, flexible enough to convey empathy in her crusading lawyer in *Dead River,* the anger and heartbreak of her Holocaust survivor in *The Grocer's Daughter,* the pragmatic and loving heart of the doomed mother in *Time Remaining.* Brian was dazzled as she invited him into her heart. No, this was something purer, an invitation into her soul. She allowed him to feel that she cared about him, that she was listening to his deepest feelings with all her attention, and Brian thought: *We're all phonies, aren't we? So, of course, the pretending is what we trust.*

"I'll try to explain." Brian raised a hand to signal he needed a moment to collect his thoughts. Diplomacy wouldn't get Veronica to sign the contract. She must have already heard all the mealymouthed excuses from Lamont and Aries's people. But how to tell her Brian's wisdom? He shut his eyes to relieve himself of Veronica's mesmerizing beauty. Her challenge, or the adrenaline it provoked, felt good, burning off the foggy calm the latest psychotropic medication had draped over all sensations. He had to try something new after his relapse in December, anything to stop the longing to put his hands on the Red Head or the Lazy Intern or the Little Beast. He hadn't felt this alert, keenly aware of color and sound, in weeks.

His always cramping, gurgling stomach—especially when stressed—was tranquil. His always stiff fifty-year-old back, sometimes pierced by iron spikes, felt loose and gloriously free of pain.

When he opened his eyes again to the sun of Veronica's loveliness, he talked freely. "I'm a coward," he told her. "I would probably have chosen to collaborate with the Nazis rather than be killed—I'm Jewish on my mother's side, so they would have killed me no matter how eager I was to sell out—but despite my lack of bravery I still believe in the proverb 'A coward dies a thousand deaths, the brave man only one.' People who collaborate to survive are more to be pitied than the dead. To feel you've helped your tormentor at your own destruction, what could be worse? In a spiritual sense, deep in her soul, maybe a thirteen-year-old girl who sleeps with a world-famous director to please him was more raped than the heroine of *Sleep of the Innocent*. Your character was not even given an illusion of choice. She was helpless, strapped to a gurney, then tortured, then raped . . ."

"Sorry, but I don't buy that," Veronica said, confident she had discovered a fatal flaw. "I don't think being raped by Aries is worse than being tortured with electric shocks to your clitoris." She smiled. "Or my clitoris."

"I agree," Brian answered, admiring her willingness to be witty about rape. "Not while you're being tortured. Pain is pain. I don't mean to overstate my distinction. All I mean to say is that I believe the effects of molestation could be longer lasting. Harder to discover, for one thing. Maybe easier to talk about, in a superficial way. Certainly easier for everyone to hear. And much easier to dismiss as a trauma. But I think, ultimately, it's harder to resolve."

"Then," Veronica asked him slowly, amazed at what she was discovering Brian to mean, "you really think that what Aries did to that girl was even worse . . ." She dropped the thought.

Brian picked it up. "It's a paradox: that thirteen-year-old child may well have suffered a deeper wound than our heroine, and yet I think Aries was less of a rapist than the doctor in our story."

Veronica looked up at the double-height ceiling. Her long neck was delicious. Oh, to nuzzle and nip at that tender spot! She stared at a modern wrought-iron chandelier above their table. They would be crushed if it fell. Why would it fall? Brian wondered at his own violent image. He looked away. Behind her, about half of the hotel's luncheon patrons were gaping at the two-time Academy Award–winning actress. One woman seemed to be debating with her husband whether she dare approach. "So you think . . ." Veronica said struggling to untangle his reasoning, "what Aries did was in some ways worse than out-and-out rape, but he's less guilty than a rapist?"

"Exactly. The doctor in *Sleep of the Innocent* knows he is a monster. Aries thought what he did with that girl was naughty, nothing more. He didn't believe it was rape. He didn't *know* it was rape. How could he? He was seven years old when the Nazis took his mother. He was seven and a half when his father sent him off alone to the countryside to escape the death camps. He managed on his own until the war ended and was finally reunited with his father at age eleven. His father had survived Auschwitz. While being repatriated, he had married another woman. This stepmother, a noble Jewish survivor of Buchenwald, by the way, took one look at eleven-year-old Aries, a child who had survived the war all by his lonesome, and decided she didn't like him, didn't want to live with him. So Aries's father left motherless eleven-year-old Aries in an abandoned apartment building in postwar Poland to fend for himself. "

Veronica gasped. Brian was relieved, felt lucky that she didn't already know the full details of Aries's youth. Most people didn't; the rape charge overwhelmed the rest of his horrific past. "She . . . she actually refused to let Aries live with his father?"

"Said she couldn't stand the brat."

"And I thought my three stepmothers were bad . . ." Veronica mumbled.

Brian laughed. "Good line. Anyway, that's why Aries didn't think a nearly fourteen-year-old girl is a child. He hasn't been a child since he was seven, since the Nazis took everything from him: mother, father, friends—all of Kraków, for that matter. The idea to Aries that a thirteen-year-old is being coerced who takes a quaalude, doesn't gag while giving you a blow job, and doesn't scratch your eyes out when you fuck her is nonsense. *I* know it isn't nonsense, *you* know it isn't nonsense, the editorial page of the *New York Times* knows it isn't nonsense, but Aries didn't, and he still doesn't know. What he did to her was appalling and disgusting and it was rape, an insidious and despicable rape, the overwhelming of a child's will, but Aries is not, in his heart, a rapist."

"Okay," Veronica conceded. "I don't agree with you. But I see your point." A waiter hovered at her elbow while another removed Brian's salad. Veronica put her knife and fork on the plate over the uneaten asparagus stalks. The waiter reached for her plate.

Brian warned him off. "She's not done," he said.

"I'm finished," she explained to Brian. "I only eat the tips," she added with an apologetic shrug. "It's a shameful waste. But the stalks are yucky. Like eating soggy celery."

Brian smiled. "I'll have to tell that to my father."

"Really?" Veronica leaned her elbows on the table, the long fingers of her hands forming a plateau for her chin to rest on. "Your father would be interested in my eating habits?"

"Fascinated."

"Did you get your lovely coloring from him, your Irish father? And those china blue eyes?" She gazed at Brian as if he were the only male on Earth.

Ignore it, Brian ordered himself. That's the autonomic seductiveness of her profession. "Thank you. Actually the eyes come from my Jewish mother. I haven't answered your question." He glanced outside the tall window. New York was wearing its gray flannel sky today, the surly town of finance. "You asked why Aries wanted to make *Sleep of the Innocent.* People assume it's a kind of apologia, and I suppose some will think it's a weird form of community service, that the rapist in the play is a metaphorical equivalent of what he was accused of. That's all crap." Brian returned to look at Veronica. He was relieved to see she had dropped the flirtatiousness. She was squinting with concentration while she smiled slyly, another signature look, the scheming murderess in *Passage Home,* the desperate gambler in *Hole Card,* the brilliant scientist in *Curie.* "Aries knows, better than anyone I can think of, what it is to live a life haunted by the past. His mother, friends, family, were murdered by the Nazis. And yet he rebuilt that life, became a success as a Polish filmmaker and made a family out of the film community there. Then, because of Soviet censorship he had to flee that home, that family. And when he created a third life for himself as a director in Hollywood, that too was destroyed, first by a madman who murdered his wife and unborn baby and finally by his own act of rape. This play is about the destruction of three people's lives by evil social forces: the doctor, a healer who is turned into a torturer; our brave heroine who is left dysfunctional by his torture; and her husband who is forever branded as a coward for betraying her. The movie is about trying to resolve the past for all three of these damaged people. At one time or another Aries has been each of them. He isn't doing this story to reclaim his reputation or make excuses. Aries lived without a family from seven to thirteen. At thirteen, he got into film school. He boarded there, a child among adults, and there he learned how to act, how to write, how to operate a camera, how to direct. He grew up at last, up and out of the terror of his childhood, all the while surrounded by people who wanted the same thing: to make movies. They became his family. And they are still the only family he can rely on. He's making this picture with us, with members of his family, to heal himself."

Veronica's supple features transformed in a instant from skepticism to wonder. "To heal himself . . ." she whispered.

"To heal himself," Brian repeated.

Her eyes glistened with tears. Brian felt a heart stopping stab of pure pleasure. *I've moved her. I've moved her with my words,* he congratulated himself, then immediately conceded the possibility: *And she's a great actress.*

"Well . . ." Veronica looked contrite. "I thought I was cutting my fee in half because you can't expect a big audience for a political drama. I didn't realize I was doing psychotherapy. Now I'm ashamed I'm asking for any money at all."

Brian chuckled. *Tears in her eyes and steel in her heart.* "You should bill Blue Cross," he said.

She grinned. He noticed a single freckle nestled below the strong line of her jaw, as dark as chocolate. *Oh, no,* he thought with horror. *I'm starting to memorize her body.* He averted his head, pretending to look for a waiter. *What should I ask for—a side order of saltpeter?*

Instead he saw their producer approaching. The legendary Gregory Lamont strode with the harried confidence of a man who had been head of a studio at twenty-four, four-time Oscar-winning independent producer by thirty-three, bankrupt by forty-five, and now in the up-ramp of a comeback at fifty. He was wearing a blue blazer over a gray crew neck cashmere sweater too tight for his swelling belly. He completed his out-of-date semicasual Hollywood look of the cocaine eighties with tailored jeans and gaudy cowboy boots—a handcrafted souvenir of his top-grossing picture, *The Yellow Rose.*

"How's lunch so far?" Gregory asked as he sat down in an empty chair between them at their table for four. He smoothed his eyebrows with the index finger and thumb of his right hand, then pinched his nostrils, and lastly stroked his mustache—a nervous tic that was irritatingly familiar to Brian.

"Thanks to our brilliant writer, lunch is excellent," Veronica said.

The producer turned from Veronica to Brian, following the flight of the movie star's compliment to its object. "He *is* brilliant." Although seated, he buttoned his blazer as if the announcement demanded a more formal dress code. "I have good news," Gregory said. "Aries is available to have our video-conference call now. We can do it from my office, two blocks crosstown. I've arranged a car."

"Okay. But we haven't had our entrées."

Gregory nodded, took a moment to consider this information, and declared, "And, of course, you want your entrées."

"I know I'm supposed to keep my figure, Gregory, but even for a light lunch this is the anorexic special."

Gregory announced grimly, "I'll see about them." He stood and walked confidently toward the swinging service doors.

"He's actually going into the kitchen?" Brian wondered aloud.

"Maybe he'll make our food. Gregory's a good cook. Used to make lasagna for Scorsese no less. By the way, speaking of directors," Veronica said, leaning in again. Those shoulders and long arms—he imagined how they would looked raised above her in handcuffs. Ah, but in his arty script, there were no tasteless flashbacks to her torture. "I just finished doing ADR on *Mother's Helper II,*" Veronica said with a mischievous look.

"Oh. Right." His back ached. His stomach fluttered. *What does she know?* Surely Jeff had kept his mouth shut.

Lamont burst through the swinging doors like a gunfighter, heading their way.

"Guess who went out of his way to ask me to say hello to you?" she teased.

Hurry up! Say it! He nodded to encourage her. Unfortunately, Veronica paused for him to guess. "Your director?" he whispered.

Too late. Lamont arrived in time to overhear Veronica say, "Exactly. Jeff Mark told me you were BFF as children. In fact, he told me a funny story about how you used to tape-record his parents without them knowing . . ."

"What?" Lamont, still standing, frowned down at Brian with the irritation of a boss who hasn't been kept in the loop. "You and Jeff Mark were what?"

Veronica looked up. "Our entrées?"

Lamont sat down. "They'll be right out." He snapped at Brian, "Did you order the vegan salad?" Brian nodded. "Didn't you have a salad for an appetizer?"

"I'm vegan," Brian said. "Everything else here is cooked in butter. Or worse."

"God, you're even more of a fag than I thought." Lamont could use the F-word because he was openly gay. That is, openly gay since his bankruptcy and release from the Betty Ford Center.

Veronica defended Brian's diet: "Well, it's good for you. You look great."

Lamont stroked his eyebrows, pinched his nose, caressed his mustache and said to Brian, "What the fuck is this BFF bullshit about Jeff Mark and you?"

Veronica grinned, proud to have information the all-knowing Lamont didn't. "They grew up together. They were 'bestest of friends,' Jeff said. He was adorable about it." She turned to Brian. "Jeff said you used to put on shows together, that's how you both learned to be storytellers."

So now Jeff thinks of himself as a storyteller. Oh really.

Lamont made a face. "Brian Moran, I've known you, what? Ten years. We've done three projects together. You never said anything about knowing the Mark Man."

"I don't know him. I haven't seen him since I was eleven."

"That's what he said!" Veronica announced triumphantly. "Even though you and Jeff were best friends, he said you haven't spoken or seen each other since you were eleven."

"You just finished ADR on *Helper II,*" Brian tried to steer off this course. "Isn't that late to be doing ADR?"

"We did some reshooting after the first previews. The studio is very nervous. They've got three hundred and sixty million in it."

"Jeff can't fail. He's a genius," Gregory grumbled, as if that were a damning fault. He shifted in his chair to confront Brian. "You're in the movie business. He's the top box-office director and the most powerful and active producer in the business—the little prick. Why the fuck aren't you in touch with him?"

Brian shrugged. "I don't *not* talk to him. I just don't know him." He saw their entrées coming. "Ah, lunch."

"What happened? You fought? Please tell me you punched his lights out. Of course I love Jeffrey. He's a genius, there will never be another like him, but it would be a gas to think that, just once, a writer decked him." Jeff was notorious for hiring Pulitzer Prize–winning playwrights and novelists, pampering them during their first drafts, firing them after the second, replacing them with more compliant screenwriters who composed the script he actually shot and then later, during awards season, Jeff would only mention the famous writers because their names lent more prestige to the project. So far, although nominated four times for Best Director, Jeff had yet to win the Oscar. Brian believed Jeff would win in a landslide if the category was Best Fucking Over.

"No," Brian said. "I didn't punch him. My parents divorced and we moved away."

Lamont gave up on Brian. He turned to Veronica. "What did Jeff say our writer did to offend him?"

"Nothing. Jeff said they lost touch. In fact, he spoke fondly of our writer. Said to say hello."

Lamont tried Brian again. "Spoke fondly? Lost touch?" He shook his head as if trying to wake up. "This is the fucking movie business. Movie people work all over the world, but they live in a small town. You're an A-list screenwriter—"

"Let's not exaggerate," Brian interrupted. "I'm no better than B-plus."

"Fuck off. If I say you're A-list, you're A-list. And Jeff! My God he's an A-plus hyphenate. And you were BFF as kiddies. How the fuck could you not know him today?"

Brian ordered his muscles to form as pleasant a countenance as possible given that he wanted to kick the producer in the mouth. "Doesn't seem so weird to me," Brian commented. "We were kids who lived a million years ago two floors apart in Rego Park, Queens. My mother moved us to the Upper West Side in '69, when I was eleven. Jeff's right: we just lost touch." He smiled at the skeptical producer and sympathetic actress, and beyond them the Four Seasons audience neglecting their lunches, wondering who was this ordinary, balding middle-age man that the great Veronica Stillman was listening to so intently. "We were just childhood friends," Brian said to the famous and the bankrupt, "and let's face it, Jeff and me, we're not children anymore."

Grown-up Secrets

—— April 1966 ——

"I'M GOING, KIDS. I'm going now," they heard Hy call out. "Be back later."

Jeff gripped Brian's forearm. "Mom'll go to the bathroom. She always needs to pee after guests leave. I can get the tape back!" He nodded at Julie and Noah. "Keep them here."

Noah made a run to follow Jeff. Brian caught him around the waist. The five-year-old strained against the hold, shoes coming up off the floor. "Lemme go!" he protested. Brian held fast and watched Julie for a reaction. Since confessing that they had hidden the tape recorder under Harriet's bed, she had responded with doubtful looks, not explicitly agreeing to maintain their secret.

Noah's Buster Browns kicked Brian in both shins. He lifted Noah as high as he could and dumped him on the floorboards. The little boy looked astounded that he had been treated so roughly. "That hurt," he declared with more surprise than outrage. Evidently Julie was not a violent older sister.

"Keep quiet," Brian said, "or I'll really hurt you."

"Okay," Noah agreed. He sat up and rubbed the back of his head.

The door banged open, propelled by Jeff's foot. His arms were full, carrying the recorder: one reel empty, the other fat with tape, its end flapping loose. Brian was impressed: *We recorded a whole hour.*

"I just made it," Jeff reported, lowering the machine on his twin bed. "I heard the toilet flush and I got the hell out. Plug it in. I'll fix the tape."

Noah badgered Jeff, "What are you doing? What are you doing?" while Jeff concentrated on the delicate operation of threading the heads and Brian found an outlet.

"He has to rewind the tape," Brian explained. Julie was at the door, her hand on the knob. "You going?" Brian asked.

She froze. Her hair draped the length of her back, black and straight. He noticed the bare backs of her knees; their different, tender texture was interesting to look at. He never used to find girls interesting to look at. Last Wednesday, Nina Goldfarb, who was fat and her skin too red, was two steps ahead of him on the stairs. As she stepped up, he could see her white thighs and powder-blue panties. He wondered about what was under them. Was it like the sculptures his mother had taken him to see—a smooth nothing? *Don't be stupid—how do they pee? And his mother had hair . . .* He let this speculation lapse. He wasn't happy about these new worries; he didn't want to start acting dumb about girls, like men in movies.

"Fuck," Jeff said. The slippery tape had squirted out of the notch.

Noah giggled. "Bad word."

Brian walked up behind Julie and whispered in her ear. "You leaving?"

She turned. "You shouldn't be doing this."

"Somebody's mother is sick," Brian said. He glanced at the bumps under her bright red sweater. He was instantly ashamed. He looked up quickly. "Somebody's mom is sick," he repeated.

"Sick with what?"

"We heard—"

"*I* heard," Jeff corrected.

"Who cares who heard," Brian said. "Jeff heard his mother talking to my mother about one of them being sick with cancer."

"Oh my God . . ." A hand covered her mouth. "Cancer," she repeated through fingers. "Who is it?"

"We don't know."

"I think it's Brian's mom," Jeff said in the same casual way he might predict "The Mets will lose a hundred games."

Julie put a hand on Brian's shoulder. "I'm sorry," she mumbled.

"It could be Jeff's mom who's sick." Brian stepped away from her. Why was she touching him? And he was offended that she was in such a hurry to believe Jeff.

"She's not sick." Noah shook his head from side to side and repeated, "She's not sick." He insisted to Jeff a third time: "Your mom's not sick."

"How do you know my mom's not sick?" Jeff asked as he succeeded in threading the tape into the notch. He spun the reel manually once to ensure it would hold, then depressed the black Rewind button. Noah, Julie, and Brian were hypnotized by the spinning reels and the flow of shiny brown tape through silver recording heads.

Jeff rapped Noah on his head. "How do you know my mom's not sick?"

"Ow!" Noah complained.

"Why did you say my mom isn't sick?"

"Because Dad said Aunt Harriet's never sick. She's always in bed, but she's never sick."

"Noah!" Julie scolded, but she smiled. "Say you're sorry."

"Tell Dad to apologize," Noah said.

"It's okay, Noah," Jeff said. "We're gonna find out who's sick." A fascinated silence overcame them while they watched the tape transfer from the right reel to left, listening to its gradually changing melody, a breathy whisper becoming a rasp as it neared the finish. When the Rewind button shut off, it made a loud click. How come Harriet hadn't heard that, Brian wondered? Maybe she was too busy talking.

Jeff pressed the Play button. A lurch of distorted, warbled noise resolved into the clear sound of Harriet shuffling in on her slippers. She said, "Oy vey," and sighed loudly, which was followed by a moan from the bedsprings as she settled on her bed.

"Ugh," Harriet groaned. She talked unselfconsciously to herself in a low but distinct voice. "I have to call her. No way out of it." The springs creaked, and there was a clattering sound, followed by the rotary whirring of her bedside phone as she dialed. She interrupted after the first three numbers to comment, "God, I hope that fool Danny doesn't answer. I'll have to listen to stories of his pathetic auditions."

Jeff looked stricken. "I'm sorry," he mumbled to Brian.

"Who's Danny?" Noah asked.

"My father," Brian snapped. "Now shut up so we can listen."

"Hello, Rose? How are you?" Harriet's voice rose an octave, growl replaced by a singsong lilt. "It's been so long. We never talk anymore."

"Is she talking to your mom?" Noah asked.

"Shut up!" Jeff said.

"Noah, please try to be patient and just listen."

Harriet coughed, the bedsprings creaked in sympathy, and then she continued, "So Brian tells me—you know, he's a lovely boy, your son. He's here every day. I feel he's almost mine, the little brother Jeff always wanted. I bet I see as much of him as you do. Maybe more! And he's such a good boy. So polite. And a little shy. He's a little shy, isn't he? Where does he get that from? Danny is so big a personality." She paused to listen, then laughed and said, "I don't think you're shy. Anyway, Brian tells me you have this wonderful new job. He just mentioned it today. I could kill him for not saying something sooner. He said you've had this job for months." Jeff looked an apology to his friend. Brian shrugged. "So what is the job? Brian makes it sound like you're running *Time* magazine all by yourself."

"Jesus," Brian mumbled.

"You're an editor?" Harriet sounded amazed. "Oh . . . you're not an editor? What's an assistant editor? So how do you assist an editor? Isn't that being a secretary? I'm so confused! What do you do exactly?"

All that made Brian intensely uncomfortable. His mother must hate this conversation. She was sure to express her unhappiness to him by wondering aloud if Brian ought to be spending so much time at Jeff's. Jeff was embarrassed too. His index finger tapped the recorder's green power light impatiently.

"Reading? You read books all day? That's a job?" Harriet asked.

Jeff hit the Stop button.

Noah protested, "Hey, don't!" and reached for the Play button. Jeff grabbed the little boy's wrist and twisted. "Ow!" Noah complained, feebly punching Jeff's shoulder with his other, tiny hand.

"Don't touch!" He released Noah, pressing Fast Forward. He mumbled for Brian's benefit, "This is boring. I'm skipping it."

Brian was glad. He wished life would allow him to fast-forward through all conversations with Harriet, especially about his parents.

"Stop!" Noah nagged as the tape sped through the heads. "You're going too far."

"Shut up," Jeff said, although he did stab the Stop button and press Play. There was an electronic wail as the recorder came up to speed that resolved into human grief, Harriet mumbling incoherently between sobs. At this distressing noise, the four children got very quiet. "I'm sorry, Rose . . . I'm sorry," Brian eventually understood Harriet to be saying. His heart sank. Harriet's pitying his mother could mean only one thing: *Mom is dying.* "No, honey, no, you don't have to do that. How sweet," Harriet continued, atypically affectionate. "The doctors don't know a goddamn thing." Harriet returned to her normal sourness. "Except how to charge. I don't how we're going to pay all the doctors' bills. Even if this new treatment works, it could be a disaster. What good is it if we end up broke . . . living like animals on the street? Jeff and Saul will be better off with me in the grave." She gasped out, "Oh God, oh God, what's going to happen to my little Jeffy. His father can't take care of him after I'm gone."

Jeff hit the Stop button hard. Relieved for himself, Brian watched his friend stare at the still reels, cheeks sucked in, lips rolled together. Julie put an arm around her cousin's shoulder. Brian patted him on the back.

He felt like a big fat phony. Under the circumstances, he was glad Harriet was dying. Jeff was grim, intent. "I'm going to rewind to hear what we skipped."

"Maybe we'd better stop listening," Julie suggested.

"Are you crazy?" Jeff said. "I don't really know anything right now. We skipped too much." He punched the Rewind button defiantly.

"Yeah," Brian said, "Maybe she's not . . . Maybe it's not as bad as it sounds. Maybe they can cure her." After all, Ben Casey or Dr. Kildare often saved patients everyone said were doomed.

"That's right," Jeff jabbed the Stop button. "She said there was a new medicine or something." He pressed Play.

"Oy," Harriet's voice was loud and clear. "I have my in-laws coming for dinner and Hy is dropping his little brats off for the afternoon." Harriet chuckled. "No, not Julie," Harriet assured Rose. "Julie is beautifully behaved. Of course she's not the prize her parents think she is, and the thought of her dancing ballet coming from that family of klutzes is a scream, but she's sweet and harmless. Her brother *is* the spoiled brat, he's just impossible. But that's Hy. Hy thinks he's God's gift so his son must be too, right? Anyway, I'm grateful Brian is here to help Jeff entertain them. He can't stand them."

None of the eavesdroppers spoke. Brian wanted to tell Julie she was beautiful and could become a dancer but thought he should act as if he hadn't paid attention. They remained attentive during a long silence from Harriet on the tape, presumably listening to Rose. At one point Harriet commented, alarm in her tone, "What are you talking about? He's not a bother—" but she must have been cut off by Rose.

Harriet's next comment was "I see," said in an icy tone. "I see what you're getting at. You're not worried about whether it's a bother to me. You don't want Brian playing with Jeff, that's what you really mean." There was a brief silence on Harriet's side, followed by a startling bang. "Oh God!" Harriet cried out in horror. The frantic banging noise repeated. "I can't believe this is happening," Harriet moaned and banged something again. Brian decided Harriet was smacking the headboard. The thudding stopped. Then Harriet, through gasping sobs, pleaded, "Rose, you don't understand. I can't let Jeff out of my sight. I can't bear to miss even a moment of his life. No, no." Her voice almost rose to a shout. "That's not why. I didn't want to tell you. I didn't want to burden you. I have cancer. I have breast cancer. I'm going to die. I'm dying, Rose," and she sobbed without restraint.

The children listened in a dismal, cowed silence. Jeff lowered his head until his eyes were fixed on his Keds, a folding chair collapsing. Finally his mother's weeping subsided to sniffles. Harriet gathered herself enough to speak clearly: "They found a tumor. Yes, they're sure. They can't operate. They want to try some sort of new drug. But no surgery. Thank God. It's bad enough I'm dying. I don't want to die flat-chested." Harriet laughed bravely. Brian was impressed by the very thing that frightened him about her—unexpected and violent shifts of emotion.

Julie leaned toward her cousin until their temples touched. Noah put his legs under him and hugged himself. The recording reached the part they had heard before. They listened again to Harriet say, "Thank you, honey. Thank you. You're a sweetheart," to whatever Rose was saying. "That's true, there is hope," Harriet conceded, her voice strengthening. "I'm sorry, Rose . . . I'm sorry. No, honey, no, you don't have to do that. How sweet. The doctors don't know a goddamn thing. Except how to charge. I don't how we're going to pay all the doctors' bills. Even if this new treatment works, it could be a disaster. What good is it if we end up broke . . . living like animals on the street? Jeff and Saul will be better off with me in the grave. Oh God, oh God, what's going to happen to my little Jeffy. His father can't take care of him after I'm gone."

Jeff raised his head enough for Brian to see his friend's eyes were dry, jaw in a determined clench. On the tape they heard the front door ring. "Oh my God," Harriet said, "that's Hy and the kids. I've got to pull myself together. JEFF!" she called. "JEFF! ANSWER THE DOOR!"

It was an eerie feeling, recalling the comedy of an unwilling Hy coaxed into seeing a malingering Harriet with the irony of what Brian now understood about the real situation. He was tantalized by the thought that if only they hadn't hidden the recorder the day would have continued to be innocent fun. Of course, Harriet would still be sick. Or would she? Was the tape recording magic? If they hadn't hidden the machine, maybe she wouldn't have cancer.

Jeff fast-forwarded. At one point, he pressed Play to check on his progress—they heard Noah and Julie greet Aunt Harriet—then resumed until he reached a point where they could listen in on Harriet's and Hy's tête-à-tête.

Jeff overshot a little. Hy was in midspeech. "Saul's my brother. I loaned him the money. I'll talk to him about it."

"Goddamn it, Hy," Harriet answered, her tone nakedly hostile. "Saul told me all about it. That you've lost money playing the stock market and need the two thousand back—"

"Two thousand seven hundred. And I didn't play the stock market. Don't tell me Saul told you I've been—"

"Maybe you've been playing the ponies like your father used to—"

"What!" Hy squealed with outrage. "I'm not a gambler. I don't have to explain to you or even Saul why I want to be paid back. The point is that it was a six-month loan and it's been a year and a half . . ." He sighed, exasperated. "Look, I'm not talking about this with my brother's wife. All right? It's not appropriate."

"Why not? Why in God's name isn't it appropriate? Saul's lived with me as many years as he lived with you. *I've* known you for twenty years. If we're not family now I don't know when we'll be."

"Harriet, what has the number of years we've known each other got to do with anything?"

"I'm talking about family—"

"Saul *is* my family. Our parents are dead. We have no aunts and uncles. He's my one and only blood relative. Saul *is* my family. I lent my brother money. I'll talk to him about it. That's it. Case closed."

"No. The case is not closed." Brian looked at Jeff to check if he was impressed as he was by Harriet's boldness in facing down the blustering Hy, transformed from a pathetic sick woman into an inspiring heroine. "The case is not closed, Hy, because Saul is too proud to tell you what's really going on. You ask him for the money and he'll give it to you, even if it means he has to lose the store. He'll give you the two thousand dollars without saying a word about the fact that I have breast cancer. Without letting you know that he has no idea what my treatment is going to—"

"What?" Hy interrupted, irritated. "What the hell did you just say?"

"I have a lump in my breast. It's cancer." She hurled the diagnosis at Hy like a rebuke. The news silenced him. His quiet continued for five revolutions of the reels, a very long time for the surveillance team. Julie whispered, "Say something, Daddy."

"Harriet," he spoke at last, very gently. "When did this happen?"

"Um . . ." Harriet hesitated. "I guess I felt it—I don't know—truth is, I didn't want to know what it was. I felt it just before Christmas. That's when it was."

"Two months ago? Why didn't you tell me right away? Who's treating you? My friend, David Newberg, is a top oncologist at Sloan Kettering. He doesn't treat breast, but he can get you in to to see one of the best in the country. I want you to see him on Monday—"

"No, no, Hy. I don't want to see anyone else," Harriet said in a tone of profound hopelessness, then added nothing more, which seemed odd to Brian.

"Why not? Don't be ridiculous! You have to let me—"

"Thank you, Hy, but no," she was certain this time. "I'm in the HIP plan through the city. They have certain doctors you're supposed to see and they're very good."

"David will see you for free. Professional courtesy. I did his mother's whole mouth for nothing for exactly this kind of situation. Trust me on this—"

Jeff's door swung open with a bang.

Jeff poked the Stop button and tried to shield the machine from view while the children's heads turned in guilty unison. There, filling the doorway, was Richard Klein. He was in a tailored blue blazer, gray slacks, and a white Brooks Brothers shirt without a tie. Brian imagined he could smell Old Spice, although he was half a room away. "Happy birthday, Jeff!" he announced. "Hi there, boys and girls," he added with a mischievous smile at the sight of four children on their knees hovering with an air of secrecy over something on the bed. "What you got there?" He turned to someone behind him and commented, "I think we interrupted something naughty."

Sam the NBC page appeared, peering curiously over his benefactor's shoulder. "Hi, kids," he called in. "Happy birthday, Jeff."

Jeff stood up, revealing the object on the bed. "It's your present, Cousin Richard. I was showing them the portable tape recorder."

"That's your parents' present. I just helped get it. Sam here is going to help me get you a present of my own." Klein strolled toward the bed, a broad smile aimed at Brian. "Hello, Brian." Brian shifted behind Julie. Jeff had given no warning that he should expect Klein to show up today. It was a dreadful surprise.

Klein veered toward him, nudging past Julie. He stuck out his hand, saying in a wounded tone, "Brian, aren't you going to say hello to me?" Brian's heart was pounding. His legs yearned to run as fast as he could, but he couldn't order them to move. He was mortified Klein had singled him out; it seemed to announce to everyone what had happened in the NBC bathroom. Klein's showy greeting was a further proof to Brian that he, not the vice president, ought to be ashamed, that it was his secret, not Klein's.

"Here." Klein stuck his chubby fingers almost directly under Brian's nose. "Shake hands."

Embarrassment warmed Brian's face. Head down, he offered his hand limply. Klein grabbed it and jerked Brian into his fragrant shirt, exclaiming, "Whoops!" Klein bear-hugged Brian in a way that looked to the others as an attempt to steady himself. Brian felt a bulge at Klein's groin press against his belly, and his nose was dunked into the well of the adult's open collar. He did get a faint whiff of Old Spice while he was squeezed tight a second time, then was abruptly pushed away.

Klein stepped back, commenting, "I said 'Let's shake,' not 'Let's knock down Richard.'" He winked at Noah, who lit up like a pinball machine. "Who are you?" Klein said, peering into little boy's eager face. "I don't know you, do I?"

"I'm Noah!" he shouted, showing all his crooked baby teeth.

"Well, how about you, Noah? Do you know how to shake?" Klein offered his hand.

Noah reached for it. The instant he did, Klein engulfed the little fingers in his fist and yanked Noah's against him. "Whoops!" Klein said, repeating his burlesque of being off balance while squeezing Noah's face tight to his groin, followed by the mock discard of pushing him away. "I said 'Shake, Noah,' not 'Let's crush Richard.'"

Noah was overcome by appreciation for Klein's gag: he collapsed to the floor with laughter, doubled up into a fetal position.

"Noah," Julie said. Her comment attracted Klein's attention. He buttoned his blazer while he studied Julie, pretty as a doll in her Mary Janes, bright red sweater and short pleated gray skirt.

"Who are you?" he asked solemnly.

"I'm Julie," she said.

Klein offered his hand.

Julie stared at it suspiciously.

"Don't!" Noah managed to squeeze out between a cackle and a hiss.

"Don't be scared," Klein coaxed Julie. "You know, we're practically related. You're Jeff's cousin and so am I."

"Really?" Julie said, looking pleased by this information.

"Only I'm from his mother's side and you're from his father's, so though we're both Jeff's cousins, you're not my cousin. Does that make sense?" Klein asked with appealing innocence.

"Sure," Julie said. Noah had stopped his hilarity and listened quietly from the floor.

"So let's shake hands, Not-Really-Cousin Julie," Klein said. He stepped closer, offering his hand.

"Don't do it," Noah said, grinning.

Brian, Jeff, and Sam watched grimly as if the outcome (would Klein pull the same trick on Julie?) were of great moment. Julie looked down at Klein's proffered hand, up to his earnest countenance, and back to his hand before she at last extended her own.

Klein reached for Julie's hand abruptly—Noah cried out with expectant glee—but he surprised by not surprising: he shook her hand gently. "Nice to meet you, Julie." Klein stepped aside to introduce the page. "This is Sam, my Little Brother." He grabbed Sam by the back of the neck, pulling him close, shaking the adolescent's blond head like a rag doll's. "Sam's a little older than all of you—he's seventeen—but he's still a kid at heart. Right, Sam?"

Sam grinned. His face was smooth and pink and hairless, the load of blond curls on top of his head like a baby's. To Brian, he looked like Ricky from *The Adventures of Ozzie and Harriet*. "You bet, boss," he answered. "I'm still a little boy, just like these guys."

"Boss?" Noah asked Klein. "You're his boss?"

"Sam's taken a semester off before starting college to work at NBC as a page and I'm a vice president of NBC. So I must be his boss."

Sam ducked his head to the right, escaping Klein's grip on his neck. He said, "Dick's not my real boss, but I do what he tells me." Sam grinned at Klein. Klein laughed. Then Sam laughed.

The children did not laugh. If it was meant as a joke, they misunderstood. Especially Brian. He had retreated as far as he could, backing up all the way to Jeff's bed, and he was watching every move the adult made. Now he added Sam to his surveillance because he was sure, even then, before he knew anything, before he knew everything, Brian was sure that Sam always did exactly what Richard Klein wanted.

Witness for the Prosecution

—— February 2008 ——

BEFORE JULIE ENTERED Lincoln Center, she hid in the cold shadows of Sixty-fifth Street, near the underground garage entrance, shivering along with a few others of the addicted and the ashamed while she smoked her second cigarette from the first pack she had bought in fifteen years. Adding self-deception to sin, she had chosen a bright yellow American Spirit brand that claimed to be "additive-free." She was a clear-eyed sucker. She knew the appealing package with an Indian in a headdress taking a toke on a long pipe was intended to provoke a perverse rebelliousness in teenagers and that the absurd claim of being "natural" allowed smokers to subconsciously convince themselves that these cigarettes weren't deadly. She was certain that she was shortening her life with each inhalation, which made each draw all the more delicious.

She smoked three before going upstairs to resume the represervation of Boris Aronson's production sketches at the New York Public Library for the Performing Arts. Eleven years ago Amelia Waxman, a friend from her Hunter College days, had hired her to work part-time on the private collections, an interesting job that dovetailed nicely with Zack's attending preschool, helping pay the household bills and satisfying her need to fulfill some role other than mother and wife. Originally she had intended the work as temporary while she decided whether to get a graduate degree in art history or take up something entirely new. For a while she had a vague longing to be a psychologist. "Talking therapy is dead," Gary said when she raised the idea. "It's all pills now." He was right. She was on Zoloft and a hormone patch to keep hot flashes at bay. Besides Wellbutrin, Gary was taking Klonopin to help him fall asleep ever since he had been weaned from Ambien. Most of Julie's friends, at least all the ones she asked, admitted they were staving off anxiety or depression or both with the help of a pill. Yeah, talk was not cheap but definitely dead. Besides, how arrogant to think she could help anyone.

Other ambitions had faded as the years passed, especially after Amelia made her archival job permanent. Julie relished the quiet solitude of her windowless room, kept at a constant temperature and humidity for the sake of preservation, empty but for drawings and models of Broadway's golden days. She felt more at peace in that tomb than anywhere on earth. Gary complained endlessly about bad luck in his career, but it seemed to Julie they had always found a way to cobble together a prosperous middle-class New York life without much effort, thanks to Gary's "inheriting" his mother's obscenely inexpensive rent-controlled apartment, then getting a chance to buy it at the "insider's price" when it went co-op, in effect a fifty percent discount. Then there were the odd well-paying cases, especially his successful defense of the Freiberg widow against the charge that she had deliberately left her wealthy senile father-in-law sitting in their Westchester garage all night so that he died of exposure. Meanwhile her brother, Noah, cleverly managed Gary's profits, swelling them especially after 9/11, thanks to the Lower East Side real estate boom. He put the Widow Freiberg's fee into converting two Orchard Street tenements into tiny monstrously priced condos that tripled their nest egg, paid for Zack's outrageous thirty-thousand-dollar-a-year tuition and would put him through college. And with real estate going up and up with no end in sight, there might even be enough to pay for a generous retirement.

Julie didn't speak to her financial wunderkind brother often. She had phoned Noah yesterday, asking whether he would come to a Seder if she were to host it, but that was a pretext. When she was fourteen, attendance at family Seders had been halved by the horrendous quarrel between the Mark brothers (really between Harriet and her father) over Saul's failing to repay a four-thousand-dollar loan, and another consequence of that rupture was the blissful disappearance of Richard Klein from her life. In her twenties, following her mother's sudden death from an aneurism, Seders were inconveniently transferred to her mother's sister's house in suburban Chicago and then brought to a complete halt by her father's death nine years ago. She hadn't attempted to convene her own Seder and didn't really feel like putting one together now. Her true motive in placing the call was to find out if Noah remembered Sam Rydel or Richard Klein, assuming he had come across the latter's name. Two days since her discovery and Klein was still cited only as part of the background story of Rydel's success and philanthropy.

Noah apparently hadn't remembered Sam. When she commented that Gary was very busy with the *Rydel* case, he mumbled, "There's always some sex abuse shit going on. There are so many sick fucks out there. Speaking of sick fucks, I've got a contractor on the other line I've got to kill. Talk to you later."

She was relieved. No need to make up a story to discourage her brother from mentioning the coincidence to Gary. She loved Noah, especially admired his self-confidence, but there was no subtlety in him. When he wept over their mother's early death (Noah was only thirteen), they were efficient tears that actually drained him of pain.

She shouldn't have worried, she decided afterward. Why would Noah remember Sam or Klein? He had been very young, five and six, when they had their encounters with those monsters.

Being at work, as always, was soothing, a real pleasure handling Aronson's sketches for *Fiddler on the Roof.* They were lovely variants on Chagall: pretty childlike colors, shtetl homes as cunning and quaint as dollhouses. She remembered the production vividly. She was nine and it was her first Broadway show and a pure joy. She had adored Tevye, wished her pompous and unaffectionate father were more like him. And she particularly admired Hodel, the noble daughter who followed her betrothed, the handsome revolutionary, into exile in Siberia. For two years, she tried to imitate the actress's posture, as severe as a ballerina's, her manner dignified. Julie too longed to love a brave man of convictions, to help him triumph over injustice. People would laugh now, but that's how she saw Gary when they first met. He was a Legal Aid lawyer, denouncing rogue DAs, battling what he labeled a police state, under the guise of a war against drugs, instituting apartheid against inner-city black youth.

For an hour, she removed sketches from old encapsulating polyester sleeves that were now thought to contain a trace of acid and transferred them into the absolute safety of Solandar boxes. At ten thirty, Julie pulled off her white cotton gloves, dashing outside for two more cigarettes that she gulped desperately while shivering on Sixty-fifth Street. She popped a Certs and stopped in the bathroom to wash off the cigarette smell from her hands. *You have to quit,* she told the guilty face in the mirror for the hundredth time that morning. Highlighted by Lincoln Center's halogen spots in the restrooms, she poked at her short gray hair and wondered why she resisted dyeing it. When she used to be salt-and-pepper that was her favorite phase: mature but not decrepit. She was the only woman in her set who wasn't coloring out the gray; Amelia scolded her about it at least once a month, but she still resisted. It seemed like a futile effort, a drop in the bucket of deterioration.

Age was a reason to quit smoking. A single cigarette at fifty-three had to be more dangerous than hundreds consumed in her twenties. Perhaps that last one, inhaled with the Hudson's cold wind, would activate a cancer cell in her breasts, too tired now to fight, no longer needed for nurture. The irony was that Gary had quit, really and truly quit, while she and Zack had taken it up. She must stop. How could she confront Zack about his smoking—she hadn't; nor had she snitched on him to Gary—while she was weak? She felt guilty sitting on the closed toilet seat at home, guilty blowing smoke at the window, guilty as she hurried away from the sight line of her doorman while on a trumped-up errand for a "forgotten" supermarket item to sneak a cigarette between the corner deli and her apartment building. She felt guilty and also very glad to have such a respectable secret.

"Gary called on the landline while you were in the bathroom," Amelia said as a greeting when she returned. "Said your cell went straight to voice mail. Are you okay?" she asked. "You were in there for a while."

"I went out for some air." Julie averted her head in case the dank smell lingered on her breath. "What did Gary want?"

"Not to worry, he said, nothing's wrong but he did want to talk to you ASAP. Want to call from my office?" Amelia offered her privacy. She was a doll. All of Julie's friends, and the women she knew casually from Zack's school, as well as the wives of Gary's friends, all were free of her faults. They were openhearted with Julie. They gossiped freely and in glorious detail about their marriages and children, while she offered dry facts with none of her true feelings—except when she rejoiced in Zack. She certainly wasn't going to be graphic about her disgust with Gary's B-cup breasts and pleated folds of belly fat. And to confide any disappointment in Zack, such as discovering he smoked, hurt too keenly, as if the confession made his fault real. She couldn't shake the superstitious belief that if she never spoke of it, then the pain would not exist, would never have existed.

"Hi, Jules," Gary answered. "Wait. I'm on the other line. Hang on," he said and then added emphatically, "Don't hang up!" The line went dead. Her throat was dry with anxiety. What is it? Could he have found out about her connection to Rydel and Klein? Not from her. She had never breathed a word about either of them. She intended to tell him what had happened when they were first dating but couldn't figure out when was the right time. Certainly not before they made love. And then, since sex with Gary felt good, normal and comfortable, why add an aftertaste of illness to their love? Soon after, Gary stampeded her into marriage and she stopped thinking about what had been done to her in the excitement of making a home together. Not a willful amnesia. She did not forget. She archived it, like memories of other men and earlier romances, something you don't unpack in front of your husband, especially when, after a blissfully contented year, shortly after their first anniversary, the shameful longings came back. And then Zack arrived. Tell him after Zack? What if Gary blew up? No. She had at last found a man with whom she could live a normal life and she wasn't going to mess that up.

And their lives *were* good. Except for Zack's exposure to adult vices, things were better than ever. Gary was a success. He had even quit smoking. And she would soon be back on the straight and narrow herself. "Honey," Gary's voice returned in a hushed, solemn whisper. "Did you know your cousin Jeff was an original investor of the American Broadcasting Academy? He was on the board for five years."

She shut her eyes against panic. "The what?"

Gary sighed, the long-suffering complaint of a man saddled with an inattentive wife. "I was talking about the *Rydel* case the other day. Remember? I mentioned he's the president of this somewhat sleazy so-called school—actually it's flat-out sleazy—that lures credulous working-class kids into student loans with promises of jobs in radio and TV? Your cousin Jeff was on the board for five years back in the eighties. You know why? Because it was founded by a relative of his, Richard Klein. I guess he's also a relative by marriage to you. Did you ever meet him?" He waited for her to comment. She waited too. "Honey, you there?"

She opened her eyes. She swallowed to get the spooked sound out of her voice. "I don't know anything about what Jeff is doing. I haven't talked to him since my father died."

"I know that!" Gary sighed, suppressing exasperation as best he could. "Look, there are rumors from the DA's office that there are new accusations about to come out about this Richard Klein and I just found out Klein's not only a blood cousin of Jeff's, he was also important to him. Helped his career. At least when Jeff was starting out."

"I don't . . . know . . . about that," she stammered. She didn't. If Klein had been a booster of Jeff that was news to her. "New accusations about what?"

"That Klein also molested kids. Boys and girls. Back in the eighties and nineties. At Huck Finn Days and at the academy. They're just rumors now, I can't get a DA to confirm, and probably they're all past the statute of limitation. And Klein's old. He's eighty-four, very ill, maybe not worth prosecuting."

"There's a statue of limitation on . . ." Julie hesitated.

"Stat*ute* of limitation," Gary corrected her. "Yeah. Look, here's what I know. First thing this morning I finished a draft of a column I really like and the point I make is that whatever the truth of these disgusting molestation charges, the broadcasting academy is a rip-off. So before handing in the column, I do my due diligence, checking the board of the academy—and Jeff's name pops up big-time. Earlier in my research, I had noticed he was a donor to Huck Finn, but that didn't set off an alarm. Like all Hollywood big shots, Jeff gives to lots of charities and he wasn't on the board or active in any way. But being an original investor in the broadcasting academy and sitting on its board for five years, that's a real connection and an endorsement. I tried to reach you, couldn't, and then I found out on the academy's website that way back in 1983 Jeff gave the commencement speech there. That's a really big endorsement. So then I found the text of Jeff's speech on the website. In his speech, Jeff said the founder, his cousin Richard Klein, put him through college and got him his start in show business. So then I look up your cousin, and since his mother's maiden name was Klein and she had a brother, I assume Richard Klein is Jeff's mother's brother's son. He was Jeff's first cousin. He's really nothing to you. So . . . you never met Klein at some family thing? I mean, when your dad was still talking to his brother?"

Julie's brain was racing, but she couldn't figure out what had to be said, what should be said, what she wanted to say. She said nothing.

"Honey? Are you there?"

"I'm here. Let's talk about this when I get home. I'll be there at three," she said, a lie. She could be home by one, had planned to be, in fact. And Amelia would let her go immediately if she asked.

"No, babe, I can't wait. If this is a story I have to recuse myself from writing about, I need to know that now. I blogged a teaser about my column and I'm already in a blog shoot-out with some right-wing schmuck who—can you believe this?—blogged that child molestation has become epidemic because our society espouses homosexuality, as if being gay is the equivalent of raping children. Jesus!" Gary cleared his throat. "Anyway, I've got to know right away if this is something I can't write about. Not 'cause of Klein—he's not a relative—but because of your cousin Jeff."

"You can't." The words came out without her considering the ramifications.

Those arrived immediately. "Why not? What do you know about his involvement?"

"I don't know anything about his involvement. I don't know anything about him. You know that. We haven't spoken at all since my father died and before that I hadn't seen Jeff since I was a teenager. That's two conversations in thirty years."

"So then I can write about it. Right? I mean, there's no conflict of interest if he's a virtual stranger. Remind me. What was the fight about? Something about your dad owing his dad money?"

"No," Julie said. "Other way around. His father owned a store and my father loaned him money and Saul didn't pay it back in a timely fashion so the brothers stopped speaking, and so we stopped having Seder together." Amelia was hovering outside the glass partition, pretending not to be looking through.

"Well, that's gonna sound loopy. Your father, Hy, who died almost broke after all those stupid real estate deals in Florida, claiming one of the richest men on earth owed him money?"

"Not Jeff. Jeff didn't owe him money. Jeff was a child at the time. It was his father."

"I know that, but that's what it's gonna sound like. Anyway, the point is, you don't mind if I write about it, right?"

"I do mind," she snapped. "I just said you can't. Aren't you listening?"

"Why?" he demanded, a willful toddler. "Why can't I write about it?"

She spoke without thinking it through: "I have to speak to Jeff. I never quarreled with Jeff. It's not fair to him. He's still my first cousin."

"Okay. So when will you speak to him?"

"When? I don't know . . . I don't how long it's going to take for me to get in touch with him. I don't even have a number for him."

"I do," Gary said, pouncing as if he had been waiting for her to step into this trap. "I have a number for his private personal assistant, not some receptionist at his company, so he'll get your message quick. I'll give you the number and wait for you to call him, but first, I just want to understand why you think you have to talk to him? If you don't have a relationship with him and you don't care about him—"

"I do care." Her mouth dried out. Her upper lip stuck to her teeth and she licked them so she could go on. "Someday . . . I don't know. Maybe someday Jeff can be of help to Zack." She grabbed for that blindly, but she was delighted by the discovery.

"Help . . . Zack?"

"What if Zack's interest in acting keeps up? Who knows? Someone like Jeff, he's so important, who knows in what way he might help Zack, right? For college, maybe a letter of recommendation? No matter what school Zack wants to go to, a letter from Jeff Mark will help, right? Who knows?" She sounded so unlike herself, eager to sell an idea. To Gary of all people. When had she ever convinced Gary of anything?

Now. "You're right. When you're right, you're right," he said. "Okay. You should call him first. But listen. You gotta do it fast. You can't procrastinate, like usual. You really can't. These days this stuff goes around the world in minutes. Any second someone else could stumble on to Jeff's being on the board, then I might have to comment if they Google him and see your family name and eventually bring it back around to me, so I need to know. Anyway, I can't keep quiet about the case unless I shut down altogether and I'd have to do that today. Okay, sweetie? You'll call him right now?"

"Yes," she hissed, furious now. "Bye." Pushing her. Always pushing her. She hung up, took a step to the door, saw Amelia entering, and turned her back to hide her rage.

"Everything okay?"

She nodded. She had to think, figure this out.

Amelia came around to peer at her face, saw distress. "You sure you're okay?"

Her cell buzzed against her thigh. She dug it out. Gary. When she answered, he scolded, "You didn't ask for the number I have for Jeff. Pretty hard to call him without it. Do you know how to put your phone on speaker so you can copy it in?"

"I'll write it down." She looked at Amelia, pointing at her memo pad. "Can I . . . ?" Amelia nodded. "Give me the number." She wrote it down, folded the paper neatly, slid it into the back pocket of her jeans.

"Do it right away like you promised, okay?" Gary said, talking to her as if she were five.

She hung up without a good-bye. "Fuck," she said. Her voice warbled, more pain than anger in the curse.

Amelia's jaw set. Her tone was harsh. "Is Gary being a shit again?"

"No, no, it's not that," she said in a hurry to forestall Amelia from a misapprehension provoked by what always remained uppermost in Amelia's mind about Gary and their marriage: his affair five years ago with a young assistant district attorney, his tearful pleas for forgiveness, and Julie's quickly granted pardon. Amelia had not and would never forgive Gary for a betrayal of Julie that didn't truly bother Julie—as long as Zack never found out. After all, she couldn't blame Gary for wanting more than she could provide. "Gary's just dumping his family's nuttiness on me. I have to go home early. All right?"

"You're the best wife in the world. He's lucky to have you," Amelia said. She let her go with a kiss on the cheek and a pat on the shoulder. Didn't even press for details. What a doll.

An hour later, Julie was at home, smoking while she kept an eye on her cell, waiting for Jeff to return her call, as promised by his assistant. She hoped the message she had left would be provocative without being indiscreet: "It's his cousin Julie calling about a family emergency."

During her vigil, she perched on her bedroom window's ledge, neck and face chilled by a steady wind off the Hudson, legs and butt baked by the radiator while she took a drag and exhaled. *Last puff,* she thought in sadness. *This is my last puff ever.* She crushed the ember on the mortar between the bricks, using the filter to brush the remains away before she flicked it into the alley below. She watched to make sure it didn't hit anyone.

Now that her eyes weren't on the phone, it rang. Caller ID read "Satisfaction," the name of Jeff's producing company. Her heart began to pound. "Hello . . . ?" Her voice was faint and high, a shy little girl.

"Hello," answered a brash woman's voice that echoed slightly, as if the speaker were in a tiled room. "Julie Mark, please. I have Jeff Mark returning." It had taken twenty-two minutes. That was quick. "Hello!" the woman standing in a shower demanded.

"Uh, yes, this is Julie—this is her. This is she, I mean."

"Hold on for—"

A clattering noise interrupted the secretary and Jeff's voice came on, deeper than when he was a child, yet still nasal and congested by complaint. "Who died? Just tell me straight out. I can take it. I'm terrified. But I can take it. Who died?"

"What?"

"The message was family emergency and I haven't heard from you since the last family funeral. Who died?"

"Oh." Julie attempted a chuckle but instead made the noise of a stalled car. "No one. Everyone's fine."

"Your brother?"

"Yeah. He's fine—"

"Your husband? Your kid? Your dog? Your goldfish?"

At last he got a laugh from her. "They're all fine, Jeff."

"And you? You're fine?"

"Well," Julie reached for one more cigarette, to survive this conversation. "I've been better. I'm still kind of recovering from the shock of—"

"What?" Jeff interrupted. She heard noise in the background. Sounded like lots of people walking in a circle around Jeff and telling him things. "Recover? Recover from what? Were you in an accident?"

"I wasn't." Julie paused to light her cigarette.

"Oh thank God!" Jeff addressed someone with him. He made no effort to mute his voice, inviting her to eavesdrop. "We're about to get on a plane and I thought she was telling me she was in an accident. I swear I wouldn't get on, Grace. I would not get on this plane if she told me she'd been in an accident. It's a bad juju." He returned to Julie, so loudly she moved the receiver away from her ear. "You mean you were grief-stricken. You had to recover from being grief-stricken."

"Grief-stricken?" Julie repeated, puzzled. She exhaled a thin stream of smoke at the open window and repeated, "Grief-stricken?" Over Rydel and Klein?

"From losing your parents. What's it been? Five years since you lost your father?"

"Nine," Julie said.

"Nine! I'm old. Well, don't be embarrassed by it taking a long time. Your parents were great. Your mother was really great. Smart, witty, and holy shit, what a great cook. I can still remember her *rugelach.* She was somebody to grieve. Not like my mother." ("You're terrible!" a woman chided in the background, followed by laughter.) "I'm terrible," Jeff informed Julie, and then answered his companion (or companions—Julie heard several people in the background). "She knows what I'm talking about. This is my first cousin Julie. She knows what a horror I grew up with. The reason Julie and I didn't see each other outside of funerals for thirty years is because of my horror of a mother, the compulsive liar." To Julie, he commented, "Isn't that right, Jules? The family quarrel was all my mother's fault?"

This bravado he was displaying, glibly summing up the painful truth about his mother with easy mockery, was that a bluff? Had Jeff really learned to embrace his past in public hallways? Was Julie the straggler, a little girl stuck in her pathetic closet of shame? "Uh, well, I think, my father was also a little to blame—" Julie stammered.

"You don't have to be nice. I remember that about you, Julie. You're very nice. Well, I'm not nice. How could I be? I was raised by Eva Braun. So, what's up? If nobody's dead, what's up?"

Julie's stomach grumbled. She took a long draw on the cigarette to calm herself. She exhaled away from her cell, then chose to start with the most cowardly of her alternatives. "My husband, Gary, a lawyer, I don't know if you know, is also a TV legal analyst and columnist and he's been investigating the Rydel story—"

"Are you smoking?" Jeff interrupted. "Are you still smoking? I'm talking to a white middle-class mother who is smoking," he commented to the others. "You are a mother, right?"

"Yes, I have a son. Zack. He's fifteen."

"Wow. Fifteen. Wow. I have four kids, you know that, right? Oldest is sixteen, the baby just one. And you're smoking? How did you get away with it? You don't live in LA, that's how. They'd shoot you in LA." (His audience enjoyed that; there was a chorus of laughter.) "They would." Jeff milked the joke. "A mother who smokes? They would shoot you. No, I'm sorry. I'm wrong. First, they would take away your illegal Nicaraguan nanny and then they would shoot you." (The female laughter got raucous; someone called, "Jeff, you're hilarious.") "I'm on my way home to LA now," Jeff continued. "We just tested in Houston. Can you believe it? Houston fucking Texas. In fact, I have to get off, we're about to board. So, can I call you back? What were you calling about, anyway?"

"I was calling because my husband tells me it's not going to stop with Sam. It's going to come out about . . ." She was about to say "your cousin," but Jeff was talking nervously over her: "You said something about your son. What's his name? I'm sorry, I forgot."

"Not my son. His name is Zack."

"Zack, that's a good Jewish name." (A woman giggled and said in a southern accent, "He's terrible, he's god-awful terrible.")

"Actually, his father's not Jewish," Julie said.

"Really. Married a goy, eh, Jules? Smart move. Jewish men are too much work." ("You can say that again," a woman with a baritone voice called out.) "Look, I have to turn the phone off because I'm about to board a plane with the most powerful scumbag in Hollywood." (She heard a man grumble, then laugh.) "And he expects me to hold his hand during takeoff. Actually for the entire flight. Can I call you back after I land in LA?"

She should say no; she had promised Gary.

Like Gary, Jeff didn't wait for her to agree. "Glad nobody's dead. After we land in LA, I'll call you. That is, *if* we land." ("Don't say that!" the deep-voiced woman said. "That's real bad juju.") "Talk to you later, *bubelah*."

When the line went dead, it felt to her that not an individual but an entire world had disappeared. Despite his bitter jokes, he was full of confidence—that certainly was a contrast to her. Was this the true value of being world famous: no more shame, no more guilt? She shivered at a gust off the Hudson, pressed out a second this-is-my-last cigarette, and decided to confess to Gary that she was smoking. And to Zack. How could she expect them to quit (*Gary has quit,* she reminded herself) if she continued in secret? Besides, she knew that only by removing the guilty pleasure of the secrecy would she be able to surrender the narcotic.

The front door banged. She slammed the window shut, a fleck of paint flying off. "Honey!" Gary called. She tossed the pack of American Spirits into her pocketbook while his feet tramped in the hall, heading her way. She dashed into the bathroom and shut the door. "Honey! You here? Why aren't you answering your phone?" Gary called as he entered the bedroom. She turned on the faucets, grabbed her toothbrush and the tube of Colgate. She squeezed the container too hard—shooting out a two-inch stream of blue and white striped goo that vaulted over the bristles and onto the mirror, adhering to the glass like a dying worm.

"I'll be right out!" Julie called, trying to scoop up the creature with her toothbrush.

The door opened. Gary opened the door! She was in the bathroom and he brazenly came in as if she had no right to privacy. "Did you reach—?" Gary paused as he took in the spectacle of his wife scraping Colgate off the mirror. "What are you doing?"

She pushed past him into the bedroom, had a wild thought of fleeing from him, running out of the apartment and never coming back. But that was nonsense—abandon Zack?

Gary appeared, squawking at her like an outraged duck, "What the fuck is going on? You haven't called, right? Is that why you're hiding from me?"

She needed one now, she couldn't wait. She reached blindly into her pocketbook, perched on the night table. In her haste to remove one American Spirit yellow she crushed the pack, but at least she didn't destroy the cigarette selected. She put it between her lips, dry with fear, and moved at Gary while opening a book of matches. He gaped at her while she lit up. She inhaled deep and exhaled fully, walking through the cloud she had created. "I'm smoking, you self-centered motherfucker," she informed him.

For once, he was silenced.

"I'm smoking," she repeated, ready to cry. She took another draw and blew in his direction. Tears subsided. Her head throbbed. She didn't want the cigarette anymore.

The smoke between them had dissipated by the time he walked straight at her, eyes narrowed with rage.

She back away until she whacked into the wall. "Gary . . ." she pleaded for mercy.

He pressed flush against her and enveloped her lips with his, tongue pushing all the way in. He ran a hand roughly down over her breast, squashing it as if he were performing a mammogram. He pushed a thigh between her legs, quadriceps on pelvic bone. He mumbled over her lips, "I can taste it." He turned his head to search for her hand with the cigarette. He took hold of her wrist and moved her hand toward his mouth, lips parting in anticipation of the filter's arrival.

"No." She fought to keep the cigarette at arm's length.

"Gimme," he pleaded.

"No, I'm quitting."

He kissed her again, slobbering, not his usual firm peck. His lips were a stranger's, greedy, hostile. He jerked away, perhaps also feeling her lips to be alien, and buried his head in her neck. He licked from her collarbone to earlobe, a hot wet sensation that tickled. She arched away, head thudding against the wall. "I can taste it on you," he croaked. He buried his head in the cleavage of her sweater and inhaled with noisy satisfaction.

"I'm quitting." She pushed free, into the bathroom. She tossed the half-smoked cigarette in the toilet and flushed. Deciding to take a shower, she pulled up her sweater. As her head emerged from the wool blindfold, she discovered Gary had once again entered without respect for her privacy. He took her right hand, raised it to his nose, sniffing her fingers, kissing their smoky tips.

"I'm taking a shower," she said, trying to pull free.

"No." He pulled her out of the bathroom, toward their bed for a few struggling steps, finally flinging her at it. He pulled his shirt out of his pants and unbuttoned from the bottom up. His swollen belly appeared, covered with swirling black hairs. "How long?" he asked.

"How long?" she repeated, wondering with horror if he meant how long he could fuck her, for that was obviously what he intended as he proceeded to lower his corduroy pants, revealing the full splendor of his belly's overhang, a cantilevering so severe that his underpants were obscured by its shadow.

He kicked out of his shoes and dove at her, still wearing black socks. The bed sagged when he landed beside her. "How long have you been smoking?" he said as he pulled her blouse out of her skirt. He sniffed the collar while undoing her buttons and watched the unclothing of her body with a hunger she hadn't seen for two decades.

"A few weeks," she lied for some unfathomable reason.

"You bitch," he said with an admiring smile. He cupped her right breast, encased in the satin support of her wire bra. "I love you," he said. He pecked at the outline of her nipple, sniffing as he did. He pushed her down gently, but firmly, and ran his tongue the length of her exposed midriff.

Her head lolled back, eyes wandering to the open window, blackout shades up, curtains pulled back. She was wet. All of New Jersey could see her, loose and fluid and helpless. She was so wet. How long? How long since her body was young like this? "Gary," she called.

"Mmm," he answered while plump fingers crawled between her back and the bedspread to unhook her bra.

"I love you," she lied.

White Lies

— April 1966 —

RICHARD KLEIN UNBUTTONED and rebuttoned his blazer while he surveyed the roomful of children. "How about we all go for some good deli? Hot dogs, pastrami, knishes—what do you say, kids?"

Noah scrambled up from the floor and cheered, arms aloft.

Klein smiled at the sight of the excited boy on tiptoe, back arched to reach as high as he could. Brian studied that smile as if it were a Rosetta stone to the urgent mystery of Richard Klein: puffy cheeks raised, mouth parting to show small, evenly spaced teeth, as he enjoyed the spectacle of Noah. All Brian could decipher in the smile was the benign delight of a grandparent. He concluded, not for the first time, that what happened in the NBC bathroom had been unique, because of something about Brian or the circumstances: the violation of the set, the potted plant spilling, his penis's keen reaction when it was touched. Even Klein had noticed that: "You like it when I touch you there, don't you?" But how did he know in advance that Brian would like it?

"Come on!" Noah grabbed his sister's hand. Julie allowed herself to be towed to the door. "Come on!" Noah called to Jeff and Brian.

Brian tried to catch Jeff's eye, to signal they needed to confer. Brian wanted to tell him they had to skip lunch and deal with the secret recording—which was true enough—plus it was a convenient excuse for Brian avoiding being with Richard Klein without telling Jeff why he wanted to avoid him. Unluckily, Jeff's eyes remained down while he trudged after the group gathered near the door.

"I can't," Brian blurted out.

They all turned his way, except for Klein. He shoved his hands in his pockets, noisily jiggling change while he peered at his highly polished black loafers.

"You can't?" Sam said.

"We're gonna have hot dogs! Hot dogs, hot dogs!" Noah chanted.

"Noah," Julie warned.

Brian pointedly moved his eyes to the tape recorder on the twin bed, then back to Jeff. He repeated the signal twice, so blatantly he felt fortunate that Sam didn't pick it up. Unfortunately Jeff didn't either. He stared hopelessly at nothing.

Brian said, "I gotta have lunch with my mom," which made no sense but was exactly what he felt.

"Okay, Brian can't come," Richard Klein took his hands out of his pockets. The cold indifference in his voice amazed Brian. Maybe he was angry. Maybe Klein thought what happened in the NBC bathroom was Brian's fault. Maybe it was. "Come on, kids," Klein said. "Let's have hot dogs!" He swallowed little Noah's hand in his chubby palm and led the way out. The rest followed.

Brian was left alone with his confusion. He heard Klein say, "We're going to lunch, honey. We'll be back soon!" as the group passed Harriet's door. "Hot dogs, hot dogs!" Noah chanted, fainter and fainter, until the front door slammed shut and there was silence.

Brian felt tremendous relief at the absence of people (his preference for being alone would last a lifetime) until he heard Harriet sigh, a surprisingly loud sound considering that it had to travel the distance from her bed and down the intervening hallway. Harriet sighed a second time and exclaimed, "What a cheap son of a bitch!"

Brian froze, dumbstruck by the stupidity of what he had done. He was trapped. Harriet assumed he had gone with the others. She would be angry that he hadn't; she had asked him to help Jeff entertain his cousins. Brian listened to her furious dialing of the phone's rotary, unable to hear what she was mumbling bitterly to herself.

Go! he urged himself. *Go while she's distracted.* He crept down the hallway toward her room, hoping to get there before she made her connection.

"Saul," Harriet said as Brian's nose reached the edge of her doorframe. She invariably talked on the phone with her head on pillows propped against the headrest, maintaining a constant surveillance of the hall, preventing him from escaping the apartment unobserved. "You can't call me back, Saul, I have to talk to you right now. Hy's not there yet, is he? I have to talk to you before your brother gets there."

Brian smelled the peculiar dank odor of Harriet's lair: a blend of perspiration and potatoes, a stew smell like Grandma Maggie's cooking, but not of beef and vegetables, a boiling off of Harriet, an evaporation of her persona.

"Forget about your customer. Let Billy deal with a customer for once in his life. Now listen, Hy's on his way to you. I talked to him about the money. Because I had to! He brought it up. Yes, I'm telling you, he brought it up. Why would I bring it up? I don't remember how. Saul, will you stop arguing and listen to me. Of course you're arguing. I told him I have a lump in my breast. Yes, I told him I have breast cancer. No, not benign. I told him it was malignant. Calm down. Saul, calm down. Calm down and listen!" she shouted furiously, which was strange to Brian considering the subject was her death. Her raging made him cringe. Everything about her terrified him, especially her illness. "Listen to me, Saul!" she yelled. "Will you listen to me! Do you want to lose the store? Is that what you want?

Fine. You tell him I don't have breast cancer and you'll lose everything and Jeff will grow up to be a *shmendrek* salesman while your brother's bratty little kids will live like kings. The thought of that little shit Noah becoming a doctor, driving a Cadillac, living on Park Avenue while my Jeff has to kiss his *tuchus* every High Holiday. It makes me sick. I'd rather be dead than see my Jeff humiliated."

Brian, appalled and confused by Harriet's reason for lying, was also profoundly relieved that she wasn't dying, at least for Jeff's sake. But what preoccupied him above all was an inspiration that came to him during Harriet's weird speech about Noah's future. It occurred to him that a relatively short time had elapsed since the others passed Harriet's door to go to lunch. What if he had stayed behind to use Jeff's bathroom and was supposed to meet them at the deli? Then his sudden appearance, dashing out in a hurry to catch up, would make sense.

He settled on that plan while Harriet continued to shout at Saul, describing a bizarre future in which Julie married a rich man and gave Hy beautiful grandchildren while Jeff remained unmarried, lost his hair, and worked in a pool hall. (*Why a pool hall?* Brian wondered.) Brian stepped on the floorboards nearest to the wall, believing they creaked less readily there, and ducked into the hall bathroom. He flushed the toilet, and while the rushing water was at its peak he ran as if propelled by the explosive sound, dashing past Harriet's door—"Who's that!" she shouted. "My God, who's that?"—turned the corner into the main hall—"Brian? Is that you—"

He called out, "I'm late!" as he reached the foyer, opened the front door, exited into the building's hallway, and hustled down the stairs so recklessly that he missed a step as the staircase turned a corner, whacked into the wall, and ended up sprawled on the landing, unhurt, breathless, and full of triumph. He was free. He was safe.

No one answered the bell at his apartment. His mother must have gone out shopping and his father was probably rehearsing too loudly in the bedroom to hear his ring. He had been told to make sure to ring before using his key, something about a scary story of some kid he didn't know who had been followed home by a robber—it didn't really make sense to him. He let himself in and called, "I'm home!"

No response. He glanced in the kitchen and living room on his way to the hall to his and his parents' bedrooms. Their door was open. No one was in there. "Dad?" he called. When he turned, he saw the door to the bathroom at the end of hall was shut.

As he approached, he heard a soft slapping of water. His mother must be in the tub, soaking, as she liked to when tired, or upset at his father for staying out very late, sometimes so late he slept over at an actor friend's apartment. Brian knocked.

"Oh, I'm so glad you came back, honey. Come in. It's open," Rose said in a lilting voice. Years later, when an adult Brian thought back on the many mysteries of this day, he realized she reserved that singsong for her husband.

Brian entered. His mother lay in a tub of clear water, wrinkled toes in the air, pubic hair afloat, as if levitating off her white belly. "Mom," he leaned on the glass doorknob while staring at the curious sight of the black patch of hair swaying in the water. "When you get out, could you make me a grilled cheese sandwich?"

No answer was forthcoming. Brian raised his eyes to meet his mother's. They were wide with alarm. Her hands were on either side of the tub's rim, as if she were about to push off to rise, but she didn't move, didn't appear to draw a breath. "You okay, Mom?" Brian asked. Her eyes were red rimmed and swollen.

"Uh . . ." His mother glanced at the towel rack. Instead of reaching for one, as Brian expected, she lowered herself as much as she could, nipples sinking below the clear water's surface. *Periscopes down,* Brian thought to himself. She met his eyes, then immediately looked away. "Go to the kitchen while I'll dry off, and I'll come make you lunch."

"Can I have grilled cheese?" Brian persisted, to make sure she understood that he definitely wanted grilled cheese and not tuna fish.

"What?" Her hands continued to grip the porcelain rim as if she were about to boost herself up. But she made no other move to rise; the opposite, in fact, slipping lower, water up to her chin, knees rising to put her back flat, drowning the floating black forest.

"I want grilled cheese. Do we have grilled cheese?"

"I—don't—know," she stammered. "Why don't you look in the refrigerator and see?" She nodded at the door.

That was the moment he understood. A faint message that she had been transmitting since he entered the bathroom was finally received. He wasn't supposed to see her naked. Worse, he was supposed to know he wasn't allowed to see her naked. Lingering at the door, studying her body was wrong. Now that he understood how important it was for him to get out of there, he was too overwhelmed to leave. He wanted to explain that he hadn't meant any harm. "Go," she ordered.

In the kitchen, he tried to make amends for his error. He took out the tin-foil-wrapped American cheese, removed the butter from its tray, searched in the lower cabinet for the small frying pan she used to grill sandwiches, and set a plate beside the stove. He prayed she wouldn't say anything about his mistake.

Could he distract her by telling her that Harriet had lied to her about being sick? *No, stupid.* The only way he could know Harriet had lied was because of the secret taping. Besides, he wasn't sure he wanted his mother to have this latest information on Harriet. Harriet was so nutty Rose might forbid him from playing with Jeff at all.

Brian sat down to wait at the white Formica kitchen table. Almost immediately he got up, worried if he was doing nothing when she entered the kitchen that might invite a lecture. He spied one of his Superman comics, bought and read yesterday. Not a good one. It featured Mxyzptlk, a villain Brian didn't enjoy, a whimsical imp who used magic to confound the Man of Steel, creating more dangerous mischief than actual harm. Brian preferred his bad guys to be made of sterner stuff. He sat at the table and opened it, pages high to cover his face.

Rose appeared in a long red robe, hair damp. She silently surveyed the kitchen. "You put out everything I need," she noted with surprise. "Thank you." Brian kept his eyes on a panel depicting a befuddled Superman flying upside down, cape flopped over his face, blind to the fact that was about to collide with a plane. He heard crinkling of tin foil, whoosh of a gas burner, sizzle of butter hitting the skillet. The yummy odor of cheese cooking reached him as his mother said, "I thought you were having lunch with Jeff."

"He went out," Brian said. He didn't want to talk about that either. *Why didn't you want to go to lunch? Because of Mr. Klein. Why? Don't you like him?* "Dad went out?" he asked.

"Yes. To yet another reading in *Greenwich Village,*" she emphasized the location as if it were damning. "Jeff went out for lunch with Harriet?"

Brian shook his head.

"With his cousins?"

"Yeah. That smells good, Mom. You make the best grilled cheese sandwich on earth."

The compliment wasn't enough to detour her. "Didn't they invite you?"

Brian had an answer ready. "They were going to the deli for franks. I wanted a grilled cheese sandwich." He dropped the disappointing Superman comic, got up, and stood beside his mother to observe her virtuoso technique. "I wanted to have *your* grilled cheese sandwich." He rested his head against the soft shoulder of her robe.

She tensed. "But Jeff wanted you to go to lunch?" She shifted, shoulder slipping away.

Brian took the hint and straightened. "He didn't care, Mom."

"Today's his birthday, right?"

"Not really. Monday is his birthday."

One side was browned, the cheese oozing, sticking to the pan. Rose flipped the sandwich and pressed it flush with the spatula, forming stripes on the bread. "Aren't Harriet and Saul having a party for Jeff today?"

"They're not having a party, Mom."

"You know what I mean. His cousins from Riverdale are there. And isn't that cousin of Harriet's, that nice man who took you to NBC, isn't he coming over?" She turned to him, spatula up, a fencer ready to spar. He lowered his eyes to the bubbling cheese. "That's what Harriet told me. We were talking on the phone less than an hour ago and she told me they were inviting you to stay for a special dinner to celebrate Jeff's birthday with all his family. Didn't Jeff invite you?"

He hadn't. But he probably just assumed. Brian's weekend dates often lasted through dinner. "I don't know," he said.

Rose pressed: "Harriet told me he invited you."

Brian returned to the table and shielded his face behind the inferior Superman comic. "Probably," he mumbled.

There was a long silence broken only by the sizzling pan. Brian considered asking her to take his temperature. If she looked away while the thermometer was in his mouth he could hold it under his tensor lamp; Jeff claimed that had worked for him once. She wouldn't suspect a faked illness on a Sunday. The plan seemed sound. He thought it through again, mostly just for the pleasure of contemplation. He didn't have the nerve to try.

She turned off the stove. Her robe appeared at the periphery of the comic book. He was presented with an evenly browned sandwich, just like the picture on the Broadway Diner menu. He took a bite, tongue pressing the mix of warm soft cheese and crunchy toast against the solid roof of his mouth.

"You know, honey," his mother said as she ran a hand through his hair, "you shouldn't come into the bathroom while I'm using it."

Brian nodded. He had no desire to make the accurate defense that he had been invited into the bathroom.

She kissed him on top of the head, then sat in the chair opposite, watching as he took another bite. "Mmm," he said. "This is good."

"Brian," she said in an ominous tone and waited.

What is it now? "Yeah . . . ?"

"Jeff is your best friend," she pointed out. "He may not have said anything, but this is a special day for him, the day they're really celebrating his birthday. So after you finish your sandwich I think you should go back upstairs. In fact, I have to visit Aunt Helen this afternoon. I also don't know when your father will get back so this would be a good night for you to have a sleepover with Jeff."

"But I have school tomorrow."

"So? You'll come downstairs when you wake up. I'll give you breakfast. You'll have plenty of time to get ready for school. You're the one who's always saying you should be allowed to sleep over on school nights." He didn't answer. She stroked a lock of his hair off his forehead. "What's going on, honey? Did you have a fight with Jeff?"

"No!" He was vehement. Fight with Jeff? Sometimes they argued about whether to pinch hit for Whitey Ford, or whether *The Outer Limits* was really scary, but they never really had a fight. Brian took another bite of cheese and toast, tongue cradling the soft and the crunchy. He could fake getting sick by sticking his finger down his throat. Jeff said that would make you throw up.

Rose stood. She picked up the white phone mounted on the wall. "I'll call Harriet," she said as she dialed, "and arrange it."

Unfortunately Brian hated throwing up. He would go. And he would sleep over. Anyway, the sleepover wouldn't be a problem; by nighttime, Klein would be gone. Brian resumed reading the inferior Superman comic. The citizens of Metropolis laughed at the Man of Steel as he walked down the street with his famous uniform on backward, tripping over his cape. That was stupid. It made no sense. People wouldn't laugh at Superman no matter how confused he got.

Childhood's End

—— February 2008 ——

FINISHED WITH HER, Gary rolled onto his back, and asked, "Why?"

"Why what?" Julie looked away from her horrified fascination with the beach ball of his belly, up to the plaster ceiling, brilliantly illuminated by the afternoon sun. She noticed cracks, flaking, and a dark spot where a leak from somewhere had penetrated before their grumpy superintendent stopped it. We have to repaint. *When can we do that? Everything will have to be packed up.*

"Why did you start smoking?" Gary asked.

She didn't want to add another charge to Gary's indictment of Zack as criminally adolescent. "I don't really know. Just happened." She yanked the top sheet up to cover her breasts, flattened by gravity and aging. They had been a constant focus of anxiety throughout life: when they would appear, then their size, then nurturing, then death. The latter was the most time-consuming anxiety: probing, mammograms, confusing articles in the Science section of the *Times,* the disappearance of one woman she knew fairly well from ten years of morning drop-offs at school. Breasts: start to finish a worry.

Gary groaned as he made the effort to rise from the bed. She looked at his back's expanse of pale flesh, dotted by three enormous moles that were a yearly dermatological concern. *We are repulsive creatures lumbering to our deaths.* "You don't know. How can you not know what the impulse was?" He reached for his pants. He wondered out loud, "Do I have to take a shower?" then returned to his interrogation. "Don't you think it has something to do with me quitting?"

"Definitely not. Everything I do doesn't have to do with you, Gary. It's just that at work I see all the young people on their breaks smoking outside and talking together so intensely. They all looked so . . . I don't know . . ."

"Young?" Gary offered, looking out the window at the Hudson, naked but for the draped fig leaf of his relaxed-fit corduroys. "Why should I quit if you're smoking?"

"I'm stopping," she said firmly.

"You'd better. Or I'm starting again." He stared as sternly as he could from above the essential cheerfulness of his chubby cheeks and the essential neediness of his brown eyes. "I mean it."

"I'm quitting," she promised, and meant it.

He considered that for a long moment, then commented, "Although the sex was good," before ducking into the bathroom.

She lay there, relaxed and happy to feel cool air on her still warmed skin, glad to be free of clothing, listening to the faint waterfall of Gary's shower. She wished for summer: to bake in the sun with eyes shut, head encased by heat and light, ocean roaring, worries silenced. The beach. *Is that where Cousin Jeff lives? Malibu?* The Colony she had read about? He was so rich he probably owned houses in all the major cities. But whom did he have sex with?

With his wife, she reminded herself. Jeff had a wife and four children, although not all with that wife. *Four children.* It amazed her that a boy who was so much a child could evolve into a parent. She got up, put on her robe and slippers waiting for the bathroom to be free. In the meantime she could clean.

She wandered into Zack's room, deciding that the pile of books, magazines and video game cases could no longer wait for that hoped for day when Zack would spontaneously neaten them. Why worry about Jeff's sex life? He was a big Hollywood success. They got to fuck whoever they wanted.

Zack's books and papers were in an ungovernable pile on his Ikea desk. She dug into it. Did he know his chemistry book was under a mound of *Rolling Stone* magazines, a fourteenth-birthday subscription she had renewed even though he claimed not to read them, and . . . My God, a copy of *Variety!* Zack's love affair with acting must be more than a high school romance. Still it shouldn't be taken seriously, she decided. Didn't every teenager dream of becoming a movie star?

Although in Zack's case she judged the ambition made sense. He was handsome. Take your breath away handsome. God had cherry-picked otherwise ordinary features of hers and Gary's and rearranged them into a flawless miracle of beauty and strength, the soulful face of a tragic Prince. He had Gary's sturdy bones, her lean, limber flesh. And he had his father's voice: a resonant, confident instrument that invited you to listen uncritically. She suspected her husband's success as a legal analyst could be credited more to a felicitous stringing of vocal chords than Columbia Law School.

She thoughtlessly, she later told herself, removed an unlined black bound sketchbook from the bottom of the pile, opening it casually (not realizing she was invading his privacy, she would have sworn) scanning a page of black ink produced by Zack's compact and surprisingly—given the condition of his room—neat handwriting. She saw the word—*Cunt*—and forgot every other concern but the rest of the sentence.

S.'s *Cunt*—Zack had capitalized the word, as if it were a proper noun, a personality to reckon with—*smelled. Not like V's. V's didn't stink. I thought I was going to gag, but S. was so wet, I took a deep breath through my mouth and got to work. After a minute I got used to her stink. Even got to kinda like it. I'm getting good with my tongue because she came. Came hard.*

No faking. Couldn't be faking. She arched her back, pushed her Cunt up at me like a bitch in heat and grabbed my hair. She pulled so hard I thought I was gonna end up as bald as Dad.

When she discovered Zack's cigarettes, she had staggered until she was forced to sit on his bed to avoid fainting. This time she remained on her feet. Seventy-two hours had made her impervious to the shock of her son's capacity for depravity; a teenager who ruined his lungs was capable of any degradation. She wasted no time on imagined alibis, this was unmistakably her baby boy's hand, the same tight letters he used to write from summer camp. *Dear Mom & Dad. Last night was Campfire. Uncle Tom told a really really scary Ghost story. I toasted lots of marshmallows. Yum. Miss you, Zack.*

She flipped to another page. More despicable writing: *F. gave me head. Her teeth were a little rough on my Helmet, but she's pretty good. Better than S. She swallowed all of it . . .* Was this a grotesque joke? The girls Zack knew were bright, well educated, choking with self-esteem. Maybe this was Zack's attempt at pornographic fiction? She read on in a hurry, hearing Gary had shut off the shower. *Afterward, she asked if I liked her. So pathetic. Brandon*—no, this was not fiction, Brandon was his closest male friend—*says I should try to get her to take it in the ass. That's too gross. But it's great how she'll do anything to please me. I am truly evil."*

"Honey!" Gary called. She shoved the notebook back under the chemistry text. *I am truly evil,* she echoed, hustling out of her son's room, down the narrow hall to the kitchen where Gary entered from the other side dressed in his favorite traveling outfit—a safari shirt and L.L. Bean cargo pants whose endless pockets he filled with an iPhone, a charger, earphones, a reporter's notebook, two pens, and lots of gum. "Here you are," he said, sealing the flap over his iPhone with the intense concentration of a toddler. "Where did you go?"

I am truly evil were the only words in her head, so she kept mum.

"Honey, the reason I came home is to make sure you get ahold of Cousin Jeff today. My source in the DA's office says they're getting formal statements today from other witnesses. And guess what: they may indict Klein too. Probably not for a few days, but Paula"—Gary was referring to the producer of *American Justice*—"wants me at the scene to answer questions remotely from outside the gates of Rydel's mansion, so if I'm begging off this story I have to do it tonight. She's booked me into the Dis-Comfort Inn in East Hampton. He's out on bail and supposedly Klein is with him, but that's not confirmed. I thought about asking Bill and Sue if I could use their place, but—I don't know—then I'd have to feed them tidbits and where the fuck do I stand, right? Can I cover this or not?" The afterglow of sex had dimmed; he was back to his usual state of anxiety, competitiveness, nagging, fault finding. "You gotta get some clarity about this situation with your cousin Jeff for me by tonight. So, please, please—"

"Maybe you should just tell Paula you can't cover this story," Julie said. *They don't need my two cents,* she thought. *No one needs to know about me.*

"What?" Gary put his hands on the hips of his ballooning cargo pants, astounded. "Why would I do that? How do we know Jeff will give a shit whether I write about it? And if he does, as you very astutely pointed out to me, shouldn't we get something out of it? Jesus, I'm giving up a great story that I have an original angle on. This is lots of columns, lot of TV appearances, maybe a book, maybe a raise." He stared, in a stubborn pose, indicating he would wait for an answer until hell froze over.

There was no point in trying to debate Gary. She confessed: "I called him. I spoke to Jeff."

At first, Gary was delighted. Then his exasperation and anxiety worsened when she explained that their conversation had been interrupted; and he wasn't reassured that Jeff had promised to call back after he landed. "For chrissakes, he flies in a private plane. He didn't have to hang up. They make schmucks like me turn off their cells, not Jeff Mark in his very own plane! He was stalling you."

"Stalling me about what?" she argued. "I never got around to explaining why I was calling."

"Oh." That gave Gary pause. Not for long. "Well, my point is he can talk while on the plane. Even if they didn't let him use his cell during the flight, his private plane must have a goddamn phone. Call his office. Say you can't wait until he lands, you have to speak to him in flight."

"Okay," she stalled. "I'll take a shower and call him." She moved to push past him.

He took her arm and bussed her. "I love you," he apologized.

He loved her but didn't trust her to place the call to Jeff's assistant. After her shower, while she dressed in the closet, he stood a few feet away, focused on his iPhone. He said, "Here's the number," twice, to prod her. She dialed on their landline while he mouthed suggestions of what to say to convince the director's gatekeeper to let her, a nobody relative whom Jeff hadn't talked to in years, through immediately. Hopeless. No concession other than "I will give Mr. Mark your message."

Even Gary gave up, leaving for the Hamptons. After he was settled at the motel, he texted her twice asking if Jeff had called, before her cousin finally did call back, six hours after their first contact.

Julie was mindful that everything he said was more or less a lie. Her father used to say about Jeff, after the famous quarrel when he learned that Harriet wasn't dying of anything except the acute desire not to have Saul repay him, "Lying's in Jeff's genes. Harriet was the biggest liar on earth, so you can't blame the poor kid. He can't help himself."

Jeff lied, "Julie, that was the worst flight I've ever been on. It was a total nightmare—" He interrupted himself to interject to the caravan around him, "No way that was turbulence. An engine must've fallen off the fucking plane." His voice returned to speak to her—deeper than when he was a boy, to be sure, yet still imbued with a kid's energy and lack of reserve. "Julie, believe me, that was the worst experience of my life. I've got to get out of this business. Too much fucking flying. Nothing is worth being that scared. Do you like to fly?" he asked before supplying her answer. "Of course you do. Everybody loves to fly except for me. Or at least everybody says they love it. Yeah, they do!" he squawked to the murmur of a female voice in the background. "Everybody says they don't think about it. Lies. All lies. As soon as the plane hits a little bump, everybody's praying to God. What's the line about foxholes?" A female voice mumbled something. Jeff shouted, "Right! Well, it's true of jets. There are no atheists during takeoff. so . . ." Julie moved the phone a few inches from her ear. He had returned to speaking directly to her. That, and some other improvement in his cell phone's broadcast amplified his voice into a shout. "YOU HAVE A TEENAGE SON. I CAN'T BELIEVE IT. HOW OLD—?" Abruptly there was a bomb of static and Jeff was gone.

By the time he called back, she had moved to the maid's room, settling at the little desk in the pantry/office. She didn't turn on a light, intently watching a window directly across the wide courtyard of their prewar apartment building. That apartment's kitchen and maid's room had been renovated to make one large eat-in kitchen. It looked very clean and new: recessed halogen lights, granite counters, super-high-tech appliances with glowing LED lights. A handsome young man—late twenties, she guessed—dressed in a conservative gray suit stood at a black laminate round table under a brilliant spotlight, unloading take-out food from the new Thai restaurant around the corner on Broadway.

"Julie! Sorry." Jeff spoke without a hello. "Cell phone networks in America are like a third-world county. So . . . what's your boy into?"

"What's he what?" she asked, watching the young man open a bottle of beer and sit down to deal with a pair of tin foil containers. He seemed to have big hands. Or long fingers anyway, since they wrapped around the bottle with room to spare. His head of black hair was thick. She couldn't really see his features but they were strong. From this distance he vaguely resembled the actor who played Don Draper in *Mad Men*. He removed his jacket, tossing it with a boy's sloppiness over a chair. There wasn't a hint of a bulge at his belly. The shirt was flush, disappearing seamlessly into narrow gray pants. He was too handsome to be alone. Since he moved in a year ago, she had never spotted a girl guest, or a boy for that matter. But she couldn't see into the window of his bedroom; that faced away, toward West End Avenue. Probably his guests had better things to do than eat. Still, a solo dinner seemed a lonely activity for such a looker.

"Your son. What's he interested in?"

"Acting," she admitted reluctantly.

"Acting! Shoot him. Take him to the pound. Put him down. Don't even think twice. Best thing for him. Merciful thing to do." There was a collection of laughs in the background—a screechy one, a giggly one, and a male snorting. It was as if Jeff were performing in front of a studio audience or had installed a laugh track on his cell phone. "Just kidding, Jules. Really. Just kidding." She heard another round of screech, giggle and snort; she presumed he'd made a face to his entourage.

"He's fifteen. Just a kid with foolish dreams," Julie said, regretting she'd mentioned Zack at all. She had raised a creep; she had to give up speaking or thinking about him. She watched the lovely young man remove chopsticks from the take-out bag, snap them apart with a flick of thumb and index finger. He did everything with the physical confidence of an athlete.

"Sure, sure. He'll grow up to be a doctor. Like his father."

"A lawyer," Julie corrected.

"Oh, right. Guess I was thinking of your daddy. But what am I talking about? Uncle Harry was a dentist. Of course dentists *are* doctors." Another snorting laugh in the background. Jeff must have rolled his eyes. Julie was taken aback by Jeff's mockery. If he wasn't at least a little scared of her, why had he returned her call? "They are doctors!" Jeff insisted, then couldn't stop himself from laughing. He tried again to be sober: "Jules. Listen, I'm almost at my editing room. And speaking of editing, I have to cut to the chase. Why did you call?"

He seemed to take it for granted everyone would do his bidding and on his schedule. *Because he's famous and rich? Maybe I'm just being irritable.* She hadn't had a cigarette for four hours, maintaining her postcoital promise. "Your cousin. I'm calling because they're going to indict him."

Jeff vanished. The background sound of traffic, electronic whoosh, mumbled voices, and Jeff's cackle—all gone.

"Jeff?" she asked dead air but knew better. Quite an advantage talking on a cell. Plausible deniability about hanging up. Her eyes drifted across the dark courtyard, to the brilliantly lit tableaux of a vigorous young man in shirtsleeves, chopsticks funneling food into his hungry mouth. Only hours ago she'd had the first orgasm she'd allowed herself in three months—and with Gary no less! It had been lovely, a wonderful surprise, but what good had it done? She just wanted another.

For a long minute, she felt utterly alone. She hadn't felt so alone in this way since the weeks after her mother's death. And it was same kind of loneliness: feeling herself small, standing solo on the skin of the earth, with no soul on the horizon approaching to comfort her.

She had to get rid of this miserable feeling. She walked into the hall to see if Zack's lights were on. They were.

She turned out the living-room lamps, retired to her bedroom, undressed, took a long bath, brushed her teeth, washed her face, and slowly rubbed Ponds moisturizer into her pores. Although it was February, she chose her thin white cotton robe. She left her bedroom walking noiselessly in bare feet. En route to the kitchen, she saw Zack's lights were out. She didn't bother with the extra precaution of putting the chain on the front door, in case Gary came home unexpectedly. Hearing him unlock the doors had always provided sufficient warning for her to draw her robe close, shake off a glazed look, turn on a burner under the stainless-steel kettle, pretending to brew a soothing cup of chamomile tea.

At her desk, she turned the chair to face the window squarely, sat, and straddled the sill with her feet apart. A thin line of air, entering through a crack, striped her arches, a pleasant, tickling sensation. She was glad to see the young man's kitchen lights were still on. She could anticipate an appearance. He might come in for dessert or another bottle of beer. At the very least he would have to turn the lights off before he went to bed. She spread her legs, which opened the lower half of her robe, and idly stroked her tummy with the bath-softened fingers of her right hand, as if she were soothing a child's upset stomach.

She scanned the other floors across the courtyard. She saw a light in the penthouse, but its residents wouldn't have a good viewing angle to see her unless they turned out their own light, moved close to their window, and deliberately scanned down. And who would do that? She had long ago calculated the risks. The windows to the right, the dining rooms of the C line, might have a view of her legs, but that angle was too severe to see more. The line of window to the left were the bathrooms of the A line, all made of frosted glass to provide their own privacy. The kitchen line of windows across the courtyard were in the best position, especially those four floors above and below her own, but his, the handsome young man's, had the best vantage, being level. Eyes naturally sought illumination directly across the way, as had hers a year ago when he entered, removing a pin-striped jacket from his broad shoulders, with the slow grace of a bullfighter unfurling a cape, then rolling up the white sleeves of his shirt to unpack bachelor's groceries—beer, chips, a small orange juice, a box of cereal, and a can of shaving cream. Remembering her virgin sighting, her hand dropped, fingers netting across her right thigh, a quivering web of warmth on cool skin.

She was in the dark. The shadows would protect her from her recklessness. She was not absolutely sure what he could see, just as she had never known what his predecessor, a much less attractive middle-aged married man, might have been able to see. For her to judge, neighbors across the courtyard would have to sit in a dark kitchen while she watched them and they had never sat in the dark. Why would they? Why would anyone? Which was why for twenty years no neighbor had ever given her unilluminated window more than a glance. She was exposed, not visible. Besides, it was the threat that she liked, the possibility that he might glance up and see a naked female form in the shadows, the restless movement of her hand, and the finale, her head thrown back, mouth open in choked ecstasy.

He entered the kitchen! It was the only lucky event of her day. She had begun, resigned to a fantasy of his presence when the reality showed on cue. And there was a bonus. He was wearing only his red and white striped boxers. His tall body had definition, the lines of classic sculpture, a dream lover, and he presented a 360-degree view while making himself an eccentric dessert of cereal. He reached for a bowl from an upper cabinet, then from another fetched a box of what appeared to be Raisin Bran, and while bending over to fetch a quart of milk from the refrigerator side door showed off globes worthy of a male underwear model. He poured cereal and milk into a white bowl and sat. She was thrilled. She didn't have to hurry. He was going to eat at the table virtually nude, while her robe fell open and her thighs sighed apart, longing for him, displayed for him.

He settled at his round table with the bowl, broad shoulders slightly hunched, muscles in his right arm rippling while, in a thoughtful steady pace, he opened his mouth to engulf a brimming spoonful. Her keen reaction, like the surprise of Gary's smoking-inspired lust, was a reminder of her first orgasm: quick and delirious. She didn't want to climax that fast, expending pleasure without savor. She paused the motion of her hand, but soon her body yearned for more and she resumed, the ache quickly reaching an unsustainable intensity. She gave up fighting its urgent need to release, felt the waves rising, about to engulf and crash her on the shore. The roar of their approach got loud in her head, too loud to hear a warning noise of movement if Gary or Zack approached. This was her true climax, of abandon, pleasure overwhelming shame, so that if someone glanced out a window and could penetrate the dark to see her naked and writhing in her spotless kitchen, she wouldn't stop and cover herself. At last she was reckless, wanting to be seen by the beautiful man if now, right now, he lifted his eyes. It was thrilling to ride the cresting wave without fear.

But she never reached shore. As if she had missed her train, she was stranded on a platform of anticipation. Nothing she did, not imagining lightly pressing her lips on his washboard stomach, no alteration of speed below or a hard pinch of nipple, nothing pushed her over the edge; she remained expectant, unable to ride the wave of oblivion to the relief of shore.

She was furious at herself, as irritated as she would be with any incompetent lover. The self-absorbed young buck remained at the table, methodically spoon-feeding himself. The promise of joy receded, the ocean a glassy pond. Finally she dropped her hand, allowing her feet to slide off the sill and trail down the wall, skin squeaking as they descended. Her muscles remained clenched, running a phantom race. Her body was covered with a fine sheen of sweat, nipples tingling, every inch of skin independently touched by air—she was all nerve endings, no central control, body painfully alive, head numbed. Look at that stupid man feeding himself, indifferent and young. *Stupid and young.*

She reached back for the light switch and flipped it up. The ceiling globe drenched the room with light. Her eyes winced. She shrugged off her robe and stood at the window naked head to toe. *Look at me,* she demanded, eyes boring at him. *Look at me,* her eyes screamed.

He must have heard the shout of her stare. He raised his head and, because he was facing the window, looked right at her. He appeared to accept her presence as unremarkable. Seen at last, she expected to be mortified. She had always assumed that when this day came, after thirty-odd years of remaining in shadows, she would bolt or at least shut off the light. If she moved quickly, the incident might still seem innocent: a woman wandering late at night in her kitchen for a snack, not anticipating she might be seen, hurrying to recover modesty as soon as possible. Perhaps her neighbor would presume he was the naughty voyeur, instead of she the exhibitionist.

She was not mortified. She did not bolt. She reached below and rubbed, just as she had in her head so many times. She acted out the madness.

At first he didn't react. Then the dark-haired young man seemed to wake up. His head tilted to one side. He dropped the spoon. He sat up straight. He craned forward. He squinted.

Again she had a chance to take it all back. Shut off the light, dive for her robe, run from the kitchen. She didn't move.

She rubbed and felt nothing. Her limbs ached, with tension, not pleasure. She was drying out, the numbness in her head anesthetizing all of her. She persisted, although it began to hurt. She had committed to being discovered—at least she wanted that to be a success.

He squinted as hard as he could, narrowing his eyes to slits.

He can't see me, she wondered with horror. She'd never noticed that he wore glasses, but what if he wore contacts, took them out before bed, and had come for his late snack in the full glory of his nearsightedness and she was nothing but a pink blur?

She stopped molesting herself. She stood at the window, a naked sentinel, and waited for him to figure it out.

He squinted so hard he made a pig's face, a hand coming up to shade his eyes, forehead pressing against the glass, a lookout trying to spot a distant vessel.

He can't see me, she confirmed in a rage, disgusted. She turned off the light. She put on her robe, went to the sink, washed her hands, and only then returned to her desk, straightening the chair and opening her computer.

The disappointing young man was gone and his kitchen lights were out. At least now her head was calm, all the unsettled questions floating peacefully through her thoughts, easy to contemplate without the anxious feeling that she needed to do something, anything, right away. What finally roused her from this meditative state of mind was the image of another dark-haired male, a boy from long ago.

What did he make of all this?

She typed Brian Moran into Google and found his Wikipedia entry, which included the information that he lived in the West Village. She typed Brian Moran, West Village into WhitePages.com and found him on West Ninth Street with a 212 number. She was about to dial it when her phone rang. Caller ID read: "Private Number."

"Hey, Julie, it's Jeff." His voice was low but transmitted very clearly. He had forsaken cell for landline. *Was he home?* "We got cut off again. Sorry. Why did you say you were calling me? What's up?"

Can't help it. Raised to be a liar. "I was calling about your cousin and his boyfriend, Sam. I assume he was his boyfriend—but that's wrong of me, isn't it? Sam was about to go to college, so he was, what, seventeen? Still just a minor. So not a boyfriend. He was being molested by your cousin." She heard Jeff breathing hard through his mouth, like he was running too fast. "And that's going to come out. Or—I mean, not that, not what he did to Sam. Gary, my husband, says they're close to indicting your cousin for molesting children at his school and at that Huck Finn camp."

"Really?" he said finally. And so lamely.

"He molested you too, right? I mean, when we were all little."

"No," he said much too quickly.

"You can admit it to me, Jeff. I'm not going to tell anybody."

"Julie, I really don't have time for this!" he complained. Without an audience all his comedy had vanished. "I've been making this fucking monster of a movie. You don't know what that's like. When you're directing a picture you don't have time to take a shit. I haven't spoken to or seen Cousin Richard since 1988. That's twenty years. And I don't know Sam Rydel. I didn't even know he was alive or running anything. I haven't been following the case. I probably know less about all this than you."

She had to admit he sounded convincing. Remarkably so. "Jeffrey," she said as gently as she could, "Gary says your commencement speech at the American Broadcasting Academy is on their website. It's on the website that you said your cousin got you your start in the movie business."

"He paid my tuition at USC! That's all." There was a silence. "He didn't give me a start in the business," he added in a disgusted tone. "I was exaggerating. Being kind. Jesus, that was in 1983! I did that stupid speech for my mother. Soon as she died I never saw or spoke to Cousin Richard again. And I stopped having anything to do with that fucking school."

"You sound angry, Jeff." Despite his money and fame she wasn't intimated by him. That surprised her. "If your cousin never touched you, why are you so angry?"

"I'm not angry," Jeff said in a whine.

"If he paid for you to go college, if he was so nice to you, why did you stop talking to him?" Julie pressed.

The beautiful young man returned to the window wearing thick, nerdish glasses. She did not want him to see this Julie, a drab middle-aged woman in a robe. She turned her back on him and shut off the desk lamp to further impede him.

Meanwhile Jeff sighed. There was a long pause, followed by another sigh. Julie waited patiently for his admission. She felt for him. Like her, he must have followed the case with horror and fascination, worrying (with even more reason than she) that Klein's behavior would come out, that some reporter would make the connection and drag him into it. "Julie," he said at last, "I'll be honest. I've been expecting you to call for some time. You know. Our parents are dead, we're all in therapy, and we examine the past. We hope to . . . you know." He shouted: "FUCKING REDEMPTION!" He went on in a hoarse, exhausted voice, "I was just a kid. I didn't understand what Cousin Richard was into. I mean, sure I knew he was weirdly interested in kids, but you know what my mother was like. She got Richard to pay for my college education. So she insisted I had to help him when he got canned by NBC, but as soon as she died I had nothing to do with him. And Sam Rydel, I swear, I knew nothing about him. He was there when I gave the speech, but I just said hello to him and that was the last time we talked. Okay?"

The okay was a mistake. For a cover-up his speech wasn't bad, but the "okay," asking for immediate release, gave him away. It was barely possible—she didn't believe it—but his fans might think it possible that he didn't fully understand what had happened to her, and that nothing had happened to him, but the plea in that hurried "okay" was desperate and guilty. "Listen, Jeffrey, it's more complicated than just you and me. My husband is Gary Stein. If you don't remember who he is or don't know what's been going on with him, Google him. He's a legal columnist for *Manhattan Mag. American Justice* has him under contract as a TV analyst. He's going to cover the investigation wherever it leads and he says the DA's office is about to indict Klein for molesting children at the school and at the camp. He asked me to call you before he goes public with the info about your connection to the school."

"Does he know?" Jeff's voice had changed: panic—accusation too.

"Know what?"

"About . . ." Jeff hesitated. "You know. What did you tell him?"

There it was. An admission he was lying. He had understood what had happened to her. How could he not have understood? "I wanted to talk to you first, Jeff. I told him I had to talk to you first."

"Huh," he said. She heard Jeff open a can. Beer? She didn't picture him slugging a Bud. He definitely sipped something. After a swallow he asked, "How long have you been married to him?"

"Twenty-three years."

"Don't trust him, huh?" She could hear the smirk on his face. *Why is he making fun of me? That's not smart.*

"How about you? Does your pretty wife know?" She threw in "pretty" as damning sarcasm, although now that it was out she had no idea how it qualified as a put-down.

"No!" he almost shouted.

"How about your first wife?"

"Jesus Christ, she doesn't even have my cell number. And I didn't tell my second wife either."

"Tell them what? You just said you didn't understand what your cousin was into."

"I didn't even tell them what I don't know." He grunted at his joke, a feeble grim laugh. "They don't know the half of how crazy my family was." Another grunt. "They don't know ten percent."

"So why are you surprised I haven't told Gary?"

"'Cause I assume you have a real marriage."

"You don't?" This was interesting.

"Come on, you must have talked to somebody about this," Jeff said, evading again.

No point in tugging at the will of this man. She laughed scornfully, then admitted, "One girlfriend, one boyfriend. Both were a big mistake." It was during her third year at the University of Pennsylvania, after taking a course in psychology. He was a lean dark-eyed boy, the kind she liked, or thought she did until she decided the lumbering puppy of Gary's broad body was cozier. The rising senior at UPenn listened solemnly, wasn't satisfied by her general description, wanted graphic details, seemed (maybe she was paranoid) disappointed that they weren't worse, brutal. She had hoped telling him would bring them closer, relax her when they made love. Instead she lost all interest in sex. Distressed by his reaction, she told her roommate, a sweet, ditzy blonde from Minnesota who listened and nodded solemnly, said she was sorry and that she had an organic chemistry test she had to cram for. In a month, she caught boyfriend and roommate screwing. He didn't apologize. He labeled her frigid. The roommate asked to be moved. Soon after, all the women she had been friends with became creepy, some with oily sympathy, the rest shunning her. One of the touch-your-arm-with-a-sad-face girls said, "I heard about your trauma. Have you experimented with women?" Julie never decided if that was a come-on or a veiled insult.

"You never told your parents?" Jeff sounded anxious. Did he think that's why their fathers had quarreled?

"No, of course not." Her father would have . . . she couldn't decide how he would have reacted. Beaten the shit out of Klein? Pretended it never happened? She didn't know, but certainly she would no longer have been an object of pride for him—the only paternal emotion she had ever received from him. Anything she failed at, or didn't succeed at brilliantly, her father never mentioned again. As for her mother? She had planned to tell Ma, when it was far enough away from the event that she wouldn't feel she had to tell Dad, but then Ma dropped dead during Julie's freshman year. She wished she had told her. If anyone could have wiped the slate clean, it was Ma. "How about you? You ever tell your mother?"

"My mother! Jesus. I didn't talk to my mother about anything. Didn't have much to do with her or Cousin Richard or any of my family as soon as I was out of film school. Once I got my first job, I sent the monster a check once a month and stopped answering her calls. Dad I'd see on the side, like we were having an affair."

"Did you tell your dad?" She thought: *Gary would be proud; I'm coaxing him into tacitly admitting he was molested.*

"No," Jeff said. "No," he repeated in a regretful tone.

"I told a shrink," Julie offered. "Someone I saw after mom died."

"Yeah, I told my shrink. That's all he wanted to talk about for a good ten years. Then he became a Buddhist. He still brings it up but only to say it's archival trauma."

"Archival?" Julie laughed, thinking of white gloves and dehumidified rooms.

"Yeah, you know, it's no longer relevant except as a point of origin. Anyway, he's an idiot. I'll give him another twenty years and then I'll see someone else. What did your shrink say?"

"Mine thought it was a distraction from my deeper father issues." Julie laughed scornfully again. That fat, old, droopy-eyed Freudian. He had been useless. She was better off with Zoloft. Maybe that's what she needed. Double to a hundred milligrams of Zoloft. Maybe a thousand. That would dry her up. "So you only told your shrink, Jeff? No girlfriends?"

"No! Never. All my girlfriends were actresses. Tell an actress something about your sex life and you might as well print it on the front page of the *New York Post.* Only my shrink and"—he hesitated—"another therapist. So listen, for both our sakes, tell Gary to back off. I resigned from that school in 1988, and if someone asks why I was on it in first place I'll tell them the absolute truth: it was all a favor to Cousin Richard."

"You mean a favor to your mother."

"What? Oh yeah, right."

He couldn't keep his own lies straight. He hadn't helped Klein solely for Harriet's sake. He had felt obliged too.

"And what will you say about Sam Rydel? He's the one who is actually indicted."

"No! I keep telling you. I didn't know about him, I knew back in 1983 that he was around, but I didn't know what he was doing. I still don't. Listen to me, Julie, as soon as I got my first TV movie to direct, I stayed as far away as I could from Cousin Richard. I don't know anything about what happened to Sam or what sick shit he's into. I saw him at one black-tie dinner for Huck Finn over twenty years ago. I didn't even know what Cousin Richard was up to. I didn't even fucking think about what he was up to."

He never, ever thought about Klein?

"Jules?" Jeff prompted. "You there?"

"What about Brian?" she asked.

"Brian?" Jeff sounded thrown by this. "Brian Moran? What about him?"

"You must've talked to him about all this."

"I haven't seen him since I was eleven." Julie was profoundly surprised. It seemed incredible. But why would he lie about it? Into her silence, Jeff amended, "Actually I met him for coffee, once, when I got my first job, but that was a mistake."

"You're really . . . not friends at all?"

"You mean cause he's in the business? No. I don't know him at all."

"But . . . how could . . . ? You were in love with him."

"What!" The way he said the word it almost a squeal of pain. "What the fuck does that mean?"

"You two were like glued together."

"Yeah, we were best friends as kids. So what? Jesus, that kind of friendship never survives. Do you know anybody who's still really close to their childhood friend? Isn't that why BFF is always said ironically? Are you still friends with your girlhood BFF?"

"I probably would be if I were on Facebook." Julie chuckled. "I hear she loves Facebook and can't believe I'm not on it. But I haven't seen her more than a couple times since her family moved to Texas when I started middle school. We wrote some letters for a while but then lost touch and, well"—she laughed again—"I'm not on Facebook."

"That's more or less what happened with me and Brian. His parents split up and a year later his mom moved him away and we lost touch. Listen, Jules, you gotta keep Gary away from this story. You haven't told him, so it's obvious you don't want him and three hundred million of his closest friends to know what happened to us. And why should you? Won't do any good. What Cousin Richard did in Queens forty years ago has nothing to do with whatever Sam Rydel did today. So Jules—let's talk about how I can help your family, which is also my family. What does Gary want? He's on TV. You said he's on *American Justice*. What network is that?"

"MSNBC." Julie grunted at the irony.

Jeff didn't. "I know just who to talk to over there. And I can do it casually so it won't be suspicious. I've got a TV production company, maybe we can create a show around Gary about the law. Maybe a reality show. I mean, Jesus, we're the most litigious country on earth, there's gotta be a TV show in it."

"You mean like making him Judge Judy?" Julie pictured Gary in black robes scolding people.

"He should be so lucky. Judge Judy makes twenty-five mil a year. But no, not Judge Judy. Something classier. Interview show, maybe. We'll figure it out, Jules."

"You know what?" she said, having thought it over many times during the six-hour wait for his callback. "That's not necessary. All I have to tell Gary is that if he lays off, you'll owe us. You know what I was thinking you might help with in a couple years? Maybe you can help get Zack into a college, maybe a drama school if he—"

"I can get him a job on a movie!" Jeff was excited. "I can definitely give him a small role. He'll get a SAG card and an agent. I'll find him a good Young Turk at CAA to rep him, get him started. I can't make him a star, nobody can do that—just ask my three wives—but I can give him a real shot at it."

"I know," she said with a sigh. Zack was corrupted anyway. Why not make him a permanent resident of Sodom and Gomorrah? "I'll call off Gary. But I should tell you he says it's just a matter of time."

"What's a matter of time?"

"Someone in the press seeing you were on the board."

"So I was on the board twenty years ago. Look, honey, what's the story with you? Half the time you get the joke, half the time you're a straight line. I'm not worried about what Gary can tell the world. I'm worried about what you can tell Gary to tell the world."

Across the way, the light went out. She checked: the tall drink of water was gone. "What about Brian?"

"What . . . ?" Once again Jeff was startled by her mentioning him. *Why?*

"Will Brian say something?"

"He hasn't said anything for forty years."

Again she felt utterly alone, as if she were the hero of one of those movies about the world ending: the sole survivor with nothing to look at but empty rooms.

"Jules," Jeff said into her gloomy silence, "Brian didn't call me, you called me. So don't worry about Brian. I gotta go. I'm late to the editing room. We okay, Jules?"

"We're okay."

"Let me know if I should find something for your boy in my next picture. Either way, I'll call you soon. We should stay in touch. We're family. Bye." The phone clattered, then silence.

In the dark of her loneliness she thought about the arrangement. Convincing Gary wouldn't be a problem, sadly. So it was all neat and tidy, stowed in the bottom drawer again. Only one messy item left to dispose of, the memo paper in her hand with Brian's phone number, the dark-haired boy of long ago. He was only a phone call and sixty streets away.

First Cause

— April 1966 —

BRIAN SEARCHED FOR Jeff at Zolly's Deli. Catching him there, he might be able to wave for his best friend to come out and discreetly make sure Richard Klein wasn't going to stay all evening. And if Jeff insisted Brian join them, at least he could have a hot dog. Mom's grilled cheese was great, but a kosher frank with sauerkraut and slathered with spicy deli mustard was a treat beyond equal.

Brian hurried to Alderton Street, slowing as he approached Zolly's one window, dominated by a yellow neon HEBREW NATIONAL sign. Between the *N* and the *A*, Brian saw Richard Klein on a metal chair that was usually placed at one of two freestanding tables. He had moved it to the open end of a red vinyl booth to serve as a fifth seat. Presumably Sam, Julie, Jeff, and little Noah were inside the high wood walls of the booth; they weren't visible.

Brian was grateful to be able to watch Klein from another environment through a pane of glass, a television-like perspective that allowed Brian to satisfy his curiosity from a safe vantage. He scrutinized every detail of this puzzling and disturbing man, settling on Klein's pudgy hands, ceaselessly punctuating his talk. When Klein paused to listen to the booth of children respond to his animated conversation, it was with an expression of pure delight, at one point throwing his head back to laugh openmouthed at something one of them said. While Brian wondered at how happy Klein seemed to be, the executive turned his head toward the window casually. Then his eyes found Brian.

Brian ran to the corner, heart pounding. A wood-paneled station wagon braked hard a few feet from Brian, car lurching to a stop. The woman driver stared at him angrily, although he was on the sidewalk and in no danger of being under her wheels. Maybe she thought he was about to cross, since Brian kept turning his head to check on whether he was being pursued.

At that point he did see the deli door being opened from the inside. He bolted again, back to Sixty-third Street. He thought he heard his name called repeatedly, but the wind and traffic made it impossible for him to be sure.

He decided to head back to Jeff's while waiting for them to return from Zolly's. Harriet's interrogation would be terrible, but that would be better than sitting with Richard without other adults around. He had already been with Klein in a place not drawn on the map of his day-to-day world; he wouldn't make that mistake again.

Brian was in no hurry to face Harriet. He stayed on the far side of Sixty-third, went past his building, and decided to climb up the low part of a concrete wall that rose until it joined at a right angle to an overpass above a forbidden place to horse around, the perilous elevated Long Island Railroad tracks. At the wall's base, Brian placed one Keds' heel flush to its mate's toe, imagining that he was walking a tightrope as it gradually rose from two to over six feet off the pavement. Farther along, on the overpass, it would rise even higher and to fall off there meant you would tumble onto the deadly tracks. Some of the older boys made that climb and, in a feat of daring, leapt down immediately after the last car of a train passed, madly climbing back up using struts, garbage, and their strength, racing to see who could be first. Every mother had warned the boys against that stunt and Brian had never attempted it, although tempted. He chose not to again, especially after a chilly gust had him wobbling for a few seconds to maintain balance. He sat down on the wall, putting his legs over the sidewalk side, and was about to slowly slide down when an amused voice asked, "How's the view?"

It was Sam. He looked much younger out of his NBC page outfit. He had no sign of a beard, not even a wispy blond mustache. He was just another teenager in a beige windbreaker, Levi's and Converse sneaks; one of the slightly older boys who sometimes let you play stickball with them.

"Hi." Brian started shimmying down.

"Don't get down 'cause of me," Sam said.

"I was coming down." Brian let go. Sam moved fast to the spot, catching Brian by the waist. While suspended at eye level, Sam put his lips on Brian's and kissed gently. They smelled of smoke.

Brian averted his face and shouted, "Leggo! Leggo of me!" He kicked his legs.

Sam eased him to the pavement and stepped back, shoving his hands into the back pockets of his jeans. "Just trying to help," he said.

It had happened so fast, Brian immediately doubted whether it had.

Sam certainly showed no sign of embarrassment. He was at ease, smiling ingratiatingly as he asked, "That was you sneaking a peek through the deli window, right?"

"What?" Brian stalled, looking away.

"Why didn't you come in?" he continued, as if Brian had confessed.

"It wasn't me." Brian moved quickly to the corner to cross to his building's side of the street.

Sam appeared by his side, hands in his pockets, head bowed. In a low voice, he commented, "I'm just like you."

"What?"

"I know Richard likes you. He likes me too."

His heart raced. The light turned green. Brian hustled across onto Sixty-third. During winter, especially during a snowfall, on his level street

Brian and Jeff liked to imagine they were scaling Mount Everest. When coming home after a really fun day of playing Slug or Running Bases, he and Jeff paused midway, shielding themselves from the wind by crouching low next to parked cars. They peered out at the swirls of flakes and told each other that they were starving climbers pressing on against hopeless odds to become the first boys in history to conquer the world's highest peak.

But that day, trudging in the feeble sunlight and chilling breeze of April, he had Sam, not Jeff, for company.

"Can I tell you a secret?" Sam caught up. He nudged Brian with his hip.

Brian nodded reluctantly. Brian was ashamed to be talking with Sam about "It" but didn't want to discourage him. For one thing, he was very curious and relieved that It had happened with someone else besides him. At least he hoped that was what Sam was implying.

"Promise to keep it a secret?" Sam tapped Brian on his head.

Brian tried to avoid the contact. Jumping back, he lost his balance, toppling against a car.

"Whoa." Sam snagged his arm to steady him. "Take it easy."

"I'm all right." He jerked away, heart pounding so wildly it felt like it was coming out through his chest.

"I'm not gonna hurt you," Sam said. "I like you."

Brian was humiliated he was spooked by the contact. Why was he afraid of Sam, who was almost a kid like him? Brian tried to make amends: "I'll keep your secret."

"I went out for a smoke. Dick doesn't like me to smoke. That's how I saw you peeking in the deli. I was across the avenue having a dromedary."

"A what?"

Sam grinned. He pulled a pack of Camels out of the right pocket of his pants. "Dromedary," he said. "That's another name for camel. I've been building up my vocabulary. Dick says that will help me get into a good college."

"I thought you were already going to college."

"Nah." He looked down, embarrassed. "Dick tells people that so they'll think I'm older. You're not supposed to be an NBC page unless you're already in college. Saying I was seventeen and about to start was stretching it anyway, but I'm fifteen, not seventeen. I am a junior, though, 'cause I skipped a grade! 'Cause I'm pretty smart. One of the smartest in my class."

He's stupid, Brian decided. Smart people didn't tell you they were smart. Concluding that Sam wasn't bright made Brian no longer fearful of him. Many years would pass before Brian learned the folly of believing superior intelligence could protect him. "He really doesn't know you smoke?" Brian asked.

"Dick thinks I quit. He hates the smell on my breath. That's why I suck on these." Sam stuck his tongue way out—cradled in its center groove was a half-melted Life Saver. The long pink snake retracted. "Dick says smoking causes cancer. He says everybody, you know, like scientists and newsmen, knows that. The tobacco companies know it, Dick says. I don't know how he knows what the tobacco companies secretly think."

"Yeah," Brian said, bringing in a true authority. "My mom says it's bad. And Dad knows it's bad for him, but he says it's an addiction."

"What?" Sam stopped their climb to lodge a protest. "An addiction? You mean, a *habit*. It's a habit, right?"

"No. Dad said it was an addiction, not a habit," Brian said, stopping and turning to argue this point.

"Your dad's wrong. You get addicted to stuff like heroin. Smoking is just a habit."

"No, he's not wrong." Brian was deeply offended that Sam dared to contradict his father. "He explained the difference to me. He meant addiction."

"Oh yeah? So what's the difference, smarty-pants?" Sam put his hands on his hips, like a little kid. He really wasn't very smart.

Brian resumed walking, bored by Sam, eager to reach Jeff's. "An addiction is something you gotta keep getting more and more of, like being a drunk, Dad says. You keep wanting more even if it makes you sick. Same thing with cigarettes. No matter how long you stop yourself from smoking you still want to."

"So?" Sam, catching up, tapped him on the shoulder. "How is that different from a habit?"

"That's kind of obvious. You can change a habit." Brian vividly remembered how much he missed sucking his thumb for the first week he stopped. The wanting ached like a deep bruise, then got weaker day by day and finally faded altogether. "You may miss it for a while, but the missing goes away." While he explained Brian half-turned to Sam. He awkwardly tripped over his Keds. He tried to right himself by putting his arms out. He listed one way then the other.

While Brian recovered his footing, Sam said, "I just can't believe they would do that."

"Who?" Brian said, resuming the climb, Sam tagging along a step behind.

"The tobacco companies. I don't believe they would make cigarettes if they knew they would make you sick."

Brian shrugged. "Why not?" he said. His father and mother had told him all advertising was a lie. "They're lovely lies, don't ya know," Danny Moran had said, imitating Grandma's Irish lilt.

"It's . . ." Sam hesitated, then said helplessly, "I just can't believe they'd do that."

Brian was puzzled. That bad guys will do anything for money was a principle widely accepted in comics, TV, movies, and the handful of novels he'd read. "Why not?" he insisted. "They got no choice. Even if cigarettes make people sick they can't stop making 'em, right? They'd go bankrupt." He finished as they reached his apartment building. He opened the door and held it for Sam, who was gaping at him, astonished. He didn't move, so Brian, in the style of his exchanges with Jeff, encouraged him. "Come on, stupid. Don't just stand there."

Sam hit him. Later Brian tried to figure out whether Sam used a fist or an open hand or maybe he just pushed Brian's face with the flat of his palm. It happened too fast to be sure. Abruptly he was on his ass on New York pavement. His nose stung. It didn't hurt.

"Jesus," Sam said. He bent over Brian. "You okay? I barely touched you . . ."

Brian jumped to his feet and in one motion—a feat he had mastered dodging bullies in the playground—scampered around Sam, jerked the door open, ran to the stairs, taking them two at a time up to the sixth floor. Years later, obliged to analyze every detail of this day, it occurred to Brian his dashing upstairs probably implied that Brian was planning to tattle on Sam. He had no such intention. He hoped getting inside would forever erase his mistake of calling Sam stupid and the disgrace of Sam's knocking him over so easily.

He reached Jeff's, breathless, and leaned hard on the doorbell. It opened to reveal a delighted Richard Klein. "Brian! There you are!" Brian was shocked but still in running mode, so he scurried around Klein, down the long hall, past the invalid's door—"Brian!" Harriet croaked as he got an impression of a crowd around her—and banged into Jeff's door, crashing into his friend's room. What he saw shoved aside all thoughts of Sam and Klein.

Jeff was sitting on a low stool whose original use (now forgotten) came from when he was a toddler and needed extra height for the toilet. His back was to the door, face in his hands, shoulders trembling. Without looking, he said, "Go away," his voice breaking with tears.

Brian shut the door. "It's me," he said. "What's wrong, Mr. Jeff?" he asked, using his nickname for his friend, inspired by the talking horse on *Mister Ed.*

There was a silence. Jeff's shoulders quieted. "You know," he mumbled.

It took Brian a second to remember. "Oh! I gotta tell you something. I got good news." He was very pleased that this time, unlike any other occasion he could remember, he was sure he could make someone feel better. "Your mom's not sick. She made it up."

Jeff raised his tearful face, hope dawning. From the hall Klein called, "Boys? You in there?"

"Lock it," Jeff whispered.

Brian hurried, fingers fumbling at the task. Klein's voice came close and loud: "Boys?" Brian slid hook into eye a split second before Klein pushed from the other side. Klein whispered through a slight crack the hook and eye allowed, "Brian, don't be upset. Sam's sorry. He says he's very sorry."

Brian moved across the room, next to Jeff.

He mouthed, *What is Sam sorry for?*

Brian stuck to his good news, whispering, "I heard your mom talking to your dad on the phone while you were at Zolly's. She didn't realize I was here. She said—"

"Boys?" Klein rattled the door.

"ONE SECOND," Jeff shouted, so near Brian's ear Brian winced. "Go on," Jeff said.

While Klein said something about locking doors and called out an answer to a query from Harriet, who could be heard shouting from her bed, Brian whispered, "Your mom called your dad to warn him not to say anything to your uncle about her not having breast cancer."

"What?" Jeff shook his head to indicate he wasn't following. "What was that?"

"It's got something to do with money. Your mom told your uncle she has breast cancer so you wouldn't have to grow up poor. Or something. Anyway, she doesn't have cancer. It was just something she made up for your uncle."

Jeff wiped away a lingering tear from his left eye. "Yeah, but she also said it to your mother," he pointed out.

"Yeah," Brian agreed. "Why'd she do that?"

"She's crazy," Jeff said, rather sadly, as if that were a matter of regret more than anything else.

Klein shook the door again, harder. "Come on. You heard your mother, Jeff: Locked doors are rude."

Jeff shouted, "JUST ONE SECOND." He grabbed Brian's bicep, squeezing to emphasize the crucial nature of this detail. "Did she talk about the money Dad owes my uncle for starting his store?"

"Yeah, that's it!" Brian agreed. "She didn't want your dad to pay him back—"

Jeff interrupted, "He can't pay him back. The store's not making any money."

"Oh," Brian said, understanding now. "I guess that's why she told him she has cancer. It doesn't really make sense. But that's why she made it up."

Jeff's eyes were clear of tears. "She's crazy," he said, sounding himself again.

"Jeff! Your mother says you should—" Before Klein finished, Jeff crossed to the door, flipped the hook up, and opened the door.

"Well, well . . ." Klein entered with a knowing smirk. Old Spice immediately snaked into Brian's nostrils. "What were you boys doing in here"—he flicked the dangling hook playfully—"with the door locked?"

"We were talking. Is Dad home?" Jeff spoke imperiously, as if the vice president were his secretary.

Klein appeared ready to object but then frowned and reported dutifully, "Everybody's here. Your cousins, your aunt, your uncle. Everybody's in your mother's room."

"Great." Jeff pushed past him, disappearing into the hall.

Brian was stunned to find he was suddenly alone with Klein. Before he could recover and dash out, Klein said to someone obscured from Brian's view, "Come in. Don't be shy, Sam."

Sam appeared, eyes downcast. Klein put his hands on Sam's waist and positioned him in front of Brian. "Well? What do you have to say?"

Sam glanced at Brian from lowered lids, barely able to sustain the contact. "I'm sorry I lost my temper. I don't like being called stupid. I'm sorry. I didn't mean to hurt you. I just . . ." His eyes seemed to lose all hope, falling to the floor permanently. "I just got upset for a second," he said, a whisper. "I'm sorry."

Klein nodded at Brian. "Sam was a bad boy. This is what we do to bad boys." He raised his right arm high, holding it up in the air long enough for Brian to anticipate what he was going to do and then brought the flat of his hand down on Sam's behind, hard. The teenager's jeans muffled the noise of impact. Sam blushed but didn't wince or object. "That's what we do, right, Brian?" He ordered Sam, "Turn around." He gave his back to Brian. "Why don't you spank him, Brian? That way Sammy will know you forgive him."

Brian was appalled. "But he didn't hurt me!" He moved alongside Sam, talking to his profile. "You didn't hurt me. Understand?" It was very important to make them understand that the whole thing was something no one should talk about. "Nothing happened." Brian made this point to Klein. The adult cocked his head, regarding Brian with a puzzled frown. "It was no big deal," Brian insisted. "Okay? Don't talk about it."

Klein considered this carefully. He nodded once, pursed his lips, nodded again, then looked very solemn. "Of course, Brian, we won't talk about it." He put a hand around the back of Sam's neck, lowering the teenager's head enough to speak directly into his ear. "Right, Sam? You understand? Brian doesn't want us to talk about it."

Sam seemed to smile a little but then looked very serious. "Okay."

Klein released Sam. He grinned at Brian. "It'll be our secret, Brian."

"It's not a secret," Brian said, irritation in his tone. "I just don't want people talking about it." His cheeks felt hot: the strain of expressing himself was almost unbearable. *Run,* he thought. *Just run.* But that had failed before. And then there would be more talk, more questions, more lies.

Richard raised a hand to the corner of his mouth. "Our lips are sealed," he said, then zippered them shut. He turned to Sam. "Now that you two are friends again, why don't you give Brian a hug? Show him you're sorry."

Sam opened his arms and came toward him. Brian stuck out both hands and said firmly, "No."

Sam stopped, looked at Klein for direction.

"Okay," Klein said. "Sam has to go now anyway. You'll be gone for an hour, right? Running that errand?"

"You bet!" Sam was abruptly very cheerful. "Thanks again, Brian, for understanding. See you soon." He walked around Klein and pulled the door shut behind him.

Brian was appalled. He was exactly where he didn't want to be. Despite his best efforts, he was all alone with Richard Klein.

Whom Do You Trust?

—— **February 2008** ——

BRIAN DIDN'T RECOGNIZE Julie; he recognized her eagerness to see him. As soon as he entered the restaurant, a silver-haired woman's head bobbed above a customer who was blocking her view of Brian; then she weaved around an obstructing waiter to maintain her sight line. *What's happened to her?* he thought with dismay as he approached her table, then reminded himself, *Of course. She's forty years older.*

He offered a smile of welcome, cautioning himself not to reveal any awareness she had aged. "You look great," he planned to say no matter what. Perhaps she did. His habit of meticulously assessing physical attractiveness was momentarily impaired by the shock that Julie's long raven locks were gone, replaced with a cropped gray hairdo that bordered on butch. As she stood up to greet him, he was favorably impressed that she had retained as much of her lean, girlish body as could be reasonably expected. Her narrow face was fuller, but that was an improvement; she looked less stern, friendlier. More good news came as he got close enough to see that she was genetically very fortunate. He could tell it wasn't Botox or surgery that allowed her skin to look a decade, maybe two, younger than her age—parentheses around her mouth but few wrinkles elsewhere. Her black eyes were still bright with that intense curiosity he remembered. Her smile was eager too. She hadn't subsided, as had so many of his friends, into the frowning smugness of middle age. Best of all, although she had put on a makeup base that dulled the two beauty marks under each eye, they were still there—old friends.

He noted all that while he leaned in for the obligatory peck on the cheek between the sexes expected by all New Yorkers—unless the person you were greeting had recently made an attempt on your life. Julie stiffened as his lips came near the beauty mark at the point of her high right cheekbone. She relaxed when, as was Brian's custom, he kissed air, not flesh. He assumed he knew why she was shy of contact and felt sorry for her, but then immediately scolded himself: *Don't be a hack writer. You don't know that Klein had any effect on her. Not everyone is a fragile flower like you.*

"You look great," he said and, as it turned out, meant.

"You look so different!" Julie exclaimed. "You're a man." The latter was said as if that were an unlikely development.

"I doubt that." Brian eased himself onto the tippy metal chairs of Not Your Mother's Kitchen on Hudson, a block from his expensive, very cramped so-called two-bedroom apartment. (He couldn't fit more than a twin bed in the second room in which he had installed his father this past January, when Danny's health began a severe decline.) Not Your Mother is where he preferred to meet someone he didn't know well. The espresso was strong and—an amazing bonus in a hip emporium—they offered a vegan version of Linzer cookies. They were as thoroughly covered in confectionery sugar, and the raspberry jam center was as sweet as his idealized memory of Zolly's Linzers, but of course spelt, sunflower oil, and agave nectar didn't reproduce exactly the butter and egg yolk base of the old neighborhood treat. Still, pleasant memories, even imperfectly reproduced, were in short supply. And the virtue of meeting at Not Your Mother was that should the person prove, as people so often did, to be hostile or a bore, the espresso would keep Brian awake while the Linzer cookie salved his wounds.

"I didn't mean that the way it came out." She nervously brushed the short white hairs at her temple as if she too missed her long raven hair. "It's just that last time I saw you, you were a little boy and now you're a tall, beautiful man." She got very flustered. "Handsome. I mean, handsome."

"I didn't know you were in the movie business, Julie. Your flattery is so good you could be a member of the academy," he said.

Julie winced. "I'm not flattering you."

Brian patted the top of her hand gently. "I'm sorry. I guess I spend so much time listening to insincere people, I can't hear a true melody anymore." At his touch, her fingers reacted skittishly, fanning out, on alert. He immediately registered that reaction as further proof she had shut down sexually, confirmed by her mannish do, sparing makeup, and menopausal clothes—jeans a size too large to properly show off her lean body and a shapeless wool sweater.

A waitress appeared to ask what he wanted. He surveyed her thoroughly: two toned hair, half pale blue, half straw yellow; a line of pimples across the ridge of her forehead; left nostril pierced three times to accommodate the decoration of three thin silver-colored rings, an elaborate floral tattoo that covered her right shoulder like a skin tight epaulette, then flowed down, wallpapering her forearm. He looked away from those desecrations to the purer Julie. She was drinking a cappuccino. "That all you're having?" Brian asked. She nodded, rested her chin in her hands, and studied his face with disconcerting meticulousness. A taste of his own medicine. He didn't care for it. He ordered the espresso and Linzer cookie. "My madeleine," he explained.

She was following her own train of thought. "Is Jeff good at flattery?" she asked.

It took Brian a moment to catch up. "I have no idea. Haven't spoken to Jeff in twenty-five years. At least. And even that was only a two-minute phone call to congratulate him on his first picture. I really haven't spoken to him in any depth or at any length since we were eleven years old."

"So you really don't talk to him. That's what he said."

"You've spoken with Jeff?"

She nodded guiltily. *Guilty about what?*

"So that was a trick question?" Brian asked. "It wasn't especially tricky. If Jeff and I really were in touch, he could have called me and warned me to pretend we weren't."

Julie laughed, very pleasantly. "That *was* dumb of me."

Brian thought her clumsiness at deception endearing. "Julie, why would we lie about being in touch? Of all the things to lie about, why that?"

"I just can't believe it. I know it was forty years ago, but . . ." She paused.

He was intensely curious about what she might say, but his Linzer cookie arrived. "Your espresso will be right up," the waitress said.

"Could I have a glass of water?" he asked, looking up at the waitress' beringed nostril and wondering how messy it all became when she got a head cold. Once she was gone, he prodded Julie, "Go on. Why can't you believe we're no longer friends?"

"I don't know, I guess it's all frozen in time for me. That's crazy, isn't it? Also, you two were so close," Julie added wistfully, as if she missed their friendship.

"We were," he admitted. "I think I saw Jeff every day of my life from when our mothers pushed us in baby carriages in Rego Park until I was almost twelve. A mere eleven years. I mean, I've had lots of friendships that lasted longer, but there's nothing quite like the intensity, the complete trust you feel for that first best friend you make. Think about it. After puberty, you look to one sex for more than friendship and to the other for less-than-complete intimacy." His espresso appeared. He took a sip, mostly to stop talking. He had said way too much.

"You're right. And even for best childhood friends, you two were really close. I remember that so well. You were very important to Jeff. He loved you."

Brian's throat closed. He blinked back tears. How humiliating. *Now*

I'm a sentimental hack. Maybe it's the new meds. Maybe I've let the doc go overboard on de-balling me. Next thing I know I'll be menstruating. "You really think I was so important to him?" he asked coyly.

"Oh yeah. Jeff was not a popular little boy. You were. And you were a good athlete. You were smart and handsome and popular. Weren't you class president?"

"We didn't have a class president. It was a public school in a working-class neighborhood. We couldn't even afford a class clown."

"But you were popular. Right? I remember Jeff bragging about how popular you were. Don't be modest. Tell the truth. Weren't you a seriously popular kid?"

The question felt like a trap. He agreed quickly, "Yeah I was popular." And was quick to retract, "Wasn't hard, in that group of misfits."

"So why did you stop being friends?" She was earnest. She was a very earnest woman. He didn't really care for earnestness. It wasn't the same as honesty. In this case, for example, he didn't think she was being sincere. She knew why. "I'm afraid by eleven, for reasons I'm sure you understand, I decided dealing with Harriet and Richard Klein was not worth the effort of being friends with Jeff."

Julie nodded. "But why at age eleven? Did something happen when you were eleven that was different from what happened when you were eight, nine, ten?" She put her chin in her hands and waited with the determination of a child to get an answer.

She was asking without asking, like a clever interrogator. *But this isn't an interrogation,* Brian thought. *It's her mystery too.* He focused on the Linzer cookie. They had supplied a knife and fork for its consumption. That was misguided. Cutting it would scatter the confectionery sugar and crack the top layer off the bottom, eventually breaking the whole into pieces. The true pleasure was in biting through the two hardened layers to the sweet layer of jam. He usually acquiesced to decorum and spoiled his own treat by using silverware. Confronted by Julie's naive gaze he picked up the cookie and chomped. That left a line of white sugar on his mouth.

When he spoke, sugar sprayed and flecked Julie's blue sweater. "Around when I was ten—after almost two years of fending him off—I finally figured out the only way I could handle Richard Klein was not to be in the same room with him. Sorry," he said, pointing to her sweater and dabbing his lips with a napkin. Julie glanced down at the damage, demurely wetted the tip of her pinky, and lifted off the dots of sugar. Brian drank some of the water, then took a sip of espresso, composed himself, and resumed, "So I told Jeff not to invite me up when Klein was around. In fact, I told him we should always play at my apartment." Brian sighed. He had no desire to continue. Without regret he could rise from the table and walk away from her forever. What sentimental insanity had made him think any good could come out of talking with someone who had shared his past? She was as ignorant about all this as any civilian.

"And what happened?" she asked.

"What happened! He kept doing it." Brian heard his anger, still green. He sighed. He wanted to stop but forced himself to go on. "It would happen every few months, spaced out so I'd sort of forget that it might happen again. I'd speak to Jeff in the morning about what we were gonna do that day, like always, we'd make plans for me to play at his apartment, like always, and then Klein would be there."

"And Jeff never warned you he'd be there?"

"No. He'd let him ambush me. First time it happened I yelled at him. He promised it wouldn't happen again. Then a few months later it happened again. Again, I yelled at him. Again he promised. Then it happened a third time. That ended our friendship as far as I was concerned. Eventually I went to Horace Mann, a private school—"

"Sure," she said. "I know Horace Mann."

"Yeah, well, Richard Klein turned out to be a good preparation for that place."

Julie frowned. "What do you mean?"

"Oh there were a couple of Kleins there, but I could spot them immediately." Brian chuckled. "That was the only favor Klein did for me—he prepared me to deal with our world of predators. I can't tell you what a dimwitted boy I was. It took me way too long to realize that Richard Klein wasn't all that unusual."

"What!" Julie sat up straight. For a moment, in that pose, he saw the proud, striking girl who wanted to be a ballet dancer. She's really a handsome woman, he decided, high brow, black eyes and pale skin suggesting an old-world grace that evoked not the Jews of Riverdale but the doomed artists of Prague. "Klein was a monster," she declared.

"Exactly. The world is chock-full of monsters. Anyway, with me at Horace Mann and Jeff going to the public junior high we were no longer in the same school, and that, as far as everyone else was concerned, ended our friendship. When I was eleven, my parents, after two trial separations, finally legally divorced, and just before my twelfth birthday Mom moved us out of Rego Park." Brian paused. He realized that this collection of facts about his life, told in this way, had never been discussed outside of the soft couches of therapy. There they had become commonplace, the chitchat of trauma: easily said, easily understood, easily accepted. Not here. Telling Julie, the words scalded his throat and left a foul taste. He felt as if he'd vomited. "I'm sorry."

"For what?" She frowned. Crow's-feet appeared. He liked those lines. They lent her earnest face a needed dose of skepticism.

"Being flip. I don't mean to be flip."

"I don't mind. But I'm confused. I thought you said you saw Jeff once when you were both grown-up. In your twenties, maybe?"

"No, I didn't."

"Really? I thought you did." Once again, she didn't do a good job of lying.

"I'm sure I said nothing of the kind. Where did you get that tidbit? From Jeff?"

Julie confessed, "Yeah, he said he saw you after he graduated from film school."

"I bet the fucker didn't tell you what happened," he said, the ancient anger new again. He wanted to apologize, then balked. *Apologize for facts?* "Jeff came to see me when he got his first job directing a TV movie. Wanted to know if I'd do a polish on the script—I had already had two plays on at Playwrights Horizons and I was making a living writing for *As the World Turns*—so he wasn't doing me any favors. On the contrary. But I was pleased. I admit it, I was a fool, my heart skipping with delight to have my old buddy back. So we met at my apartment. It was just like the old days for about half an hour. Then Jeff, remembering I was a Knicks fan, asked me if I still liked them. Those were days when nobody had cable and you could only get the Knicks on cable. I said I was obsessed with them. So Jeff offered to take me to a Knicks game. He said we could use Klein's seats, that he had great seats. Said that Cousin Richard would be happy to give them to us whenever we wanted."

Julie blanched. "You're kidding," she mumbled.

"I was so shocked I couldn't answer him." He laughed grimly. "I stared my shock, my slow horror, my idiotically naive outrage." Brian leaned back and mused, having thought about this moment a thousand times, "It would take a great actor, a total genius like Brando, to reproduce the complexity of what went on in my eyes in just a few seconds, the seamless shift from shock to understanding to disgust. No," he amended. "That's wrong. Betrayed. I was betrayed all over again, as if no time had passed, as if I were still a dumb, trusting child. Anyway," Brian snorted with disgust at that former self, "Jeff's face suddenly changed, looked like he understood. He got it, I was convinced. Like when we were boys, he got what I was feeling just from my look. But I was desperately wrong. You know what he said? It speaks volumes. Jeff said, 'Oh! No, no. You don't understand. Don't worry. Cousin Richard's not interested in us anymore. We're too old.'"

"Oh my God." Julie covered her mouth with both hands.

"I think until that moment I had forgiven Jeff," Brian said. "Actually, until that moment, I don't think I was wise enough to know there was anything to forgive." Julie lowered her hands to ask exactly what he had forgiven Jeff for, but Brian interrupted with his own question: "So you haven't been in regular touch with him? Just as cousins, family stuff?"

"What?" she said, momentarily stalled, accustomed to not telling the whole truth. "No. But everyone thinks that's because of Dad's fight with Uncle Saul after he finally figured out Harriet couldn't possibly be dying of breast cancer."

"So you never told your parents she was lying about that?"

"No. I never told them anything. Not even that." She sighed. "Mom and Dad figured out Harriet wasn't dying soon enough. I mean, my God, she didn't have any surgery, she didn't lose her hair, there was absolutely no sign of treatment. I guess it took a year, but Dad finally challenged Uncle Saul and he admitted she'd made it up to buy him some time to repay Dad. And he did repay Dad—in fact, he repaid him with interest—but still, you know, my mother and father were easygoing up to a point, but once you lost their goodwill, you kind of lost it forever. So my dad and Saul stopped talking altogether, much to my mom's relief. And then, when I was in college, my mom died suddenly and Dad really didn't want to talk to Harriet, the fake-fatal-illness-lady."

"Oh, Julie," Brian said, instantly sympathetic. It seemed obvious that this woman needed her mother to be strong and alive. "I'm sorry about your mom."

"It was a long time ago," Julie said casually. "Even losing Ma was a long time ago."

"I'm sorry. I lost my mother five years ago," Brian said. "It was hard. Very hard. Much harder than I expected. I don't know why. Yes, I do. Before she died, in some way death simply hadn't been real."

"Did you ever tell your mother about Klein?" Julie asked.

"No," Brian said. He reflected on the questions again and repeated, "No." He thought some more and said, "That would have been cruel."

"Cruel?" Julie was puzzled.

"She was already beating herself up for ruining my life by divorcing her faithless ne'er-do-well husband." He sighed. "I guess we should straighten this out right away—outside of shrinks, no one knows about me and what happened. And you?"

"Not really. I told two people in college, but I don't know them at all now, so no one who is close to me knows about me." She grunted. "That's a really sad thing to say, isn't it?"

Brian nodded. "I wanted to talk about it at one point. With Jeff of all people. When I got into therapy for the first time, in my midtwenties, I was all hot to talk it out, you know heal myself." Brian laughed derisively. "I was so desperate for a happy ending, a so-called normal life, I was even prepared to forgive the Knicks ticket business. I called him a few times. He never returned my calls. Of course, by then he was a really hot director so I thought maybe he was just dodging me for career reasons." Brian took an enormous bite of his Linzer cookie, white dust and crumbs collecting on his lips.

Julie offered her napkin as if he were her very own messy boy. She was pleased he took it and cleaned himself up. "It's funny," she said. "While waiting for you here I realized I never really knew if Klein . . ." She grimaced rather than say the word.

"You didn't know if Klein molested me?" Brian said very loudly.

Julie ducked as if he'd thrown something at her, and she put a finger to her lips. Brian looked around. At eleven, too late for breakfast, too early for lunch, the place was nearly empty. Only the nose-pierced, blue and yellow hair waitress, standing behind the counter near their table, was near enough to have heard him. Judging from the way she was staring at him Brian decided she had heard, and he understood her surprise. He must look the picture of staid middle-aged respectability in his sensible Ecco walking shoes, his Banana Republic chinos, his Paul Stuart black cashmere crew neck sweater, covering all but the collar of his Armani white shirt, balding hair neatly trimmed, face carefully shaved with the white-tipped beaver brush and cream for sensitive skin from the Art of Shaving. Hearing such an obviously square man declaim "molested me" had jarred the tattooed lady. He met her young eyes with a knowing smile and asked in his head, *Want to sit on my lap, little girl?* She intuited his look, dropped her eyes, and pretended to fuss with something on the counter.

"How would I know for sure?" Julie asked Brian. "I didn't see him do anything to you. I assumed it eventually, much later. I thought about it and figured he must have. That's why . . ." She didn't finish.

Brian completed her logic aloud: "That's why I didn't tell on Klein about what I saw." He winced at this realization. "Jesus, before you figured out I was also a victim, you must have hated me."

"Hated you?" Julie looked so surprised he was relieved. "Why?"

"For not rescuing you."

She smiled tolerantly. "Oh no. I didn't expect you to save me. You were a little boy."

"Who then?"

Her eyes flickered. *Was that mischief?* Then they dulled into disappointment. "Me, of course."

She was lying. *Who was supposed to rescue her? Her pompous father, probably. Little girls always think their fathers will save them. Women know better.* He let it go. "Here's something I don't know: did Klein bother you more than that one time?"

Julie rolled her lips inward and nodded. Fear came into her eyes and they slid away to the door.

"Do you not want to talk about this?" Brian asked, flooded with pity for her. "I'm sorry, I thought that's why you wanted to meet."

"No. I mean, I'm glad to talk to you about—well, not glad—but it's a relief to talk with someone who really understands. But no. I called you to talk about the *Rydel* case." She paused, looked right at him with dread, as if she were faced with a high dive into cold waters.

"Well, sure, I guessed that much," Brian said. "Since it broke in the paper last week of course Klein's been on my mind too. I gotta say, I'm not happy to be thinking about him again. I stopped thinking and talking about him in therapy twenty-five years ago. And of course since I never followed what Klein was up to—I didn't even know about his dumb-ass school and charity—it never occurred to me to get in touch with you, but my excuse is that until today I assumed you never saw Klein again." Her expression made it clear that was quite wrong. Brian waited for her to volunteer more. When she seemed to be waiting on him to speak, he continued, "Revolting about Rydel, isn't it? I read today, in a sickening background piece in the *Times,* that after Klein founded that phony school he adopted Rydel. At first I assumed that was a gay legal workaround to get the equivalent of marital rights in the eighties, but when I got to the end of piece I realized, no, it's because he was proud of Sam. After all, Sam's a real chip off the old block." He chuckled. Julie looked horrified. "What?" he asked.

"That's what you thought," she said, unable to conceal her disgust. "That's all?"

"What else is there to think?"

"He's alive. Klein is alive," she said.

"Yeah." Brian remained puzzled. "I was surprised by that too. He's been dead in my head for years, so I assumed he really was dead."

Her black eyes flashed what looked like outrage. *Does she expect me to do something? I'm Batman, she's Catwoman, and we'll avenge our childhoods? No. Stop thinking like a hack writer. She can't be here for something practical.*

"Tell me, Julie. I can't guess what you're thinking."

Still looking offended, she held his gaze for another long beat. When at last she spoke, she answered a question he had asked earlier: "Klein became a patient of my father's. A favorite patient because he knew celebrities. So he was invited to our house in Riverdale four, I don't know, it may even have been five times over two years. I'm older than you. When I met you I was eleven, so I was thirteen the last time Klein showed up. I had breasts, real boobs by then. Each time he managed to get me alone. He was really clever about figuring a way to fool my parents into leaving us alone long enough for him to . . ." She paused. She frowned. "The first two times he came without Sam. He just used his hands. I didn't fight. He stopped each time because somebody was coming. But then one Sunday he showed up with a dental emergency that turned out to be nothing, a cap had fallen out, on very short notice, and that time he brought Sam. After fixing Klein's cap my father decided to start a barbecue and Mom had to clean up . . ." Her voice had been a calm monotone until this phrase. It broke without warning, threatening tears. She swallowed hard and then resumed in that emotionally neutral voice. "Noah had squirted ketchup all over himself and Mom had to get him changed. While they were all distracted, Klein and Sam both, they both came into my room, where I had gone specifically to stay away from him, and he put it in my mouth. With Sam watching. He put it in my mouth. I don't know why I didn't bite it off. I really don't." She looked at Brian as if he knew.

"You were protecting your parents," he offered.

She dismissed that quickly. "Yes, but not just them. It sounds crazy, but I was protecting me too."

"That's not crazy to me," Brian said.

Julie nodded. "There was a lot I was afraid of. So many things I was afraid of. I don't know if I'll ever know what all my fears were. But it still makes no sense to me that I did nothing that time, because the very next time, when he trapped me in the basement, I was getting a spare folding chair in the basement, he trapped me there and I threw the chair at him and ran upstairs and stood next to my mother, one inch away from Ma, for the rest of the afternoon. And that stopped it." At last there was something other than gloom and self-recrimination in her expression. She looked faintly and distinctly proud. "He never came to the house again," she said.

"You stopped him, Julie. That was brave." *This is what she wants. Absolution. And approval.* "You were very brave, Julie."

Both hands came up and covered her eyes. "I'm not brave," she mumbled. "I'm not brave," she repeated, her shoulders quaking, voice breaking up with tears.

While he watched her struggle for composure he wanted to get up, kneel beside her chair and hug her, but he couldn't budge. He remained stuck in his chair and felt a fool, an utter fool. All along he had thought he was the worst wounded at this table, but there was her old pain staring him in the face, much worse than his, and now there was fresh pain in the world, worse than both of theirs. *You see, I'm not the hack. God is. And the Old Fart doesn't know how to write a conclusion that'll satisfy his audience. He leaves that to us, his lost children, doing his dirty work, inventing uplifting endings to erase his mistakes.*

HE'S A MAN, Julie observed, and was surprised. Not surprised that Brian had aged but that he had matured. Men were usually adolescent or boyish: on the phone Jeff sounded like a teenager; her husband rarely showed more restraint than a toddler. Yet when she blurted out that Brian was a man, he said, "I doubt that." Self-deprecation only made him seem all the more grown-up. Indeed, Julie was soon persuaded that at least about the subject of Richard Klein, he was wiser than she. The question was whether his wisdom would be of any help.

Is he gay? she wondered as she probed him over coffee and the Linzer cookie he ate with a kind of desperation after she said that Jeff had loved him. Was she unsure about his sexual preference because he had been molested by a man? Or simply because he was single and unmarried at fifty?

After she told him what Klein had done to her, had embarrassingly wept into her hands and confessed that she was a coward, she continued to muse in the background about Brian's sex life while she told him some—not all—of what Gary had found out so far and all about her agreement with Jeff to keep their connection to Rydel a secret. She held back the bombshell, the latest news about the case that Gary had phoned in from the Hamptons last night. Meanwhile, watching Brian react was fun. With each twist and turn, his expressive face shifted rapidly from world-weary nods to wide-eyed surprise. He listened without interrupting. Even when she was finally done, he paused for a moment before commenting, "So if Jeff told you to forget about me, and you agreed to keep quiet to jump-start your son's acting career, why are you talking to me at all?"

"Because of new information Gary has about the case. No one knows it. It's not public."

"What? What did he find out?" Brian, like her, was instantly panicked. Was that because he knew all along this could never end easily for them? *Why do we keep hoping for a way out?*

At last she took the risk, her great leap of faith. "In the past forty-eight hours I've lied to both Gary and Jeff. I haven't lied to you so far, and I don't want to, but you shouldn't trust me."

Brian broke into a grin. "Julie . . ." He tried not to, but then he laughed hard enough for tears to well. When he composed himself, he said amiably, "I don't trust anyone, and by the way, you shouldn't trust me. But I hope that doesn't stop you. I'm dying to know what you've been lying to Jeff about."

"I told Jeff I would stop Gary from covering the case and I haven't. I told Gary that Jeff didn't care whether he covered the case and he should stay on it."

"Wow. Good for you. Jeff won't see that coming. I'm sure he thinks offering your boy a career is too good for you to pass up."

"Zack would probably kill me if he knew. So Gary stayed on the case all day yesterday. And he called last night with really bad, really upsetting news." Before she continued, she wanted to impress Brian with how much trust she was placing in him. "I'm not supposed to tell anybody on pain of death, so you can really mess me up if you tell Gary's rivals. Right now he has this exclusively." She waited.

"Okay. I can really mess you up. Do you want me to swear I won't?"

"No. I wouldn't believe you anyway. Here's the scoop: Gary's source in the DA's office says they may not be able to make the rape and sexual molestation charges stick. Only the most recent cases . . . You know about the sta . . . *statute* of limitations on child sexual abuse?"

Brian nodded wearily. He said in a disgusted tone, "Five years after the child victim turns eighteen. If the victim doesn't come forward by age twenty-three, it's history."

"Amazing," Julie said. That legal nicety, which apparently was old news to Brian, was shockingly new to her. "Anyway, yeah, so there are only four witnesses under twenty-three. Two of the four are . . . what's the word? Impeached. One has a long criminal record, the other is a meth addict. And yesterday, the two who were considered good witnesses suddenly changed their story, made it sound like it was just consensual sex games going on between the boys that Sam Rydel covered up, or something like that. It's pretty lame but good enough to create reasonable doubt, Gary says. Rydel's lawyer is offering that he'll plead to contributing to the delinquency of a minor, that he's willing to go into rehab for his Percocet habit—"

"Percocet? Seriously?" Brian laughed bitterly. "That's so nineties. He should at least update his addictions."

Julie didn't care for cynicism and now she tried to discourage it with stern urgency. "Listen. They're negotiating with Rydel's lawyer now. If he can keep his broadcasting school, Rydel's willing to check himself into some kind of psychiatric program for six months. The deal hasn't been made because the DA also wants him to agree to take a drug that some sex offenders are put on. I can't remember what Gary said it was . . ."

"Cyproterone?" Brian offered.

She shook her head. "No, that's not it.

"Depo-Provera?"

"That's it. Depo- . . ." She hesitated.

"Provera. That makes sense for a DA to demand in lieu of jail time because it's verifiable. Depo-Provera has to be given by injection and it stays in your system for ninety days. So once every three months you have to come in for an injection. That way they can be sure a sex offender is on the drug and presumably harmless."

"I see." Then a terrible suspicion arrived and she couldn't keep it to herself: "How do you know about these drugs?"

Brian spread his arms to encompass the universe. “Wikipedia!” He made a Bronx cheer. “Also, serial killers, child killers, they’re hot, they’re the new cool kids, the new vampires, the new zombies, everybody’s favorite spook monster. In just the past year, the studios must have sent me two dozen books to adapt about the fascinating subject of child sexual murderers.”

“Is that really why you know so much about them?” She didn’t let his eyes go. She was naive enough to believe that if he lied to her about this, she would see it in his eyes.

He frowned with disgust. “I’m not on Depo-Provera or cyproterone, Julie.” She didn’t release him. He met her stare and testified solemnly: “I’m not a child molester.”

So, as it turned out, even more than she had assumed, she was still walking on the thin ice of trust. She had gone too far out to worry about falling through now. “Brian, the point I’m trying to make is that one way or the other Rydel’s going to get away with it.”

“I agree. I expected him to get off even if they charged him. He can afford great lawyers.”

“And that’s not the worst part,” Julie said. At last she had arrived at her real point: “Klein’s going to get away with it.”

“Klein? Of course. He’s eighty-four.”

“No, it’s not that he’s too old. This is something only Gary knows from his source in the DA’s office. So again, I have to trust you.” Brian nodded. “More than a dozen witnesses, boys and girls, have come forward that Klein molested them at the academy, and at the camp too, but mostly at the academy in the past twenty years. All but two are too old, but using the two who still are younger than twenty-three, the DA was going to nail him too, Brian. They were going to get Klein. But the witnesses against Klein have the same kind of credibility problems, so they’re going to let Klein go too. And even if the witnesses who aren’t too old decide to sue, Gary says both Rydel and Klein will settle out of court with them in exchange for not admitting any guilt.”

"Sure." Brian rubbed his temples as if he had a headache. "The *Times* piece said that even with the academy's stock dropping like a rock, Klein's still worth a fortune."

"They're going to get away with it, Brian," Julie insisted. Her black eyes gleamed. "And I've decided that's not acceptable."

Brian stopped rubbing. He squinted at her. "Not acceptable? What does that mean?"

"We have to do something."

"No, we don't," he said, his answer like that of a schoolteacher: a mild, amused correction. "In fact, 'something' is exactly what we can't do. There's no 'something' available to us."

Julie lowered her voice to a whisper, to make absolutely sure the waitress couldn't hear. "If I'd blown the whistle on Richard Klein years ago, God knows how many kids he molested would have been spared."

Brian interrupted. "Give me a break, Julie. Give yourself a break. By the time you were twenty-three, it was already too late."

"Doesn't matter!" Julie caught herself shouting. She lowered her voice, again to an intense whisper. "It would have put the spotlight on them. And maybe whatever sickness he did with Sam would have come out. Maybe our talking then could have helped Sam . . ."

"And that could have stopped him? Saved those poor black and Hispanic kids?" Brian's Linzer cookie was gone. He wetted his fingertip and picked up the few remaining crumbs from his plate, licking them. *How could he eat?* Julie wondered. She felt sick to her stomach. Since she had heard from Gary the full, detailed accounts of what Klein and Rydel did to those poor orphaned boys, the disgusting way they were seduced and bullied and perverted . . . sickening. For years, she had been haunted by the responsibility of not telling on Klein—Rydel was proof her fears had been justified. Saying it aloud made her feel even worse. As an unspoken guilt, in the company of all her other shameful secrets, its ugliness had remained in shadow. Now she couldn't look away from the revealing spotlight: she bore a portion of the blame for all those ruined lives.

"So we're murderers." Brian sucked the last dot of sugar from his thumb. He didn't have old man lips, thinned and downturned. He looked his age, but there was something preserved about him, an old child. That was how she had remembered him and chose to recall him when she was in heat, sometimes imagining him as an adult in a suit, sometimes insisting on his thin boy's face: but always his eyes understood her, feeling what she was feeling, seeing what she could not.

"What?" She hadn't really taken in what he said.

Brian casually repeated, "So we're murderers. Aren't we—if what you say is correct—responsible for everything Klein and Sam Rydel have done? I don't know if Gary has different info, but I heard on TV one of the Huck Finn boys hanged himself in a cabin on the camp grounds. Before that, another OD'd on glue or some household product or other, right? I mean I did my best not to listen, but I did hear something like that. So if we're responsible for Rydel raping those boys, then we're responsible for their deaths."

He might as well have punched her. She bent over until her head nearly touched the organic honey dispenser. Brian's judgment hadn't occurred to her, not consciously. *He's right. We're responsible for those deaths.* For decades, they had done nothing about Klein and Rydel, so now they were a party to every crime they had committed, to every boy and girl who had been broken.

Brian touched her forearm briefly. She sat up. He looked stricken. "I'm sorry. I'm being a drama queen," Brian said. He tried to retract his awful indictment. "That's what the studios pay me to do: raise the stakes; increase jeopardy, heighten conflict. All that bullshit. Don't pay attention to me. It's just storytelling. In the real world, only lunatics believe in that melodramatic crap."

Despairing, Julie stared into the middle distance: rows of pastries blurring, an espresso machine catching light, blinding her for a moment. Brian tapped her arm again, lightly, voice urgent: "Listen, I was exaggerating. Okay? I like to play around with this shit in my head, that's all. Any first-year psychology major will tell you we were kids, just kids—none of it is our responsibility. And any first-year law student will tell you there was nothing we could have said, even if we were miraculous human specimens who could get it together to make our accusations before we turned twenty-three, in the 1970s the chances our testimony alone would have prevailed is really really questionable. In fact, we could have been sued for slander, and with a guy like Klein, I bet he would have sued. And as for today? These new charges? We have no evidence, none at all, against Klein or Rydel about what they did. What I said makes a good dramatic speech, but in the real world it's just bullshit. Nobody, nobody in the history of the world, would have done anything differently than what you and I did. Nobody. What I just said is sentimental melodrama. Don't give it a second thought."

Julie was grateful he wanted to relieve her of guilt. But he was wrong. She did not judge him harshly for his longing to remain passive, the cynical bystander. He was willing to accept her without judgment and deserved the same from her. For better or for worse, she felt sure there was no one else on earth who could do for her what Brian could. Others could offer sympathy, empathy, soothing explanations. But only he knew or could know the truth of her experience. She could trust him. She was convinced she had found a reliable ally. That was what today's meeting had to settle for her.

Julie sat up, head straight above her spine, chin forward, neck long, shoulders relaxed. "An exclamation point, that's what you are," her ballet teacher used to say. Julie summoned her from long ago, that good girl who knew right from wrong, to tell the solemn boy of yesterday, "I'm not a child anymore. That excuse doesn't work. And I don't care if what I have to say is of any use in court. I won't let Klein die unpunished. I won't let Rydel bury what they are. I'm going to the press. I'll tell Gary about it, about all of what happened to me, or as much of it as he needs to know, and he'll figure out the best way to go public. And I'm not going to warn Jeff because I think he's helping Klein and Rydel cover up—"

"Of course he is," Brian said, interrupting. "He tried to buy you off and now the victims are being bought off. It's got to be Jeff who's behind that strategy."

"I know!" Julie nodded, pleased they had figured that out. "But why? Why is he protecting them? He's not . . ." She couldn't say it. "You don't think he's also . . . ?"

"Jeff? No! It's his reputation. He's the most beloved director in America. Or the most successful, anyway. If all this comes out, that he got his start thanks to a child molester, you know what they'll do to him. Nothing on earth is more vicious than a disappointed American public."

Julie nodded. *Yes, that would be unfair to Jeff,* she thought, *very unfair, but shielding Jeff isn't worth ruining a single child's life.* She took her final, her greatest, leap of faith with Brian: "I'm going to tell what I know about Klein and Rydel, although it's not evidence, although probably no one will care or do anything about it. I'm going to tell what happened so they can't hide anymore." Julie panted. She felt as if she had been running as fast as she could for as long as she could. "I'll also be exposing you. So I came here today to figure out if you deserved a warning. If I'm wrong to trust you, and you go to Jeff, maybe you can mess me up, concoct some story about how I'm unstable, discredit me or whatever, but . . . well, I trust you. I didn't think there was anyone I could trust. But I can. And it's you."

Original Sin

— April 1966 —

RICHARD KLEIN SHUT the door. He lifted the hook off Jeff's lock, aiming it at the eye without letting go, as if figuring out how they worked together.

"Don't do that," Brian said.

With a mischievous smile, Klein let the hook dangle freely. He turned to give the boy his full attention. "Why not?"

"You're not supposed to lock Jeff's door unless he's here."

Klein pointed at his chest with a smirk. "*I'm* not?"

"Nobody is. Jeff isn't supposed to lock it without permission from his mom."

"Then what's the point?" Klein laughed. He took a step toward Brian, who took a step back. Klein took three more steps forward and Brian retreated three. Klein noticed. Brian saw he noticed. "Why have a lock if you can't use it to keep your mother out?" Klein chuckled.

Brian shrugged. "She has to knock."

Klein nodded. "You're very smart, aren't you?" He veered away from Brian, seeming to be abruptly fascinated by Jeff's bracketed system of shelves. He ran his fingers across the colorful spines of Landmark in History books. "Harriet was just telling me you're very very smart. Actually she said you're smarter than Jeff." Klein smirked, as if they were sharing a joke. "I didn't know Harriet thought it was possible for anyone to be smarter than her precious Jeff."

Brian shrugged. That he was smarter than his best friend was hardly news. He ought to go find Jeff, presumably in Harriet's bedroom with all the others, but he didn't. He wasn't in danger. Everyone was just a few feet away. The door was unlocked. Still, he wished Jeff would return.

Klein turned, facing the shelves, his wandering eyes dropping down a level to a deeper shelf where Jeff had stowed the portable tape recorder. Klein's hand hovered above the machine for a moment before he depressed the Play button. The large plastic reels jerked to life, the lax tape tightening to begin their journey through the heads.

"Don't!" Brian raced over to shut off the recorder before Klein could hear a syllable of the secret recording.

Klein's hand closed around the back of Brian's neck. He twisted Brian's head up, bringing the boy's abashed face close to his delighted one. "What a reaction!" He put his index finger on the bridge of Brian's nose. With insinuating gentleness, he trailed slowly down to the tip while he said in a teasing lilt, "Have you boys been doing something naughty with my present?"

Klein's Old Spice aftershave enveloped Brian. Brian squirmed against the hand on his neck. Klein held on by slightly emphasizing his grip, as if it were a leash. He reached across Brian's body with his free hand, threatening to press the Play button. While doing that he locked his forearm around Brian's chest and shifted his feet to stand directly behind him, pressing tight against Brian.

Brian's body wanted to free itself. It could have. Klein's grip on his neck felt firm, not imprisoning, but Brian was preoccupied by the urgent need to stop Klein's other hand from turning on the tape. He grabbed at the adult's chubby fingers with his skinny, smaller ones, tugging on the knuckles, trying to lift them clear of the Play button.

Klein could easily have won the struggle and turned on the machine.

Instead, he splayed his fingers and captured Brian's. Brian brought his other hand over as reinforcements. Klein matched the maneuver, letting go of Brian's neck. He captured this new contestant by the wrist and pushed up tight against Brian's back.

Brian froze. He felt Klein's Thing, stone hard and impossibly long, nestling into the groove of his spine. Klein leaned his chin on Brian's head. His aftershave fell over Brian like a caul. Brian didn't move. He could break free only by abandoning the recorder, but that wasn't what held him there. He was unable to think. There was this amazing and appalling object that made nonsense out of everything. Klein's voice whispered, suffused with pleasure, "What have you bad boys been up to?"

"Nothing," Brian mumbled.

Klein covered the back of Brian's hands with his own and moved them away from the tape recorder to Brian's Levi's. He was a skinny eight-year-old. The gap between skin and waist easily accommodated the double thickness of the quartet of hands that Klein forced, his fingers wiggling, digging below for It.

For the second time in his life, Brian's body reacted in an astonishing way to being touched. On this occasion, there was confusion in the overwhelming sensation, confusion about whose fingers were teasing It. He was touched and touching. Richard Klein no longer existed and Richard Klein was all that existed. There was tremendous heat pulsing in his chest, his belly, throughout his groin. His mind shut off. The world was his body's remarkable reaction to those twenty fingers, irrevocably altering his understanding of what the universe could offer.

He felt a whoosh of air from the direction of the door as it opened. Klein's head twisted to look. Brian jerked to get away. In that moment, he learned two lessons. First, his body, although hesitant to fight to free itself, was instantly willing to fight not to be discovered. Second, Klein easily held him in place, destroying the illusion that he could always escape. Klein spoke in the direction of the door, voice husky: "Hi, Jeff."

Brian opened his eyes. He hadn't realized until then he had shut them. He violently tried to pull his hands out of his Jockey shorts and Levi's, but they were stopped by the obstruction of Klein's forearms at his waist. Klein's fingers remained. He continued to stroke Brian's Thing, which felt so hard and jumpy he worried it would break off.

"Come in, Jeffrey," Klein whispered. "Shut the door."

Brian expected horror and disgust from Jeff. The only secret he had ever kept from his best friend was exploded.

Jeff, head down, solemnly shut the door.

Klein took a firm hold on Brian's Thing, fat hands enveloping It, as if he were taking ownership. He whispered to Jeff, "Lock the door."

Jeff put the hook in the eye. He spoke to the floorboards. "Mom wants us to be with everybody."

"Come here." Klein's breathy voice was hardly audible, but it was infused with command. Eyes averted, Jeff obediently moved toward the awkward embrace of adult and child. Klein roughly removed his right hand from Brian's jeans; the left remained anchored there. With Klein's withdrawal, Brian's hands exited gladly, but then they did nothing with their freedom, hanging limply. He watched as Klein took possession of Jeff's elbow, dumbfounded that his friend did not protest. Klein stepped sideways, one hand in Brian's pants, the other towing Jeff, forcing them into a clumsy group walk to the twin bed against the wall, a maneuver as silly as anything out of *The Three Stooges,* only it wasn't funny.

Brian tried to meet Jeff's eyes. They remained downcast. He's not happy about this either, Brian realized, and couldn't understand why he obeyed. This wasn't the whiny, argumentative Jeff he knew. Brian counted on Jeff to resist grown-up craziness on his behalf, especially from members of Jeff's family.

Klein sat on the bed, pulling Brian down beside him on his left, tugging Jeff down with his other hand to lie on his right side. Out of the corner of his eye, Brian saw Klein reach into Jeff's Levi's. Brian looked away, to the windows. Framed by the city's sky he saw the top floors of their public school. They were double height to accommodate the gym and its glistening wood floor. He thought: *I'm not going to think.*

"I know you boys play with each other," Klein informed them. "You like doing this," he said, accompanied by the clink of Jeff's belt buckle being released.

"Don't take them off," Jeff pleaded.

"The door's locked," Klein answered in a soothing tone. "You boys like doing this. All boys like playing with themselves. When you have sleepovers, you like playing with each other, don't you?" Klein stopped stroking Brian. He pulled his hand out of Brian's jeans. The relief—and the confusion that this relief was accompanied by a loss of pleasure—was short-lived. Klein flicked opened Brian's waist button, pulling one side down, unzipping him. His white Jockeys and the lump of It were exposed. He looked away to the school's roof.

Klein gripped Brian's right wrist, pulling it toward Jeff.

This time Brian resisted. He jerked violently, sure his hand would come free. But Klein didn't give an inch. He tugged harder, painfully forcing Brian's fingers at Jeff's opened pants. Brian's eyes went to the struggle. His friend's white Jockeys were pulled halfway down. The head of his Thing was sticking halfway out, smooth and very swollen, looking too large for its own good. Above his captured hand, Brian saw Klein's other hand towing Jeff's fingers toward the lump in Brian's underpants. Lying between them, Klein's ridiculously big Thing was making a tent of his gray slacks.

If Brian had known the word *grotesque,* that's how he would have thought of the scene, everything distorted like a comic book's drawings. For the first time since Jeff came in, their eyes met. Jeff's eyes looked as if they were covered by cellophane: dimmed and sad.

Brian stopped resisting. Klein placed the palm of Brian's hand onto Jeff's Thing, half on cotton, half swollen flesh. He was surprised that It felt like regular skin. Klein pushed Jeff's fingers under the elastic to touch Brian's. The boys didn't move their hands.

"Rub like this." Klein put his one hand on top of each of theirs, forcing their hands to rub each other's Things back and forth a few times. Then he released them, Klein's hands burrowing underneath his own belt, inside his tent, frantically jerking the pole up into the fabric in a way that looked like it must hurt.

Again Brian's eyes met Jeff's cellophane-covered eyes, a stranger he didn't want to know. He removed his hand from Jeff's Thing, not caring what Klein would do.

Jeff's hand also departed from Brian's body and he was quickly on his feet, zipping his pants, fastening his belt. "Mom's calling," he said, a preposterous lie. The only sound was the friction of Klein's hands moving furiously underneath his slacks. Otherwise the silence in the room was profound, the silence of places Brian had not yet been: gazing at the lifeless body of a beloved, the echo of a lost illusion, the tinnitus of betrayal.

Jeff crossed to the door.

"Don't go," Klein commanded in a low voice.

Jeff halted. He kept his back to them, head bowed, shoulders slumped.

Klein's chubby hands reappeared. He leaned over Brian, tugging at his underpants, his aftershave rolling in like a fog. Brian pressed his ass down on the bed as hard as he could to prevent Klein from lowering his Jockeys. Klein pulled the front elastic band away with his left hand, stretching the material to its limits, while his right showed Brian a part of Brian he no longer recognized: once soft, now swollen; once wrinkled, now smooth; once shriveled, now long. He was mesmerized by the sight of the transformation. He had felt Its stiffness once before in the NBC bathroom but not seen it. That day Brian had kept his eyes up the entire time, looking at his face in the mirror. Now Klein displayed It thoroughly, cradled in the warm hollow of his hand while he whispered compliments, "Yours is very long for a little boy. And your stomach is so flat, so soft. I like how your belly button goes in. And I can see your hip bones!" He touched the peak of one. "And I like that you have no hair," he said, running the back of his hand lightly over the boy's concave stomach. Klein closed his fingers around Brian's Thing and began to stroke it roughly. That the pumping felt very painful and also very good was stupefying. Brian stared at his body, the features Klein had pointed out, as if he had never seen them before. He hadn't, this way, and forever more he would see himself through his molester's eyes.

"Turn around, Jeff," Klein said. "Look how excited Brian is."

"Jeff! Where are you?" Harriet's screech penetrated the door. Klein's hands released him. Jeff pressed against the door as if to barricade it. Brian stopped breathing. "Dick! Are you with the boys? Bring them here!" Brian realized she hadn't moved from her bedroom.

Jeff pleaded in a whisper, "We have to go." Then he shouted. "COMING MA." He fumbled with the hook and eye to undo it.

Klein released Brian, standing up and moving fast despite the bulge in his slacks. He paused to button his jacket, using the fabric to cover his Thing's shape. He followed Jeff out.

Brian had the most trouble repairing himself. While zipping up he was distressed that this time, unlike in the bathroom, the manifestation of his excitement wasn't subsiding once Klein let go. Was he permanently damaged? Would everyone know just by looking at his Levi's?

He pushed his swollen Thing to the side. He punched It. He tried to walk nonchalantly while looking down to see if It was visible. He tried to convince himself It could look like a Swiss Army knife in his pocket—only he knew the position at his groin was hopelessly wrong. He paused outside Harriet's bedroom door, squeezing the bulge through the denim, hoping to compress It down to unobtrusive utility. As he strained to squash It, he sensed someone coming out of the room and managed to get his hand away only a second before Julie's solemn face appeared.

"Hi, Brian," she said with a chime of delight, smiling in a wonderfully friendly way. She had a tiny beauty mark below her right eye at the point where her cheekbone appeared. It was interesting. And there was another one directly beneath her left eye. "There you are! Everyone was wondering." She twisted toward Harriet's door. Brian's eyes roved over her long raven hair, cascading down her red sweater. "He's here!" She turned back. "I'm making tea for Aunt Harriet. Want to help me?"

He nodded. Recent events made him wish to be a mute from now on. He followed her past the open door of Harriet's room, which was experiencing a rush hour of unprecedented proportions. Noah was perched on the bed next to Harriet, his legs crossed while peering intently at a Superboy comic. The Mark brothers, Saul and Hy, were seated in folding chairs arranged beside the invalid, squeezed into the narrow passage between dresser and bed. Richard Klein was occupying the most comfortable seat, the wing chair on the far side of the bed, in the corner, in front of heavily draped windows. He was angled away from a direct view of the invalid, favoring another of Klein's gifts, the RCA television console, its curved glass screen currently a dormant gray. Jeff sat on the floor near his father, back propped against the closet door, as far from Klein as was possible in his mother's cramped bedroom.

As Brian passed the open doorway he was acknowledged by Saul's sad beagle face: watery eyes peering from above dark half-moons, permanently tattooed by the insufficient sleep he was granted as a partner in a failing business and as occupant of a queen-size bed with lesser rights to its expanse than his wife. "Hi, Bri." He raised a hand in greeting. He rarely had much to say to Brian but he always seemed glad to see him.

Brian nodded, hurrying down the hall after Julie's white legs, flashing ahead of him through the dark foyer, the almost never used dining room, and on into the kitchen. She walked with her head held high. He was fascinated by the graceful flutter of her long black hair against her straight back. He felt safe as long as he was with her. Or safer.

The kitchen was a long galley with dark green cabinets, lit by a circular fluorescent fixture that gave off a sickly yellow light. "Do you want tea?" she asked while filling a kettle. Brian shook his head. He sat at the Formica table by the window where he and Jeff would savor Nestlé instant hot chocolates in the winter, egg cream sodas in summer. The window looked onto the building's interior courtyard.

He scanned down to find his kitchen window. He couldn't see much inside, but he knew the light was a bright globe, the cabinets and walls white and cheerful. His father had gone out and his mother was sad about it. He sort of had understood that earlier; he thought it through now. He wished his father would stop trying to be an actor. He decided he didn't want to go home right now. He was content to remain with Julie and never speak again.

Abruptly Brian realized It was gone. No sensation down there—the nothing felt wonderful.

"I want to talk to you about something, okay?" Julie turned on the right front burner. He waited for it to ignite with a whoosh, then stayed focused on the caress of flame and metal, wary of her question. "Brian?" She ducked to meet his eyes. Hers were as black and shiny as her hair.

He evaded them. He studied the sweep of her long hair as it came together briefly under her chin while she was bent over, then parting as she straightened. She smelled a little of pine needles.

"You listening?" she insisted.

Brian nodded. How long had it been since he spoke? It wasn't hard, staying silent. Julie was satisfied with his nod and continued, "I think we have to talk to one of the grown-ups about . . . you know, about what we know about Aunt Harriet."

It took Brian a moment to remember what Julie knew and didn't know. *She thinks Harriet is dying,* he reminded himself.

Julie sat in the chair opposite. Her knees touched Brian's. Her legs were way longer than his. He noticed a beauty mark on her left thigh, very dark chocolate, like the one under her left eye and at the jutting point of her high cheekbone. There were more. Above her right knee. On her left forearm. At least six more. He searched for each one. She whispered, "Jeff's very upset. I can tell he's very upset. We have to tell somebody he knows about Aunt Harriet. I don't want to get you in trouble or anything about the tape machine, but maybe we can figure out some other way, like . . . maybe you overheard by accident or something? And of course you told Cousin Jeff. I mean, you're best friends. You tell each other everything. Like I do with Nancy Weiss. She's my best friend. I tell her everything."

Tears gathered, clouding vision, choking him. How could he undo the knot of misunderstandings, lies, and confounding behaviors? And It. How to explain It?

The kettle whistled, then screamed. Brian covered his ears until Julie turned off the burner. He kept them covered while she poured. When she finished, she tapped his knee. "Brian. Could you take your hands away?" He lowered them. "We have to tell his parents. It's not fair to Jeff. He must be very scared. We have to tell his parents that he knows so they can make him feel better."

He was going to have to speak. He was sorry to. "She's . . ." His voice was an unrecognizable croak. Shocked by the sound of himself, he stopped.

Julie prompted, "What? She's what?"

"She's not sick. She made it up 'cause they can't pay your father back. Some money they owe him for the store."

Julie looked at the hallway, then back to Brian. She was pouting as if he'd hurt her feelings. Brian expected she was going to argue. Deciding she didn't understand, Brian continued, "Your uncle Saul owes your father money and your father wants it back so she made it up about the cancer so he won't want it back. *I think.* I don't really know." He stood up. "I don't want to talk about it." He looked out the window to his kitchen below. *Go home. Tell Mom you feel sick.*

The sound of someone walking their way from the hall brought Julie to her feet. She moved close to Brian, whispering, "Does Jeff know it's a lie?"

"I just told him. We can't tell Harriet we know. We'll get Jeff in trouble, " Brian insisted, spooked by the prospect of more attention focused on the tape and the secrets they know. Less. He wanted less of everything.

"Why are they like this?" Julie pleaded as if he really could answer.

Brian studied her lips; they were curvy and soft. He wondered about kissing a girl. Not wanting to. Curious. What would that feel like?

"Julie? Need help making Harriet's tea?" The low rumble of Saul's exhausted voice reached them from the foyer. They moved apart, Julie to pour, Brian sitting sideways on the windowsill, staring down at home.

Julie stepped into the dining room, showing off cup and saucer. "I've got it, Uncle Saul. Does Aunt Harriet want milk or sugar?"

"Just lemon," Saul said. He waved to Brian. "Hey, Bri, come here."

Brian dutifully crossed the dining room to the foyer. "I'm gonna pick up Jeff's birthday cake from Zolly's. Make sure he stays in the bedroom until I return. So he doesn't see me bring in the cake? Supposed to be a surprise."

Brian nodded. Saul rubbed Brian's thick black hair, then gave it two pats. "Good boy," he said, then left.

Julie appeared, carrying the tea. "Did he hear us?" she asked.

"No. He's getting Jeff's birthday cake. We're supposed to keep him busy. That's all."

"Oh." She bit her lip. They looked down the hall, reluctant to begin the journey to Harriet's sickroom.

"JULIE!" Harriet shouted hoarsely.

"I've got to give this to Aunt Harriet," Julie said. Brian followed. No matter how much trouble she might cause with her mania for telling grownups everything, he definitely felt safest with her.

As Saul had feared, Jeff did try to leave the bedroom, rising when Julie arrived with the tea. "Here's your tea, Aunt Harriet!" Julie announced in an overly cheerful voice while Jeff slid behind his cousin, heading for the door. Brian stopped him. "Where you going?"

Jeff's wouldn't look at him. *Why is he angry at me?* Brian wondered. He didn't think it was fair for Jeff to be angry at him for touching his Thing. Jeff had touched his. Jeff shook off Brian's hand and sidled out to the hallway.

Harriet was saying, "Thank you, darling. What a sweet girl. Taking care of your poor sick aunt. Thank you. This is just what I need. I'm so nauseous." Harriet belched. That triggered a staccato string of giggles from Noah. He was sternly rebuked by his father.

Brian hustled after Jeff, catching up as he reached the foyer. He raced ahead and blocked his progress. "Where are you going?"

"Looking for Dad." Jeff met his eyes only for a second; they drifted off to the wall of art books and sets of classics that were never removed from the floor-to-ceiling shelves, a larger version of the bracketed system in Jeff's room. "I want to ask him if we can go play Slug downstairs until dinner."

"You want to go out?" Brian was surprised.

Jeff stared at a wide spine with *Cézanne* written in tall red script letters. "I don't wanna stay here and listen to my crazy mom complain." He sounded bitterly angry at her, which puzzled Brian. Harriet was bad, but she wasn't the worst of their problems. Since Brian didn't answer, Jeff persisted, "Mom won't let us, that's why I want to ask Dad. He'll let us." Jeff stepped to the side, preparing to go around Brian.

"Your dad went out," Brian said.

"Where?"

"He went to get your cake at Zolly's. You're not supposed to know."

"That's stupid," Jeff whined in his nasal voice. Brian was relieved to hear his honk return. He had been speaking in an unnaturally gloomy tone. "They always get me a cake from Zolly's." Jeff moved past. "Let's go. Let's meet him."

"No!" Brian stamped his foot. "He doesn't want you to know."

"That's stupid!" Jeff yelled. "That's so stupid!"

"What's stupid?" asked Richard Klein. He ambled toward them on polished black loafers that made the floorboards creak. Brian's heart pounded wildly.

"Nothing," Jeff said. He walked boldly right at Klein. Brian was amazed, then appalled as he watched Klein allow Jeff to go by without so much as a glance, instead continuing his progress toward Brian, those greedy hands appearing from his slacks.

Brian bolted. His long, skinny legs had always allowed him to get a good jump, that's why he almost always won at Running Bases in the school yard. From standing still he could be at full speed within a second, stopping and reversing direction on a dime. With a dollop of malicious pleasure he saw the look of surprise on Klein's face as Brian rapidly arrived at Klein's position, apparently blocked, turned sideways, back skimming the wall past Klein, turning hard and fast into Harriet's bedroom.

Jeff had stopped in the doorway. Brian bumped into him. Jeff stumbled toward the foot of his mother's bed where Harriet was perched, sipping her cup of tea. "Watch it!" she screamed as Jeff caught himself by grabbing the arm of Uncle Hy's chair. Harriet's cup wobbled, sloshed a little tea into the saucer, but was essentially preserved. "What is the matter with you?" Harriet complained bitterly. "Can't you see I have hot tea in my hands?"

"Tea in my hands!" Noah repeated, and dissolved into a fugue of giggles. Hy shushed him.

Brian smelled Old Spice wafting from behind him. He fought off a sneeze. Klein passed him, waist rubbing against the boy's back. "I took your seat," Julie said, rising from the wing chair near the drapes. Klein accepted her offer and in a quick graceful move sat while simultaneously hooking her by the arm. He tugged her down, saying, "Sit with me. There's plenty of room in this big old chair."

Her father, Hy, didn't pay attention to what was going on, but Brian's eyes went straight to Klein. He never wanted to see the man again and he wanted to make sure to see everything he did.

Julie sat on the armrest. Klein commented, "That's not comfortable." He urged her onto the cleared edge of the seat. That meant her waist was wedged in while her back had no support, forcing her to lean forward, which appeared to be even less comfortable than perching on the arm.

Meanwhile Jeff turned to his mother. "Brian and I want to go outside and play Slug."

"What's Slug?" Hy asked.

"You want to go outside!" Harriet groaned as she maneuvered to put the cup and saucer on her crowded night table: tissue dispensers, several smudged empty glasses and a bottle of Alka Seltzer.

"Until dinner," Jeff insisted. "We want to play Slug."

"What the hell is Slug?" Hy asked.

"It's Chinese handball," Brian explained.

"Absolutely not!" Harriet said.

Hearing that healthy a no, Brian gave up all hope of escape from the sickroom. He consoled himself that no matter how boring it was in Harriet's lair, he would be safe from Klein's hands. Brian put his back against the wall beside the TV console and slid down to his haunches. From there he had a upward angle view of the two people he most wanted to keep his eyes on: Julie and Klein.

"Ma!" Jeff honked. "We don't want to sit around listening to you talk. We want to play."

"No," Harriet said firmly.

Jeff stamped his feet. "It's my birthday!"

"It's not your birthday. Your birthday is tomorrow. We're just celebrating today."

Richard Klein laughed. "That's right, Jeffrey. We're only celebrating your birthday. Don't expect to have any fun."

Noah was delighted by Klein's irreverent remark. He lifted the Superboy comic high and brought it down on the bed over and over while chanting over and over, "It's your birthday! Don't have fun!"

"Stop it, Noah," Hy said by the fourth repetition, and he reached for the comic. Noah ducked away, tumbling back until his head whacked into the wall. He moaned piteously. "Serves you right," said his father.

Harriet twisted toward the wing chair and Klein. The movement was impressive, since for her to perform it required a full ninety-degree turn of her neck, a neck reputed to be always very stiff and painful. Lying a few feet away in her closet was a neck brace she wore at least a few hours every day, prescribed by a HIP doctor in lieu of another refill of Valium.

"What I meant, Dick, is that today is for Jeff to celebrate with his family. He had a treat with his friends yesterday."

"I did not!" Jeff complained.

"You and Brian went to the movies to see the late show."

"Late show!" Jeff was outraged. "It was six o'clock. That's not the late show."

"Jeff, stop it. Stop it this instant." Harriet glared as if powering up a death ray.

"Fine," Jeff said bitterly. "We'll wait until Dad gets back with the stupid cake from Zolly's and then we'll go out." Having played this ace of trumps, Jeff collapsed onto the floor. He folded up: chin on his chest, arms crossed, knees rising, until he was hardly larger than a footstool.

"Your father told you about the cake?" Jeff nodded. Harriet turned to Hy. "What's wrong with that idiot brother of yours? It's supposed to be a surprise!"

Jeff's head popped up. "Dad didn't tell me. I knew anyway. You always get me the same cake." Jeff's neck dissolved, head drooping.

"Not always!" Harriet explained to Hy, "Last year was the first time we ordered a cake from Zolly's. They're so expensive," she added. "I can't believe you figured it out all by yourself." She looked at Jeff's lifeless body. "Your father must have told you." Back to Hy: "Your brother can't keep a secret. That's why he has so much trouble in business. I keep telling him. In business, you have to keep your cards close to your chest."

"Vest," Klein corrected. Hy twisted on his folding chair—he needed to shift ninety degrees to see Klein in the wing chair. Now that Hy was looking at Klein, to Brian's surprise (although with Klein, the surprises were so many they no longer shocked) Klein put an arm around Julie and tugged her closer so that one of her legs rode up partway on his thigh. "That's more comfortable, right?" he asked Julie, then continued speaking to her father: "The expression is *vest,* right Hy? Keep your cards close to your vest. Comes from the Wild West days—poker players in fancy duds."

Brian saw Julie was squirming a little at the awkwardness of Klein squeezing her shoulder a second time, drawing her closer. She slid up higher on his thigh. Her short skirt flared on that side. Brian glimpsed her white panties, decorated with little yellow birds, before she reached over and smoothed her skirt down.

Hy was looking directly at his daughter and Klein, but he didn't complain about Klein's maneuvers. He was delighted to be asked a question by the NBC executive and eagerly agreed. "You're right. Close to the vest, that's the expression. Although I never played poker for real money. Just penny ante stuff. How about you, Dick?"

"In college," Klein said. "I was in a high-stakes game. And some of the guys at the network, especially the guys in sales, they get a serious game going every once in a while. Especially when we entertain the affiliates. But I'm not a gambler. I take risks, calculated risks, but I don't like to gamble. Don't like to lose control." He gave Julie's shoulder another affectionate squeeze, scrunching her. Her bare thigh slid all the way up on Klein's so that she was straddling his leg. Brian noticed a self-conscious look join the already pensive cast in her eyes. He watched as she brought her other leg onto Klein's thigh and pushed her knees together, which was a much more demure posture—perched on Klein's thigh instead of riding it. That also lowered her skirt, covering her thighs. A look of relief crossed her face at having hit upon this solution.

Meanwhile Hy chuckled and smiled at Klein. "Me too. Just the way I am. Can't stand to lose control."

"Ugh. You men." Harriet waved her hand in disgust. She reached for her teacup, groaning at the effort. "Being in charge all the time. All that garbage. Forgive me, Richard, it is such *mishigas*. But"—she paused to sip her tea—"since we women have no hope of ever being in control of anything—"

"Not for lack of trying!" Klein said gleefully, and again he squeezed Julie. This time—Brian noticed with mounting amazement—Klein dropped his arm to her waist and pulled her squarely on his broad lap, her head seemingly growing out of his chest, raven hair flowing from under his chin, a shiny beard. "That's better," he brazenly announced to the room. Julie winced out a polite smile. Brian understood why uncertainty clouded her expression—it was the confusion he had felt, that something you couldn't name was going wrong. And for Brian, a new paralyzing mystery had been added: *What is he doing with her? In front of everybody?*

"Nonsense!" Harriet declared. "We've given up trying. You men will never give us a chance."

Hy wasn't interested in his sister-in-law's topic. "Tell me, Dick." Hy leaned forward, looking past the worried eyes and halfhearted smile frozen on his daughter's face. "There must be tremendous stress in your job. I mean, with the constant battle for viewers . . ."

"And listeners," Klein amended with a broad smile. "We're TV *and* radio."

"Listeners. Of course. But it's the same battle for the audience, isn't it?"

Klein dropped a hard-and-fast curtain on his smile. Wearing a grave face, he spoke solemnly. "Absolutely. One point in the ratings is life and death. Worse. Much worse than life and death. It's millions of dollars." Klein looked off sadly, a combat veteran reliving the tragedy of war.

"Incredible," Hy said. "One point is worth millions of dollars?"

Klein shifted, moving his head beside Julie's, apparently to have room to nod. Brian knew she could smell his perfume, that his husky voice, right at her ear, would sound as if he were inside her skull. "Three points in the ratings could be the difference between General Sarnoff making a profit or loss for the year."

"Tell me," Hy's began, his voice dropping to a lower register, signaling he was about to broach a confidential matter. "I know this is getting a little personal, but out of scientific curiosity, to confirm a theory of mine, when you wake up in the morning, do you have jaw pain?"

Jeff stirred, stretching to peer at his uncle. "What?" he mumbled. Brian also thought the question was very odd, but he was distracted by keeping track of Klein's hands. The adult's arm had virtually encircled Julie's waist. Three fingers on his right hand were slipping through a space created by the bunching of fabric at the lip of Julie's skirt, snaking under it. Brian could almost feel those hot fingers on his own tummy, insinuating, an intrusion but one that wasn't quite rude enough to justify a complaint. He tensed, as if somehow that would stop Klein's action. He watched for Julie's reaction. Her curious shining eyes weren't taking in the world. They were focused inward, flitting back and forth as if hunting for an intruder. Her lips parted, about to speak. Brian was in dreadful and thrilling suspense. What if she jumped up and complained? He hoped so! What would happen?

"Jaw pain?" Jeff honked derisively. "What's that?"

Hy ignored his nephew. "Sorry, don't mean to pry." He looked past his daughter's puzzled expression to peer at Klein's mouth while he explained, "I have a theory that people like yourself, who have important, demanding jobs, who are under great stress, tend to grind their teeth at night." To illustrate, Hy moved his lower jaw around in an exaggerated way, opening his lips ghoulishly to reveal he was gnashing his molars.

Klein maintained a straight face while he watched this goofy display. Brian saw that the adult's eyes were twinkling mischievously, but that wasn't as significant to Brian as his noticing that Klein was tightening his arm around Julie's waist, pressing her flush to his lap.

Julie opened her mouth as if she were about to shriek, but Klein immediately relaxed his vise. Once she calmed, then he squeezed again, and again let go when she tensed. He repeated this cycle three times. With each encore, she reacted more passively, until it was clear to Brian that she had given up the impulse to object, no longer sure what she could protest.

Brian was astonished. He could see Klein's maneuvers easily from behind Julie's father. Hy's view was also unobstructed, but he wasn't noticing, he was too busy silently studying Klein's mouth.

The person who spoke up was Klein. He looked up earnestly at Julie's father and, after a pensive pause, while squeezing the girl tight to his lap, conceded, "I think you're right, Hy. I do have jaw pain in the morning."

JULIE WATCHED HER father's face loom large as he bent over them while Klein wiggled his finger closer and closer to There. ("Your vagina," her father had told her to call it—to her mother's horror. She hated that word. She thought of it as There.) Julie was too startled by all the strange things going on to worry about the right word. For one thing, she didn't quite recognize her father. Being Hyram Mark's daughter, and not his dental assistant, she had never witnessed his manner with a new patient whom he wanted to impress, the solemn medical expert concentrating on his work. "May I?" the dentist asked, hands pausing inches away from examining Klein's jaw.

"Sure." Klein crossed his forearms completely across Julie's tummy as if he needed to make room for her father's fingers. He pulled her even tighter to his waist. She slid her eyes up and to the side to watch her father gently cup each of Klein's cheeks, index fingers probing at the jaw's joints. Meanwhile a startling addition joined their threesome. Julie felt Klein's long hard weenie (that's what she and her best friend Nancy called penises) against a butt cheek.

She wanted to jump up and run. But how without a big fuss? His hands held her fast. She'd have to yell something about his weenie, which was unthinkable, or pry his hands apart, equally appalling behavior. And her father was right there. He wasn't objecting. She comforted herself that it would soon be over.

But it continued. Her father probed Klein's jaw with his fingers spread in a variety of weblike grips. He then asked Klein to open wide and peered at his teeth while Klein's finger wiggled farther below, past her belly button, making feints There. He tugged the tender skin up, which almost felt like he was touching There. Was he? A radiating tingling made her legs feel unstrung. She couldn't figure out what was going on exactly because Klein seemed to be absorbing her into his skin. His aftershave filled her nostrils and she was partially deafened by the heavy breaths he took in, then released with a tickling heat across her right ear. (Years later in college, a well-meaning boyfriend licked her earlobe, then blew on it. She screamed. Poor kid was deafened for half an hour.)

"Is that sensitive?" her father asked.

"Yes," Klein's answer whooshed into her ear.

"Sore?"

"Uh-huh." Klein shifted her a little. His hard weenie nestled between her cheeks. Was it really his weenie? It was too hard, too big.

At last her father stood up, stepped back. "Well, I'd have to do a complete examination and a set of x-rays to confirm it, but you're grinding, Dick. You're a night grinder."

BRIAN'S VIEW, MOMENTARILY blocked by Hy's weird survey of Klein's mouth, was cleared as the dentist returned to his folding chair. Julie remained captured in Klein's arms. She stared ahead, her eyes not seeing anything, looking inward at the sensations. Brian knew. Never again in his life would he feel that he so thoroughly inhabited another's mind—he was living in concert with her soul.

It was just at that moment of utter synchronicity that Julie's eyes found him. He could almost hear her cry out: *What do I do?*

Brian had no answer for her. He looked at Klein, whose placid expression appeared to be absorbed by the ongoing consultation with Julie's father, and heard him declare, "You know, Hy, I don't really have a dentist I trust."

JULIE LOOKED AWAY from the solace of Brian's china blue eyes when Harriet sang out, "Dick, you have to see Hy! He's a great dentist. You should have told me you were looking for a dentist . . ."

Klein laughed. Julie felt its rumble all along her spine. "Well, no one's *looking* for a dentist. No offense, Hy. But I've never heard anybody say, 'Can't wait to get to the dentist!'"

Noah opened his mostly toothless mouth and cackled. Klein couldn't resist playing to that audience. "Right, Noah? 'Ever hear anybody say, 'Oh gee, I can't wait: cancel my theater tickets I want to go to the dentist!'" he said, blowing across Julie's cheek a hot wind that this time gave off a whiff of the Zolly's spicy mustard. She tried to wriggle up and away, but his weenie, his hands, his grip, weren't easing as she had expected they would when her father was done. Meanwhile Noah adored the elaboration of Klein's joke, laughing so hard sound ceased to come out of his gaping mouth.

Hy suffered being teased with a resigned air. He mumbled, "We're not too popular," glumly watching his son's toothless derision. "But people sure are glad to see us when they get a toothache. Then they cancel their theater tickets, Dick. Then they're begging to see us!"

The doorbell rang. "And here they are!" Klein adeptly commented. "They've all come for root canal."

His audience was not amused. Noah didn't grasp the comic significance of root canal, Julie and Brian were preoccupied, and Hy never saw humor in his profession.

Jeff scrambled to his feet, announcing, "I'll get it."

"Stay right where you are if you know what's good for you," Harriet commanded. "Hy, would you go?"

"Sure," he agreed, glad to go, flustered by his exchange with Klein. The NBC executive's sudden addition of mockery to friendliness was not an equation Hy could easily comprehend.

"You know, Richard, you really should see Hy," Harriet said to Klein while Hy was moving toward the door. "And you should send him some of your show biz friends."

"You bet," Klein said. "I'm going to Hy first chance he can see me. And I've got plenty of friends who need a good dentist. Especially in TV." Klein squeezed Julie, confiding in a spiced whisper, "Lots of my friends need your father's help to make their smiles perfect. Perfect like your smile." He pecked her on the cheek. His lips parted as they landed, leaving a wet impression, and his hand snaked closer, right to the edge of There, tugging, almost tickling, almost not.

Hy, all suspicion of being ridiculed dispelled, paused at the doorway. "Anytime, Dick. Whatever time works for you. Just tell my secretary when you want to come in and we'll clear it for you." The bell rang again. Hy hurried off.

"Would you like more tea, Aunt Harriet?" Julie asked, trying to sit up straight and escape politely. Klein's arms tightened across her waist, making that impossible. She fell back against him. And he was not forced to let her go because Harriet, reaching for a tissue said, "No thank you, dear," and blew her nose.

"Can I turn on the TV?" Jeff asked, moving to the console.

"There's nothing on," Harriet complained.

"Mets game," Klein said in Julie's ear. At least, with her father gone, the fat fingers settled down, resting on and below her tummy, near There, but no longer reaching for more.

"THAT'S RIGHT!" JEFF exclaimed. "I forgot." He shimmied on his knees to reach the power dial. Brian felt the vibration of the picture tube awakening through the cabinet. Normally he would have changed position to have a better view, but he was transfixed by the spectacle of Richard Klein with Julie in his lap.

Brian watched her troubled eyes shift to the television. A moment ago, he knew exactly what she was feeling. Now he lost her. She appeared to be thoroughly engaged by a Schaefer beer commercial. She looked uncomfortable, but Klein's arms weren't moving. Brian couldn't know exactly what the fingers of his right hand were up to, but he had enough of an angle to determine that the most they could be doing was touching her tummy. Anyway, even if he touched her . . . what? He had no real understanding of female anatomy, or a vocabulary for it, other than words older boys used and whose correct usage he didn't know. While the roomful of faces settled into the slack-jawed poses of spectators, besides not knowing what Klein could touch on Julie, he wondered if there was anything wrong about any of it anyway. Maybe everybody knew about being touched down there. Maybe, like some other activities of adults, it was understood and not talked about.

While Brian watched the Mets take the field, everything seemed likely to return to the boring normal of being with adults. But then Sam Rydel's Converse sneakers appeared beside Brian. "What are we watching?" asked the teenager. "Not the Mets. They never win." He was carrying a rectangular box, gift-wrapped in blue paper with yellow script that read *Happy Birthday!*

"Is that for me?" Jeff asked.

JULIE WAS RELIEVED the young prince had returned. Sam Rydel had the fair skin, broad shoulders, and narrow waist of Peter Martins, the best male dancer in the world and the man she hoped to marry someday, although her mother smiled slyly every time she said so. Sam was even more beautiful than Martins, she decided on the spot. With those curls and baby-smooth skin, he looked like the illustration of Prince Charming in her favorite volume of fairy tales, which she sometimes still read when she felt sad.

Aunt Harriet also seemed glad to see this handsome lad. She sat up from her layers of pillows, a hand touching her flattened hair, trying to fluff it. "Sam! You're back. I thought you had to go somewhere . . ."

"Dick sent me on an important errand." Sam showed off the birthday gift.

"That's for later," Klein said. "After the"—he tightened his arms around Julie's waist and squeezed three times as he said—"you-know-what." He pushed all the air from her lungs. While she recovered her breath, his fingers, quiescent for a while, came alive. They spread and reached lower, almost There. Maybe a little There? She arched and managed to slide down some, providing just enough clearance from those fat fingers.

She tried to focus on Prince Charming. Jeff was jumping at him like a puppy, hungry for the wrapped gift, touching, retreating, and touching it again. "It's a board game," Jeff guessed. "Right?" He checked with Klein. "Why can't we play it now?"

"Jeff, cut it out," Harriet said. "You were so sweet to get it, Samuel. So sweet."

"Hey." Klein's breath tickled her neck. "I paid for it." Klein patted her tummy, fingers snaking lower, middle tip reaching the edge of There.

Sam winked. "That's right, Harriet. Dick paid. For a change."

Jeff grabbed one end of the gift box, couldn't pull it free from Sam's hands. "Lemme open it," he whined. Jeff's insistence on his desire inspired Julie to try to sit up from the weenie pressing between her butt. If she jerked against and loosened his arms, she could slide down, out and away.

Klein seemed to read her mind: as soon as she tensed to make a move, his arms turned to iron. And his hands got mean: a nail pinched a tender spot just above There. The shock froze her.

But she didn't cry out. She gave up any attempt to squirm out of his grasp. He had made it clear that she wouldn't be allowed to move an inch unless she were to thrash and fight hard. She would have to "make a scene," as her mother used to say, and she wasn't supposed to make a scene. Noah made scenes, her father made scenes, and both humiliated her mother. Julie got as still as she could. Sure enough, the fingers relaxed and patted her tummy. "Good girl," Klein whispered, from right inside her ear, it felt like, and so faintly, too faintly for anyone but her to hear.

JEFF'S BACK TO *normal,* Brian thought, glad to see his friend tugging on his present. Sam didn't let go. Jeff pulled with all his might, face turning red.

"Jeff!" Harriet scolded.

Sam teased him, lifting the box up and away, but not too far away.

Hy appeared, carrying in another folding chair, setting it down between Harriet's bed and the closet.

"Open the present! Open the present!" Noah demanded, bouncing on the bed. He didn't make contact with Harriet, yet she clutched her side and groaned.

While he opened up the chair, Hy scolded, "Stop, Noah. Sit still!"

"I'd better hide this," Sam said.

"NO!" Noah cried, slamming his hands on the bed. Harriet moaned.

"*I'll* put it away," Hy said, taking the package and leaving. Noah, grief-stricken, buried his head in the covers.

Harriet gestured to the empty folding chairs. "Sit down, Samuel. Tell me all about yourself. You excited about going to college?"

This reminded Brian of another lie he had to keep quiet about—Sam wasn't seventeen and a high school senior; he was fifteen, a junior. How could he explain knowing that? Worse, if he did let it slip, in retaliation his secret—how It acted—would come out.

Sam sat in Hy's empty chair. His legs partially obscured Brian's view of Klein and Julie. Sam looked down at Brian and teased, in the same husky tone Klein used, "Am I in your way?"

"Move here," Klein told Brian, tapping the empty corner where the drapes gathered when open. "You can see the baseball game better."

Brian moved on all fours to the indicated spot. Klein wanted him to watch what he was doing to Julie and he wanted to see. Brian leaned one shoulder on the drapes, angling himself to take in both the RCA console and a view of Julie's legs atop Klein's lap. With a slight lift and tilt of his head, he could see up her skirt—if her legs parted. She was keeping them flush.

"So tell me, Sam," Harriet repeated, pausing to release a heavy sigh, "what are you thinking of majoring in?"

"Hoping to go to law school, I guess," Sam said.

"You're going to law school?" Hy picked up the conversation as he reentered. He sat in the chair he had placed beside Harriet's bed, facing Sam and, beyond him, the television, putting his back to Klein and Julie.

Sam laughed. Harriet was scornful. "For God's sakes, he's just starting college!"

Hy, bruised from the earlier dentist jokes, was quick to take offense. "I was being polite. He's obviously too young for law school. Matter of fact, you look too young for college. Did you skip a couple grades? That's what they're doing these days, skipping bright kids."

"He's seventeen," Klein snapped. "A very bright seventeen."

Sam answered respectfully, "I was laughing at myself, Mr. Mark. Law school's just my dream. I probably won't have the grades."

Klein hiked Julie up a little higher on his lap. Her eyes widened. *What is he doing with his hand?* Brian wondered. *Girls only have a hole,* Jeff had claimed. Klein said, "Don't let him talk that way, Hy. Unlike me, you've got an advanced degree. Encourage the boy. Tell him he can be anything he wants. Sam's problem is that he didn't have the benefit of a great father like you, Hy. He needs a man's encouragement."

Openly discussing Sam's psychological needs was discomforting for Harriet and Hy. She coughed, reached for her tea. Hy smiled warily while stumbling his way through "Uh, yeah . . . Richard's right, Sam, you put your mind to it I'm sure you'd make a fine lawyer." There was an awkward silence. Brian lost track of the adults for a moment, distracted by the television broadcast of the Mets game when Ed Kranepool hit a home run. "He's gonna have a great year," Jeff said to no one, and added that Kranepool had gone to James Monroe High School in the Bronx. Brian had heard him say that at least a million times. "Of course being a lawyer is always a good idea," Hy tried cautiously. "But you have to have the aptitude for it."

"Oh, Sam's got the aptitude," Klein said, drawing Brian's gaze back to him and Julie. *Where is his hand?* He could see the left on top of her skirt, at its waistband. The right was underneath, touching her. That was confirmed by clues from Julie. She wasn't moving. Her eyes were glazed, focused inward monitoring Klein's hidden hand. Brian slid down to see what it was up to. "He's a brilliant student. He's going to Columbia. I'm sure he'll graduate Phi Beta and get into any law school he wants—"

"Wow," Hy said. "Columbia. Why didn't you say so? Sure, sure, he'll get into a good law school, maybe even Columbia's. Theirs is good, very good."

Brian found an angle that allowed him to see her white panties with little yellow birds and sure enough, just above them, the tips of Klein's fingers. They weren't moving. That was good. Brian checked on Julie. She was staring past him. Klein wasn't. He was looking right at Brian, and once the boy's eyes came his way, the grown-up winked.

JULIE FASTENED ON Sam's profile. She had admired his good looks when they went to Zolly's. Now he was more than merely cute. He's really a prince, she decided, and made a wish, for this beautiful young man to free her.

Miraculously, he did. When her father examined Mr. Klein, that hadn't chased away the discomforts and surprises of sitting in the man's lap, but Sam's being in the observer's seat banished all weirdness. Klein shifted her position in some small way that meant his weenie wasn't pressing against her, and then Klein's hands joined in the discussion over Sam's future, so the restless fingers on her belly also departed. She was still on Mr. Klein's lap, but now it was only a lap.

She listened to her father, Aunt Harriet, and Klein praise Sam's abilities, debating how he could make the best use of them. She wondered, with pity in her heart, about Sam's need for a father. She was impressed by the reports of the teenager's brilliant mind, well suited to the demands of the law, Klein said. "He'll be worth millions someday," he said. Handsome Sam modestly deflected the compliments with demure shakes of his blond curls, which persuaded Julie he must indeed be a genius.

"CAN I MAKE the TV louder? I can't hear," Jeff complained. Brian was glad to hear him complain. *Things really seem to be okay again,* Brian thought, *really normal.*

"Jeff," Harriet said harshly. That was all she said.

"I can't hear it!" Jeff repeated, his whine elongating each word.

Klein pointed to Brian. "Sit with your buddy. You can hear from there."

So things weren't normal. That was a lie. Brian understood instantly

Klein was moving Jeff so he could also see Julie in his lap. Jeff obeyed without protest, which also wasn't normal. Brian twisted to avoid his best friend's Keds whacking him, accidentally improving his view looking up Julie's white legs. He forced himself not to look. For one thing, nothing was going on; for another, now that he understood Klein wanted him to see, he wanted to thwart him.

Nothing happened as two scoreless innings of baseball were played while Harriet, Hy, and Klein talked about civil rights and the war. The world *was* normal: the adults were boring, he and Jeff were being deprived of their rightful entertainment, everything was waiting on the performance of a tedious birthday ritual whose only redeeming feature was they would get to eat cake.

JULIE WAS EVEN more relieved than Brian that things had become dull and familiar. She leaned away from Klein's voice, keeping her nose out of the cloud of Old Spice, fastening her eyes on Sam's angular face while he answered random questions about his plans. From time to time Sam glanced her way, first lighting on Klein with a serious look, then dropping to offer her a friendlier twinkle of a smile.

Saul returned home from his errand. He entered the bedroom, saying low to Harriet, "Taken care of."

"Great! The big surprise is safe," Jeff said. "Now can we go play outside?"

"No!" Harriet fairly shrieked. Jeff moaned, burying his head in his lap.

Sam laughed, twisted in his chair to say something to Jeff and caught Julie's unrestrained look of admiration. He gazed directly at her for a long, long moment. She was overwhelmed by the full glare of his beauty and looked away.

Hy asked him about the duties of a NBC page. Saul settled in a folding chair while Sam described his schedule: five afternoons and evenings a week at NBC, mornings attending college prep courses. When the young man began to describe escorting guests on *The Tonight Show* to the greenroom—the mere mention of these celebrities excited her father; additional details extracted a "Wow!" from Hy—Klein's hand, nestled beneath Julie's skirt's waist, came to life.

The room was crowded. She was surrounded. Cousin Jeff and Brian were two feet away looking right at her in Klein's lap. Sam was angled slightly to the right, but he regularly glanced at her while he talked. Her father and Noah were a few feet behind, the other adults were on the far side of the bed, parallel to her, not able to see her but very near, while Klein's fingers crept under her panties, making funny little taps along the way down as if he were playing Little Piggy with a baby.

Julie attempted to turn her head in the direction of the other adults, intending to join in the conversation, get them to look in her direction, sure that would stop him. Klein leaned his chin on her shoulder, blocking that move. His forearms tightened about her waist. Two fingers pressed on either side of There, a squeeze that almost pinched, almost tickled. She froze. He wasn't going to hurt her There, was he? Her legs tensed, monitoring: the pressure intensified, then relaxed; he pressed harder still and departed; and again, returning more insistently.

She felt wet. She knew she hadn't peed because that kind of wet had happened once before, in the tub when she rubbed in a way that felt good. For a while she had assumed the wet came from the bathwater, not her, and almost asked Nancy about it but got too shy.

One finger slid right on top of There. And stayed.

She wasn't gagged. Her arms hung loose at her sides, free to strike at his face. But how could she explain?

Klein made a fist at her groin, pushing for her legs to part. They yielded. She ordered them not to, but they complied. Then she realized if she were to shut them now she would be trapping his hand tight to There.

Klein opened his fist, a fan of fingers pushing her legs wider apart until they rolled open on the slopes of his thick thighs. Then he cupped all of There, holding her like a handle in his heat of his palm. "You're wet," he whispered as faintly as any one could possibly speak but not faintly enough for her comfort. Her heart pounded. What if her father heard? One finger slid inside There. "Goes in easy now," Klein whispered. "You really like this." *What's the matter with me?*

Her Mary Janes swung free; she could dig their sharp heels into his slacks. Instead she prayed he wouldn't whisper more things about her. She looked at the boys. Jeff was twisted away, trying too hard to see only the TV. Not so the dark-headed boy with china blue eyes: Brian was watching Klein's hand—he could see what she could only feel.

She looked to her prince. She had Sam's profile while he talked about famous people. He was so beautiful. *Look at me. Save me.* The young man's voice faded into background noise while she worried about what was going on There, overwhelmed by the restless fingers—rubbing, tickling, sliding in and across. She couldn't delineate what Klein was doing—waves of sensation drowned their individual action. She looked down to check. Her skirt hid his maneuvers from her sight. But then she saw in Brian's fascinated eyes, glowing like a cat's, she saw that she must be thoroughly exposed to him.

Shame warmed her cheeks, mixing with the discomforts and pleasures below. She decided to endure it. *Don't feel.* Then one finger briefly, but distinctly, went very deep inside her.

She jerked her head up. She shouted through her eyes to the room. The boys were too young, they were useless, but Sam was tall and strong. Her father was telling a story about his one celebrity patient, a violinist in the New York Philharmonic whom he often bragged on at home, so Sam was free to linger on her. His gray eyes dropped to her skirt. She looked down with him. Klein's hands were busy under the pleats: his left tented her skirt to show Sam some of what was going on. The little boys could see everything: Cousin Jeff's eyes spookily shifted sideways to watch without turning his head; Brian stared.

Sam looked into her eyes fully and frankly. And the miracle she had wished for happened: Klein's fingers departed.

It's over! Her heart soared. *I'm free.*

Then she felt her panties being nudged down, the cool air highlighting her nudity. On both sides of There, Klein's fingers pulled her skin apart in a way she had never, no one had ever done. Klein held her open, displaying her.

She couldn't speak, but she talked in her head to Sam. She pleaded for him to stop this.

The prince watched without expression. Her father asked him something. Sam looked away to answer, but the absence was brief. When his indifferent gaze returned, he was in no hurry. His eyes moved down to the tented show below, inspecting her, then up to study her dispassionately until, after a long long time, so long that she felt it would never end, Uncle Saul announced that everyone should move to the dining room for a big surprise.

To Tell the Truth

—— February 2008 ——

BRIAN STARED AT the entry for Jeff Mark in his once beloved Hermès black leather address book, buried two years ago in the bottom drawer of his desk in favor of his even more cherished smartphone. He hadn't transferred Jeff's numbers into his electronic contacts. In the discarded Hermès there were two numbers, for an office in LA and his home. They had appeared in Brian's mail not long after his first movie premiered, embossed on a thick linen card with the heading: JEFF MARK'S NEW LA NUMBERS.

At first, Brian had puzzled over why Jeff chose to inform him of his home number. He had searched for a clue in how it was addressed. Not in evidence were the extra four digits on the zip code that business correspondence, such as talent agencies, liked to include. Brian deduced that an assistant had been handed Jeff's address book of friends and was told to mail this more personal information to them. That would explain why Jeff's home number was included.

So he kept me listed as an intimate, Brian thought at the time, with a teaspoon of self-satisfaction added to the cup of bitterness labeled Jeff Mark he carried everywhere. *He thinks we might be friends one day.* Brian had marveled at that piece of emotional stupidity and nearly tossed the numbers. Nearly, because on reflection Brian reminded himself that Jeff was one of the most successful box-office directors in Hollywood and that in the face of some tomorrow of penury Brian might no longer be able to afford today's virtuous shunning.

So he had copied the numbers into the Hermès. Whenever his eyes had happened to light on them he regretted that he had. But rather than tear out the offending page Brian had devoted an entire therapy session to why he chose to keep the Mark contact info, seeking two hundred dollars' worth of insight from his shrink. "You want to be reminded," the doctor pointed out in a bored tone. Brian was bored too. It was merely another example of what was plentifully illustrated in their sessions—Brian had not, could not, would not, and will not discard his past.

Moving on had at last seemed to be accomplished, at least when it came to discarding contact info, after Brian started taking Paxil, which, as his psychiatrist had predicted, along with killing his bothersome sex drive, tugged him clear of wallowing in the rut of his past. So when he purchased his iPhone, Brian had decided to live in this Brave New World without Jeff Mark's phone numbers in his pocket.

But he hadn't thrown out the Hermès and now he was grateful. He couldn't ask Julie for the number she had successfully used because he had promised her that he wouldn't call Jeff. Another way would involve asking his LA agent or Gregory Lamont, and any lie he invented to explain why he wanted to speak to Jeff would lead to awkward questions. Worse, with his agent it would provoke a greedy excitement that Brian was finally making profitable use of the connection, a sore point between representative and screenwriter ever since Jeff had told Brian's agent that they used to be best friends. From then on, Jeff's name was raised by Brian's agent repeatedly as a possible buyer for Brian's story ideas until Brian supplied what he liked to think of as a lie full of truths: "It's really my problem. I can't imagine taking notes from the same guy who used to wet his bed and scream at spiders." His agent laughed and never again raised sending scripts or pitching to Jeff. Brian could hear him conclude: *My client's too proud to accept his childhood buddy's being his boss.* Brian had long ago learned the trick to a successful lie: don't bother to seem to be telling the truth; provide your listener with a false insight to discover for themselves.

The time had come. Julie, in her innocence, had handed Brian the perfect opportunity to break the nearly thirty-year moratorium on calling the great Jeff Mark. He lifted the receiver while glancing at his desk clock, subtracting three hours for the coast and noting that at two forty-five they should be back from lunch. A young man answered after one ring: "Satisfaction," the irritating name of Jeff's production company. Brian had read in Jeff's *New Yorker* profile that it was a reference to the Stones' iconic hit; presumably Jeff's movies were providing a satisfaction obtainable nowhere else.

"Jeff Mark, please," Brian said. "Brian Moran is calling."

There was no human reply. He heard another immediate ring, as he was relayed from switchboard to a female assistant with an English accent (hiring a Brit was the latest pretention these days). She announced briskly, "Jeff Mark's office."

"Jeff Mark, please? This is Brian Moran calling."

Hollywood assistants were all aspiring filmmakers, or at least aspiring studio executives, and knew the names of currently employed screenwriters (an increasingly rare specimen), so he was not surprised by the lowered register of respect with which she said, "Please hold, Mr. Moran. I'll see if he's available."

He steeled himself for actual conversation with Jeff. She was gone for more than a few seconds, another hint Jeff would be coming on as soon as he finished zipping up or whatever other important task . . .

"Uh, Mr. Moran?" The assistant sounded cowed, as if she'd been scolded. "I'm terribly sorry. I completely forgot Mr. Mark is traveling today and tomorrow. In fact, he'll be unavailable through the weekend. May I have your cell—we don't seem to have that on file—and we'll get back to you on Monday?"

Brian was stunned that Jeff was deliberately avoiding him. Not merely avoiding him, Jeff was hoping to prevent him from calling until next week. Why? Would the cover-up be complete?

"Bri? Where are you?" his father demanded from down the hall.

"In the study!" he shouted with his hand over the receiver, and then uncovered to say, "My cell is . . ." He rattled off the number and hung up abruptly, flipping the Hermès shut as if he were hiding porno.

He certainly didn't want his father to know he was calling Jeff. Twenty years ago, after the first of Jeff's box office hits, Danny Moran had become obsessed with why Brian wasn't in touch with "your dear old buddy, best buddies you were, until your mum messed that up with her self-righteousness about that lunatic Harriet. Just like your mother, causing more trouble where there's already plenty to go around." For the next ten years, Brian had to deflect weekly questions about why he hadn't resumed the friendship, mostly because Danny felt his son ought to be reminding Jeff Mark that Danny Moran was a damn good actor. His father finally blew up at his evasions. "You don't want him to hire me, that's it! You're afraid I'll be the More Famous Moran," he said, turning sideways as if modeling for a bust.

"Are you writing?" his seventy-eight-year-old father said from the hall as he approached. Danny appeared at the doorsill, panting as if he'd been jogging. "You're not working," he accused, once he had a clear line of sight. "So I can talk to you about my idea, then."

Despite the always high color in Danny's ruddy, vein exploded cheeks, Brian was struck once again by the overall grayness of his father's face, alarming in a old man who had survived a heart attack ten years ago. Danny leaned against the doorframe, too weary to remain on his feet while nagging his son. Because of these symptoms of rapid deterioration despite all the medications he was on, Brian had arranged for his father to see a cardiologist who Gregory Lamont insisted was "the most brilliant heart guy on the planet." The showbiz endorsement seduced Danny into agreeing. "Since he's a doctor to the stars, I'll see him. If I can't be a star, at least I can die like one."

"You feeling all right, Dad?" Brian couldn't stop himself from asking, although he knew any suggestion of infirmity would provoke a nasty reply.

"I tell you I feel fine, Brian. Stop being such a biddy. You like the lads, all right I accept that, but does being homosexual mean you have to turn yourself into an old Irish biddy?"

As always when his father brought up his sexuality, Brian changed the subject. "Dad, why don't you come in and tell me your idea?"

"Don't mind if I do," Danny said, propelling himself across the room with a push off from the doorjamb. He staggered to the couch, landing so heavily its feet squealed and slid on oak floorboards that Brian had walked, in one New York apartment or other, all his life.

Brian couldn't forestall "Jesus, are you okay?" from escaping.

"Stop that," Danny said, putting up his hand like a traffic cop. "I mean it. It's very boring." The palm of his father's hand was usually very pink, flushed with the pulse of his restless energy. This was a ghost of that hand.

"Sorry. So what's your idea?"

"It's really quite a stunning coup. It came to me while I was rereading your very stunning script for Aries and the glorious Miss Stillman. While marveling over your characters, I had the most thrilling idea for a brilliant stroke of casting."

Brian braced himself for his father asking to play the elderly chief justice of the Reconciliation Tribunal in *Sleep of the Innocent*. The part consisted of merely two scenes, but two featured scenes was a lot in this day and age of fewer big-budget features and almost no parts for actors over the age of sixty. There was talk of casting Anthony Hopkins or any number of world-famous elderly actors, especially Brits, happy to work with Aries for a few weeks in Paris. They wouldn't even hold auditions for this part—it would simply be offered to one of the greats. "What is it, Dad?" he asked faintly.

"You should cast me"—Danny paused to drop his chin, speaking from under a lowered brow, a mannerism he affected whenever he wished to grant a portentous authority to a line—"as Veronica's husband."

Brian blinked, replayed the words. Even for his father, this had to be a joke. He waited for a clue that he was allowed to laugh.

"Think of it." Danny gestured to the heavens. "Women like that, serious intellectual political women, often marry men twenty, thirty, years older, especially successful lawyers like the chap in your script. And you get the father–daughter subtext of her wanting to be taken care of emotionally in some way because of the rape." He leaned forward. "Then the character of the husband, who seems to me a little underwritten, gains some authority if he's my age, which lends more credence to the polemical aspects of your stunning, just stunning, dialogue."

Brian spoke in a deliberately measured monotone, to keep mockery at bay. "Dad, you're forty years older than Veronica, not thirty."

"Don't be silly. Makeup, toupee, and Spanx"—Danny sucked in his cheeks and presumably his Guinness stomach, although it didn't shrink an inch—"and I won't look a day over fifty-five."

Brian was enraged. He knew that to be an insane reaction. He couldn't wait to be able to laugh about this, probably by telling the story to Pamela Wright, his cattiest and closest friend in the business. Pamela was a gifted and unusually modest actress who, after a good laugh, would console him by saying, "Darling, please forgive your father. He can't help himself. He's a toddler. Like all of us actors, he's just a child who wants to play."

"Dad . . ." Brian paused to inject some gentleness into his crabby tone. "We can't get financing for the movie unless we have an international movie star playing opposite Veronica. Presales to foreign markets, cable, that kind of thing—we have to have a big male star in that part."

Danny raised an eyebrow. He could lift the right one a full two inches while keeping the left down. He used this mannerism when cast in one of his small off-off-Broadway roles, usually playing an officious bureaucrat or a shocked grandparent. "I thought when you got Veronica to sign the contract last week that meant you had all the financing."

Brian was ready for this; in fact he had led Danny to believe he had uncovered an inconsistency in order to refute it and end this humiliating discussion. "Because with Veronica in hand, the financiers assume we'll have no problem getting a big star. All the biggies want to play opposite her. If, by some miracle, we don't get George Clooney or Matt Damon or the like, then you're right, we'll lose our financing."

Danny goggled. He retracted his double chin, jaw hanging open, rheumy eyes opening wide, brows shooting up—a parody of a horror double take. This was his favorite mannerism, in life and on stage: Danny Moran astonished. "Well . . ." he sputtered, "I, for one, don't think Clooney or Matt Damon are up to the demands of this part. They'll ruin your script."

Brian's iPhone buzzed in his jeans pocket. Brian's heart skipped: Jeff had thought better of dodging him. "I'll take this in the other room, Dad," he said as he hurried out toward the kitchen, the room farthest away from Danny's nosiness.

When he whispered hello, "Brian," he heard Julie say his name with alarm in her voice. Hers was part of a chorus coming through the earpiece of his iPhone. He heard an urgent American news broadcast in the background, that peculiar combination of resonant, measured voices speaking with the hurried staccato emphasis of someone on the verge of hysteria. "Have you heard?" she asked.

"What happened?"

"They're dropping the charges against Rydel! It took even Gary by surprise that they're just dropping them altogether. No psychiatric supervision, nothing. All the witnesses, they . . . I can't think of the word, damn it! They took everything back."

"They recanted," he said.

"Right! And there's nothing about Klein. Not even that there were witnesses against him. Turn on your TV . . . Rydel's lawyer is reading a statement. He's resigning from the Huck Finn board, which doesn't make sense if he's innocent. There! You can see Sam. Turn on your TV."

"I can't right now."

"Why can't you turn on your TV?"

"My father lives with me, remember?" he said, irritated.

Danny called from the study, “Bri! Are you on the phone? Who is it?”

“My agent,” Brian called out.

“How’s your father? Feeling better?”

“Not good. He’s really not breathing right and he can’t stay steady on his feet. My guess is that second-rate cardiologist in SAG’s network doesn’t know his ass from his aorta—why am I talking about this? What does Gary say? Have you told him yet?”

“No! I haven’t even seen him since you and I talked three hours ago. He called on his cell while running to the press conference. This is Jeff, right? He’s got to be part of this cover-up, right?”

“I dunno. Let’s give him the benefit of the doubt. I hope not. He doesn’t have to be.”

“Right.” Julie was quick to agree. “Rydel and Klein are rich. They don’t need Jeff’s help buying off those kids.”

“Right. But—” Brian cut himself off.

“But . . . ?”

“Klein must know that if Jeff spoke up he can’t get away with a whitewash. Statute of limitations or no, if Jeff talked the world would listen.”

“So why won’t Jeff talk? I was thinking about what you said, you know America turning on him. Really? Just because Klein paid for him to go to film school? Or do you mean ’cause Jeff was molested too? They’d hate him for that? Really?”

Brian sighed. He knew and he didn’t know. He was sure and couldn’t be. But he was sure. Basically.

“You know why,” she said. “Please tell me. Don’t keep secrets from me. You don’t have to. I swear. You don’t have to keep secrets from me.”

Brian couldn’t show his cards to this lovely, kind woman who was hopelessly in over her head. Too much was at stake to trust someone this decent. “There might be more to it. I can’t talk about it on the phone right now.”

“Can we talk later tonight? Gary’s coming back from East Hampton. I’ll tell him over dinner what I’m going to do, what I hope you and I will do together, and then I'll try to call you. How late can I call you? It means so much to me to be able to talk about all this with you."

"For me too, Julie." He felt strange about her tone, however. There was ardor there, implying more than talk was promised.

"Bri!" a hoarse Danny called from study.

"One minute, Dad! Julie, I have to go. And remember, the first step is for you to tell your husband."

"But can I? Can I really do it, Brian?" she asked earnestly. "If I can't tell my own husband, how am I going to tell the world? God, I'm such a coward. I know you said I'm not. But I am. All my life I've been a coward. Do you think I can be brave, Brian?"

Her tone was so utterly sincere Brian laughed. He cut it off. "Actually, Julie, I don't think the reason you're not telling Gary is cowardice."

"You don't! Wow." She was delighted. "What is it?"

"You don't want to give up your secret because your secret is what makes you superior to Gary. He's the big dope who doesn't know what's going on in his own life. He thinks he's the star of the marriage, pushing you around, but really it's you who know it all. You don't want to tell him because then you're merely equals: he's got problems, you've got problems, you're both *shmendreks* trying to figure it all out." He was proud of this speech. He waited for her to thank him, hang up and rush off into the movie climax of her life, boldly telling Gary her secret and resolving all the story problems.

She wasn't impressed. "Honestly, Brian, keeping this secret doesn't make me feel superior to Gary. I feel stupid and cowardly. I kept it secret all these years because Gary can't really understand. And because he'd tell his friends about me."

"Tell his friends about you?" Brian was surprised. "Why?"

"He just would. Eventually he'd tell them, to get sympathy or just to be a little more interesting to everybody."

Brian was accustomed to disagreeing with people's explanations of themselves. Typically he would listen to a speech like Julie's and discover self-delusion or self-aggrandizement or sentimentality or some other understandable yet corrosive agent in their self-regard. Julie struck him as essentially unexamined, a woman who had allowed too much of her life to go by without the sort of analytic filtration he valued so highly, the professional as well as self-directed self-study that he believed had saved his sanity during the tumultuous years of adolescence and raw youth. And yet his reflex was to trust her instinct, not his expensively acquired by-the-book psychology. After all, like him, she was a scarred veteran of a nearly invisible trauma whose aftereffects had no true experts.

"Brian!" his father's impatience had brewed into action. He tramped heavily down the hall. Brian worried every step Danny took might provoke a fatal strain on his faulty heart.

"I gotta go. Call me after you tell Gary. Bye."

Danny appeared, leaned on the kitchen wall, skin ashen. "Was . . . that . . . Wallinski?" he gasped out.

"No. I told you. Just my agent. Sit down." Brian pulled a Bentwood chair clear of his butcher-block table and urged his father onto it.

Meanwhile Danny gasped out, "Okay. I guess if you and Aries don't have the balls to pull off the brilliant stroke of casting me as Veronica's hubby, I'll have to settle for the chief justice. Just two dull expositional scenes, but I can do something with them."

Brian stared down at his father, not bothering to conceal his resentment at his father's delusional grandiosity. "I'll talk to Aries about it, Dad. But no promises. Even that part will be offered to stars. But there is a part I'm pretty sure I can get you. The court clerk. It's a one-liner, but you're in the background shots for two weeks, so that's a pretty decent payday. Since Aries wants me there for the shoot, they'll rent me a two-bedroom apartment in Paris. I'll pay for your ticket over and back, so you'll be a local hire and won't cost the production much."

Danny goggled again, a hammier version, adding a groan: "Court clerk! That's practically being an extra!" The surprise and outrage were fake. One-line parts were the only kind Brian had been able to arrange for Danny on his other movies, and his father had been grateful to get them. Up close, his father's goggling emphasized the wrinkled skin of his forehead, damp and translucent, and showed off a turkey neck that with his recent weight loss had replaced his double chin. *He's ill,* Brian scolded himself. *Cut him some slack.*

"But why won't you pitch me to Aries as the chief justice?"

"I said I would talk to Aries about it."

"Bri, for once just be straight with me: you don't think I'm good enough."

He wanted to kick his father. Instead he turned his back on him. *Calm down,* he urged himself. His mouth was dry, lips sticking to his teeth. He pictured the Red Head waiting patiently while his manicured nails reached for a tender pink nipple.

Jesus, isn't the Paxil working anymore? He looked out the kitchen window facing the backyard of a nineteenth-century townhouse with a plaque that claimed Edgar Allan Poe had lived there. Two years ago, an investment banker had gutted it. The neighborhood rumor was that he had poured twenty million into the renovation. From Brian's daily observations, that was likely: the contractor had built a full swimming pool in the basement and two levels of gracious porches—the wood looked to be teak or something equally costly—jutting out over the elaborately landscaped garden. He focused on the denuded branches of a pair of cherry trees. Last spring their blossoms burst like floral fireworks.

He spoke but kept his back turned. "Dad, I think you're perfectly capable of winning an Academy Award as the chief justice, but I have to talk to you about something else right now. There's something very important I have to tell you. Immediately. It can't wait." Brian glanced at his father. Danny was mugging a question mark out of his expressive features so the last seat in the back row of the mezzanine could see he was in great suspense. It never failed to amaze Brian how clownish and over the top Danny was in real life. His father couldn't even give a convincing performance as himself.

"Don't be scared to tell me," Danny said, filling the silence. "Is it AIDS? Are you HIV positive?"

That shoved Brian past caring whether he was going to upset his father. "Do you remember Jeff Mark's older cousin? A middle-aged man, worked at NBC?"

Danny overacted recollection: hand on chin, eyebrows furrowed to a line, eyes blinking as if changing slides of memory until he found the right one. "Oh!" he exclaimed. "Executive at NBC who gave you a tour of the television studios? And he gave you a record album, didn't he?" Brian nodded. "I remember," Danny continued cheerfully, "because it was a very thoughtful gift. Irish folk songs, right? Pretty good memory for an old man, eh?"

Of course Danny remembered. His father had called Harriet after the album arrived to ask if this NBC vice president had anything to do with casting TV series. Years later, Brian had to explain to his shrink, but never to himself, why his father didn't think it peculiar that a grown man had bothered to give a little boy who wasn't a relative a gift designed to make a definite connection. Danny had certainly enjoyed Klein's present. He played the LP right away, singing out of tune to the ditties. And when Harriet called, inviting Brian to accompany Jeff and Klein to a young people's concert at the New York Philharmonic, Danny agreed without first asking Brian. Klein was a showbiz success; that was the only bona fide Danny Moran required to hand over his son.

The acceptance led to Brian's being alone for ten minutes with Klein while Jeff was supposedly in the bathroom, before they went downstairs to get into a hired car. Klein sat on Jeff's bed while he lowered Brian's pants and put the boy's little wrinkled penis in his mouth, where it swelled into a paradox of pleasure and terror: was he going bite It off?

Brian didn't speak for a while. Danny decided to fill the silence with more recollections about those happy times: "You were a very charming, very talented boy. The NBC chappie must've picked up on your abilities right away. I remember that madwoman Harriet telling me he was very taken with you."

"He molested me, Dad." Brian met his father's eyes briefly. He couldn't hold them. The embarrassment he felt, at fifty years of age, overwhelmed as much as if he were eight. He hurried on, "Nothing horrendous. Just"—Brian gestured at his groin—"played . . ." Shame covered him like a hangman's hood, forcing his eyes down. He stared at the narrow oak boards, gouged from use, darkened with age. "Anyway," he said, breathing out, expelling the stupid embarrassment. "He molested me and Jeff, and I know of two others, a girl and a teenage boy, whom he apparently . . . I guess the teenager was his catamite. "

"What?" Danny's theatricality had fled in favor of a movie actor's mumble. "I don't understand. He had a lover? He was gay?"

"Catamite doesn't mean that, Dad. It means a boy kept for unnatural purposes."

"I know what catamite means," his father said haughtily, a little of Broadway restored. "I've worked in the theater for fifty years. Some gay writers don't use it pejoratively. They use it to mean an older man's young male lover."

"Richard Klein was a pedophile, Dad. He took charge of this teenager when he was much younger, a ten-year-old orphaned boy. Even as a fifteen-year-old he still looked very young. He had no beard at all, he was immature and . . . well, like a boy. Klein molested boys and girls. He didn't care what gender they were. He was a pedophile. Maybe he was primarily a pedophile who liked boys, but that doesn't make him gay. He wasn't gay anymore than it would have made him heterosexual if he were only molesting girls and fucking a very young looking fifteen-year-old girl. He was a pedophile. He wanted to have sex with children. He was a pedophile!" The repetitions were angry and angrier, escalating to rage. At their crescendo, Brian was finally able to meet his father's eyes, only now Danny refused the contact. It was his turn to gaze at the multimillionaire's winter garden.

Brian waited for a response. When none seemed forthcoming, he told his father's profile, "The teenager, the catamite, was named Sam Rydel. It's the same guy who is all over the newspapers and TV, the man accused of sodomizing and raping all those disadvantaged boys at the charity camp he runs."

"I don't understand," Danny mumbled. "I'm not following." His eyes flitted about the room, landing everywhere but on Brian. "You mean, the catamite of this man who bothered . . ." Danny gestured at Brian before continuing in an irritated tone, "What did that NBC exec do? Masturbate children, is that what we're talking about?" He said children as if they were speaking of strangers.

"Yes. With Jeff and me and a girl, more or less, that's what I witnessed Klein do. I don't know how far he went with Jeff or others out of my sight. There was no penetration with me, if that's what you're asking. In fact, to finally answer your stupid suspicions, no man has put his dick in my ass or my mouth. I'm not gay, Dad. I wish I were. That would be a normal thing to be." Brian knew he must be wounding his father. He wanted to, to flay him with the information. "I don't know the extent of what Klein did with Rydel. But he had control of him physically, financially, and psychologically through all of his formative years and ever since, as far I can tell. So I'm sure it went much farther, horribly farther with Sam, and I assume Klein got Rydel to participate in molesting children with him, but that's speculation." Brian paused, then answered a skeptic: "But not very speculative. I had one hint of what young Sam's life with Klein was like and I've read a lot about all this and it's not surprising that Sam became a child molester himself because of his prolonged experiences with Klein and his emotional dependency on him. Lots of people like to think this kind of monstrous behavior is genetic. I don't. I'm willing to keep an open mind about the existence of God or whether or not Joyce's *Ulysses* is a great novel, but I have no doubt that one way or another child molesters are nurtured, not born."

This drew Danny's eyes his way. The fear there was not playacting.

His mouth opened, presumably to ask a logical question about Brian. Brian had never married or had roommates. There had been putative girlfriends during his tumultuous adolescence and raw youth but only platonic friends since. Brian knew Danny thought he had settled the mystery of Brian's sexuality when the old man had switched from saying "fags" to "gay" fifteen years ago; but this other appalling possibility was brand new.

"No!" Brian fairly shouted. "Not me!" Brian glared, displaying the rage he felt at his father's lack of faith in him. Danny Moran had skipped from what had been done to Brian to worrying over what Brian had become without pausing for even a beat of sympathy. "No, I'm not a child molester," he said, more calmly. "Very little happened to me, first of all. Second, you may have noticed I've been in therapy for twenty-five years. And I'm on medication that happens to kill my sex drive." Brian laughed. "Mostly."

Danny bowed his head and seemed to observe a minute of silence. When he straightened, he had the air of a man who had settled something to his satisfaction. *Has he mourned me so quickly?* "Medi—" The old man choked partway through the word. He cleared his throat and tried again. "What kind of medication? Does it do something . . ." He nodded in the direction of Brian's groin.

"God, no. Jesus. Paxil. It's a widely prescribed antianxiety drug. Usually for extreme phobic behavior, shut-ins who won't leave their apartments, or any other form of social anxiety. But I take it primarily as a sexual suppressor. Because my libido is both the source and the nexus of my anxieties." Danny sagged in the chair, crushed. Abruptly Brian pitied his father, having to hear his only son's loins were handicapped. Brian had wanted to be cruel to his father; he was sorry to have succeeded so well. He patted Danny's knee. "It works really well for me, Dad. Don't fret about it. Used to bother me that I needed to take a pill. Last Thanksgiving I even tried to stop. For a week, I felt in control, full of energy, myself again. By the second week, I couldn't think about anything else. I can't have my whole life only be about this idiotic incident, this fucking circumstance of my childhood that I can't get out of my head. I'm much better this way. I'm not always seeing things through the . . ." Brian hesitated. He hadn't, as writers often do, mentally written out how to describe the different states. "I don't know. It jumps the tracks for me. I'm lifted out of the groove of unhappy feelings and self-destructive acts of . . . I don't know, rage or punishment or guilt. I don't know. Whatever the hell it is, it stops." Brian tried a friendly smile. "I'm not a child molester, Dad. Don't worry about that." It was sad and absurd that he had to make this reassurance; at that moment, it seemed more absurd than sad.

"Of course not," Danny said, head up, back straight. The curtain was up; he was recast as a defender of his son. "Who would think that? That's preposterous. Utterly preposterous. Lots of people are taking psychiatric medicine. In fact, from what I can tell, practically all truly talented people are on Prozac."

"Yeah," Brian said, playing along. "That's why all the books and movies are so fucking bland. Everyone's medicated into reassuring sentimentality."

Danny grinned. "I should take Prozac. Then maybe *Law & Order* would hire me again." Over the years, Danny had landed three bit parts on different iterations of the hit show, just enough to allow him to feel he had a career. Those gigs had dried up seven years ago. A lifetime of striving to be a working actor and he had the résumé of a hobbyist. Danny Moran sighed: he had abandoned Brian's troubles and returned to the comforts of his tragedy.

Brian put a reassuring hand on his father's shoulder, a body he could always touch without the fear, to guide him gently to the end of this painful conversation. "I may have to talk about being molested, Dad. There's a chance someone will force things very soon, so that I may have to write something about it, or go into court even, God knows what. That's why I'm telling you. I don't want you to be taken by surprise."

"Go public?" Danny repeated with a bewildered expression.

"Because Klein and Rydel are going to get away with their latest crimes. The DA's dropping the charges against them, so someone you don't know may put me in a position where I'll have to tell what happened to me."

"Did this Rydel fellow do anything to you?"

"No. He was the catamite, remember?"

"But you're saying that Klein is still alive?"

"Yes."

"But what happened to you was a long time ago, wasn't it? Can they still prosecute him for that?"

"No. The idea is to raise hell. Then maybe others will come forward. Or the DA will go ahead with prosecuting."

Danny took his time responding. Brian's thoughts drifted. He wondered if Julie would be inspired by learning that he had finally told his father. Or would she take it as a rebuke? Danny cleared his throat to make sure he had Brian's full attention. "In fact, what you can testify to, what happened to you, doesn't have anything to do with this Rydel chap, correct? And they can't prosecute Klein for what he did to you?"

Brian groaned. "Yes," he said angrily.

"So what's the point?"

Brian's irritation that his father had still offered no sympathy or apology, for the circumstance if nothing else, erupted: "I don't know what the point is, Dad! But I may have to go public anyway."

"I don't see the necessity of . . ." Danny began.

"For my sake!" Brian interrupted angrily. "Okay? For the sake of my immortal soul."

Danny fixed him with the kind of penetrating look actors are regularly asked to produce: announcing the wisdom of the third act, providing a truth that will send the audience home sadder but wiser. "Brian, if you tell, that's all they'll ever think of you. You realize that, don't you? Your lovely plays, your brilliant movies—that won't be what they'll think of when they hear your name. They'll think of some man diddling you. A lot of them will get confused and think you did the diddling. But what's worse . . ." Danny lowered his register a scale, to punch the payoff: "What's worse about all the ugly attention you'll have to endure for merely telling the truth, is that everyone will think the only reason you talked about it at all is to help sell your scripts."

Confession

— February 2008 —

THEY'RE GOING TO *get away with it,* she thought, fighting the urge to flee, as if Klein and Rydel were coming to kill her.

"Mom! Are you here?" Zack appeared from his room. His door had been shut for an hour after he came home with a whore named Gabby. Julie couldn't remember if she was mentioned in his loathsome diary as the one who gave him a blow job. He walked right up to his mother, stopping too close, as if he were suddenly severely nearsighted. "We want to make cookies." His eyes were bloodshot and unfocused. He hadn't bothered to disguise either the sour stink of weed or the dank odor of cigarettes. "Chocolate chip cookies," he said, hair falling softly over his high brow. "She likes, you know, chocolate chip cookies to be hot." He blinked rapidly as if trying to clear the fog from his drug-addled, sex-soaked brain. "You know, I mean . . . fresh-baked."

She nearly asked, "Isn't it dinnertime?" as if they were children spoiling their appetite. Instead she answered in their vernacular: "Whatever."

"Great. It's okay to use the baking stuff and chocolate chips?"

She nodded and walked away. She couldn't bear the sight of his sloth, his depravity, his impurity. She shut the bedroom door behind her and paced restlessly. She felt trapped although for the first time since she recognized Rydel she wasn't cornered. With the charges dropped, Jeff would never find out that she hadn't told Gary to give up his intention to write about Rydel. She could pretend to have done Jeff's bidding and he'd launch Zack's acting career. All else could remain as it is, as it had been for decades: her secret safe but for the boys, now men, who had witnessed her degradation; her marriage a lie she could easily endure. All she needed was to calm her nerves.

Unfortunately her son was occupying the space where she would usually seek refuge and soothe herself with the orderly fragrant and tactile pleasures of cooking. She resorted to her late-night comfort, a hot bath.

She made it so hot her belly reddened, as if she were a boiled lobster. The enveloping heat worked its magic: neck melting, muscles softened. Her mind drifted back to those troubling days and landed somewhere neutral, a vivid memory of her mother's having found out Harriet had lied about dying of cancer. Ma had ranted in front of Julie, exposing her true opinion of Harriet for the first and last time, denouncing her sister-in-law as a destructive, selfish monster who should have her son taken away from her. Hy had remonstrated that she was "going overboard," that Harriet loved Jeff and took pretty good care of him. At the time, Julie had agreed with her father. Today she marveled at how correct her mother had been without possessing one-tenth of the information that would have proved her right. What a wise and moral woman her mother was, patient to a fault with her self-absorbed husband, maybe, but always sure of her moral compass, always bold in the face of evil. How she missed her! She needed her mother's care more than ever, although she was older now than her mother was when she died.

She cried a little, gently and pleasantly, splashed the tears away, then sank lower in the tub, soaking in a reverie of admiration for her mother until Gary thumped on the bathroom door. She listened to his fist and voice as if she weren't occupying the same dimension of time and space. "Jules! You in there?" Framed between her toes poking out of the bathwater, she saw the glass doorknob turn.

"No!" she cried out.

"You're not decent, eh?" Gary asked, suggestive, frisky. Since her confession of smoking and her excited response to his lovemaking, he had a new confidence in his seductive skills.

"I'm in the bath," she called. "I'll be right out."

The door opened a crack. Gary's voice snaked through. "Now I *really* want to come in."

Julie slid out of the tub like a bar of soap, flopping on the floor, feet hydroplaning as she reached to push the door shut before Gary could come in.

"Hey, what are you hiding? A lover? Open up, babe. I'll help towel you off . . ." he murmured, through the keyhole it sounded like.

She wanted to shout, *Don't you dare come in,* but she had no right to refuse him. *I am a whore,* she reminded herself. *I was Klein's whore, I was a show whore for Sam and Brian and Jeff.* All these years, disgusted by Gary's appetite for food and for fucking her, she had thought his grossness justified her rejections. Wrong, hopelessly wrong. Gary was a righteous man, frank about his lusts, and they were the lusts of the righteous: for sugar and fat and the succor of a wife.

"Honey?" Gary was abruptly meek. "Is something wrong?"

"I'm toweling off. I'll be right out." She pulled a towel off the rack. Her right side, where she'd landed on the tiles, was immediately sore. She searched for a bruise. She stretched, twisted, examining breasts, hips, back. No crenulation. No cellulite puckering. Still an ass that could tempt a man's hands. But look at that mournful face and droopy breasts. And worst of all, the loose withered neck . . . *Oh God, I'm old and I've never been young.*

"Listen," Gary called. He hadn't moved from the door. "Frankenthaler thinks I should go ahead with a series of columns about Rydel. You know, a lynching story. And *American Justice* agrees. They'll pit me against Kelly who'll want his balls cut off and we can argue it forever since there's not going to be a trial . . ."

Julie wrapped the towel around her and pulled the door open. "A what story?"

"You know, the public hysteria about all this. Let's face it, Sam Rydel nearly got lynched. And the old guy too, Klein, Jeff's cousin, although nobody knows about him and I can't blow my source. But two unsubstantiated child molestation stories and the cops were all over both of them, assuming they were child rapists. Even I bought into it—a little. It's obvious now that the cops never vetted these witnesses. Turns out both of them had tried to blackmail Rydel and Klein with the threat that if they didn't pay them off they would tell these lurid stories. One of them even accepted a thousand dollars, but he wanted more, fifty thousand to send himself to college, he claimed, though really he's a meth addict. Anyway, the cops were sloppy and the media were all too ready to believe any sexual abuse story. People hear child abuse and they freak out. Scream for blood. Mob vengeance."

The sharp edges of her short hairdo were glued onto the back of her neck, wet and chilling. She shivered.

"Maybe we should take a bath together." Gary stepped close, a hand reaching as if to strip away her towel, although thankfully his greedy fingers stalled halfway, flicking at the air. "We won't be interrupted. Zack's got his own girl." His brows went up and down lasciviously.

"He's a pervert," she said.

Gary laughed. "He's a teenager. All teenagers are perverts."

"Rydel is a pervert," she repeated in a toneless voice, a dull fact. She felt utterly different than how she had imagined she would when she finally told Gary. No shame, only the tedium of explanation: "When I was eleven years old, Sam Rydel watched a grown man play with my genitals. That grown man was Klein. When I was twelve, Rydel watched Klein shove his dick in my mouth. He watched as if it were normal, as if it were something he had seen many times before. And then he . . ." She couldn't finish. "Sam was fifteen and he was already a pervert. What do you think he's become after forty years of indulging himself?" The edge of the towel came loose, falling away. Cool air struck her left breast, the nipple hardening.

Gary's eyes locked onto it, but he obviously wasn't focused there. He frowned, then stammered, "What? Klein . . . ? You were eleven . . . ? You know Klein? Go back. I'm not following . . ."

"Listen to me carefully," she interrupted. "Don't make me repeat things until you've got every little fact memorized and ready to be checked. I can't stand to say it over and over, so listen." She suddenly realized that she was yelling, "SO FOR GOD'S SAKES, LISTEN!"

Gary winced, put a finger over his lips, and said through gritted teeth, "Calm down. I am listening."

She took a deep breath, then returned to a bored recitation. "Of course I knew Klein. I met him at Jeff's apartment. He was a crazed child molester, unbelievably bold. I think that was part of it for him, he enjoyed that he might get caught. I still can't believe he was never caught! Sam Rydel was his . . . I don't know what to call it. He was his main victim, I guess. Klein brought Sam along like they were a tag team. He molested me three times right in front of Sam. Those poor victims of the media you feel sorry for treated me like their plaything. Sam Rydel watched while Klein fingered me. He even smiled. And a month later, because Klein starting seeing my father as a patient, and was sending him celebrities . . ."

"Klein was a patient of your father's?" Gary interrupted. Julie must have glared at him with an intent to kill. Gary raised his hands in surrender. "I'm sorry, but I'm catching up, you didn't tell me any of this . . ."

"Yes, for a couple of years Klein was my father's patient and a family friend, if you can believe that," she said, cutting off his complaint. "Klein and Sam even came to Thanksgiving one year. Another time he made up some excuse to show up in Riverdale, a fake dental emergency, I'm convinced, and he brought Sam along and . . ." She sighed. "I can't stomach going through the whole story, but he maneuvered things so I was alone with the two of them and Klein took out his penis and he made me . . ." She shook her head, shrugging the memory off. "Sam watched and touched himself and then Klein told him to put his . . ." She didn't finish. She was immediately sorry she had said this to Gary. She hadn't been willing to let go of this detail even to tell someone as sympathetic as Brian, that in addition to not stopping Klein from raping her mouth, she had failed to stop Sam too. "They're perverts . . ." She burst into tears. She hadn't felt the urge to cry. The tears came without warning. She doubled over and covered her face, listening to herself sob, and she kept thinking, *You're a phony. You're not upset about this anymore. You're a big phony.* All the while she blubbered, "I was eleven." She felt only frustration, but her voice was saturated with anguish. "I know you love being on TV and you can't say it 'cause there's no proof, but these men are monsters." Her chest was quaking and she keened, forehead touching knees.

Gary's shoes appeared. A hand landed on her neck. "Honey," he whispered. "It's okay." He kissed the top of her head, then her cheek. "Shhh," he said into her ear, hand sliding down to pat her back. She felt like his pet.

"It's not okay." She straightened, unaware his chin was right above the crown of her skull. She caught him with a devastating uppercut.

Gary staggered, toppling backward. One hand grabbed at a glass shelf and collapsed its brackets. Cosmetic jars smashed on the floor, makeup powder swirling, colored glass flying. His other hand reached for the tub's edge. His palm slid off the slick surface and sent him falling faster that way, left cheek and eye slamming into the black-and-white tile floor. The deafening noise of bottles exploding and Gary smacking hard onto tile was terrifying.

He lay completely still on the floor. "Gary?" she whispered. She wouldn't have been surprised to discover he was dead.

Zack called from just outside the bedroom door. "Mom? Dad? You guys okay?"

She bent over her husband. He was unconscious. Alive—chest rising and falling—but out cold.

She ran out of the bathroom door—passing her son and the slut as they entered the bedroom. She made for her closet, fumbling for clothes.

She heard the girl scream. Zack said, "I'm here, Dad," so she presumed they were tending to him. *Good,* she thought, *because I'm not.* She dressed in the closet's darkness, then made a run to the hallway.

Glancing back, she saw Gary was awake, propped up in Zack's arms. Gary's swollen left eye was all red. A devil's eye.

"Mom?" Zack called plaintively.

"Honey?" Gary cried, bewildered.

Even the slut looked to her for rescue.

"Put ice on it! There are green peas in the freezer." Worried Zack might try to catch her while she waited for the elevator, she hustled down nine flights of stairs, arriving breathless on the street, profoundly relieved to be clear of the mess of glass and muck that needed to be swept, scrubbed, bagged, and thrown out.

The air was freezing and the sky heavy with gray and black clouds. They filled in the narrow clearance between the Upper West Side's brick towers, but she was not hemmed in. The first drops of an icy rain tapped on her skull. She lifted her face to the needles of water. She was free. She was free of lies she had told Gary all their married life. She was free and she had nowhere to go.

Best Friends Forever

—— February 2008 ——

AFTER JULIE ALERTED him to the news of Klein and Rydel's legal escape, Brian called Jeff's office a second time, although that was a breach of Hollywood etiquette. He was told snappishly by Jeff's English secretary that Mr. Mark absolutely couldn't return his call until next week. Then he really crossed the line of proper film hierarchical behavior and tried the director's home number in LA. Much to his surprise, Jeff's third wife, Halley, picked up. He recognized her voice from her aborted career as a sitcom actress and her cameo in Jeff's hit *October Surprise,* immediately prior to their becoming a couple. He did his best to sound very relaxed. "Hello. Is this Halley?"

"Yes," she said.

"Hi. We've never met, but I'm a childhood friend of Jeff's. My name is Brian Moran . . ."

"Oh sure! I've heard all about you, Brian. Jeff'll be sorry he missed your call. Do you still live in New York? 'Cause he's there now. Poor boy—tomorrow they're doing another test preview in Jersey." Not a trace of nervousness, and she was completely open about Jeff's schedule. *She doesn't know a thing.* Brian was not surprised by her being kept in the dark. That confirmed his suspicions about Jeff.

Brian told Halley that unfortunately he wasn't in New York, he was in Paris on a movie, but he'd love to call Jeff to arrange something soon, and was this Jeff's current cell number. He rattled off the contact info from his Hermès.

It wasn't, of course. "Jeff has to change his cell every couple months," Halley said. "The number leaks out and crazies call." She didn't give him a current one, lamely alibiing that Jeff hated talking on cells. She suggested Brian try calling him at the Four Seasons hotel. "Ask for Saul Klein," she said, and a chill, an actual shiver climbed up and down Brian's spine hearing an amalgamation of Jeff's father's first name and his mother's maiden name. "That's his alias on the road so fans can't call his room," Halley explained. *At least he's not calling himself Richard Klein,* Brian consoled himself. Halley advised him to try Jeff's hotel right away because he was heading out soon to have dinner to meet the cast of *Mother's Helper II* after they had all been shown a final cut. She added, hilariously for Brian, "I bet Jeff would love you to see *Helper II.* It's brilliant."

So Jeff was in New York. Brian could confront him physically, much better than over the phone, perhaps as Jeff came out of the restaurant, tipsy and fattened up. He was tempted to ask Halley where Jeff and his cast were eating but feared that would seem very suspicious. He thanked her and hung up.

There was another source he could try, someone certain to know where the stars of *Mother's Helper II* were having dinner with their director. He called Veronica Stillman's personal cell, not her assistant's. This hallowed number had been generously provided to allow him to stay in close touch while he rewrote her monologue at the climax of *Sleep of the Innocent.* He could pretend to be giving her an update about how that was going and casually ask where they were eating if her evening plans came up. That is, if she answered when she saw who was calling. He had no choice about disguising his number; a blocked one certainly wouldn't be picked up.

"Brian! I'm so glad it's you!" Veronica said without a hello and with convincing enthusiasm. "Guess who I'm about to meet for dinner?"

"You're flying to Paris to have dinner with me and Aries at Taillevent."

She chuckled. "I wish. No, I'm eating with your childhood buddy Jeff."

"No kidding. I hope you're making him take you somewhere very expensive and very very chic."

"We're going to Our Place, which everyone says is the new hot restaurant. Have you been?"

"Yeah, it's great. I won't keep you. Just wanted to say your suggestion for including a more detailed description of how our heroine's genitals were tortured, contrary to my misgivings, really does work. Works wonderfully. So thanks for the note. It was a great help."

"Oh, I'm so excited. I'm so glad I'm doing our serious movie." She lowered her voice. "Especially after this big-money, no-brains Hollywood sequel. One for them and one for us, right? So when can I see my lovely new lines?"

"Well, I'm in Paris. It's two a.m. here and I can't sleep, of course . . ."

"You weren't kidding! You lucky dog, you really are in Paris."

"Had to meet with Aries about the changes we're making for you. I'm going to take a pill and pass out—I hope. I'll e-mail the pages to your assistant tomorrow morning after I've had a chance to read them over and do a little polishing, but please, I beg you, don't tell Aries I sent them to you before he's approved them."

"Never! Of course not. My God, I'd never do that. How could you think I'd betray you like that?" *Hmm,* Brian thought. *She isn't so good at lying in real life.* Veronica asked if she could say hello for him to Jeff. He gave permission. That would confirm his telling Halley that he was out of the country and thus relax Jeff.

He gave his failing father dinner, cleaned up, and settled Danny in front of the TV with DVDs of *The Wire.* Brian then walked in a leisurely fashion to Our Place's neighborhood, doing his best to keep his eyes from lingering on New York's sexy pedestrians. He found the architecture no less stimulating. Brian watched the belly of a lingering storm cloud, bleached white by the city's lights, pass languorously through the lance of the Chrysler building's spire. The nude building was passive, its attitude like an artist's life model, unimpressed by New York's lunge through its generous stomach, all the more seductive for its bored display. Even the weather felt voluptuous to Brian, the air scrubbed and electric. The evening's cold rain had deposited puddles that shimmered green and red from traffic signals, Christmas lily pads on the black pond of Park Avenue South. Again and again Brian had to force himself to avert his eyes from relishing painted faces and bare throats. He watched leafless trees waving their branches—streetwalkers beckoning customers to pleasure and to danger.

As he neared Our Place and the great confrontation, his eyes could no longer resist staring hungrily at New York's dolled-up boys and girls. Since starting Paxil, he had stopped his nighttime prowling, but he was glad to be a hunter once again on the anonymous streets of his hometown where, as at a masquerade ball, you could become anyone, including your real self. Should he have just one more taste, a last fling before asking his shrink to double his dosage? For a farewell, he could instruct the Red Head or maybe train the Black Beauty or even, if they weren't available, put the Chubby Cheerleader through her paces.

But he only looked, and soon the ache faded. Just as well. Later, with any luck, he would be busy with a reunion. He settled across the avenue from Our Place, waiting patiently for twenty minutes until he spotted a clue that Jeff would soon come out: a black stretch limousine lumbering on uneven New York paving, too long and wide for the narrow side street as it turned in fits and starts onto the more commodious Park Avenue, resting at last by the corner near the restaurant's glass doors.

"How far we've come, Jeff," Brian whispered to the cold, wet streets. "How far the geeky boys have come."

As Jeff, Veronica, and five other cast members emerged, they were immediately swarmed by autograph hounds and paparazzi who seemed to sprout, like overnight mushrooms, from the damp concrete forest. A second long stretch awakened, lights coming on, its driver pulling out from a discreet parking space to join the other, the pair effectively cutting off a lane of traffic. Each star responded differently to the fans and photographers. A few—not Veronica—posed and signed autographs. Not for long. All continued to maneuver to the two limousines, accommodating celebrities efficiently scrawling signatures while they walked. Brian crossed Park Avenue South halfway, stopping at the center island for a better view. He stood shoulder to shoulder with the gawking rubes, the civilians, the outsiders, thrilled by fame in the flesh. And truth be told, like a rube from the sticks, Brian was fascinated to discover which stars Jeff would choose to ride back to his two-thousand-dollar-a-night suite, to sleep the sleep of the successful in the world's most successful city, a city that had once paid the young Jeff Mark no mind, if not deliberately wished him ill.

None was the answer. Brian goggled as the once goofy Jeff kissed the hand of the star of *Critical Care,* the gorgeous twenty-two-year-old Kate Hooper, and actually helped her into the limousine as if he were Sir Walter fucking Raleigh. Brian shook his head to see the once unpopular Jeff embrace the supercool Steven Zaban, fresh off his smashing debut as the latest incarnation of Spider-Man, as if they were blood brothers. He grunted as his once skinny friend with a honking voice, now a bald middle-aged auteur with a good start on a substantial paunch, tousle young Billy Frederick's blond hair (*How Richard Klein would envy him that,* Brian thought), and he watched, astonished, as Jeff seemed to have a funny or warm-hearted comment for each of the spouses, mothers, and celebrity dates of his stars. He even did a funny dip of tall Veronica, pretending to hurt his back so she could playfully punch him on the shoulder. With his stars in the vehicles Jeff signed three autographs with a gracious flair and posed long enough for the paparazzi not to become angry or frustrated with him, but not long enough to seem desperate for their attention, then stood calmly on the corner as they all departed—movie stars, limos, paparazzi, and autograph hounds—as if he were master even of his own vanity, as if he not merely enjoyed fame, but could watch it recede with a philosophical air.

Brian had planned to hail a cab, follow Jeff's limo to the Four Seasons, and catch him in the lobby, demanding a tête-á-tête in his room. He was about to take advantage of Jeff's lingering on the sidewalk, watched respectfully from a distance by a few fans, when Jeff did something unexpected. He reentered the restaurant.

Brian was still debating whether to go in after him when Jeff reappeared, now wearing a Mets cap low over his head and a very long raincoat that nearly touched pavement. He deliberately looked up and down the avenue, evidently checking that all fans and paparazzi were gone, then abruptly turned onto a side street, walking west briskly.

The Four Seasons was uptown, didn't require walking west to hail a cab. If Jeff wanted to be a true proletarian and take the subway, he would head for the Lexington Avenue line on Twenty-third. But he was heading west. To ride the E? The long ride to Queens and the old neighborhood? No one lived there now. They were all gone: Jeff's mother and father, Brian's mother, everyone. The parents of their school friends had escaped to the suburbs in the seventies. Everyone was gone. Even Mrs. Rosen in 5A, always in that floral nightgown, smelling of onions, permanently at her post, leaning on her windowsill watching them play ball as if they were her particular business. Their neighborhood was erased by a tsunamis of Latino and Asian immigrants who had replaced the eastern Europeans. The city eroded every mark, washed the sand smooth of all human tracks, including the powerful. Jeff's newest picture could outgross *ET* and sooner or later the city would forget him.

Jeff appeared to welcome New York's cloak of obscurity, choosing a deserted route crosstown, hugging the dark buildings, disappearing into their shadows, still walking, despite the pear shape of his middle age, with a hint of his youth's awkward bony gawkiness, moving past half-gentrified blocks of brownstones and low brick office buildings partially converted to lofts. They had long ago ceased to house the old New York of tailors, bakers, and candlestick makers but were not quite fully ready to accommodate the short but brilliant life span of that fragile butterfly, the childless young investment banker. At night, most of this neighborhood wasn't residential, hosting modestly illegal activities—high-stakes poker, low rent brothels—nothing that ought to be of interest to one of the world's hottest directors, which made it all the more puzzling when Jeff stopped at a public phone (forswearing his cell), first looking around as if to check on whether he had company, and produced a piece of foolscap from his pocket before feeding it a quarter. Brian concealed himself in the cubby of a doorway with an overpowering smell of urine. He watched closely as Jeff consulted the paper before he dialed each digit. The number was unfamiliar.

When Jeff reached the other party, the conversation was short. Before he hung up, he leaned out of the booth, searching for a landmark being described to him, and then made a beeline across Fifth Avenue, into a loft building twenty feet on the other side. The short, chubby director moved so fast that Brian barely reached the corner in time to notice which of the dark, rather ominous doors Jeff had chosen.

He waited for a few minutes, in case Jeff exited, before finally taking the chance of crossing the avenue, empty except for taxis hurrying passengers through this deserted barrier between the busyness of midtown to the delights of downtown. Brian strolled past the building in question, glancing casually at the door. Jeff could hardly have chosen a more forbidding and unwelcoming entrance, a dented metal door, covered with thick black curlicues of graffiti meaningless to Brian. It looked like a service entrance. He wondered for a moment if he had made a mistake. Could this really be where Jeff had gone? He tried to think of an innocent explanation. Perhaps these were his old loft digs, where the young, struggling film student had lived and which the famous rich director had never sold?

No. Why would Jeff need to phone ahead for directions to his own place? Okay, he was up to something sleazy, unwilling to risk summoning a call girl or call boy or she-boy up to his Four Seasons' suite where a nosy paparazzi might spot a sex worker entering Jeff's room.

So what? Who cares what self-indulgence Jeff Mark is up to? I have my playmates, he has his.

But he wanted to know. Brian's frustration at the blank obstacle mounted. He tried to reason it away, reminding himself his objective was to expose Klein and Rydel, not Jeff. But he decided to confront Jeff when he came out and that's when he noticed the intercom: a small black plastic box, set discreetly into the brick to the left of the door, nearly invisible in the shadows of the night.

He moved into the well of the doorway to study it. There were six buttons, marked crudely One, Two, Three, and Three-A and two others not marked at all. Beside One was a cheap stick-on label that read STUDIO, the *S* and *T* peeling off from the top edges. Two and Three had spent the money to have a slide-on nameplate made that covered both spaces to read BROADWAY PRINTING, and Three-A had also made the effort to get a nameplate, which read RICHARD REISER, CPA. Two, Three and Three-A were obviously daytime businesses, except perhaps Mr. Reiser during tax season. Only the mysterious studio could be a nocturnal enterprise. And Brian knew well what studio was a euphemism for.

It couldn't be just a regular hooker, male or female. This had to be at least a tranny, someone Jeff daren't risk summoning to his hotel, who couldn't be alibied as a masseuse, because venturing to this dingy location was no more discreet than indulging in his room. And far less safe. Leaving a star-studded dinner, gutters awash in paparazzi, to walk through deserted streets, phone for directions, and disappear behind a metal door was really dangerous, a terrible risk. No, this was self-hatred and self-destruction, this was Jeff Mark acting out a perverse need, and Brian was pleased, very pleased, to discover that Jeff wasn't unscathed.

He should play it safe and wait. The general knowledge ought to be enough to give him leverage when he confronted Jeff. He could probably bluff the truth out of Jeff or at least provoke him sufficiently to learn the general neighborhood of the poor sap's lusts.

But he wanted to *see. I always want to see, that is the cause of my tragedy,* he had rhymed as a teenage poet.

Brian dialed information on his iPhone. He asked for a listing of a "Studio" with that building's address. The operator immediately objected to the vague name, but Brian insisted that since he had a particular address it oughtn't to matter. The operator relented, was silent for a moment and then, with some satisfaction, informed him there was no listing for "a Studio at that address."

He glanced at the time. Twelve forty. He guessed Jeff had been inside for ten minutes. He returned to the anonymous door, moved into the darkness of its well and stared at the Studio button, trying to calculate how stupid what he was about to do might be.

Embarrassing, he decided, surely not dangerous. He pressed the intercom. He didn't have long to wait. "Who is it?" a harassed and irritated female voice asked.

Brian leaned close, almost kissed the grill of the intercom to reply, "Hi, I've lost your number. I'm sorry, I know I should call ahead, but I lost your number and I was in the neighborhood, so I was hoping you could squeeze me in tonight now. Or I can come back in a half hour and buzz again. Or you could give me your number and I'll call in half an hour. Whatever you prefer."

There was a beat, presumably of confusion, before the harsh, hoarse female voice demanded, "Who is it?"

"Richard," he said. "It's Richard Klein." He wondered for a moment if this indulgence of irony was a mistake. What if Jeff were listening in? But then there would be a certain satisfaction in having revealed his presence with that moniker—imagine the horror on his friend's face hearing Klein's name in the middle of whatever revolting act of sexual gratification he had chosen for his flabby middle-aged body. "I haven't been in New York for a year. That's why I can't find your number—"

"Do you have an appointment?" she demanded. She sounded like an ill-tempered scold, a remarkably unwelcoming voice for a prostitute. He was disappointed anyway that a woman had answered. It would have been a pleasure to discover a homosexual Jeff cowering in the closet, a cowardly closet in 2008, especially in show business, unless you were an action star or a femme fatale. For a director, being gay wouldn't be a drawback at all. What a pleasure it would be to discover that Jeff Mark was living in a hell largely of his own making.

"No," Brian said. "That's why I'm buzzing you. I want to make an appointment and I don't have your phone number."

"Go to my website. DDNYC dot com," she said. "The number's there." She hung up.

He walked under an amber streetlamp, typed the address into his iPhone browser and waited for her webpage to load. The animated image appeared in jerky lines from the top down: a buxom middle-aged redhead in a pale gray jacket and long skirt, her business attire and somber expression made mischievous by a hairbrush she held in her right hand, the wood side tapping her left palm. A line of text at the bottom was the last to appear: "Domestic Discipline Administered by Katherine Stern." He tapped the link for Services, although he was confident he already knew what it would reveal. "No BDSM and Definitely NO SEX," her website explained. "Just the Spanking you Naughty little boys Deserve," her ad admonished with arbitrary Victorian capitalization.

He moved into the shadows near the metal door, leaning against the frame, prepared to wait. He would embarrass Jeff when he exited. He pictured the surprise and mortification on his old friend's face, imagining his own grin and laughter.

But in the darkness of his ambush the prospect didn't blossom.

Anticipating humiliating Jeff brought him no pleasure. *Who am I really shaming?* he wondered.

Walk away, he urged himself. *He suffers. Jeff also suffers.*

Brian looked again at the spanker's ad. He wiped it off his screen and pocketed his iPhone. He began a lonely walk home, sad and satisfied by knowing that he and Jeff were yet sharing the bitter brew of their past, each trying to control what had once controlled them, still connected like best friends, desperate to make painless theater out of their ruined childhoods.

THE MEN IN HER LIFE

—— February 2008 ——

THE MORNING WAS bright and cold. Too cold to enjoy shade. Julie stepped from under the Four Seasons' covered entrance to feel the sun on her face. She was waiting for Brian. She had been awake all night, unable to sleep on Amelia's pullout couch. She had retired to her guest quarters immediately on returning to the apartment, pleading that she was too upset about her "fight" with Gary to talk about it, which she expected Amelia would assume was over her discovering that Gary was having another affair. She had left at 5:45 a.m. to avoid a breakfast interrogation, waiting in a coffee shop for a decent hour to try Brian's cell. He had beat her to it, calling her at seven. "Get your ass down to the Four Seasons in a hour," he'd told her. "Wait for me outside the front entrance."

"Why?" she had asked.

"We're having breakfast with Jeff," he'd said, and then hung up.

When Brian eventually appeared from a cab, she tried again to find out. "What's happened?"

"Nothing. Just that it's time to confront him." He yawned. Maybe out of tension, but his eyes looked as if he too hadn't slept. He guided her toward the uniformed hotel doorman, already pushing the revolving door for their benefit, and then led her though the imposing and somewhat gloomy lobby, better suited, she thought, to a modern cathedral than a hotel. He stopped at a counter near the front desk, picking up a matte black phone with no dial or buttons. He said, "Penthouse A, please." There was a pause. A slow smile dawned on Brian's face. He said with an obnoxious air, "Yes, I can tell you whom I'm trying to reach. I'm trying to reach Saul Klein. Thank you."

Brian put a hand over the receiver. "His wife told me to give that name as code. He's using Klein as an alias, can you believe that shit?" He uncovered and said with brittle cheerfulness into the house phone, "Jeff! It's Brian! Yes, Brian Moran! Can you believe it? It's really me. I'm in the lobby of your hotel and I'm starving. I want to have breakfast with you. What a surprise, no?"

Certainly this was a surprise to Julie. They were crashing? She had assumed Brian had already made a date with Jeff. She couldn't hear Jeff's reply. Brian maintained his sarcastic gaiety, "Yes, I did tell Halley and Veronica I was in Paris. Guess what? I lied." He met Julie's eyes while he added, "But I'm not the only surprise, Jeff. Guess who's here with me? And she's also dying to have breakfast with you. No guesses? Well, it's your long-lost cousin, the beautiful Julie, the daughter of your dead father's brother, probably the closest living relative you have. What do you say, Jeff, do you have an hour to spare to meet your oldest friend and your closest relative in the world for a yummy breakfast? All you have to do is throw on a *shmata* and take the elevator downstairs." There was a longish silence, a little too long for comfort. "Forty-five minutes?" Brian said. "Come on, you don't have to shower and shave for us. We're family. Get down here in fifteen minutes, Jeff, or you'll regret it." Brian hung up with a bang.

"I can't believe you did that."

"You wanted me to do that," he said.

At the reception desk of the hotel's dining room, a solemn young man in a black jacket with too many buttons and not enough shoulder padding greeted him on arrival. "Good morning, Mr. Moran. Welcome back to the Four Seasons. Who are you joining today?" Julie was profoundly impressed he knew Brian by sight.

"Jeff Mark," Brian mumbled, as if he were ashamed of it.

Although this young maître d' had already seemed to have exhibited as much deference as possible, he summoned more from a reserve of servility: "Very good, Mr. Moran." He checked his book. "I'm afraid I don't have a reservation for Mr. Mark—"

Brian cut him off. "I just spoke to him in his suite. He said you'd find us a table and he would be down in fifteen minutes. He's going under the name Saul Klein. You can call and check with him."

"That won't be necessary, Mr. Moran." He signaled a tall, thin blonde who until then Julie had assumed was a world-class fashion model waiting to be seated for her own power breakfast. "Ann will take you to your table." The extraordinarily thin and lovely young woman escorted them to a table big enough for six, set in near isolation at the rear of the double height room, beside an enormous recessed window. Nothing about how Jeff was treated ought to have surprised Julie, but the reality did anyway.

The blonde asked if they wanted juice or coffee. Nearly simultaneous with their affirmatives, a solemn young man, wearing a well-fitted striped vest, immediately appeared with a pitcher of fresh-squeezed orange juice while she handed them menus large enough to be the tablets on which Charlton Heston had received the Ten Commandments.

Brian caught Julie's eye as she watched a fourth attendant arrive with a carafe of coffee. "Regular coffee all right, miss?"

"Yes. Thank you." Julie grinned at Brian.

He nodded for the waiter to give him coffee. "Remember, while we're talking to Jeff, that this is how he is treated twenty-four hours a day, seven days a week."

"Even by his wife?" Julie couldn't resist trying to puncture Brian's hyperbole.

He wasn't deflated. "I'm sure she has a staff of ten to pamper him for her. My point is, he's not a real person anymore. He doesn't have the faintest idea what real life is like."

Julie respected Brian's obvious desire that she take this observation to heart, so she considered it while sipping coffee. She argued gently, "But you haven't seen Jeff in almost thirty years."

Brian sighed. "Okay. I don't really know Jeff today, but I just want you to bear in mind that he hasn't had to lift a finger for himself for decades, that there are hundreds of thousands of people, a few million if he bothered to seek them out, all willing to tell him everything he does and says is brilliant. Maybe there is someone on this earth on whom that would have no effect, but I'm certain if I was treated that way, for just three weeks, I would soon feel I was an equal of Da Vinci's. And not just as an artist. The sciences too."

She studied Brian's handsome face for a clue to whether he really meant what he said. He returned her scrutiny. For a long moment they gazed at each like fascinated lovers. "I don't think you would," she said at last. "I think you'd decide they were sycophants. I don't think you'd trust them."

"Well," Brian said, "that just means my self-esteem is so low I can only enjoy abuse."

"Maybe Jeff's just like you," Julie argued. "Maybe the only thing he finds convincing is abuse."

Brian laughed abruptly, as if she had surprised him. "You're right, Julie. You're absolutely right. Probably the only thing Jeff thinks is real is when someone abuses him."

Julie was pleased to win this argument. Brian was much less interested in besting and correcting her than Gary. Maybe only lawyers were irritating in that way. She was unaccountably happy. Her life had unraveled and she felt not undone, but relaxed. If the small secrets of her quiet life were about to be pinched and zoomed onto everyone's iPhone, at least having Brian along was entertaining.

Brian said, “Let’s order. I told him fifteen minutes, but Jeff’s a director. He could keep us waiting for two hours.”

While they waited she told him about Gary’s terrible fall and her running away. She had plenty of time for a full account. Jeff took thirty minutes to appear and he arrived with a surprise. He was accompanied by a tall, elegant woman who Julie guessed was in her early forties although her precise age was difficult to assess. Her face looked unnaturally smooth—Julie couldn’t decide if that was Botox or surgery. Her long, flowing hair also projected a convincing and impossible youthfulness, a rich tapestry of colors ranging from auburn to chestnut, the weave sufficiently subtle that Julie knew each strand had been dyed individually. She wore what Julie recognized as one of that season’s Armani ensembles—delicate knee-length cashmere cardigan over a shimmering and yet casual white silk blouse, a black wool skirt extended seamlessly by boots whose buttery thin leather implied they were skinned from a pedigreed calf raised on a strict diet of caviar. That had to be at least fifteen thousand dollars’ worth of clothing. Julie didn’t attempt a guess at the cost of the double strings of pearls draped about the woman’s implausibly smooth neck, cascading down into the crinkled folds of her blouse, coming to rest on a bosom whose impressive size Julie assumed had been augmented. Nor could Julie make an informed estimate of the value of an antique silver ring on her wedding finger, set with a large emerald encircled by glittering diamonds. Julie watched with fascination as the woman, confident and predatory, crossed ahead of Jeff to swoop at Brian, dark red manicured talons extended, reaching for purchase on the bruised man.

Meanwhile Jeff stopped in his tracks, jaw dropping, opening his arms wide in astonishment. “Julie, you look great! You look so young! I can’t believe it. How do you do it? Is there a painting of you somewhere?” He lowered his voice to add, “I’m sorry I didn’t let you know I was in town, but I can explain—we’re testing *Helper II* tonight and things have been crazy.”

Julie didn’t answer, absorbed by Brian’s reaction to the extraordinary woman's approach. He stood up as she made a beeline for him, putting out a hand to ward her off. She grabbed it with both hands and brought it to her bosom. "Brian Moran," she announced as if introducing him to a crowd. "I love you so much. I love everything about you and I've never met you. I can't believe I've never met you! I feel like we're brother and sister, that we're soul mates, that I've known you all my life. Your words . . ." She shook her mane from side to side, a show horse's proud display. Julie forgot all about Jeff and his compliments. She was profoundly impressed by the woman's talent for flattery, praise so bold it was like a storm surge, drowning natural skepticism. She was impressed also by her utter freedom from any trace of shyness. She continued drenching Brian with praise. "Your words, my God, your words in *The Lost Man,* they echo in my head all the time. I can't forget them. And I don't want to forget them. Ever." Finally she stopped hugging Brian's hand, releasing him to say to Jeff, "Isn't that the truth? Tell him I'm not being a full-of-shit Hollywood producer."

"She *is* a full-of-shit producer," Jeff said. "But she's not being one now."

Brian grimaced, shaking his hand in the air as if she'd put it to sleep. "I believe you," he said glumly. "But who are you?"

Now that Brian had finally spoken to her, she ignored him, addressing Julie confidentially as if they were old friends, "I didn't tell him my name. Can you believe it? You'd think I was raised in the Bronx Zoo." She still didn't introduce herself to Brian. She offered a bejeweled hand to Julie. "I'm Grace Meyer," she said, a name that meant nothing to Julie but certainly did to Brian.

Although Brian had pretended otherwise, he had met Grace Meyer years ago at a screening. He wasn't surprised or offended that she didn't remember him. At the time, he was an unproduced screenwriter whose name wasn't likely to stick to the brain pan of one of the most successful women in Hollywood. Grace was the first female to head a studio, back when she was just a youngster in the seventies. She wasn't in her forties, as Julie assumed, she was sixty-three. As an independent producer, she was credited with four of the ten top-grossing films of the last decade, one of a handful of people who could make a screenwriter's dreams (and nightmares) come true. He knew Grace couldn't possibly remember all the anxious and hopeful faces that had been thrust into her field of vision. But now that Brian was no longer unproduced, he relished the perverse pleasure of obliging Grace to introduce herself all over again.

While Jeff, Brian, and Julie remained standing, Grace sat down at their table opening her arms to Brian as if welcoming him into her bed. "I got permission from Jeff to crash your breakfast because this is Kismet. I was about to call your agent this morning. I need your help desperately. I've got a book, one of the most beautiful books ever written, that's going to make a fantastic, moving, extraordinary movie and you have to write it for me. You're the only writer . . . well"—she smiled knowingly—"not the only writer, but the best writer for the job. Can I pitch it to you?"

Brian didn't reply. He rudely looked away to study Jeff, taking advantage of his greater height to inspect, in an insultingly overt manner, Jeff's spreading bald spot. Julie, from her angle on his other side, noticed that Jeff was carrying something in his left hand, drooping by his leg as if he hoped to conceal it. She leaned over enough to see it was a small, inflated pillow in the shape of a lifesaver, discreetly housed in a black suede covering.

Jeff spoke first, demanding of Brian, "How rude can you be? Aren't you going to answer her?"

Brian finally looked at Grace. He gestured at Julie and Jeff. "I'm afraid I meant this to be a reunion. Not business."

"Yes, of course, Jeff told me all about it. It's so charming that you haven't seen each other in so long. But like all producers, I have no manners when it comes to a passion project and passion is a weak word for what I feel about this one—it's like my own heart beating . . . I don't know what I'm saying, but I swear I'm crashing your lovely reunion for only a few minutes," Grace said, still the only one seated. "I'll have a cup of coffee with you . . ." The busboy and waiter were already assembling another place setting. "And make my pitch and get out of your hair so you old friends can enjoy each other over a long scrumptious breakfast." She turned to the waiter, intercepting him as he was about to pour. "Is that decaf?" she asked, which sent him hurrying off to fetch a different carafe.

Meanwhile a waiter pulled out a chair for Jeff. The director tossed the black suede doughnut on the seat and lowered himself gingerly.

Brian's unpleasant smile broadened into a malicious grin. He asked loudly, "Painful hemorrhoids, Jeff?"

Jeff nodded as he settled onto his cushion. "Yeah. Test previews. For a week before you can't stop shitting, and the week after you can't take a shit."

"Lovely talk," Grace commented as her eyes widened at the plate of blueberry and walnut pancakes arriving for Julie. She told Julie, "I envy you."

"You . . . envy me?" Julie stammered.

"You can eat that and keep your cute figure? Just watching you eat one I'm going to have to do another hour on the Stair Beast." Julie laughed. Brian and Jeff reacted with the stern expressions of schoolmasters. Grace focused on Brian without a preliminary. "It's *The Ice Pond.* We're going to make a movie of *The Ice Pond.* Can you believe we managed to convince Tony Winters to give us the rights? I'm so excited. Everyone's been trying to seduce him for ages and he's finally agreed—"

"Yeah," Jeff interrupted, "he's generously allowed us to make a film out of his book for a mere one million bucks."

"Well," Grace said, "let's face it. None of us are exactly not for profit." She lowered her voice. "Although with the deal we've made with the studio, we won't make a dime. We'll win twelve Oscars, but I'll have to pick up mine wearing a potato sack."

"Now you are being a full-of-shit Hollywood producer," Jeff said.

Brian turned to him, "And you're beginning to sound a little bowel-obsessed."

"Don't get me wrong." Grace took hold of Brian's wrist, fingers encircling and caressing his skin. Brian returned his attention to her. "It's a dream project. For everyone. For Jeff and me and for the writer." She patted Brian's hand twice and then rubbed it vigorously, as if he were a magic lantern. "Which we desperately hope and pray and want to be *you*." As Grace massaged Brian's hand, Julie noted a strange reaction in herself: she was irritated by this beautiful and successful woman claiming Brian. *I'm jealous?* she wondered.

The seduction seemed to be a failure: Brian yanked his hand free and snubbed her. "You're going to direct *The Ice Pond?*" he asked Jeff in an insulting tone of disbelief.

"Fuck you," Jeff said mildly.

"Touché," Brian smiled. "The only reason I'm surprised you want to direct *The Ice Pond* is that it doesn't have any special effects. No cute furry monsters, no amusingly hideous aliens, no multifanged amphibians, no Nazis!" Brian added to his list with an emphatic exclamation that provoked a laugh from Grace who immediately covered her mouth. Brian wasn't done. "No witches, no cartoon characters, no zombies—"

"All right—" Jeff tried to stop him.

Brian's energy for his itemization seemed boundless. "No chase scenes! No hydrogen bombs, no Ebola virus—"

"All right! You've made the joke. It was funny the first twelve times. Now you're overplaying it. Don't beat the laugh to death."

"Thank you, maestro." Brian bowed his head. "Thank you for the note."

"I do know a thing or two about movies," Jeff said, whining like when he was a boy, his voice rising an octave.

"*A* thing," Brian responded with an eight-year-old's malice. "Not two."

"Now, boys," Grace said, wagging a scolding finger. She adjusted quickly from femme fatale to tolerant mother. The deft transition increased Julie's awe of the woman. "Stop squabbling. Everyone in Hollywood knows it's time you two work together. If you'll quit being babies about admitting you're both brilliant at what you do, you'll make a great film together. Everyone knows that."

At last she had Brian's complete attention. He mocked: "Everyone? Every single soul in Hollywood?"

Grace wasn't fazed. "Yes. It's going to be the greatest achievement of my career. I'll be the producer who brings the world's most inventive and humane director together with the world's most perceptive writer about the human psyche. Both genius artists, who would be working together, who would have worked together years ago, if it weren't for the amazing accident that they knew each other as boys and are still a teensy"—Grace screwed up her face, tasting a sour lemon—"bit jealous of what the other one doesn't have."

Jeff and Brian looked at Grace as if she were raving mad. They answered her in a chorus. Jeff said, "You think I'm jealous of Brian?" at the same moment that Brian exclaimed, "You think he's jealous of me?" Jeff then shut up, but Brian added for good measure, "You're out of your mind. Jeff wouldn't trade places with me for all the tea in China. For chrissakes, he already has all the tea in China!"

"You're wrong," Grace said. Again, much to Julie's irritation, she encompassed one of Brian's hands with both of her own. *I need a manicure,* Julie thought, admiring how Grace's long fingers captured and stroked the writer while the producer leaned in, close enough to kiss him. She cooed, "If Jeff could write beautiful, deep, complicated characters like yours, he'd give all the tea in China *and* all the Botox in Beverly Hills." Julie's admiration for Grace's flattery grew exponentially. At first she had been awed by its shamelessness; now she was delighted by its self-conscious irony, a gentle self-parody that made swallowing the implausible praise easier and clarified that the brewer was no fool.

"Is that true?" Julie asked of Jeff, genuinely curious.

Jeff seemed startled that Julie had spoken, as if he had just been alerted to her presence.

"Of course not," Brian said, not an argument, supplying information.

"But it's a lovely thought, Grace," he conceded, and much to Julie's irritation, although he had seemed repelled by Grace's presumptuous acts of physical contact until then, he covered her two hands with his free one. Thus encouraged, Grace captured this one too, fingers interlocking with Brian's and squeezing affectionately.

"It *is* true," Grace insisted. "Will you do it, Brian? Will you adapt *The Ice Pond* and make me the happiest and luckiest producer in the world?" She gave his hands another, harder squeeze for good measure.

Brian squeezed back. "Absolutely not," he said. "And now, if you'll forgive us, we really need to be alone with Jeff." He brought her hands to his lips, kissed the air above them, and let go, casting her off.

Grace's eyes immediately fastened on the director, waiting on him to instruct her.

Jeff said, "Go. We'll talk him into it later."

Grace obeyed without further ado. She stood, saying to Brian, "I won't take no for an answer."

"Then take never for an answer," Brian said. Julie winced at the spitefulness in his tone.

"Great line," Grace commented. She turned to Julie, "Nice to meet you. Enjoy breakfast!" she said, her long cashmere sweater billowing in the wake of her departure.

At last the trio were together and alone. Jeff shook his head slowly and sadly at Brian as if he had made the gravest mistake of his life. Brian returned the disapproving look with a predator's grin. Julie was acutely aware that, at this moment, she hardly existed for them.

The silence became intensely uncomfortable. When Brian broke it, he added more discomfort by saying in a threatening tone, "You know why we're here."

"I was going to call you," Jeff said to Julie, turning away from Brian. "The test is tonight. Until then, I'm useless. So I was going to call after that."

"What is this test you keep talking about?" Julie asked.

"Test screening of *Helper II*." Jeff sighed. "In a New Jersey mall," he added with disgust and doom in his voice.

Brian turned to Julie. "Before a movie is released, the studios test them with audiences they select to represent key market groups." He asked Jeff, "This a suburban-mall test?"

"Yeah," Jeff said gloomily.

"So it'll be skewed middle class, white, and young?"

"Supposedly." He focused on Julie. "Speaking of the young, I'll be shooting a picture on the East Coast this summer. I think there's a two-liner for a fifteen-year-old."

Brian snorted. Jeff reacted by turning his attention to him. "Speaking of actors, how's your dad? He's still working right? You know there's the grandfather in *The Ice Pond,* a small but decent part for a man his age. He's welcome to it. Okay!" Jeff announced as if that was settled. "Let's get down to business."

"I thought you were already doing business," Brian mumbled.

"Cousin Richard is senile," Jeff said, briskly, frowning regretfully. "He's gaga. Totally out of it. Doesn't recognize anybody. He'd be in an institution except Sam Rydel is paying for round-the-clock nurses. And you've heard the news about Sam Rydel, right? That he's getting off. So there's nothing we can do. It's terrible, it's disgusting, but at least the cops are hip to Rydel. He wouldn't dare bother any kids again, and if he does, he's sure to get nailed. Anyway, here are copies of the medical reports on Cousin Richard." Jeff maneuvered gingerly on his pillow as he reached for something in his right pocket. He was in the dressed-down uniform of a successful director: stressed tailored jeans, retro Converse sneakers, brushed white cotton T under a black V-neck cashmere sweater. It took some squirming before Jeff produced a letter that had been folded in half. He placed it on the Four Seasons' linen and pushed it in their direction, skimming on the arch of its folds. "That's just a summary. I have the full eighteen-page report in the room. I didn't want to schlep it out in front of Grace—I had promised I would have breakfast with her, and when I tried to cancel and she heard it was you, Brian, she insisted she come by. Anyway, we can go upstairs to my room and I'll show you the whole report."

Brian angled the letter for Julie to read along with him. IS was embossed in huge gold print at the top. Just below, in normal size, the initials were spelled out: INTERNATIONAL SECURITY. Julie skipped the opening paragraph of self-congratulation on how much information they had gathered to read an itemized summary of confidential medical tests they had somehow copied, including a photocopy of a brain scan of Klein, a doctor's chart with a diagnosis of Alzheimer's and affidavits from three nurses who had taken care of Klein in the last year.

"Cousin Richard doesn't even know who Sam is. He wouldn't know us from Adam," Jeff said as Julie's eyes reached the last lines. "In the reports from the nurses, they say he masturbates, or tries to, compulsively. But he had prostate surgery eight years ago and is impotent and incontinent." Jeff took a long swallow of coffee and added, "So I guess in some cosmic way, he's being punished."

Julie felt as if the building was shifting beneath her. She put both hands on the table to steady herself. There had been such a terrific struggle to become willing to tell the world about Klein. And it had been wonderful convincing Brian to help. She had felt more than mere relief, true joy that at long last she was going to be brave and do something tangible. Once she had heard Klein was alive, that she could at least shame him, maybe see him die in disgrace in prison, she had been thrilled to have a second chance to do right and to be right. But Klein was beyond her reach, as good as dead.

In the background, she vaguely heard Brian ask questions about IS. They sounded off topic. One wasn't even a question. He commented he didn't realize they did this sort of investigative work. "I thought they only supplied bodyguards to pitiful helpless giants like Arnold Schwarzenegger." She was dismayed to hear Brian make showbiz jokes as if nothing had changed the situation. What an idiot she was, demolishing or possibly demolishing her marriage for nothing.

Brian shifted from meandering questions about IS to comment, "You know, Jeff, I think you should have stuck with the bribes. Was this really the best you could come up with? A bogus medical file."

She was still catching up to Brian's meaning as Jeff said confidently, "I'll go up right now and get you the complete file. It's in my suite. It's got everything. Even the MRI of his brain. I'm telling you, he's gaga."

"The bribes were a much better choice," Brian insisted. "Although I have to say it was idiotic to try both the bribes *and* a cover-up. Just like you to be over the top *and* indecisive in your storytelling. Either you're paying us off, or you're conning us. Pick one or the other."

"Look, wise guy, come upstairs, I'll show you the originals—"

Brian talked over him. "Seriously, the bribes were a much better choice. This cover-up is pathetically transparent. Makes me think your bribes aren't big enough. What's it really worth to you to shut us up?"

Jeff, trying to contain anger, addressed the center of the table in a growl: "Come on up and look at the evidence."

"Please, stop bluffing," Brian said in a pained voice while he dug in his pants pocket. He produced his iPhone. "I don't know if it'll load here, but thanks to Julie's tip about your speech on the broadcasting academy website, I found a lovely clip of Klein's reminiscing about his exciting career at NBC radio. In the clip, Sam Rydel is interviewing him and Sam conveniently introduces it by telling us they're filming on the occasion of Klein's eighty-third birthday. Just last year." He paused. When Jeff said nothing, frowning at the tablecloth as if it had insulted him, Brian continued, "You were much better off with the bribes, Mr. Jeff. A big fat paycheck for me and prestige too, adapting a National Book Award–winning novel, while Zack gets a huge step up for his acting ambitions. By the way, just so that Julie can make an informed decision whether to accept your bribe, would part of Zack's job be that if the studio is hassling you he has to let the president of production play with his dick so they won't cut your budget?"

When he came into the restaurant, Jeff's face had looked boyish. No more. He stared at Brian with the cold, depthless rage of an adult, tossed his napkin on his plate, and stood up, about to go.

Brian's voice apprehended him. "You walk out and I'm going straight to the *New Yorker, Vanity Fair, New York, Rolling Stone,* every magazine still standing and pitch a long and *very* detailed piece about the curious connection between Jeff Mark, Richard Klein, and Sam Rydel." Jeff had twisted slightly to depart, but he remained, feet rooted. Brian continued idly, as if musing aloud, "I'll even offer to indemnify them against a lawsuit. Not that I think they'll be all that nervous. After all, as I'm sure your lawyer can tell you, in a libel suit the truth is an excellent defense. I realize that as Harriet's son it may be hard for you to appreciate this nicety, but my story is actually the truth. Well, perhaps 'truth' is too grand a word. But at least my story is factual. Not only factual. It qualifies as evidence. I've got Julie here to confirm every word I write about Richard Klein, the fascinating mentor of the great auteur, Jeff Mark."

Jeff's torso remained committed to departure, but his eyes slipped back, like a hawk seeking prey, to fix on Julie. Brian's eyes went to her too. "Right, Julie?" Brian prompted when her reverie went on too long.

"You're wrong, Brian," she informed him, having had time to think it through.

"What?" Brian looked as if she'd stuck a knife in his back. Jeff smirked.

Julie said to Brian. "It wasn't overkill of Jeff to offer bribes and also make up that Klein is gaga." She looked up at Jeff. "You wanted to give me a way to rationalize taking a payoff to cover up for a sexual monster. I could take your bribe and kid myself I wasn't doing anything really bad. That was a clever psychological ploy."

Jeff's face fell. A busboy and waiter had hurried over to say "Sir?" in an anxious chorus. Jeff waved them away.

Brian said, "If you're going to take your paddled behind out of here, don't forget your pillow. And send my best to Miss Katherine Stern next time you see her."

Jeff staggered, a hand steadying himself on the chair. "Oh shit," he said.

"Why don't you sit down, Jeff?" Brian said. "Nice and easy, of course."

"You wouldn't," he whispered through gritted teeth.

"Why not?" Brian snapped at him. "Why the fuck not? If you sue me for slander, then it'll all come out. Every sordid detail."

Jeff straightened, face flushed. "Do what you want. You want to destroy my marriage, humiliate my children, go ahead. You want all my shit and all your shit to come out, fine. I'll find out what's up with you, a fifty-year-old bachelor. You want us both to be national jokes, go right the fuck ahead." He picked up his suede pillow and left.

Brian blinked. He watched his old friend disappear and blinked again.

"Brian." Julie tried to make her voice gentle, but she was angry and getting angrier. They had agreed that when it came to Jeff and his cover-up for Klein and Rydel they would be partners, not keep secrets. But he had kept something about Jeff from her. "Brian, you have to tell me right now what that was all about."

"I thought I had him." He lowered his head. "I thought I had him," he repeated, heartbroken.

Mother's Helper

— April 1966 —

JEFF STUCK HIS head out his front door, letting it close against his neck, a decapitation.

No one waiting for the elevator. No echoes from the stairs.

He retracted like a turtle, a Ked wedged to keep the door ajar. He turned the Fox bolts so the door won't shut behind him. Now GO!

Runs at top speed. Past dark elevator porthole. Around stairwell to incinerator chute. Jerks black handle down, tosses in yucky Jockeys, and releases. He spins a one eighty, skids on black and white tiles. BANG! *Chute closes as he passes barred window, black bannister, gray steps, tiles again, porthole again, front door propped by Fox lock looms, shoulder into door,* BOOM! *Shut and lock. Home free.*

"Jeff!" She sounded like the parrot in *Treasure Island.* His mother's beak grew, squawking down the hall until it found him. "You just go out and come back in? Where are you? Come here."

He didn't answer, walked slowly toward her bedroom, Keds toe to Keds heel, contemplating the paradox of February 29. Billy Zucker doesn't have a birthday three years out of four. Sure, his dumb parents celebrate anyway on the twenty-eighth, but that's cheating. Like Mom said: "He's really just two years old. And he acts like it." A two-year-old in fourth grade. Crazy. What if everyone except for people born on February 29 disappeared on the twenty-ninth? What if, to make up for not having a birthday for three years, for twenty-four hours on the twenty-ninth they got to have the world to themselves? So boss!

"Jeffrey, don't play games. Get in here. Don't make me get out of bed. I'm in agony."

No school, no parents, no stupid grown-ups: leap year kids could have a great birthday with everyone else gone for a day. Yeah, but no friends to have fun with.

"What is it?" he asked as he crucified himself in his mother's doorframe. He was like Samson chained to the temple columns in *The Illustrated Bible.* He could pull down the pillars. *Mom would die, smelly Mrs. Greenblatt, and the ugly little dog in 2A too.*

"I'm telling you to clean your room today, no arguments, move that castle or whatever it is you and Brian built and put it in your closet—"

"It won't fit in the closet!" Jeff shrieked.

"Then take it apart neatly or Hattie will have to break it up. She has to vacuum your floor. It's like the Sahara of dust in there."

"How do you know that?" Jeff asked. "You haven't been in my room since the Cretaceous period." He had learned that phrase at the Museum of Natural History when he visited with Cousin Richard—the only good thing about that day—and used it whenever possible.

"I went in there just now and nearly choked to death," his mother said. "What is that thing you and Brian built supposed to be?" She was wearing her neck brace today. The cream-colored hard plastic rested on her shoulders, covering her bosom, ending right up against her chin, where it pinched some loose neck skin. She looked like a weirdo version of an armored knight. When she wore her neck brace, she was in an even worse mood than usual.

"It's Alpha Centauri, an Earth colony in outer space."

"Was it his idea?"

"My idea," Jeff said. It was both their ideas, but he was tired of his mother's always telling him Brian is so bright. "I rolled a paper into a cone around the magnifying glass Dad brought me from the store. Looking through my magnifier-telescope, you can skim over the blocks and LEGOs. They get big and strange, just like another planet." A civilization, Brian kept bugging him to call it since that was their idea, to build a better civilization on another planet because Earth had been destroyed in a nuclear war. Brian was right, but annoying. "Civilization. Another civilization," he repeated to his mother, hoping that might convince her to spare it. They needed a name for their civilization, he kept telling Brian; calling it civilization was dumb.

"Put as much of it in the closet as you can. And put back the things you took from the kitchen. You can rebuild it with Brian when he comes over. He's coming over today, right? You told me he's keeping you company today."

Instead of speaking the lie, Jeff nodded.

"Good. Cousin Richard said he would take you both out to lunch when he stops by. He was very disappointed Bri didn't come to the museum after he went to all that trouble to arrange a special tour."

Defeated, Jeff walked to his room, moving slowly, the slowest ever, intent on making sure that he placed heel to toe with no space at all, a line of Keds. He didn't look up until he could see Alpha Centauri. The wooden blocks, LEGOs, frying pan, Heinz baked beans cans, and Matchbox cars looked pretty good even without squinting through the paper cone and magnifying glass. Best thing they'd built so far. He was very sad to destroy it. He felt like crying, but he wasn't a cry baby.

He decided he wouldn't destroy Alpha himself. Maybe he'd leave that to Hattie. This was a terrible, bad, really bad thing. No way he and Brian could ever put it back together and make it look so good. If only he could take a photograph. No! A Polaroid. Then he and Brian could rebuild later that day! Cousin Richard owned a Polaroid Land Camera. Such a boss name. Sam had used it . . .

But he didn't want to think about that anymore.

What if he owned his own Polaroid Land Camera! *Wow. Instant pictures. The way I saw it. Just now. You say I didn't. There it is. I win.*

It was itching again. He backed up against the doorknob and rubbed. That didn't reach the spot. He scratched through the denim with his hand, but even touching it that way felt really yucky.

The phone rang! This early had to be Bri. "I got it!" he shouted. GO!

Races out, past pirate's cave. "TAKE IT IN HERE!" the parrot screeches. GO top speed. Faster than fast. Skids WAY OUT WIDE from hall to living room, staggers on rug, starts to . . . FALL . . . catches dining table corner, and . . . DOESN'T!

The phone had stopped ringing. Ma must have picked up. GO!

Top speed to white kitchen phone, FLIPS receiver way UP, catches it neatly in palm. "Bri! Come up!" he yells loudly, hoping to break her nosy ears.

"Stop shouting!" Ma shouted from bedroom extension. "Brian, where did you say your father was taking you?"

"To visit my grandma in the Bronx."

"You're going to church?" she accused.

"On Wednesday?" Brian sounded confused.

"Don't Catholics have Mass on Wednesdays?"

Jeff couldn't stand this. "Bri! Come up. Alpha Centauri is in danger. We have to save her."

"Don't be ridiculous," Ma said. "So you won't be here for lunch, Brian?"

"I can't come up today," Brian said.

Jeff spoke really fast before Ma could stop him. "Bri, before you go to your grandma's come up and help me put Alpha Centauri away so we save as much of it as we possibly can, okay?"

"Good-bye, boys. Jeff, don't stay on the phone. I have to make a call." On the line, there was clatter, like dishes being stacked, his mother hanging up. Maybe. He had seen her bang the phone like that against the night table, then hold it up to her ear, listening in while his father was on the kitchen extension with Uncle Hy. So he chose his words carefully: "Ma says I have to get it off the floor so Hattie can vacuum. You have to help me take it apart neatly so we can rebuild."

There was a silence.

"Bri?"

"Is your cousin there now?"

"Just me and Mom. Dad's at the store, like always, and Ma has to go out at ten. It's not a school holiday for them." The boys had all week off, a combination of Passover and teachers' break. Already two days of the heaven of no school were gone.

Brian asked his mother for permission to come up for an hour, got it, and hung up.

Jeff opened the front door. He angled himself to see a portion of the stairs. He tried to guess which part of Brian would appear first. He decided the head.

But no. *Bri's left arm appears first, pulling him up the bannister. Just the arm. Then head. Body. Legs last*—the opposite of what you'd think!

Brian was all dressed up for a visit to his grandma in gray wool pants, white shirt, a stupid-looking tie, too long for his body. His hair was all slicked down. He looked like one of the Little Rascals.

"Mom said I can't get my clothes dirty so I can only tell you what to do," Bri said while they walked to his room. Brian called in a hello to Harriet. She stupidly asked again about why Brian was seeing his grandmother on a Wednesday.

When they reached Jeff's room, they stopped and stood and stared at their creation of wooden blocks, frying pan, two Heinz cans, LEGO buildings, Matchbox cars and plastic soldiers. It took up three-quarters of the room's floor. Brian said, "Oh! I forgot. We should call our civilization New Athens."

"Why?" Jeff demanded.

"Cause it's an Earth colony founded by America. Athens was the first democracy and it's a real democracy. All the citizens make decisions, like in Athens, no leaders. So—New Athens."

Jeff thought the name was very boring. Brian could be like that, like a teacher, no fun. "So how we gonna save it? Ma said I was allowed to put as much as we could in the closet."

Brian tried to make a Bronx cheer. Sounded more like a fart. "That won't work."

"I know," Jeff said. "We should just let Hattie destroy it."

"Wait!" Brian got excited by some idea which Jeff could tell he really liked because as he explained it he kind of hopped and flung his arms about like a spaz. Brian inspired was a goofy sight. "We could just slide this part under your bed and separate this side, put that in your closet," he said. "Then see? We'd only have to—"

"Break up the highway and park!" Jeff got it. "That's the easiest part to rebuild."

Brian was so eager he forgot his promise to his mother, got down on his fancy pants' knees, and carefully began separating a third of the wooden blocks from the rest. Jeff concentrated on making sure the frying pan, cans of beans, LEGOs buildings and Matchbox cars were completely on one side of the separation. His bed had been stripped by Hattie so they didn't have to lift blanket or sheets to clear a path to push it under the box spring. They flanked the severed section, ready to push together. "On three," Jeff said. "One, two, three . . . GO!"

Doesn't slide. Tumbles. Blocks clack hard on floor, a BIG *crash.*

"WHAT WAS THAT?" his mother shouted after the crescendo: frying pan whacking into a Heinz can, denting it badly. Jeff squinted, narrowing his vision to the *NZ* of the label and the pathetic dent.

"Fuck," Brian said. He kicked over the one tower still standing, a Heinz can surrounded by blocks, topped by a plastic soldier.

Jeff put out his hands and arched. He dove at New Athens like it was a swimming pool. He kept his eyes open until he hit. His hand plowed through most of it and broke his fall. One of the blocks caught him in the cheek. That hurt. New Athens collapsed gently around him. He rolled onto his back, a Matchbox car digging into his spine; he looked up at Brian.

Brian grinned at Jeff lying in the wreckage. "It's the end of civilization," he said, and that was so funny Jeff couldn't stop laughing the first time he tried to.

Brian said, "We'd better clean this up."

"Let Hattie do it," Jeff said, thinking that would serve Mom right because Hattie would be angry. Maybe charge extra for staying longer.

They went to the kitchen and drank Yoo-hoos. They argued about last night's *Batman and Robin* episode (Brian thought it stupider than usual; he thought it was pretty funny) until the phone rang and Ma called out that Brian had to go home.

After Bri left, Jeff went to his room to fetch the new Batman comic, which featured the Riddler. He didn't really like this issue because riddles were like school problems: no fun, just tricks to make you feel stupid. Maybe he would like it better the second time. Fetching it, he dashed in and out of his room, eyes half shut so he wouldn't have to look on the wreckage.

He settled down to read in the living room. Hattie came back from the laundry machines in the basement. She had a blue hairnet over the stiff mass of rusty brown hair that looked like it had been ironed. She stopped for a moment in the foyer with her basket of folded sheets and stared at Jeff. She seemed about to ask him something.

Did she count the underpants? That's stupid, she doesn't know how many I have. He returned her suspicious glare without any trouble: she didn't know anything. Sure enough, Hattie never said a word. She groaned, bending her round body over as best she could, picking up the laundry and heading toward the bedrooms.

He moved to the kitchen to get himself a second Yoo-hoo. That was one too many. His mouth was too sugary and his stomach got tight—he felt a round little ball inside, a Spalding pinky, like when it wasn't happy. He wanted to be in his room but didn't want to watch Hattie pick up the end of civilization. He had to keep shifting on the twine bottom of the kitchen chair because he was so itchy up in there.

He read all of the Batman again and didn't like it again.

"Your mama wants you," Hattie said in a very sad voice. He hadn't heard her come into the kitchen. She didn't look at him. She waited until he got up and walked past her, making sure he went.

Ma was going to make him put New Athens away. He had known all along that would happen, but he wanted her to have to make him. For doing it himself, he could get something out of her.

His mother was sitting up at the foot of the bed, not on the side like usual. Her back, neck, and head were thrust straight up by the neck brace. She was staring in his direction but not at him, as if he were invisible. Then he noticed his fitted bottom bedsheet was on her lap, folded up like a flag.

For the rest of his life Jeff could recall perfectly the still image of his mother in this pose. At first, he was baffled by why she was holding his bedsheet. He also remembered this sensation for the rest of his life, a spooky lack of unawareness of danger at the very height of being in danger. "What do you want, Ma?"

She unfolded his bedsheet. There were three pale, round red stains and a fourth paler, thinner, just a streak. "Jeff . . ." she began in a quiet voice, unlike herself, and unlike herself she didn't go on. He had not noticed the stains when he woke up and immediately wondered what he could have done to hide them if he had. She lifted the bloody sheet. Underneath was a pair of his Jockeys, not the one he threw out, this one was from Monday, after his Sunday with Cousin Richard. He had rolled that into a ball and shoved it deep in the hamper because it was a little poopy. She turned it inside out, tilting it at him. Beside the brown stain there was a deeper color, a crescent of red he hadn't seen. He looked at the floor.

"Is your tushy bleeding when you go to the bathroom?" she asked.

"I don't know." One of the oak boards was two shades darker than the others. Its edge was splintered.

"Are you bleeding today?"

He shook his head. He counted seven-and-one-half floorboards until Mom's bedspread shadowed the rest.

Her voice was gentle and strangely calm. It scared him. "Go to your room, Jeffrey, take off your clothes, put on your bathrobe and bring me the underpants you're wearing."

He shook his head.

"Jeffrey, I'm not angry. If you're bleeding from your tushy, that's very serious. I have to check."

"Hattie," he mumbled.

"She's cleaning in the kitchen. She won't come back here until I call her."

His robe was on the hook in the bathroom so he undressed there. His Jockeys were clean, white and perfect. He felt more confident there was nothing really wrong as he returned to his mother's bedroom.

She had put the dirty sheets and underpants on the floor all balled up so you couldn't see the yucky parts. "Give them to me," she said.

He handed over today's Jockeys. She turned them inside out and brought them closer to her bedside lamp. Because of the neck brace she had to move her entire upper torso, moving stiffly like Frankenstein. She put them aside and returned to him.

"When did you start bleeding, Jeffy?"

He looked at her knees, following a blue vein running along one side and down her calf. He shrugged.

"Sunday? After your day with Cousin Richard?" Now she sounded like herself—angry.

"Ma, can I go now?"

She put her open hand on his cheek. He flinched, but it was a caress. Her palm lingered. He glanced up. She was all teary. He looked down at her knees. "It's okay, sweetie," she said, leaning close. The hard plastic of her brace bumped his shoulder. "I need to check your tushy," she whispered, then tugged at the robe's belt, undoing it. "Lie facedown on the bed, sweetie. I have to make sure it's stopped."

Putting his face on the scratchy afghan blanket, he smelled potatoes. She lifted his robe. The air was cool on his behind. He clenched. "It's okay, Jeffy. I'm just going to make sure you're not hurt," Ma said. Two warm hands landed on each cheek. They parted him gently. His legs shot out, knees locked, toes pointed. "Relax, honey," she said. Her hands tugged him apart. "I need to make sure you're okay." He dug the edges of his top front teeth onto the bottoms so hard they hurt. He opened his lips and champed down even harder. The edge of the scratchy afghan slid into his mouth. "Relax, sweetie. Please. I'm just going to look."

He stopped pointing his feet, unstrung his calves, bent his knees, let his belly sag. He took a deep breath of the potato blanket.

The cool air touched him there. The itchiness got worse, just for a second. He felt her lean in to look. She moved his cheeks a little up, a little down, to one side, the other. Then she let go and covered his behind with the robe. "Okay, sweetie. You can get up."

Back on his feet, he kept his head down. He tried to figure out why the blanket smelled of potatoes.

"Did Cousin Richard hurt your tushy, baby?" she asked in that weird, kind voice.

He nodded up and down, eyes focused on pale oak floorboards.

"On Sunday?"

He nodded. "Can I go?" he asked.

"In a second. At his apartment?"

He could look up now. Ma's eyes were squinting still but no longer wet. Her painted brows were in an angry line. They were above where her real eyebrows should be. He wondered whether her real eyebrows would have made a line. He nodded.

"Wasn't Sam also there?" she asked irritably.

That pushed his face back down to his toes on the oak. He nodded.

"The whole time?"

He nodded, squeezing his eyes shut. "Can I go?"

The gentle hand returned, caressing his cheek. "I love you, Jeffy."

He nodded and kept his eyes squeezed shut.

She held his chin and leaned close. She kissed his cheek so softly it was like the wind was kissing him. "No one will ever love you more," she whispered. "You're the whole world to me."

"I love you, Mommy," he whispered back, still blinded.

She let him go. "Close the door and play in your room until I call for you. Don't worry about your tushy. It'll feel better soon."

He shut his door but didn't lock it. He got started on rebuilding New Athens. Hattie hadn't vacuumed, but he was sure Ma wouldn't make him take it apart again.

All his worries fell away while he worked. Until he heard the doorbell ring and knew it was Cousin Richard. But he didn't worry about him for long because the reconstruction was going great. He was sure he could remember how to fix all of it. His confidence remained high until he did something wrong with the underpass entrance to the Hall of Government. He couldn't make a smooth circle. It kept breaking. Probably Brian would remember. He never forgot anything.

Jeff went to work on the other side, where the outer buildings were easy to do. He was almost done with them when Ma knocked and opened his door. Her neck brace was off. She was wearing a dark blue and white patterned dress she usually wore to temple. Cousin Richard was behind her, hanging back in the hallway.

"Hi, Jeffrey," Cousin Richard called. "I have to go right now, but this weekend I'll take you and Brian to a Yankees game. I can get us seats right behind home plate. Maybe get Mickey Mantle's autograph. Okay? Bye for now!" He left.

Ma stayed. She stared hard at the wooden blocks, LEGOs and Matchbox cars. One cheek twitched uncontrollably, as if only that piece of her skin were angry. "You're putting it back together," she said.

His stomach got tight and hard. Was she really going to make him take it apart again?

"Sweetie," she continued in a very angry voice, "I had a long talk with

Cousin Richard. He is very sorry he bothered you. He promised me it will never happen again. He's going to make it up to you."

He thought about the Land Camera. If he had had one today, he would be able to fix New Athens all by himself.

"And that . . ." She paused for a second, then went on. "That Sam, he won't come here anymore. You will never have to see Sam again."

He nodded. That was really good news.

"From now on, sweetie, I'll tell you the day before Cousin Richard wants to visit you. And when Cousin Richard is going to be coming over, I want you to make sure Brian will be here. The whole time. Okay?"

He pushed the Matchbox English taxi down a ramp. It skidded, got stuck. "Brian doesn't like Cousin Richard," he said.

"That's not your problem," she snapped. She was back to normal, annoyed at him. "Promise me you'll make sure Brian is here when Cousin Richard comes."

He nodded.

"Say it out loud. I really want you to promise me that you'll make sure Brian is here when Cousin Richard comes over."

"I promise," he said. Then she left him alone.

Jeff tried to repair the central tower, but Hattie had taken the tin pan and Heinz baked beans cans back to the kitchen. Anyway, it made more sense to wait for Brian's help tomorrow. Together they could make it right.

Cleaning Up

—— February 2008 ——

THE BATHROOM HAD been swept. Still needed to be vacuumed to make sure every shard of glass had been cleared, and mopped to soak up every mite of makeup powder from the tile's grouting. That took only twenty minutes, so Julie continued cleaning while waiting to tell her husband she wanted a divorce. She made the bed, puffed up couch pillows, carried a half mug of caramelized coffee from Gary's study to the kitchen, left it soaking in the sink.

She decided against straightening the mess in Zack's room. She stood at the doorsill, nearly gagging at the musk of male adolescence, and chose not to cross into his swamp: crumpled boxers; soggy towels twisted into agonized abstract sculptures; T-shirts tortured, expiring inside out, sometimes housed within a similarly mangled sweater, stitching and labels exposed. Also scattered on floor, desk, and bookshelves were crumpled papers that she knew if investigated would turn out to contain a hurt teacher's complaints that Zack's paper showed little effort. Or, more painful, that he had at long last lived up to his potential and thrilled with his insight into Oedipus or the causes of the French Revolution, soon to be followed by other papers with comments lamenting that recent progress hadn't been sustained. He was as careless of praise and success as he was indifferent to advice and criticism. Gary was right about their son. He was determined to fail in order to annoy his father. Her love, her support—they counted for nothing.

That's his problem, she decided. If he wanted to live like a pig as a rebuke to her, that was his prerogative. If he wanted to squander his talents to insult his father, also his mess to make. What she had realized in these past few, tumultuous days is that she could provide an example of something much more useful than cleaning up after yourself: to be honest, no matter how painful; to be who you are, no matter how scary.

Still, the boys were astonishingly sloppy. After rinsing the coffee mug, she discovered the dishwasher was loaded sloppily, bowls upside down, all the silverware in a single compartment, and the dishes had been left overnight, food becoming encrusted. She took the worst examples out and rinsed them thoroughly before neatly stacking them back in proper positions.

And the cabinet doors! Half of them were open as if raided by starving cats. Shutting them, she spied all the items Gary insisted she keep stocked for him: pretzels and Orville Redenbacher's light-butter popcorn; in the freezer were Skinny Cow fudge bars and in the fridge no-fat Swiss Miss chocolate puddings. Gary seemed to think *no fat* meant no calories. Whenever she "forgot" to buy one of these favorite items, in the hopes of reducing his girth, he would demand restocking. Looking at his supplies, she felt pity, not the usual disgust. *Of course, he fills himself, because I can't. He's trapped in a bulimic marriage.*

Her despair over her shortcomings was so complete she didn't hear him tumble the locks, didn't realize he was home until the door shut behind him. She rushed to hallway to ask, "How's your eye?" when she saw the surrounding tissue had faded to a tinge of purple. The brilliant eye of Satan was gone, although there were still a few lightning bolts of red.

"I'm just fucking great," he said. He took off his Burberry and slung it on a hanger casually. The trench coat immediately slid off, onto the closet floor. Gary stared at it, then left it there. "We have to talk," he said before she could. He nodded at Zack's door. "Is he here?"

"No," she said.

"Good," Gary said. "Let's talk before he gets home." He announced, "I'm hungry. Is there anything to eat?"

She offered to make him a dinner out of what they had: spaghetti with clam sauce, microwave defrost and broil a steak, or a favorite impromptu meal of his, a Nova and onion omelet. He listened thoughtfully as if she were a waitress listing the specials and announced, "I'll have a PB&J."

"Let me make you a real meal," she pleaded.

He ignored her, removing chunky Skippy from a cabinet door he left open, jerking the fridge door, rattling its metal rack as he dragged out a jar of Sarabeth's strawberry preserves. He pulled apart, rather than untied, an Arnold's rye, nabbing six slices. He nodded toward the hall where he had left his computer bag. "I've got copies of the retracted statements from the Huck Finn boys. And two other statements accusing Klein the press knows nothing about." He spun the Skippy lid with a finger. It soared off the jar, crashed on the counter. He jerked open the cutlery drawer, removed a knife, and bumped it closed with his stomach. "I got them out of my source after swearing on Zack's life that they would remain private, and even that wasn't good enough until I explained about you." He plunged the knife into the peanut butter as if stabbing a villain's heart.

"Explained about me?" she repeated, appalled he had exposed her.

"Yeah, I couldn't get them to let me have copies of the sworn statements until I explained I had a personal stake in their confidentiality. To do that, I had to explain about you."

"You told somebody in the DA's office about me?" She wasn't really surprised, but she was outraged.

He pulled out the knife with an effort, bringing along a rock-sized lump of Skippy. "Not the DA's office," he said. "The state attorney general's office. They have broader powers than a DA, and that's important. They can subpoena all kinds of things a DA can't. Klein, Rydel, Jeff, or whoever can buy off witnesses, but he can't stop the state attorney general from subpoenaing documents that might lead them to more boys or families that he's bought off, and maybe, just maybe, one of them will regret having agreed to keep quiet." He tried to slide excess peanut butter off the knife back into the jar. It remained glued on.

She said, "Let me do it." He surrendered the jar and knife. "How could you tell them about me, Gary?" she asked, then proceeded to make his sandwich.

"Not *them.* I told David Sirck, the assistant AG—"

"And he's going to tell his boss, his wife, his best friend, and they'll each tell three people they trust. Jesus, Gary, I'm not that naive. I can't believe you are."

"Listen to me!" he pleaded, voice quavering. "I'm trying to help you. I really am, Jules."

"How?" she asked, genuinely puzzled. "How are you helping me?" She handed him the PB&J.

Gary took a bite, chewed thoughtfully, and then said, "Your story isn't evidence of a crime because the statute of limitations has run out on all aspects of it. Klein can't be charged. Rydel was a minor at the time, probably couldn't be charged because of that, but even if he didn't have use of the excuse that he was acting under the influence of Klein, the statute of limitations has run out on him too." He didn't finish. He added quickly, as if she were about to hurl something at him, "It shouldn't, there shouldn't be a limitation on molesting a child, but there is."

That dispelled her anger at his meddling. For Gary to say the law was wrong was unprecedented—and not convincing. Obviously he was conceding that out of consideration for her. *He still loves me?* she wondered. On second thought, she marveled at another, impossible possibility: *He feels compassion for me?*

"Does it help," she asked, "if I went public about it with some others who saw it happen?"

"Others?" He frowned. "You mean Jeff?"

She explained about Brian, including an account of their reunion, Jeff's attempt to bribe them, and the phony medical report. Gary interrupted eating his PB&J to comment, "Your friend Brian was very smart to see through that. Jeff must have gotten the idea from Rydel. Sure, since the investigation started, Rydel's been claiming Klein is suffering from severe dementia, but there was nothing about it before then—Klein was still appearing at Huck Finn and academy events. It's a typical dodge. The DA's office takes for granted any eighty-year-old accused of a crime will throw up medical excuses as to why he can't be tried."

She resumed her account, that Jeff blew them off in spite of Brian's threat to write about it, and finally that she and Brian resolved after the disastrous Four Seasons breakfast to go public anyway, to force Jeff's hand if nothing else.

Gary had finished his PB&J by then and was washing it down with Diet Coke. He swallowed. "Don't." He took another slug of soda and swallowed hard. "Don't go public yet. With or without this Brian guy, let's you and I go to Jeff and talk this through with him. Sounds to me like Brian blew it, got too angry at Jeff. Call Jeff. Tell him you and I want to meet with him."

"You'll go with me?" She was surprised by his helpfulness, until she remembered he didn't know she was divorcing him. "How's that going to change Jeff's mind about covering up for Rydel?"

"I'm a lawyer. I can scare him. I've got the suppressed sworn statements of other molestations. I know the state attorney general. I can be convincing that it's all going to come out anyway and Jeff had better fess up. Call Jeff. Tell him I have info from the state AG that he needs to know about. That'll get his attention." He crumpled the can of Diet Coke as if demonstrating his power and tossed it in the garbage.

She didn't want to threaten Jeff. She wanted him to go public voluntarily. Gary would think that naive. But she didn't want to argue with Gary. He was being sweet and chivalrous. She felt sorry for him and said the hurtful words she had to say sadly, "Gary, before you help me, there's something we really have to talk about."

"What?"

"I can't be your wife anymore."

Gary blinked. Stared. Blinked again. There was a long silence. Finally he said, "What?"

"I've been—it's so unfair to you—I'm sorry, but I just can't be married." Her legs were shaking. She leaned against the counter, she was so unsteady.

"It's not me, it's you," he mocked.

"I shouldn't be married. I'm not capable of a normal relationship."

"With me? Or with anyone?" He was cross-examining her, arguing, not listening.

But in fact, his question was clarifying for her. At that moment she understood how much she had always wanted to be married, for the lie of her life to be true. She didn't want to say, *Not with anyone.* She couldn't give up hope. Yet she couldn't say the cruel *Only you.* She had to lie to Gary even while being honest. That was the problem: she couldn't be truthful with this man. She evaded. "Gary, I've been hiding all my life and I've hurt other people by keeping quiet. I'm responsible for what happened to those children, those poor kids. I've got to deal with that. And I can't deal with it by pretending . . ." She got stuck. Pretending what?

Gary was looking at her, but he didn't seem to be focused on her. He was staring through her. "Not wanting to be married. That's about sex, isn't it?"

Was it? It couldn't be. Was her whole emotional life colored and controlled by sex? Would she be happy with Gary if only she weren't a pervert?

"You don't enjoy sex with me?" he asked.

"I don't enjoy sex with anyone," she said, relieved to not make it personal. "I'm sorry. What I did to you was awful. I shouldn't have married anyone. I've done a terrible thing to you. But I want to stop it. That's all I can do now. I can't change what I've done. But I can stop doing it." Tears dripped off her chin and jaw. She hadn't felt them release, had no sense she was crying. "You don't have to give me a penny. I don't deserve anything from you. I'm sorry. I'm a terrible person." She covered her mouth to stop the mean words.

Gary tossed his head back, throwing off a burden, and spoke in his lovely voice, the persuasive tones that had swayed juries and booked him on TV. "I don't care what you like in bed or if you don't like anything in bed, if that's what you're talking about, and I think that's what you're talking about. I love you. We can have any kind of sex you want or no sex at all. I love you, Jules. Being with you is all that matters to me."

"You don't understand," she said, pleading as she staggered backward into a chair, bending over, head in her hands. In her imagination, told what she had just told him, Gary was supposed to throw an angry self-righteous fit, to storm out or hit her. His offer that she didn't have to change at all and they would still be a couple was completely unexpected. It left her nowhere to go but to confess that she found him physically unattractive and intellectually unsympathetic. She had married what she wished she wanted, not what she wanted.

He knelt. He groaned at the effort of getting to his knees, but he went down in front of her, capturing her hands. He begged: "Let me help you, Jules. At least let me help you through this. Once we straighten this out with Jeff, I'll go into counseling with you, whatever you want. But let me help you through this."

She leaned her head on his Big Brain. Once again, her timid will was defeated. That must be what had ruined her in the first place. Klein had sensed her weakness with the intuition of a predator. Now shrewd Gary was using her fear of hurting him to get his way. She was doomed. Telling the truth or living a lie she was fated never to become herself.

The Test

—— February 2008 ——

BRIAN CALLED THE producer's office. After a long wait, Grace came on with a chilly greeting: "This is a surprise."

He didn't bother with a hello either. "I want to adapt *The Ice Pond* for Jeff. Of course I want to. It's an honor to be asked."

The line went dead. Muted? Was Jeff in the room with her? That seemed confirmed when Grace's voice, along with a background hiss, returned—her words sounded chosen for an audience other than him. "Brian, I'll be blunt. Your attitude at breakfast turned me off. I thought your being an old friend of Jeff's was an asset, but there seems to be a lot of bitterness on your side. Not on Jeff's. Frankly, he was hurt. And I was offended for him at how slighting you were about his extraordinary talent and incredible achievements. It was disrespectful."

"Jeff is the greatest director of my generation. I know that. I don't merely respect his talent—I'm in awe of it. And of course, I'm dying of envy. Believe me, Grace, it's not so easy to have a genius for your best friend as a child. Especially when you've been in the business for thirty years and he never asks you to work for him. I was hurt and I acted out. I apologize to you, and if I get the chance I'd like to tell Jeff face-to-face how flattered I am by his thinking of me at all, and how much I would like to be part of his next great film."

His abject speech was greeted by absolute silence on her end, the line dying again. Then an abrupt whoosh of background noise and Grace's voice returned, its temperature a little warmer. Without asking whether Brian was available, she said Jeff was going to drop by Brian's apartment for an hour at three to discuss the project. He said, "Great. I'll see Jeff at three."

When Brian lowered his iPhone, he saw Julie's husband looking at him with an appalled expression. "You really preferred groveling to telling her what I got from the AG?" Julie was standing beside her pompous husband. She smiled slyly. She understood the value of a plausible lie. Jeff would arrive smug, his tender white belly exposed.

They took a cab from Gary's office building to Brian's apartment. Gary and Julie waited in the lobby while he checked on Danny and how he was getting along with the day nurse Brian had hired. Yesterday the tests had come back and confirmed the doctor's preliminary diagnosis of congestive heart failure. He was also suffering from fatty liver disease. The combination meant Danny wasn't a candidate for a transplant or any other radical procedure. Drugs might keep him going for a year or so, Brian had been told. The doctor had chosen to be vaguer and more optimistic when talking to his father, offering him the solace of "a few years, nobody knows." By dinner, Danny had converted a few years into ten. The new meds, started last night, were keeping him docile and sleepy, which was good because Brian didn't much care for the dim-witted day nurse. Her shifts, and the night nurse whom he was told he would soon need, were going to eat up all of his production bonus on *Sleep of the Innocent* and a hunk of his savings. If he wanted to keep Danny out of a Medicare nursing home, he needed a job. A pity he was lying to Jeff about writing *The Ice Pond.*

Brian waited in the shadows of the awning for Jeff's limo. Its lumbering approach gave him plenty of time to prepare his move. He got a bit of luck there. The driver didn't come around to open Jeff's door; he was sufficiently self-sufficient to do that on his own. Brian hurried over before Jeff's feet appeared. "Hi, Jeff. Excuse me," he said as he climbed in, forcing Jeff to the other side. He ignored Jeff's "I thought we were meeting in your apartment."

Julie and Gary appeared from the lobby. Brian left the door open for them, shifting to the seat facing Jeff to give them room to get in.

The driver was alarmed. He lowered the partition. "Mr. Mark, is everything all right?"

Jeff looked at the trio. He didn't react except to ask his driver, "Can we park here?"

"It's No Standing, sir."

"Drive around the block and then ask me again where I want to go." Jeff raised the partition while he surveyed Julie and Gary. Gary unwound a string sealing a legal file. He produced three depositions, offering them to Jeff.

Jeff asked Brian. "What is this?"

"Just read them."

Gary was less hostile. "These are the full statements from the kids Klein and Rydel molested and raped."

"Look, I won't lie to you," Jeff said. "I've talked to my lawyer. He's made a few calls about what's going on. He says the statements are useless. They retracted them."

"Yes, but in the retracted statements they name other children whom they saw raped. The AG is looking for them. Sooner or later someone is going to testify and it will all come out. Also, as you'll see in there, Mr. Mark, your cousin is named as a participant as well. At least as of 2004, he was still healthy enough to be molesting kids."

Jeff starting reading. They completed circling the block before he had finished. Jeff ordered the driver to continue until told otherwise. When he had read the last one he said, "I don't know what you want from me."

"We're going public with what Klein did to us and what we know about Sam," Brian said.

"We want you to come forward with us," Julie said. "You know more about Klein and Sam than both of us put together."

"What we know isn't evidence of anything," Jeff insisted. "It's past the statute of limitations. Anyway, Sam was a minor. He can't be held responsible for what he did with Cousin Richard back then." He really had consulted his lawyer.

Brian began to answer, but Gary raised his hand to indicate he wanted to speak. "You know who I am?" Gary asked. "You know what I do?"

Jeff rolled his eyes. "Yeah. It's not a well-kept secret."

"The state attorney general isn't ready to close these cases. I'm going to make sure he's never ready to. You can ask your lawyer what kinds of public pressure political elected AGs are under." He fixed Jeff with a purposeful glare to make sure those words had had an effect. Satisfied by Jeff's expression, he tapped on the glass partition and signaled he wanted to be let out. As they lurched to a stop, Gary said to Jeff, "I'm an officer of the court. I'm leaving so you three can speak freely. Whatever Julie decides is what I'll do about this."

"Thank you, Gary," Brian said. Gary opened the door, saying to Julie, "I'm catching a cab home. I've got to get some sleep."

"I'll call you tonight," she said, an odd good-bye from a wife, Brian decided. And thus the childhood trio were alone for the second time in two days.

No one spoke right away. Jeff looked at Brian and kept shaking his head. "You're really an asshole," he finally pointed out. "You didn't have to lie to me about why you wanted to see me."

"Sure I did," Brian answered. "You didn't want Grace to know what we were really meeting about. Unless you've told her more than I think you have."

Jeff rubbed his face hard, as if washing all the dirt away. When he uncovered, he sighed. "Look, I don't get this. If the DA—"

"State attorney general—" Julie began.

"Whatever. If the cops are going to get them eventually, what's the point of our saying anything? Cousin Richard'll be dead soon. And Rydel's done. His school's stock is bleeding out. Huck Finn will be closed. Nobody's going to let him near kids—"

Brian slammed his hand on the leather armrest, startling Julie. "If Rydel is given any chance to slip out of this, he will! The stock can drop to zero, he's still personally richer than God from what he's taken out of it. He can buy them all off! Maybe your cousin is too fucking old to molest any kids, but Rydel's got years and the dough to ruin lots of children's lives. And that's your fault. You helped make him rich."

Jeff resumed scrubbing his face with hands. He twisted his nose all the way to one side and ended up pressing his eyes as if he trying to push them out the back of his skull. "I didn't . . ." He stopped and groaned. "I gave him ten grand in 1983, for chrissakes . . ."

"You launched that school. You spoke at the first graduation. You were on the board. You gave it legitimacy."

"I'm not proud of that any of that, but I wasn't doing it for Rydel."

Julie cried out, "Why? Why did you do anything to help Klein?"

"That's irrelevant!" Jeff said angrily. "I spoke at that school twenty-five years ago, just once, in 1983. I had nothing more to do with it after '88. I didn't know what Rydel was up to. I swear to God I had no idea what he was doing. I didn't pay any attention to either of them after 1988."

"Maybe you're as innocent as you say," Brian said, "but when Julie and I go public with our story and Gary helps the state attorney general unearth more molestations that Klein and Rydel can't buy off, no one's going to believe there's nothing to the cozy relationship between you and your cousin. People are going tsk-tsk over who gave you that early start in showbiz. Will they remember you were talented enough to have made it all on your own? I don't know, Jeff. There's nothing that cheers up Americans more than being let down by their heroes."

Jeff put the index finger of his right hand to his mouth and gnawed. All of his nails were bitten well below the rim of skin.

Julie spoke in a low, grief-stricken voice. "What happened to me . . ."

She nodded at the wheel well of the limo. "You saw my husband. He's a good man. But I'm going to have to leave him because I can't love him. He deserves to be loved." Jeff's eyes glistened as he looked out the window on his side, so darkly tinted that a ghostly reflection of him, rather than the city, filled it. "And I can't love him. I can't love anyone," she said hopelessly. Brian offered a tissue from one of three boxes in the limo—evidently the rich were often in tears. Julie dabbed at her eyes. *She's lovely in her heartbreak,* Brian thought. The nakedness of her pain was irresistible. "Klein ruined my life," she stated in a matter-of-fact tone. "Sam too. They both ruined my life," she repeated.

Brian played his last card: "Taking advantage of Klein's money and connections, that was your mother, not you. That's why you cut yourself off from his school after 1988, right? That's the year Harriet passed. Until then, you were being an obedient son by not blowing the whistle on Klein. You were still a victim. But this—protecting Klein and Rydel now—that'll be your sin. And yours alone."

"Good line for the trailer," Jeff mumbled, then put his right index finger in his mouth, chewing on the skin. He produced an indeterminate sound, a low moan or a thoughtful grunt. "I don't know," he said, not really to them. He removed his iPhone from a dark brown suede jacket, too thin for February in New York, and checked the time. "I've got to get to the test. I need to think about this and I've got this screening and I can't think about this while I'm worrying about that."

"We can't wait," Julie said firmly.

"Tomorrow," Jeff said. "Let me get through the test tonight, okay? I'll think about it tomorrow and we'll decide by tomorrow night, okay?"

"After tomorrow, Jeff, we're not going to wait for you," Julie said. She looked at Brian, a request he back her up.

"We don't hear from you by five o'clock tomorrow," Brian said, "we tell the world what we know: irrelevant, pointless, doesn't fucking matter, we tell."

Jeff nodded. "Tomorrow at five," he said.

"Okay." Brian shifted to open the door.

Jeff hooked Brian's wrist. "Stay. Come with me to the test. Okay?" He said to Julie. "I can't bring you. You're a civilian. They'd ask questions. Brian, he's there for reshoots or something." That was a lie. Jeff could bring anyone he wanted. Why did he want to separate them? Another bribe rising in the oven?

Brian looked at Julie for permission.

"You go," she said, kissing Brian on the cheek while she lay a caressing hand on his arm. It seemed like a marital farewell. "Take care of yourself," she whispered as if he were in danger alone with Jeff. Maybe he was. She opened the door. New York's car horns, a fire engine's siren and the laughter of pedestrians invaded the hush of the limousine.

"We'll decide tomorrow, Julie," Jeff said. "I promise."

She looked at him steadily, a cool survey, then slid out and onto the sidewalk without another word. When she shut the door behind her, New York left too. A tomb's hush enveloped the old boyhood friends. Jeff pressed intercom, ordering the driver, "Okay, let's go to Jersey."

As they lumbered into the traffic's flow, Brian asked, "Isn't the test later tonight?"

"Yeah, I got to check the sound and projection. No point testing it with a green tint and no bass." Jeff sighed. "You know, a year from now I'd have to make this thing in 3D? Fuck me. A comedy in 3D."

He was quiet as they slithered downtown. He became deathly still while they moved swiftly underneath the river. When daylight and Jersey appeared Jeff spoke as if they'd been talking all along: "It's funny. The Horror was always scared you'd do something like this."

"The Horror?" Brian asked, but he knew who was meant.

"Ma," Jeff said. "She read a review of your first play that said there was something in it about a child molester, and she got worried you were writing about Cousin Richard."

"Everything I write is about Klein."

Jeff shifted to face him. The weak chin, puffy pale skin, worried bug eyes at last seemed to notice Brian. "Really? I don't see that. In your films, anyway. To be honest I've only seen one of your plays."

"Yeah, in some way if you go Freudian enough, you'll find the wisdom of Klein in everything I write. He taught me my own desires can betray me. I learned from his lies, his seductions, his self-delusions, his entitlement to pleasure, and the corrosion of trust in anyone who shows me affection. Especially people who claim to love me. Worst of all Klein taught me that anyone"—Brian looked at Jeff—"even the person you love and trust the most will betray you."

Jeff's gaze wandered back into self-reflecting glass. "Really," he said.

"Yeah," Brian said. "Really."

Mother's Helper II

—— November 2008 ——

JULIE TOLD HER whole story to Amelia and succeeded in unspooling her friend's cool, sophisticated manner, the last thing she ever imagined she might accomplish. She had warned Amelia that she had something unpleasant to tell her and then began the account of her molestation and that she intended to tell the world the truth about Richard Klein and Sam Rydel. While she spoke, Amelia evolved backward from eye-lifted, capped-teeth aplomb, to gossip-hungry New Yorker, to cruise-control sympathy, to the pure shock of bewilderment, and then her earliest self, a sweet child-Amelia appeared. Face shattered, she hugged Julie too hard, squeezing her like a pain-saturated sponge she could wring dry.

Julie was amused by Amelia's ferocious empathy. She patted her soothingly, hoping that might ease her steel embrace. She tried making conversation practical, whispering into Amelia's ear, "Could you tell Suzie and maybe Cindy? They can tell everybody else." Julie extricated herself from Amelia. "I don't want any of our friends to find out from a news conference," she explained.

"Honey, we'll be there for you!" Amelia protested as if someone had denied they would. "When is this happening? Suze, Cindy, we'll all go, we'll stand beside you." Her eyebrows were inverted, beseeching. She was utterly kind, and ridiculous in her kindness.

Julie was deeply touched and had to fight not to laugh. "I don't know when we're talking to the press, Amelia. I don't know even if that's how . . ." She paused, still very uncertain whether she could wrangle two virtual strangers, both odd and difficult men, into this public act of confession. Confession? No. Accusation? Contrition? Humiliation—that's what it will feel like. "I'll let you know. I'm sorry to dump all this on you and run, but I have to go now. I need to meet Zack and tell him all about this. I don't want him learning about it on TV."

Amelia's covered her mouth. "Oh my God, of course you have to tell him," she whispered, appalled at the prospect of a mother discussing such a subject with her teenage son. She rallied to be supportive. "Zack'll be great about it. He's such a sweet young man. He'll be proud of you for speaking up." Her caretaking instinct returned: "Are you sleeping here tonight? Do you want to join Harvey and me for dinner? I'll make chicken soup, I'll make the most comforting of your comfort food, just tell me what that is. Or do you want me to ask Harvey to go out with one of the boys so we can talk?"

"I won't be staying here tonight."

"You're going home. You've told Gary," Amelia figured it out. "How was he? Was he a shit about it?"

Amelia's distrust of Gary was undiluted by what Julie had confessed. *Can't she see Gary was unfaithful to me because I couldn't give him real passion, real love?* "Gary's being great about all this." Julie changed register, to cue her friend that this next question was not as demanding as it sounded: "Is this going to be a problem for you, my working in the archives? I understand if it is . . ."

"Are you insane?" Amelia was restored to her haughtily confident self. "Darling, don't be ridiculous." She took both of Julie's hands in both of hers and squeezed. "Of course it's not a problem. You were a victim. How does that disqualify you? And you're a meticulous and brilliant archivist. I'm never letting you leave us! You're invaluable."

"Great. Because I've never really told you how much I love working there. We said it was temporary ten years ago, and I realized when I was walking over that I've never sat down and told you how much pleasure it gives me to be trusted with the sketches and diaries and personal letters. Sometimes"—and of all things, this thought filled Julie's eyes, cracked her voice—"it's like I'm with the artists while they work, that I know what they were feeling"—and now she was blubbering—"that I'm part of making all that beauty."

Amelia called out, "Oh, honey," and took her into another crushing embrace. She then proceeded to supervise Julie as if she were her daughter, insisting she fix her face before leaving, digging into her own purse and pressing her to use a mauve lipstick. "It highlights your black eyes and fair skin. I've always wanted you to put on this color, but I felt it was . . . I don't know . . . rude for me to suggest." She emitted a sigh of relief at having unburdened herself of this suppressed desire—the only kind of secret, Julie believed, that Amelia harbored.

It was not because the lipstick suited her complexion that Zack stopped in his tracks when he came out of Trinity School and saw his mother waiting for him as if he were five.

To his "What's up?" she asked where they could go for a quiet talk. He seemed agitated by that and irritably didn't make a suggestion, especially after she said she wanted to avoid any place where his friends might appear. They ended up six blocks away, in the back booth of a coffee shop new to both of them.

He fussed and tugged his locks nervously while she waited for the waitress to bring coffees and a slice of apple pie she didn't want but felt obliged to order. "This isn't about you and Dad?" he blurted before she could say a word.

"It affects us, but no," she said. Of course Zack worried they might divorce. Had any parent ever succeeded in hiding marital unhappiness from their child? Would it really be so much worse for Zack if she had kept her nerve and they were splitting up? Eventually, at least Gary would be happier with someone else. And that would be better for Zack.

"What happened? Where did you go? Dad refused to say anything. He just kept cursing and looking at his messed-up eye in the mirror and then he left." Zack scrunched up his face like a little boy trying not to cry. "I was really worried about you, Mom." He put his hand out, not on hers, but in the general direction so she would be encouraged to take it, as she did. *He is my angel, he will always be my angel,* she vowed while pressing his flesh as hard as Amelia had pressed hers.

Then let she let go and began her story. It took a while to get to the hard part. Zack knew nothing of Klein and Brian and practically nothing, other than their names, of his great-aunt Harriet and great-uncle Saul. He knew about Jeff, but the Jeffrey Mark he knew of was famous, a glittering star of today. The goofy, whiny boy with a crazy mother and dolorous father, in a dingy apartment in a working-class neighborhood was a different creature entirely. His listened distractedly, nervously sipping coffee, staring out the window, until she said Sam Rydel's name. After that he stayed on her.

It was her turn to have trouble meeting his eyes while she explained about Klein's groping her at Aunt Harriet's and, later, with Sam watching, forcing her to . . . she chickened out and let the unfinished phrase hang. Zack got very still, eyes flashing, mouth set. She decided not to tell him any more—she couldn't protect him from lurid details that might appear in the press someday, but with any luck, since she had told him this much herself, he would be merciful to himself and ignore the coverage. And she did not, as she hadn't with Brian or Gary or a shrink, not even the motherly Amelia, breathed a hint about her own odd tastes. All this honesty, after all, wasn't entirely honest. But she gave herself credit for informing Zack of the most important effect on her of the sexual abuse by concluding, "What happened has always made it difficult for me to enjoy myself as I should, as everyone should, when they make love." She wanted to look at Broadway, at the laminated menu, at her spoon, anywhere but Zack. She forced herself to. He hadn't listened so raptly to her since he was a toddler, when he would sit like a miniature king on the throne of his Maclaren stroller, demanding to know what or why or when, confident his mother had the answer.

Men are different from women. He didn't react with feeling. Like Gary, he wanted more facts. "So this happened at your parents' house? More than once?" he asked with an astonishment that to her ears was a rebuke.

She pleaded, "I was confused, I didn't know what it really—"

"No, no, I didn't mean you could have done anything." He reached for her but gave up halfway and picked up his coffee instead. Was he scared to touch her now? Was she damaged goods? He said, "I just don't understand what your parents were so busy doing. And Jeff! Jesus, I mean, he did it again in front of Jeff?"

"No, not Jeff, who was a little boy, remember. You can't expect him to have done anything about it. After the first time, only with Sam Rydel. Anyway, your grandmother and grandfather had a house full of people. He came Memorial Day, July 4, then Thanksgiving—"

Zack interrupted. "So he turned Sam Rydel into a pervert," he said with a kind of excitement at this discovery. "That's why Rydel did the same thing to the Huck Finn kids."

She winced at his labeling, the pleasure he seemed to be taking in identifying a weak and damaged person. But was Rydel weak? Maybe becoming a monster is a sign of strength.

"And why didn't your mother and father suspect anything about this weird guy showing up?"

"He wasn't weird to them. He was a success." She sighed. "People in those days didn't think it was possible that an adult would do such things—"

"WHY!" Zack half-shouted, incredulous. "After the Nazis? They didn't think ordinary people could do horrible things? Why the fuck not!" He covered his mouth. "Sorry."

"They just didn't, honey. Not in the suburbs. There were no Nazis in Riverdale." She laughed helplessly, then sighed in despair. "Me too. I didn't think it was something that happened to anybody else but me. And I felt it was up to me to deal with, that I had done something wrong, and I had to stop it. I made sure I never went to Aunt Harriet's anymore, and after Thanksgiving I made sure to be at a friend's house for the next holiday weekend barbecue. But then Klein showed up at the house with a fake dental emergency and finally I . . . I don't know why, but finally I had the nerve to risk a scene. I threw a chair at him. A folding chair." She laughed. It suddenly seemed absurd that having an object to hurl had inspired self-defense. "And I ran to my mother and I stuck myself to her like glue."

"But you still didn't tell her?"

"I never told her. I never told . . ."

"Did you think she wouldn't have believed you?"

She sighed. "Zack, you have to understand, I thought it was shameful it had happened at all. I thought I had brought it . . ." She stopped, not for discretion. She was flooded by a vivid memory of being ambushed by Klein on Thanksgiving, on her way to obey Ma's request she fetch two more seltzer spritzers from the delivery crate. He grabbed her ponytail in the pantry room off the attached garage, only one window, its shade drawn, the air stifling. He kicked the door shut behind them, turning her against the plaster wall. To this day, she could feel its coolness on the backs of her arms as Klein pressed up against her, a hand reaching down her puffy blouse to her flat eleven-year-old chest. Now in the coffee shop, a middle-aged woman with a grown son, she felt the male's warm thumb and index finger frame her nipple and squeeze, very hard, an angry pinch, a mean, invasive, entirely unpleasant sensation only . . . only it seemed to bring her child's breast to life, the first time she could remember feeling, for lack of a better word, sexy up there. Klein's fingers had mapped how to please herself there and over the years, by extrapolation, all over. In midsentence, while Zack waited patiently for her to continue, this always dimly understood revelation emerged starkly, really an admission to herself: Klein had been her introduction to pleasure; his mean-spirited act of power had been her virginal introduction to lovemaking.

"Mom, you don't have to talk about this anymore, okay? I'm glad you told me, but . . ." He bowed his head penitently. "I'm sorry, I'm really sorry all that happened to you."

His pity melted her heart. To stop tears, she looked through the dirty window at Broadway in winter, an avenue of solitary pedestrians hunched against the February chill. Her eyes burned. She squeezed them dry. She had to impress him with this next point, dangerous though it was for their relationship. "What I'm trying to tell you . . ." She looked right at him, patted the back of his hand. "What I'm trying to tell you, Zack, is that the things people do when they're young can last much longer and become something they can't get rid of or forget so easily. Of course, you're not a child. I was a child. But some of the girls you know may not be as grown up as you or they think. And what you do with them may last longer, much much longer, than you realize." This wasn't coming out right. She didn't mean to scold or scare him about sex. That was her problem. She was ashamed and frightened. No one should feel that way.

Zack didn't like her comment either. He pulled his hand free, appalled. "I don't do anything like that! Jesus, Mom, what makes you think I do anything—"

"I'm not talking about child molesting, Zack. I mean there's the body and there's the heart. What the body likes doesn't necessarily have anything to do with what the heart wants. You feel frustrated about your father and school and what you're going to do in life. You're very handsome, Zack. I know you're fifteen and you may feel some pretty odd things about yourself these days, but whatever you feel about yourself inside, on the outside you're a confident, attractive young man and young women are going to want to please you . . ." She stopped. She didn't know what she was saying. Zack's diary entry had seemed to her to be a catalog of acts of rape. In her mind, there was a rough equivalency between Klein and her son's diary, and hearing herself say it aloud she realized that was just plain crazy. He was a teenage boy bragging about getting laid, acting macho about lovemaking at just the age boys were supposed to. She reversed course: "I'm sorry. I'm not being clear. I'm implying things I don't mean at all. I'm just trying to tell you that I was hurt, very deeply hurt, by what a sick man did to me when I was young and now I've got a problem, a big problem that I don't know how I'm going to deal with, but . . ." Again, she took possession of the hand she had created. There was simply no other way she could feel about Zack, although she knew perfectly well that he would be infuriated by the notion that he belonged to her—he was her only decent, lasting achievement and therefore she ought to have control over everything he might become. "But whatever I do about it, I wanted you to know. It's a secret. It's been a secret my whole life. That day when your father fell in the bathroom, that was the very first time I told him."

She had expected this would astound Zack, and it did. He absorbed it, then nodded with satisfaction. "Wow" is all he said, his face clouding. He shifted, looked grave. "You don't have to go public about all this, Mom, if you don't want to. Let me take care of him," Zack said, his jaw set grimly.

She chuckled at his joke.

Zack's hands clenched. "I'm serious. First I'll deal with Klein. Where is he? Where does he live? Is he in New York? Don't worry, I won't hurt him, not really, but I'll scare the shit out of him." Zack tapped his fists, looking as ferocious as possible for a beardless, wide-eyed boy with tumbling locks of chestnut hair and cherry red lips.

How silly. And how wonderful. A lightness buoyed her above every sad thing. Her bones were glad. Her soul was singing. She smiled her delight.

Zack was insulted. "I'm really serious!" He shook his fists, becoming the fighter he never was in the sandboxes of Riverside Park.

She tried to suppress this ridiculous happiness. She covered her angel's hand, saying as solemnly as she could, although a little laugh of delight escaped anyway, "I know you are, honey. And I'm"—she thought this a peculiar feeling, but admitted it—"flattered. You honor me. But Klein is eighty-four, probably very frail. Anyway, the law can deal with him and Rydel much more harshly than you can." She stood up, towing her son by the hand to his feet, as if they were going to dance, and she did take him into her arms, or rather at his greater height he took her into his, and she pulled his head and its thick hair down, to whisper into his perfect ear, "Thank you. You don't have to rescue me, Zack. You already have."

The Artist's Muse

—— February 2008 ——

BRIAN WATCHED THE audience enter. Nearly every man, woman, and teenager cradled an enormous bucket of artificially buttered popcorn next to their heart, to leave their hands free for a complimentary container of soda the size of a small dug well. They were dressed in hideous casual clothes: sneakers puffed up with extra layers of rubber as if their owners were racing cars; T-shirts and sweatshirts emblazoned with ads for their manufacturers; pants with pockets big enough to swallow Job. And their various manifestations of hair, including its shaved absence on young men who would have full heads, were grotesque. Locks were purple, orange, fluorescent red, white blond, and opaque black, then sprayed to sky-scraper heights, or swirled and teased to cover baldness. No one looked the way nature had made them. *Thank God for that anyway,* Brian thought. *Without their tasteless fashions, they would have been merely ugly.*

Was it his work in the film business, surrounded by exceptionally beautiful men and women who labored day and night to sustain and improve their lovely outsides, that made the civilians seem so revolting? Had he lost the capacity to gauge normal?

He decided yes, felt cheered by this exposure to the average. After decades of spending time with dazzling movie stars and surgery-enhanced executives, Brian had been beaten down into thinking of himself as very plain. In fact, the overwhelming majority were like him: so generously endowed with ungainly features that the odd good one seemed to be a flaw. Like him, everyone was all only a few weeks of gluttony away from sickly puffiness, only months of snacking from becoming a swollen bag of mottled flesh.

"Scary, huh?" Jeff's voice cooed in his ear without preamble, startling him. "Can you believe we work our asses off for these bozos?"

Brian turned away from the mob to study his old friend. He noted that if Jeff didn't have a slight tan, if he weren't draped in cashmere, if his glasses (and why was he suddenly wearing glasses?) weren't so nerdishly hip, Jeff would look as ordinary as his fans. "But, Jeff," he said, "I read in your *New Yorker* profile that you're just one of them, that your movies are so popular because really you're the same person today as that little boy who went to Saturday matinees and couldn't figure out how Buck Rogers was going to escape next week."

Instead of Jeff's objecting that he would be a fool, worse a criminally negligent member of the Academy of Motion Pictures Arts and Sciences, if he told the truth about how he felt toward his audience in an interview, he nodded at a particularly imbecilic couple. The man was in his thirties, receding hair slicked up, as if he were an Apache warrior who had suffered a bad scare, black leather motorcycle jacket over a white T-shirt with an arrow, labeled THE MAN, pointing up to his face and an arrow pointing the opposite direction below labeled THE LEGEND, presumably intending to indicate the crotch of his jeans, only the arrow was intercepted by his inflated belly so the myth seemed to refer to his eating prowess. His companion for the evening was a bloated woman with blotchy, freckled skin. Her huge braless breasts were prevented from reaching her waist by a tube top whose orange color could not be found in nature. The rest of her quivered like Jell-O inside skin tight stretch pants.

"Check out that pair," Jeff said. "If I hadn't made it in the biz, I'd look like him and I'd definitely be married to her. And you know what's worse? As him, I'd have more to say about what's in today's movies than as a director."

"You're so full of shit," Brian said amiably. "You don't need them. They need you. You're the highlight of their year."

"I'm their slave, Bri. My last two movies have flopped. I'm one bomb away from becoming the studio's bitch."

Brian made a sour face to discourage his friend from continuing this nonsense. Was this why Jeff had insisted Brian come? To feel sorry for the poor A-list director forced to pander? "Come on. You've made billions for the studios. They'll let you flop at least five more times."

"No more. Industry's being squeezed by piracy, by streaming, most of all by video games. These days three strikes and you're out. This picture tanks, they'll take away my Get Out of Studio Notes Free card. You watch. If this mob tonight doesn't like my ending, I'll have to change it."

"Bullshit," Brian said with a smile.

"It's not bullshit. Sure, I could insist on the integrity of my ending, but I'd have to put everything on the line. Threaten to go public. To preserve a farcical ending in a broad comedy I'd have to risk a lifetime's worth of capital." Jeff snorted. "Integrity. What a fucking joke. Who am I kidding? I'm popcorn."

"Even popcorn," Brian said, "can have integrity."

"How can popcorn have integrity?"

"It can have the integrity of being good popcorn."

Jeff grunted. He nudged Brian with his shoulder. "Before they give me the Cards find me." "The Cards" referred to the most unsettling aspect of the test preview. After the movie ended, the audience would be handed index cards, sometimes a sheet of paper, with multiple-choice questions. Did they think the movie was Excellent, Very Good, Good, Fair, or Poor? Would they Definitely Recommend, Recommend, or Not Recommend to friends? And at bottom, most perilous of all for the director, were a few blank lines for them to scrawl what they wished could be changed about the picture. "You find me," Jeff said, "and tell me the fucking truth before the hyenas hit me with the numbers. So I got something to hang on to while they flay me alive. Okay, buddy? Promise? If my ending sucks, tell me. I don't want to defend the Alamo over nothing."

Tell me the fucking truth, Brian repeated to himself while he was ushered to a seat by an assistant Jeff signaled. *Tell me the fucking truth,* Jeff had begged, and as the lights came down he wondered whether he should. What if Brian thought Jeff's movie to be ghastly and told him so? How would that affect Jeff's weighing whether or not to reveal to the world that a man who had paid for Jeff's film schooling, perhaps gave him a leg up in the business, had also molested him as a child? Or that Jeff had been on the board of a company that had enriched two men accused of multiple sex crimes? And was that the worst of what would come out? Maybe Jeff had conspired with Sam Rydel to suppress the testimony of his victims. Gary said that fake medical report mirrored what Rydel was claiming to the DA about Klein's condition. Had it originated with Jeff? It was put together awfully fast. Maybe Rydel had given it to him. The reality is that he couldn't trust Jeff, so should Brian be ruthlessly honest when he needed Jeff to cooperate with finally striking a real blow in the real world for real truth, real justice, and the actual American way?

No. Brian decided no matter how awful the picture, he would tell his friend, as he was sure all of Jeff's associates did, that the movie was brilliant, the ending perfection.

Good thing Brian had decided to lie before the movie started. During the first hour, he distracted himself from its awfulness by preparing phrases of false praise. He hated the first hour so intensely that at one point he thought the swelling of loathing in his chest cavity might stop his heart. He had to restlessly shift in his chair in a vain attempt to avert his face from the blaring chaos, presented in a slow-paced, flat tone with great self-confidence as if the filmmaker were convinced that what is grotesque is funny if you also make it very dull. His head began to throb from the cranked-up sound track that pushed each overacted, slapstick calamity to be as loud as the bombing of Dresden. He winced at the parade of beautiful actors squeezed into grotesque costumes and made up like clowns—again as if exaggeration and comedy were synonyms.

Then, abruptly, in the second hour Jeff calmed his film down. He elaborated a thin and rather strange love story that had seemed a throwaway in the first half. In keeping with the picture's overall style, the lovers were a grotesque physical contrast. The boy was played by the once adorable child actor Billy Frederick, who had evolved into a thin and, in other films, appealing adolescent. In Jeff's hands, he became concentration-camp skinny, outfitted with contacts to simulate walleyes, wearing a prosthesis to sport a pair of chipmunk buck teeth. The look was reminiscent of an old Jerry Lewis character, a boyhood favorite of Jeff's. During the bombardment of the first hour, Brian had assumed it was intended as a wry homage to Lewis, but then an offbeat love story developed between the buck-toothed, walleyed skin-and-bones teenager and a very WASPy, innocent, and clumsy Veronica Stillman, cast as a nerdy scientist. Jeff's personal inspiration for this plot became clear to Brian when the mother of the buck-toothed boy, played by the comic actress Charlene Boxer in an immobilizing fat suit and makeup that simulated four double chins, learns of her son's crush on Veronica. Enraged, Boxer proceeds to whack him repeatedly on his ass with a hot waffle iron kept beside her chaise longue, from which she never rose during the course of the film. After she spanked her son, Brian realized the preposterous mother was a portrait of Harriet, and the hideously unappealing young man was disguised autobiography.

So Jeff saw himself as a vulnerable and awkward teenager, yearning for love and nurture. Since he had grown into a balding, self-satisfied, wealthy, middle-aged man, the connection probably would escape others, but to Brian it wasn't far-fetched. The walleyed, whiny, lonely, skinny boy on that screen was no doubt exactly how Jeff had felt and still felt about himself.

Brian wondered about why Jeff's character loved Veronica the scientist.

Did Jeff mean her to represent filmmaking with her technical expertise, her emotional simplicity, her ability to find Alien bones? (The plot—don't ask.) The picture evolved into shameless sentimentality about the geeky teenager's love for Veronica, building to a climax as the mother's opposition becomes murderous. She enters into a conspiracy with an Alien, played by Chris Zaban with his usual frenetic bombast. Zaban's Alien needs to consume young female organs to survive. He has come to earth in disguise as an advertising executive for TV. The evil mother decides to thwart her son's planned union with Veronica by offering his true love to the Alien as a midnight snack.

Just how block-headed am I? Brian wondered when it took him until ten minutes from the end to realize this was a portrait of Jeff's life with his mother and Cousin Richard. Perhaps it was based on a particular trauma in his teenage years, something that had happened after their friendship ended. Jeff wasn't merely obsessed with entertaining a huge audience. Like Aries Wallinski, like a real artist, he was trying to get at personal truth, to organize and illuminate life as he understood it. Maybe, as Brian leaned forward, thoroughly absorbed by wondering how the story would end, maybe Jeff, like Aries, wanted to heal.

Not surprisingly, the slower, more human storytelling of the second half engaged the audience. No longer stupefied by deafening special effects, they began to laugh, louder and longer, at a few verbal jokes about the evil mother's motivations and the awkward son's wooing. Not Oscar Wilde, to be sure, but they were genuine witticisms about the characters.

At the climax, loud special effects in the style of its unworthy first hour returned, but now Brian was emotionally invested in the action. His chest constricted and sweat broke out on his forehead as the monstrous mother filled the screen. Jeff had him now. He was awed and terrified by the unleashing of his friend's soul. All around him the audience guffawed while the mother was mistakenly consumed by the Alien because her son had miniaturized her and stuffed her into a giant box of human-flavored popcorn. (Again, don't ask about the plot's logic.) And while she was hoisted by her own petard, eaten alive by the same monster whom she had planned to feed her son's lover to, the climactic lines of the picture were shouted by her geeky son in an extreme close-up, provoking hysterical laughter in nearly every seat. "My mother's a monster," the teenager announced. "She's in the popcorn and you just ate her alive!" The Alien, who can only survive on a young female's reproductive organs, is poisoned by those of a menopausal human female. He dies while mumbling in agony, "I can't believe I ate his whole mother."

The audience loved this portrait of Jeff's mother, the monster in the popcorn, and they ate her alive with gusto. Brian didn't rise from his seat when the movie ended; around him the audience was harassed by marketing assistants: "Please fill out the cards we gave you when you came in and hand them to one of the people standing by the exits on your way out. Thank you for taking the time to give us your reaction."

Brian was stunned. No, the picture wasn't great. Probably wasn't good at all. Probably wasn't even first-rate entertainment. But it was art. Jeff had found his way through the gloom of the past—unlike Klein, unlike Sam, unlike, he feared, Julie. Jeff had learned the wisdom of perversity and made his lonely secret into art.

Jeff arrived with a lurch, past hovering studio executives and Grace, to stumble into the seat next to Brian. "I'll be in the lobby in a sec," he said to a man Brian recognized as the studio president of production. "Just want to get Brian's reaction. Fresh eyes," he explained. The studio head squinted at Brian, then shrugged and left.

They waited in silence for the audience to exit, the all-important taste makers climbing up the sloping aisle with their postcard verdicts. Several peered at Jeff and Brian, who had made themselves noticeable as the only two who lingered. One woman called to Jeff, "Awesome, Mr. Mark. The movie's awesome!"

"Thank you," Jeff said, then turned his back to the aisle until they were all gone.

"All clear," Brian reported.

Jeff still spoke in a whisper: "The truth. Remember? You promised. Is the ending worth fighting for?"

"They want you to change it?" Brian was amazed in spite of knowing better from experience. It was always the most striking scene, the best work, the most disturbing emotion and unsettling idea that attracts criticism.

"The studio thinks it's too dark."

"It's absurd, not dark."

"Absurd?" Jeff blanched. "You think it's ridiculous?"

"Sorry. Absurdist. Not absurd."

"Oh." Jeff nodded.

"Anyway, you have nothing to worry about. The audience loved it. They won't ask you to change it now."

"Yes, they will. The studio thinks the audience'll like it even better if the mother survives and apologizes to her son for all the bad things she's done."

"What?" This hurt Brian's brain. They were attacking the only thing in the film worth preserving. Worse, the suggested change was neither funny nor believable.

"The studio thinks we won't get a PG-13 rating if the mother dies."

"What?" Brian was confused by the introduction of the laughable Motion Picture Association's rating system.

"An R rating would cost us at least thirty million," Jeff explained.

"Really?" Brian was astonished.

"You don't know that?" Jeff in turn was shocked that Brian could be ignorant of this basic tenet of his own trade. "In the five top-grossing movies of all time, there are no Rs," Jeff said, reciting a cherished statistic.

"Don't you have your rating yet?" Brian asked.

"It's an R with this ending and with"—Jeff lowered his eyes, as shy as a bride—"the waffle iron stuff. The spanking has to go too. The board thinks it's too intense for children to have a mother hitting her child and then show the child murder her."

"He doesn't murder—"

Jeff anticipated Brian's objection. "What he does leads to her being killed. That's bad enough."

Brian stared off at the dizzying rows of raked empty seats. It went without saying that to remove the spanking and the killing of the mother would mean the film was destroyed for Jeff. For a moment, they sat side by side, air redolent of artificial butter. The feeling of being in a deserted theater with Jeff worrying over how they would impress the world felt familiar, but he couldn't place it exactly. The eeriness of that dislocated memory shook his resolve. Did he really have the right to urge Jeff to put his extraordinary access to the population of the earth in jeopardy? He had forgiven victim-rapist Aries for the sake of his art. Wasn't it unjust to treat Jeff, solely a victim, more harshly? No matter how much harm Klein and Rydel had done, hadn't Jeff created much more good?

Grace entered from the lobby. She kept her back against the door, speaking from twenty rows away like a telegram. "Jeff. The prez wants you. He's freaking. Thinks you're dissing him."

Jeff stood. He shook himself like a wet dog. He put a hand on Brian's shoulder and squeezed. "What do I do?"

Brian didn't want to say.

Jeff grinned. "Don't look so worried. Just tell me your opinion. Doesn't mean I'll do it."

"The ending is beautiful, Jeff," Brian said, telling exactly how he felt. "Teenagers'll love it. And young parents'll love it and they'll buy the DVD for their kids and the kids will love it because kids are not the cute, soft-hearted blank slates adults think they are. Kids know the world is full of grotesque and mean grown-ups, and they'll be very glad to see a monster they know well die and see one of their own find happiness. Stand your ground. The studio'll thank you when it grosses a billion dollars."

Jeff squeezed Brian's shoulder again. Brian forced himself to ignore the impulse to shrug off the hand. Instead he grabbed him by the wrist and demanded, "What are you going to do about Klein and Rydel?"

"Tomorrow—" Jeff began.

"Don't give me tomorrow. You know what you're going to do."

Grace, still twenty rows away, shook her fist, presumably trying to look threatening. "Jeff! They're waiting."

"Go away, Grace. Go"—he paused for effect—"away."

She thought for a moment about arguing. Then she left.

Jeff pulled his wrist free. "What's the point of our going public, Bri? It's too late and it's not proof of anything they did to those Huck Finn kids. We're just gonna look like kooks and somehow we'll come off sounding like accomplices. Especially me. Let's be honest about this. I'm the one who's gonna get hurt because Cousin Richard made me speak at his school."

"Made you? Come on. He didn't make you do that."

"Until I got my first gig, he paid for everything! Dad's stupid store, their retirement house in Florida, my schooling. I couldn't say no to going on the board and speaking and all that bullshit."

"To Harriet!" Brian shouted, losing patience. "You couldn't say no to your mom. As soon as she was dead you stopped. You already admitted that to Julie, or did you forget? You didn't deny that was the reason when I said it in your limo."

Jeff sighed. "Yeah," he mumbled. "I did it for Ma."

"So why couldn't you say no to Harriet? Why didn't you tell her what Klein had done?" Brian had been waiting to ask this. No, not waiting. He had been afraid to hear the answer to this question.

Jeff met his eyes. They were in pain, old, exhausted pain. They told Brian what he had suspected was right. He stood, as if the truth had ejected him from his seat. "She knew," he answered for Jeff. "Harriet knew. And she was blackmailing him. Right? That's why Klein paid for everything. You couldn't refuse to help him while she was alive because you were keeping up your mother's bargain with the devil."

Jeff's voice cracked as he pleaded, "What was I supposed to do, Bri? Turn my mother in? Huh? What was I supposed to do?" Tears welled in his eyes. He shook his head angrily and they subsided. "I didn't know what Rydel was up to. I'm not lying about that. It was Cousin Richard I was worried about. I should have done something about him, okay, okay. And you too! You should have done something," he accused Brian, but then abruptly let that go with a sigh. "But we don't have any evidence that'll hurt them, Bri. We really don't. We'll just make a spectacle of ourselves for nothing."

"We have you, Jeff. Your talking will encourage others to come forward. You're rich. You're famous. You're beloved. That makes you credible. If you stand up and say what Klein did to you, others will come forward and that will finish both of them."

"Rydel'll buy them off. He's got more than enough to buy them all off." Jeff retreated two steps up the raked theater aisle, regaining the high ground on Brian.

"If you speak up, one of the victims will refuse to be silenced by money or anything else."

The president of production banged the theater door open, entering in a huff. "Mr. Mark! We're trying to figure out how to make you even richer than you already are. Care to join us?"

Jeff held up a finger, silently demanding another minute. It was an impressive proof of his movie-business power that the studio head caved. "Keep me waiting one fucking minute more and I'm shooting a new ending myself!" he said, barging back out to the lobby.

Jeff shut his eyes, communing with his exasperation at studio interference before resuming, "Look, Bri, be fair about this. You don't have a wife and four kids. Halley doesn't know a fucking thing about any of this. I can't just call a news conference and dump it all on her and the children."

Brian smirked, "Ah, the new Hollywood cliché: you're only protecting your family. Okay, you want a third-act socko realization, Mr. Jeff, here it is: You've become your mother. You just admitted that she knew about Klein. That she blackmailed him. But that wasn't the worst of it. It's only taken me twenty years to be certain, but I suspected, for years I suspected. You kept inviting me up, lying to me about whether Klein was in your apartment. You did it again and again, and each time you disappeared, leaving me alone with him."

"He made me lie to you—"

"Bullshit!" Brian yelled over him. "She made you pimp me out to him, right? Come on, say it! You pimped me to him."

Jeff's mouth opened to protest, weak chin disappearing entirely, but he made no sound.

Brian closed on him, nose-to-nose, as befitted payoff dialogue. "Okay, you were a kid, a scared kid with a monster for a mother. But protecting Klein and Rydel for the sake of your reputation—you're the monster now."

There's your exit line, Brian told himself as he walked away, up the aisle.

He had reached the doors when Jeff yelled after him, "That's a disgusting thing to say. And it's a lie. It's a fucking lie. I didn't pimp you out."

"It's not a fucking lie!" Brian lost control. He turned and charged down the aisle's slope. Jeff cowered against a seat back, averting his face from the spittle of Brian's rage. "She sacrificed me to make you a star! And it cost me. I would have been a great artist except for what you let him do to me."

Brian shut himself up. He was near tears for one thing, which was humiliating. For another, he was astonished by what he had just said. That his talent had been damaged by Klein had never come into his head before. Was he sitting on that feeling all these years? For someone who considered himself analyzed—rinse, repeat, analyzed—a self-discovery this basic was stunning.

"What . . . ?" Jeff shared Brian's amazement. He remained tilted against the theater seat as if Brian were about to strike him, but he wasn't afraid, he was flabbergasted. "What are you talking about? What has this got to do with your career?"

"Not my career, you fucking idiot! I'm not talking about money and fame," Brian said. "I'm talking about being emotionally crippled. I can't write about love and trust and marriage and having kids. I don't know what most of the world feels . . ." Brian was trembling, flooded by his terrible discovery. "I can't be what I should be, what I was supposed to be, what I want to be. I've worked so hard at it, Jeff. Art was my salvation and I can't do it right, I can't get it right because your fucking mother took the real me from me—and you helped her, you helped her steal my soul." He staggered to an empty seat and fell into it, covering his wet eyes.

He waited for Jeff to come to him, to console or to argue, to justify or to apologize. He heard the lobby door open and whoosh shut. When he looked up to see who had entered to interrupt them, Jeff was gone. Brian was the only member of the audience left.

The Past Recaptured

— February 2008 —

JULIE BLURTED OUT, "Are you gay?" and immediately regretted it. "Sorry. I'm being very rude."

"Rude? Wow. A New Yorker worried about being rude." Brian rose from his desk, a slab of gray slate atop cast-iron legs outfitted with wheels that looked cannibalized from an old sewing machine. She admired his high-tech worktable: no surface to scar, no drawer for secrets. Brian shut his study's door, presumably to keep this conversation private from his father, although he had said on her arrival that Danny Moran was already sound asleep.

Brian didn't return to his space-age mesh desk chair. He moved to the couch he had assured her was a pullout and could accommodate her for tonight's vigil, waiting out Jeff's decision. It was almost midnight. They had given Jeff until tomorrow at five.

Julie sat patiently in a wing chair directly across from the couch while Brian settled himself, took his time answering. "Anyway, aren't we way past the discretion vis-à-vis matters of a sexual kind? What I do in private will soon become a public matter, right? I assume that's why you're asking: not if I'm gay but if I'm something else, something Klein can use on me?"

"No!" Julie was horrified. "That never occurred to me. I just wanted to know." She didn't have the courage to say why; then she did: "I want to know you. The real you."

"The real me. I wonder if he exists. Fair enough," he said. He looked up at the ceiling. Searching for what? Was he going to make up something?

During that pause, his earlier comment registered. She interrupted his musing. "You really think Klein will try to find some dirt on us?"

"Or Rydel," Brian told the ceiling. "If Jeff doesn't join us. Jeff would scare them. They'd make a plea, settle, whatever they have to do to preserve as much of their freedom and fortune as possible. But just you and me, two small fry whining about ancient history? Yeah, there'll be a counterattack. If they could smear us, it would cast doubt on our accusations. So I guess it makes sense to warn you what they might find out about me." He uncrossed his legs, bowed his head penitently, staring at his Persian rug. "I've never told anyone other than shrinks . . . and"—there was the flicker of a smile—"the other professionals who help me." He took a deep breath and exhaled tension. "Okay. Here goes."

Thrilled, she remained very still, not wanting to disturb his progress. In their two intense meetings, and a half-dozen long, intimate phone calls, she had grown very fond of him, his dry, embittered humor, his fussy manners and restricted diet, his persistent gloom and gentleness in everything he did, like Eeyore. He could well be the first man she had ever truly made friends with, and he knew everything about her—except the one thing no one knew and that she didn't believe a thousand of Klein and Rydel's private eyes could discover.

Brian told his secret to the rug. "I'm not gay. Everyone thinks I must be. Fifty years old and never married. Never lived with a woman or a man or even a dog. Had a cat once. Never really coaxed him from under the bed. Didn't really want to. But I'm not gay. I'm a pervert." He looked up to check her reaction. She froze, to control the thrill of hearing it. That sent his eyes away, to the room's pair of windows, glass black from the overcast night and shimmering from a light snowfall that melted on contact. Waiting for him to elaborate was unbearably suspenseful. He cleared his throat and continued in a strong voice, "I guess I'm a heterosexual pervert, if you want to be technical about it. 'What does that really mean?' you're wondering. In my case, it means the only sex I like is to remain fully dressed while I watch a woman I have paid strip, someone whose behavior I can trust because it's a business transaction, someone I have no emotional investment in, someone whom I can't hurt emotionally and who has no reason to hurt me. I have her strip naked while I watch, and then I grope her roughly, I spank her and pinch her nipples . . ." He paused, shook his head. "I don't really want to go into every detail, but it's all consensual and safe. Basically what happens is that I bring her to orgasm. They are sex workers, so that can take some time, since they prefer to pretend to climax and that doesn't work for me. I pay them extra to show me exactly what they like, which vibrator to use, which . . . you don't need to know this. Sorry. If necessary, they take over and finish themselves, although I really don't prefer that. After she finally climaxes I have her turn around so she can't see me—I don't ever let them see me—and I masturbate until I come all over her back." He had never raised his eyes from the Persian design. He swallowed hard, queasy with shame. "Pathetic, isn't it?" he mumbled.

Julie realized she had stopped breathing. Her lungs were bursting. She stood up, gasping. She steadied herself on his desk, turning away from Brian in case she was blushing.

"Julie? Are you okay? I'm sorry. That was revolting. I said it so bluntly because . . . I don't know, I've only talked to shrinks and pros about it. They're all business so I'm all business. Actually I like it better that way."

Obviously there's a God, Julie concluded.

"Julie?" he asked plaintively. "Are we okay?"

"We're more than okay." She faced him, grinning. "You have nothing to worry about."

Brian winced his surprise. "Really? Believe me, Rydel can uncover this. I pay these women by the hour. I can't kid myself that I've also bought their lifelong loyalty." He squinted, puzzled. "Why are you smiling?" he asked.

"Do they have to be young?"

He frowned. "No. That isn't important. Somewhat preferable but not crucial."

"Do you have to pay them?" She perched on the slate table. She found his eyes and held them while she undid the top button of her blouse. She paused, waiting for him. To laugh? To run? The wait was awful and wonderful.

Understanding arrived for Brian. He became very still.

"They're me," she said. She undid the second button. One more and her plain white bra would be visible. She wished she had worn the red one with a frilly trim. Or the satiny black. Her heart was rising in her throat, choking her with fear and anticipation. "You saw me being used, groped," she talked over the roar in her head, feeling loose everywhere else, pleasure looming on the horizon.

He took her seriously, thinking it through. His grave response excited her even more. "I was eight," he said at last. "I didn't know what was going on down there. I knew what he did to us. I mean to me and Jeff, but not you . . ." Brian stopped.

"And you've spent a lifetime finding out," she explained. She opened a third button, blouse falling away, utilitarian bra revealed.

"I don't think this is a good idea," he said in a strangled voice.

"That's what makes it a good idea. That it isn't good. I show myself," she confessed at last to another living soul. "I show myself to men, to strangers, but what I've been trying to do is show myself to you."

He studied her bra, deliberately, coldly, exactly the way she liked. She pulled her blouse free from her skirt and let it fall back onto the slate. She knew she must look pathetic and absurd, but she felt grand and desired.

"You're right," his voice was husky, lustful. "But I wasn't looking for you, Julie, and you weren't looking for me. We were trying to take back what Klein had robbed from us. Make it ours."

She nodded agreeably and unzipped her sensible knee-length gray wool skirt. It fell to the floor and she stepped out. Again, the wrong panties: white, utilitarian.

He roamed over her legs, her panties, her belly, her breasts. "Don't misunderstand," he told the object of her body. "I'm very glad I've found you. But what I do, what the drugs I'm taking are trying to stop me from doing, wasn't a search for you. I don't want to know the woman who lets me excite her with my hands, who gives me the gift of her orgasm, who I mark with my come. I want her to be a stranger who doesn't care about me. I want her to be someone who is using me for her own sake. I want to despise my desires."

"Why?" She slid her right hand down the stomach she had worked so hard after Zack's birth to restore to a dancer's firm source of supple strength. She infiltrated her panties and brushed lightly, teasing herself to open.

His eyes locked on her fingers, watching them restlessly shift under the white fabric while he explained, "Because they come from Klein. He put them there. They belong to me now, but he put them there, and I despise him and I despise them."

She pulled her hand free briefly, to release and drop her bra at his feet before returning below to the touch and rhythms for a witness who not only saw but understood her. She hoarsely called out her desire from far underneath this ocean of bliss. "Would you . . . do me a favor?" she managed to stammer out.

His eyes, just as she had always imagined, looked only at her hand, her stomach, her bare breasts. He nodded agreement to her body.

"Come on me." She unveiled a new desire, the first in decades. "Let me see you come. Let me be the only woman who sees you."

The Best Laid Plans

—— February 2008 ——

FIRST THING IN the morning Jeff called with what seemed to Brian to be the best possible news: after fighting with the studio over the ending for two hours, he had phoned his LA home and told Halley everything.

"Everything?" Brian said, winking at Julie who, very domestically, happened to be serving him scrambled tofu and tempeh bacon, both of which she regarded skeptically. For Danny, the Moran with the bad heart, she had run out to the supermarket and to his delight made a deadly breakfast of eggs and pork sausages.

"Everything about Cousin Richard, Sam, you, and Julie. Not everything about me and I'd appreciate it if you didn't talk about you-know-what."

"I don't really know you-know-what, Mr. Jeff. Mostly what I know are assumptions."

Jeff reported that although Halley was angry he had kept these painful childhood secrets from her, she agreed he must go public. She was frantic about how that might affect their family—she was removing their two kids from school for the week, flying to Phoenix to stay at her mother's while the media storm raged. "And she's really pissed, totally furious at me for never telling her anything about all this. She says we have to go into therapy to work on intimacy issues. *My* intimacy issues, she means. Therapy. Fuck. If only it was just therapy. I've got to start going to her spiritual adviser, her aroma therapist, and Bikram yoga."

"Yoga." Brian laughed.

"Get in touch with my body in a good way."

"That's why I'm laughing," Brian said. This hilarious report relaxed him about Jeff's commitment. With Halley's drowning him in chicken soup for the soul LA-style, and reassuring him he wasn't going to lose his children, Jeff wouldn't waver.

An hour later, he felt a fool for that confidence. Jeff called back. Brian was alone. The day nurse had arrived, given Danny his medications, made sure he didn't need help showering and dressing before taking him out for a slow healthful walk by the river. Julie had left to update Amelia over coffee before they went into work.

"Can you and Julie get to my hotel by eleven, eleven thirty at the latest," Jeff demanded more than asked. "Rydel's agreed to meet us. And he's bringing Cousin Richard."

"What the fuck for? Who asked him?"

"Me. I want to tell them, especially Cousin Richard who's old and who can't possibly want to die in prison, that after we go public that's likely to happen if they don't voluntarily confess and make a deal with the prosecution."

"I see." Brian was restored to the familiar bitterness and bleak comfort of his low opinion of humanity. Since last night, he had allowed himself a few hours of giddy optimism that his life might substantially change. Julie had relaxed the tension that had kept him clenched against affection, allowed him to hope that from now on he needn't always hold his heart in reserve from the people he loves. "So you're still trying to save your ass, Mr. Jeff."

"All our asses!" Jeff said. "Don't tell me you really want to go public.

You want every shmuck to have the Rosetta stone to your sex life? Have every fucking reviewer go: 'We can't help but look at the theme of this new play in light of his unfortunate sexual history.'"

"So what you're telling me, Mr. Jeff—"

"Stop calling me Mr. Jeff. You only called me that when you were trying to beat me at Slug."

"Trying? I used to cream you at Slug. So what you're saying is that you've arranged a meeting with the man who molested me to spare me condescending reviews?"

"To spare all of us. Sure, me. Julie too. You think she wants her fifteen-year-old son to have all his friends at high school reading about how his mother had a cock shoved down her throat?"

"Jesus," Brian mumbled. Of course sparing Julie was worth the effort. Bad enough Klein had poisoned the well of sweetness in her nature. Her black eyes shined, her soft voice strengthened whenever she talked about Zack. Why let Klein spoil everything in her life?

"Jesus, what?"

Brian did not want to explain why today he felt Julie's wounds as if they were his own. "Just disgust. At what he did to her."

"We all had something disgusting done to us. I was raped." He cleared his throat noisily. "Happened once. But it happened."

"Sorry, Jeff." He had to stop thinking only about himself, his ridiculously tender feelings. "I'm sorry."

"Not you, huh?" Jeff loudly cleared his throat again. "Glad to hear it."

"Yeah, I got off easy. I was merely . . . diddled, as my father put it."

"You told Danny!" Jeff was flabbergasted.

Brian ignored that. He was back to being suspicious of Jeff's plan. He didn't believe Klein or Rydel would admit guilt, no matter what they were threatened with. They had too much to lose. More likely what would happen during the meeting is that Jeff would find some reason to back out of his agreement to go public. As all Hollywood successes tended to be, Jeff would be adept at convincing himself that any compromise of principle was actually for the best. Klein and Rydel would agree to pay a private penance and penalty and Jeff would insist that was good enough. The face-to-face would become an about-face; Jeff, Klein, and Rydel would gang up on Brian and Julie for being stubborn. He and Julie would be put into the same hopeless position of screenwriters bullied by director, producer, and studio executive into making changes that would eviscerate their story's truth, or else their movie wouldn't be made at all. "Why don't you tell Klein what we're going to do on the phone? Why do we all have to meet? Julie and I could eavesdrop. Or even watch. You could Skype!" He announced with mock excitement.

Now it was Jeff's turn to ignore Brian. "What did your father say when you told him?"

"Like you, he worries more about critics than about Christ's forgiveness."

"He's totally fucking right. How long do you think it'll take before people start seeing creepy stuff in my movies and suddenly I'm not every American family's favorite director."

So here was the panic's source: his reputation as an artist was threatened. Brian paced his cramped kitchen, desperate for a compelling argument. When his eyes lit on the window's view of the multimillionaire's garden, he was inspired to appeal to Jeff's true love. "You know, you're being really stupid about this. Critics' finding out about your tortured childhood will allow them to reevaluate your blockbuster hits and claim they have gravitas. They'll discover all kinds of profundities in your car chases and aliens. At long last you'll win your Oscar and you can look Spielberg in the eye. Best thing: you won't even have to do a movie about the Holocaust."

"Fuck you."

"I'm serious. Sure the macho asshole agents and studio execs will make jokes about your taking it up the ass, but the rest of the world will have a reason to stop envying you and start feeling sorry for you. There's nothing that makes an artist more beloved than the audience pitying him because his work comes at a price they would never pay."

A silence. During it, Brian wondered if he believed his clever pitch. It seemed plausible enough. Of course his rosy scenario wasn't all-encompassing: contrarians would point out that Jeff had avoided treating the subject directly, thus forfeiting providing insight, and eventually someone would figure out that Jeff had covered up Klein's and Sam's proclivities long after he was a mere child, that as a newly successful young director he had lent his name to the broadcasting school and given money to Klein's charity. He claimed to be totally ignorant of what Sam was doing, but he could have denounced Klein. *Nor did I,* Brian reminded himself. *Let the self-righteous judge him. I can't.*

Jeff was having his own difficulty with setting a moral compass. "Brian, all this is still really about Cousin Richard—"

Brian interrupted sharply: "Stop calling him Cousin Richard, for chrissakes. Were you permanently infantilized by Klein? What kind of therapy were you in? Didn't your shrink at least make you examine why you can't stop behaving like an abused little boy?"

"Okay, okay, okay," Jeff said, pleading as if he were being hit. "I'll call him Dick," he said, reverting to his usual sarcasm. "Dick, Dick, Dick. That more grown-up?"

"I'd prefer Klein, but anything other than Cousin Richard, please."

"Okay, but my point is, whatever anybody else thinks, this is all about Klein. I mean, let's be honest, whatever Rydel is now, he's not that different from us."

"Really? Have you been raping children? It's something I've managed to avoid."

"Come on! He was an orphan. He had no one else. He was at Cousin Rich—Sorry. He was at Klein's mercy twenty-four/seven. You could easily get away. Julie too. Me less so, but Sam was totally vulnerable. Klein took over his whole life."

"Are you saying that anyone—you, me, Julie, anyone who suffered what Sam did at Klein's hands—would have become a child rapist? Don't you think there's some choice? Some part of who we are fundamentally that is finally able to find the strength to say, 'No.'"

Another silence. "Maybe. Rydel's not an artist," Jeff said, his voice faint. "He has no talent, no way of working through it."

"How did Julie 'work through it'?"

"She's a woman."

"So what?"

"They're nurturers. Even when they're monsters, they think they're taking care of you. Julie could raise her son. And she had a husband—you saw him, he's her big overgrown toddler."

Brian wasn't happy to be discussing Julie's marriage. "He seems grown-up enough to me," he mumbled. "And Jeff, here's a tip in case you find yourself discussing this with Charlie Rose or Oprah: don't mention this theory that women don't need to be artists because they can have children. They'll take away the Oscar you don't have."

"Jesus, I didn't mean it like that. I meant—"

"This is just delaying the inevitable. What the hell are we supposed to do in your hotel room with Klein and Rydel? Scold them?"

"I'll do the talking. You back me up, so they know all three of us mean business. They can't buy us off and they can't make all three of us look like liars."

Brian leaned his forehead against the chilly window's glass. On the second floor of the investment banker's townhouse, a little dark-haired boy was riding an enormous plastic tricycle designed to resemble a toddler's version of a Harley chopper. A very young woman, maybe a teenager, a tall colt with blonde hair halfway down her back was following him as he pedaled around the playroom, hovering as if every inch of him was precious. Was she the au pair? Imagine being a little rich boy with a beautiful loyal girl for a caretaker. *Well,* Brian consoled his envious heart, *with any luck there'll be justice and he'll grow up to be a meth head.* "I'll talk to Julie and get back to you," he said.

He didn't call Julie's cell until he was uptown, emerging from the subway at Sixty-fifth and Broadway. "I'll be right out," she said after he relayed Jeff's request.

In the raw, hopelessly gray February day, Julie immediately kissed him on the lips and snuggled against his down jacket, so he had almost no choice but to put a puffy arm around her. She beamed a giddy look of romance at him. He disengaged gently, facing her. "So . . . ? What do you think? Should we indulge Jeff or not?"

Julie nodded vigorously. "Definitely. I want to tell Klein to his face what we're going to do. I definitely want to tell him. Don't you? And I want to see him. I don't care how old and sick he is. I won't pity him. I'll spit in his face." She looked angry and disgusted: a bitter taste tightening her mouth, making her wince. Her feelings made sense to Brian but he didn't share them. He was a little frightened of meeting Klein, old wreck though he might be. He wasn't sure of what precisely he feared. Not of anything Klein might do or say. *What I might do?*

"Okay," he told Julie, "But that's not what Jeff is up to. He thinks we're going to convince Klein and Rydel to confess, like a *Law & Order* episode."

She shrugged, retook his arm, leaning on him as they walked to the curb. "That won't happen," she said.

Again he extricated himself from her clutch. "Just be prepared. If they offer some kind of bullshit compromise, paying a lot money, some kind of rehabilitation therapy but no admission of guilt in exchange for us not going public, don't be surprised if Jeff jumps on it."

"Nothing will stop me, Brian. Nothing. I'll do this alone. Even without you."

He unzipped a pocket to reach his iPhone. "I'll call Jeff, tell him we're coming over now. He's a director so he wants to rehearse."

In the cab, she slid across to his side and rested her head on his shoulder. She lay her hand on top of his, trying to insinuate her fingers between his knuckles. He moved away sharply, his hip pushing her off.

She studied him solemnly for a moment, then asked, "What's wrong?"

"Well, lots of things are wrong with me, as you know, but mostly at the moment what's going on? You're married. And not to me."

"I was just holding your hand." She thrust her strong chin forward, black eyes flashing.

"You're acting like we're lovers," he said.

She stared. The beauty marks under each of her shining eyes were clearly visible today. He had told her what they meant to him, requested she not pancake them away. "We are lovers," she said finally. "If you don't want to be, say so."

"Lovers? It was just . . ." He hesitated, ashamed of his cruelty. He gestured helplessly.

"It was just what?"

"An encounter. That doesn't make us lovers. It certainly doesn't merit threatening your marriage."

"Why do you keep bringing up my marriage?"

"You have a family. You can't throw it away because of kinky sex."

"It wasn't just sex!" she complained so loudly they both looked through the smudged plastic partition to check whether their Sikh driver was eavesdropping. His lips were moving, mumbling into a Bluetooth device that was almost thoroughly hidden beneath his headdress. Julie resumed, "You were happy. Last night *and* this morning you were really happy."

Her observation startled him. His eyes burned, his throat tightened. She was terrifyingly accurate about his happiness: all last night he had felt an easing throughout his taut, anxious soul because of Julie. Even with a female intruder in his bed, he managed a few hours of deep, restful sleep. And this morning his complete relaxation lingered during breakfast with his foolish father. In a peculiar fashion, they had achieved the intimate lovemaking of people who care for each other, something he had never experienced, he had to admit, now that he knew the real thing. It was appalling to understand that she was right to push him about their relationship. He had lost his virginity at fifty, the cherry that had never burst—Brian was in love.

HE'S SCARED, JULIE thought. *Give him a break. Let's get through this first.* They rode the rest of the way in silence to the Four Seasons. Brian relaxed physically, resting his hand next to hers on the taxi seat. She restrained her desire to take hold of it, although it would be a comfort on this chilly, anxious day.

Thinking about their status fell away once she entered Jeff's astonishing suite. Its one-hundred-degree sweep of midtown and Central Park from the fifty-second floor was dizzying. She dropped onto a black leather couch to settle her wobbly legs, mesmerized by the aviator's view of Manhattan until Jeff, pacing anxiously into and out of it, related his plan for how they should confront Klein and Rydel. Fear, blissfully absent from her system since last night's surprise with Brian, hummed back to life.

Jeff gave orders as if they were his crew, that what he wanted would be done without question. "I'll greet them. You two should wait in the second bedroom off that hall—they won't even know it's there. Let me relax them a little. Now Rydel said he has to bring Cousin—" He caught himself. "Klein in a wheelchair. And he also claims—check this out—that he really is gaga—"

"You spoke to Rydel?" Brian interrupted, his voice loaded with suspicion.

"Yeah. How do you think I arranged for the meeting?"

Brian moaned. "By calling your fucking cousin, that's who. I thought you didn't know Rydel, that you hadn't—"

"I don't! I got my assistant to get a private number for Rydel. I called it, told his secretary my name, and he took the fucking call."

"Why didn't you call Klein?" Brian asked, his tone steeped in skepticism.

Brian's suspicions seemed to Julie to be exaggerated, but she was glad he had them anyway. Jeff's answer made sense: "I did. I kept getting nurses who wouldn't put him on, and one of them finally said he wouldn't know who I was. That he doesn't know who anybody is. They're playing this Alzheimer's crap for all it's worth." He sighed and threw a bone of confession to satisfy Brian's paranoia. "Before I met you guys for lunch the other day I had found out that was their cover story. That's how I got the idea for that made up report."

"You're forgiven," Brian said angrily.

"I didn't apologize."

"No shit!"

"I'm sorry," Jeff said. He lowered his eyes. "I was panicking."

To Julie's surprise, Brian relented. "You're forgiven," he said softly.

"What if he *is* senile?" Julie said, worried it might be true.

Jeff released a Bronx cheer before saying, "Bullshit. Brian's right. I checked. He was lucid in that interview a year ago. And I saw a video of him speaking at a Huck Finn fund-raiser two years ago. That's one thing we can get done. We can get him talking coherently and blow that Alzheimer's story out of the water. So listen—I'll make them think I'm open to some kind of deal, then I'll say I have to take a leak and come get you. Don't say anything. I'll make the introductions." He snapped his fingers at Julie while keeping his eyes focused on a middle distance, seeing only his scheme, "Then you say it, what you're planning to do, tell the press what Klein did to you with Rydel watching." Jeff snapped his finger at Brian. "Then you say you'll confirm you saw him molest her and, you know, your whole I'm-writing-this-for-the-*New-Yorker*-slash-*Vanity-Fair* bit. It's a great one-two punch. And then I'll hit him with the knockout, that I'll tell the world about the deal he made with my mother."

Julie was taken aback. She asked, "What about your mother?" She saw Brian drop his head and nod slowly. He knew. He knew something he hadn't told her. "What deal?" she asked Brian.

"You didn't tell her?" Jeff asked, also surprised.

Julie felt a surge of anger at Brian, feeling betrayed the way she was supposed to have felt when she caught Gary having an affair. "What didn't you tell me?" she asked loudly, barely able to stop herself from yelling.

"Sorry, but it's not my secret," Brian said meekly. "Jeff said he was going to tell the world everything so"—he gestured at his friend—"I was leaving it to him to tell you."

She turned away from Brian, still angry with him but not wanting to be. "What about Aunt Harriet?" she demanded of her cousin. Jeff buried his face in his hands and scrubbed hard. "Jeff?" she said to prompt him.

He uncovered. His eyes were bloodshot. He explained in an exhausted voice, "That's why he paid for everything. That's how Dad repaid your dad for the store loan. That's how we moved out of Queens to the Upper East Side. That's how my parents retired to Boca Raton. And film school. He paid for all that because Mom found out that Klein had raped me. She made a deal to keep quiet." Jeff bit his lip. He looked off, to the breathtaking view of Central Park.

"Harriet knew," Julie said aloud because she couldn't believe the fact in her head if it wasn't spoken aloud. "Aunt Harriet knew. She knew what he was doing to me?"

"I don't know!" Jeff said, at once pleading and complaining. "But not that day at my apartment," Jeff said. "She didn't know a thing that day. Later. A month? I can't remember exactly when."

All the air went out of her, like taking a blow to the stomach. Her head raced to catch up with the information: *Aunt Harriet knew. She knew that Klein was a patient of Dad's, knew he was invited to our house for the holidays. She had to know what he would do to me. She knew. All right, a crazy woman, selfish and mean. But a mother. He had raped her son. She was a mother and she knew.*

Brian put a hand on Julie's arm and added, as if he had been listening to her thoughts, "She knew about me. I mean, she didn't *know* know. All she had to do was look the other way. Stay in her bed. Not ask any questions. That's why this is so hard for Jeff," he whispered.

She felt nauseated. The panorama of Manhattan wobbled against the depthless blue sky. "I have to sit down." Brian steered her to an enormous leather couch. She shut her eyes and leaned back, trying to think of nothing. Brian sat beside her. He took her hand. His was warm. Entwined with his fingers, hers felt chilled, bloodless.

"Jeff," Brian asked, "could you please explain why you're springing us on them? Why do we need to hide in the bedroom? What are you going to say to him before you have us come in?"

"You know," he said. Julie opened her eyes and saw that Jeff had perched on the edge of a leather wing chair. It looked like he was about to take a dive onto Central Park's leafless gray limbs. Still nauseated, she looked at the carpet.

Getting no answer, Brian elaborated his question: "Are you going to pretend they've got nothing to fear from you until we come out? Are you going for shock?"

Jeff scrubbed his face with his palms, pressing hard on his eyes as he groaned. "I don't know, I guess so. I was going to . . ." He uncovered, blinked. "I didn't get any sleep," he said as an explanation.

"You were going to . . . ?" Brian prompted.

"Say that I was going to go public unless they made a deal with the prosecution and a financial settlement with all of the victims."

"That's not what we want," Julie stood. She took a moment to adjust to the vertigo of the sky yawning at her feet. "That's still a cover-up."

"I know!" Jeff said, his voice squeaking like a prepubescent boy. "That's the hook, that's what Rydel's expecting me to say, that's how I got him to agree to come. He didn't even want to bring Richard because he thinks we made a deal over the phone and we're just working out the details. But I insisted no deal without Klein."

"But what are you trying to achieve by springing us on them?" Brian asked, still doubtful. "We don't have anything new to add."

"That I can't make a deal 'cause you guys will out me anyway. Richard will never believe I'm going to tell on my mother. Even with her gone. That's what he thinks protects him from what I know. But you guys prove I have no choice. You're the enforcers."

Brian let go of her hand. He leaned forward to address Jeff in a low, insinuating tone. "Are we here to convince Klein that our going public will ruin him? Or have you brought us here to strike a better deal with him than you could get without us?"

"A better deal for all of us!" Jeff said. "Look, with any luck, once they know I have no choice, maybe they'll agree to confess without any of us having to go public. You guys don't want everything to come out. Come on. Do you?"

"Jesus," Brian mumbled. "You're still protecting her. Why?" he asked loudly and incredulously, shifting to the far edge of the couch to be near Jeff. "Your mother's dead. Your father's dead. No one's really gonna care. Oh, everyone will tsk-tsk over their horror that a mother could be so evil, and there'll be loads of sympathy for poor you having such a mother, but nobody knows or cares about her. You're not ruining the reputation of Mahatma Gandhi, for God's sake."

That's when Julie's nerves unstrung. She turned her back on the dizzying view, heading for the suite's long hallway to the door. Why hadn't she seen the danger in meeting Klein? He was going to shove his cock in her mouth again—this time with Jeff's help. And Brian? She stopped, turning to stare her rage at Brian. He wasn't telling her everything. He had kept this vital fact from her about her life! She wasn't Klein's whore, she was Harriet's whore. She had been used to help Jeff become rich and famous and now Jeff was using her again! "I'm leaving," Julie said but didn't move an inch. She was too angry.

"Don't go, Julie," Jeff said. "I'm trying to trap him. Rydel would've hung up if I told him on the phone what we're going to do, or he'd talk to his lawyers and they'd talk him out of a meeting. This way, here, we've got him, but better than that we've Cousin Rich—damn it!" He caught himself. "We've got Klein, not faking being demented, totally coherent."

"How?" Brian asked. "Whatever happens in this room, they can deny it all as soon as they talk to their lawyers."

Jeff pointed to the coffee table. It was enormous, a six-inch thick slab of thick smoky glass, covered with what looked like Jeff's work on a new film. There were two piles of black-and-white drawings Julie recognized as production design sketches and four models of a prop: medium-sized statues of blackbirds, each different in one key feature. Jeff leaned forward, tapping the one closest to him.

"*The Maltese Falcon* remake?" Brian said. "What? Bogie's gonna come into the room and scare the crap out of him?"

Jeff made a disgusted face. "Miniature high-def digital video camera. We'll get Richard talking sense, admitting what he did to us, and then he's got no choice but to plea bargain and settle and he'll take Rydel down with him."

"There's a camera in that one?" Julie asked.

"There's a camera in all of them," Jeff said, grinning. He pointed behind her. "And there are two more in those prototypes of Greek urns over there. We've got full coverage. No matter where they walk or how low they talk, we'll get it."

"You were right," Julie said to Brian. "He really does think this is a *Law & Order* episode. Let's go," she said, then pleaded, "please."

"This could work, Julie," Brian said.

"No!" she said. "I'm not doing this stupid stunt. I'm going to tell the world. I don't just want to see Klein punished, I want people to understand they should talk about these experiences, I want people to understand it isn't just priests and a couple loner weirdos, this happens all the time and it's gonna keep happening unless people like us stop keeping it secret."

"Exactly." Brian pulled himself up out of the couch and walked over to her. "I don't mean we keep quiet. But if Jeff gets it all on video, then we really have something to show the world."

"I don't trust him. Let's go. We'll tell what we know and trust the world instead," Julie said all that in a whisper, not because she didn't want or expect Jeff to hear but to emphasize that the two of them were all that mattered. She had found her soul mate: the only question was whether he had the courage to abide by their love.

But he was a man and he wanted to win. Brian said to Jeff, "Here's what we're willing to do: all three of us greet Klein and Rydel simultaneously; we tell them what we're planning to do unless they confess to the cops and make a deal. The trick is for us to act like we're not interested in hearing a confession ourselves, couldn't care less, interrupt him if he starts to confess, then grudgingly let him continue. We get Klein coherent on tape, then we turn it over to the DA—"

"No!" Julie cried in agony.

Brian took her hand and pledged, "And we still go public." He turned to Jeff. "All of us tell our story to the press. Whether we get Klein and Rydel confessing on tape or not. That's the deal, Jeff. Take it or leave it."

Jeff rubbed his face. "Okay," he said, and rubbed again, harder. When he dropped his hands, he begged her, "Please, Julie. Let's not humiliate ourselves for nothing. Let's get him on film. Right, Bri? Let's at least make sure we totally fuck him." He smirked bitterly. "You should excuse the expression."

One Second of Remorse

—— February 2008 ——

THE EVIL MAN arrived in a wheelchair propelled by his adopted son, Sam Rydel. Rydel was dressed not to be recognized, wearing a New York Yankees cap pulled low, sunglasses, a windbreaker, jeans, sneakers. Richard Klein was also hard to find in his clothes. His bald skull, forehead, and both eyebrows were covered by a ribbed black beanie and his puffy down coat was pushed up to his chin. Only a stripe of the old man's face was visible and most of that was covered by the oversized frames of his eyeglasses, whose thick lenses made his eyes loom large and dwarfed his nose. He seemed deliberately dressed to send the message: dementia.

"Follow me," Jeff said, without a greeting. He turned and led them through through his hotel suite's hallway and into the vast living room, its panoramic view of a snow-covered Central Park glistening in the bright sun on the clear, cold winter's day. Rydel's head was lowered to watch where he was going while he pushed the wheelchair. Once in the main room he removed his hat and sunglasses, squinting eyes drawn first to its sweeping view, then opening wide at the surprise of two strangers.

"Who are they?" he asked. Rydel looked puffier, older in person than in the photographs. He wasn't over six feet as Julie had come to imagine;

he was no taller than Gary, maybe shorter. And the cold, remorseless eyes—they were full of fear.

"You don't remember? Ask Cousin Richard," Jeff said, pointing at Klein.

Rydel blinked twice, very rapidly as if he were toting up sums on a calculator. Then his face went blank; he shrugged, turned his back to them, bending over the wheelchair. That blocked their view of its occupant while he removed the beanie, unzipped the down coat without removing Klein's arms, and untied what turned out to be a gray scarf.

Waiting for this unveiling, Julie couldn't breathe normally. She could only take sips of air before her throat would close up, as if oxygen had become poisonous. The harder she tried to force the air down into her lungs, the quicker she choked on it. *Am I hyperventilating?* she wondered.

Brian had to pee. Waiting for Klein and Rydel, he had drunk an entire carafe of the Four Seasons' strong coffee. In the previous hour, he had gone to the bathroom three times, the last just ten minutes ago. It couldn't be that there was more in his bladder to expel, but waiting to talk to Klein for the first time in forty years, he had to tighten his pelvic muscle to squash the urge to go.

At last Rydel finished and stepped to the right of the wheelchair, revealing a frail old man in a beige cardigan sweater worn over a white shirt buttoned to the collar without a tie, and baggy blue corduroy pants with what looked like food stains on the broad lap it formed. Julie's eyes dropped to his thick-soled orthopedic brown shoes. She was momentarily fascinated by Klein's thin ankles in white compression socks. They appeared to be too skinny to stay in the shoes should he try to walk. If he ever walked. He didn't look as if he could.

While they had waited for Klein and Rydel to arrive, Jeff had been bursting with anxiety. He had settled in a chair only to jump up immediately and once again check his hidden recording devices or to press buttons on his iPhone, presumably checking e-mails. He had announced the time every ten minutes. He had seemed so nervous Julie couldn't imagine he'd follow the plan. But now, having finally gotten his cue, he looked calm. He even managed a pleasant smile as he said, "Hi, Cousin Richard. Been a while. Twenty years?" Klein's magnified eyes stared up at Jeff with the curiosity of a three-year-old. He appeared interested but puzzled, as if Jeff were speaking a foreign language. Brian thought it was a first-rate performance. Klein wasn't pretending he didn't know someone was talking to him. Just that he had no idea who he was or what this person was saying.

"I told you," Rydel said. "This past year he really declined. He doesn't know who anybody is. He thinks I'm one of his nurses." Rydel addressed Klein in a loud voice, enunciating each word meticulously. "Dick, this is Jeff. Harriet's son. You remember Jeffrey. Jeffrey Mark. You're so proud of his success as a director and producer."

Klein nodded once and managed a thin parting of his lips, revealing teeth that were either dentures or caps, Brian couldn't be sure. Then the smile faded and he looked away, as if embarrassed that he didn't know Jeff and felt too tired to keep up the pretense he did. That was another brilliant stroke, Brian decided. A clumsy faker would rely on drooling stupefaction or that he mistook Jeff for someone else.

Jeff bent over Klein's wheelchair, hands on his knees. He spoke in kind and gentle tones. "That's okay, Cousin Richard. You don't have to pretend with me. And you don't have to pretend you don't know what's going on because Brian and Julie are here. They don't want anyone to know what you did to them, either. I'm sure you remember them. They were two of your favorite victims. This is Brian Moran."

As Brian stepped up to Klein's wheelchair, he glanced at Rydel. Rydel goggled at him. Rydel knew who he was now. Brian bent over to let Klein see his face.

Klein's fish eyes came up to investigate him. The old man nodded slowly, as he had with Jeff. Again Klein smiled hesitantly, and again his eyes slid away, face expressionless, eyes focused dully on the middle distance, which happened to be Brian's chest at the moment.

"And this is Julie Rosen," Jeff said, continuing to speak in the friendly tones of a host. "Better known to you by her maiden name, a name I'm proud to share with her, Julie Mark."

Julie had been watching Klein's reaction to Jeff and Brian. She was surprised that he had light blue eyes, so light they were almost white; she had remembered them as hazel or some other brownish color. Otherwise she recognized Klein's features as a decaying version of the middle-aged man she once knew. But the confident, wheedling, energetic personality really did seem gone. She pushed that thought away. *He's faking,* she insisted to herself.

When Jeff finally said her name, she saw in the periphery that Rydel's body language had changed from sullenness to alarm and that he took a step as if to get between Jeff and Brian and the wheelchair. But they cut him off as she stepped up to Klein.

Rydel called out in a desperate voice, "He doesn't know who you—"

Before he could finish, she had bent down toward those enormous limpid eyes, rising to look at her, taking her in with a wondering puzzlement, his head, like with Jeff and Brian, nodding, a sliver of smile appearing. It was the smile, she decided later, that got her so angry she went off script. She spat on him. Only a thin stream of watery saliva came out and landed square on his pale, spotted forehead.

"Hey!" Rydel shouted, and collided with Brian, trying to reach her.

She was busy watching Klein's reaction. He cried out like a startled baby. Two bony hands that looked too big to be supported by their frail wrists came up to shield his face. They trembled uncontrollably. He made more noises of fear or pain, but they weren't words.

"Get her off him!" Rydel shouted. Brian, taller and stronger, was easily keeping him away. Jeff stood beside her, watching Klein as if he were directing him in a scene, a hand on his chin, brow furrowed thoughtfully. Julie also watched the old man's hands flail, trying both to hide his face and to push away an invisible attacker. Her disappointment deepened that faking or not, this feeble creature was nothing like the vigorous, crazily bold man who, in her own home, her mother and father a split-level floor away, had grabbed a fistful of her hair and pushed her head onto his purple swollen penis.

She stepped back and looked at Brian to signal he could let Rydel go. She had no more spontaneous anger to release. If she was going to get angry enough again to attack him, she'd have to work herself up to it. She felt utterly exhausted, her muscles struggling to support her. She would have been glad to lie down and take a nap.

"What the fuck do you think you're doing?" Rydel complained. He knelt beside Klein, a monogrammed handkerchief in his right hand while he gently lowered the old man's bony hands with his left. Klein whimpered and shut his eyes tight, wincing as if he expected to be hit.

Does he beat him? Brian wondered with horror and a trace of glee that he was immediately ashamed of.

"He doesn't know who any of you are. He doesn't even know me," Rydel insisted while wiping Klein's forehead clean. The old man stopped whimpering. His hands relaxed, dropping into his lap, but he kept his eyes shut tight. He had almost no lashes, Julie noticed. "It's okay," Rydel said softly to Klein. "No one will hurt you again. I promise."

Someone hit him recently. Brian was convinced, again appalled, again a little pleased, and then he realized he was starting to believe Klein was senile.

Rydel got to his feet. He confronted Jeff, who was still regarding Klein thoughtfully. "What the fuck is going on? I agreed to see you and you alone. I told you Dick is suffering from dementia. It's been happening to him gradually for five years. This past year he's fallen apart. I brought him to prove it to you. You said if I did, you'd agree how we were going to handle everything. Is there a problem? If there's a problem on your end, I'm outta here." He abruptly added, as if just reminded that he ought to ask this, "And who the fuck are they?" He nodded at Brian and Julie.

"You know who they are, Sam," Jeff said, back to their script. He didn't seem thrown by Julie's ad-lib. "I certainly don't have to remind you, Cousin Richard," he said, leaning around Rydel, trying to talk to the wheelchair's occupant. Jeff immediately gave that up and addressed Rydel: "You remember, Sam, giving Brian and me a tour of *The Tonight Show* set. And you also enjoyed the services of Julie's father as your dentist for several years."

This was Julie's proper cue. She almost couldn't pick it up she felt so tired, so hopeless. She had to take a deep breath—at least now she could inhale properly—to get the words out. "You watched at Aunt Harriet's apartment while you . . ." She bent down to address Klein. His eyes were open, unfocused, in the general direction of their feet. His mouth and jaw were working as if he were chewing. What unsettled her the most was that he no longer appeared to be fearful. He glanced up at her with untroubled curiously, as if he had never met her. "You put your fingers in my vagina. You did it in front of Brian and Jeff and"—she turned away from the wheelchair, relieved to be able to look from Klein's vacant gaze to Rydel's cornered, knowing eyes—"you watched. And you smiled. You enjoyed watching him molest me. But that wasn't the most fun you had. What you really enjoyed was when Klein pushed my mouth onto his penis. Remember what you said? You said, 'Put it in her pussy. I want to see it in her pussy.'"

"I never said—" Rydel stopped himself. For one second Rydel seemed to collapse from remorse and guilt. He brought his hands up to his mouth, face breaking apart from an overwhelming need to sob. Just as suddenly he mastered himself, face numbing, restored to wary sullenness. Now he backed up without looking where he was going, until he bumped into one of the fake urns. He glanced at it, surprised that it was made of papier-mâché.

"Watch it," Jeff said. "That's a prop, a prototype for my next picture."

"I've had enough of this bullshit," he said, then walked purposefully to the back of the wheelchair, grabbing the handles, releasing its brake.

"Go on, Jules," Jeff said. "Tell him."

"Tomorrow we're going to hold a news conference," Julie said. "We're going to tell what you and Klein did to each of us."

Rydel tilted the wheelchair up to turn it around. Klein's head flopped back as if he had no neck muscles. Rydel paused to say, without a trace of defensiveness, "I honestly don't know who you are."

It enraged Julie enough for her to admit in front of Brian, "I'm going to tell them how after he shoved my mouth onto his penis, he said I wasn't being fair, that I had to kiss yours, and you took yours out and put it my mouth."

Julie glanced at Brian, to check whether he was hurt that she had kept this detail from him. He nodded encouragingly. She looked back at her tormentors.

Rydel made a disgusted face. "That's bullshit," he said.

With Klein tilted back like that, the suite's floor to ceiling windows beyond the couch were front and center for his watery eyes. "Park," he said pleasantly, the first word he had spoken. "Park," he repeated.

"Yes, that's the park," Rydel said irritably but, Brian noticed, also reflexively as if he were in the habit of humoring a demented old man.

"Once we tell what happened to us, the floodgates will open," Jeff said. "Everyone in the past forty years who you and Cousin Richard molested and raped will come forward."

Brian spoke his lines: "And sooner or later the statute of limitations and your wallet won't be enough to stop an indictment."

"Cousin Richard won't go to jail," Jeff taunted Rydel. "Especially if you corroborate that he's senile. But you will. You'll lose all your money and you'll spend the rest of your life in prison."

Rydel let go of the wheelchair. Klein's head flopped forward. He moaned. "And this is all gonna happen," Rydel said in a sneering tone, "because of what you say I did when I was fifteen?"

"No, of course not just because of that," Brian said. "Think of who is saying all this. At the very least your reputation is fucked. You know what Julie can say about Klein and your relationship to him. You know what I can say. Everyone will believe us. First of all, it's true, and second of all, why would we make it up?"

Rydel reached into his jacket, removed the Yankees hat and put it on. "Good-bye," he said to Jeff.

"You're not going yet," Jeff said softly.

Rydel froze. Klein's right hand came up and made a waving motion in front of his right eye as if he were shooing away a fly. Rydel glanced at Klein, then looked back at Jeff, waiting on him.

"Let me try to make your options clear." Jeff yawned. "Sorry," he said with another yawn. "I didn't get any sleep. I was up telling my wife all about you and Cousin Richard so she would be prepared for what I'm going to say at the news conference. Such as you watching Klein rape me. And making me put your little blond cock in my mouth."

Brian and Julie both looked at Jeff, surprised.

Rydel was not surprised. He was ready to respond immediately. "Nothing I did forty years ago can be prosecuted. And I was child myself."

"You were fifteen when you—" Jeff started.

"I was a child! Emotionally I was more of a child than you." He addressed only Jeff, as if they were alone. "Are you going to tell the world what Dick was? You gonna tell the truth about your cousin?"

Jeff nodded. "Everything."

Rydel snorted. "Yeah? You gonna tell them the deal your mother made to keep quiet?"

"Yes," Jeff said, lingering on the *s* for emphasis.

Klein's hand came up again to wave at something in front of his right eye. This time he kept it raised, staring intently at nothing, then reached with his fingers, trying to catch an object that wasn't there.

"Stop that. Put your hand down. There's nothing there," Rydel told him impatiently. Klein kept it up, as if waiting to catch whatever it was the next time. Rydel refocused on Jeff. "Really? You're going to tell about all the money he gave your mother? To keep quiet about the others. How you kept quiet?" He looked pointedly at Brian.

Since Jeff had admitted his mother's involvement, Brian's thoughts had returned again and again to this point, but he didn't want to investigate it.

That Rydel was trying to drive a wedge between them, and he had found an effective way to do it, infuriated Brian all the more.

"I don't have to say I kept quiet about what I knew," Jeff said, coolly. "Obviously I did. I was a victim, that's why."

Rydel wasn't through being skeptical. "You're really going to tell the world everything he did for you?" he asked Jeff. "How he paid for your education? How he made you a star?"

"That's bullshit," Brian answered for Jeff. "Complete bullshit. So Klein paid for film school, made a few introductions. So what? Klein was a middle-management nobody in marketing. He didn't have some magical access in Hollywood. Jeff is one of a handful of the world's greatest directors. He would have made it without anybody's help and he probably would have made it sooner if Klein hadn't ruined his childhood."

Hearing this, Jeff turned from Rydel to gawk at Brian with delight and surprise.

Brian bore down on Sam. "You were the one Klein had to pay off handsomely because you were his main victim. That's mostly what I'm going to talk about, how Klein corrupted the young, stole their childhoods, turned them into his creatures. How he tried to convince his victims that they liked what he did to them, how he tried to get me to spank you, how he humiliated and used you—"

"Then why are you doing this to me?" Rydel said. "If you understand how horrible Dick was, how he destroyed my . . ." His mouth trembled. He mastered himself and said coolly, "I'm a victim. That's what you should be telling the world. That *I'm* a victim, not those boys. I was good to those boys. I loved them. I wasn't cruel like Dick." He slammed both hands on the wheelchair's handles, shaking its occupant.

Klein startled in the chair and cried out fearfully.

Rydel was still ranting. "I didn't humiliate them the way Dick—" He stopped.

Julie could see it occur to Rydel that it might not be safe to talk. He looked around as if expecting the police to show up. "I don't want to hear your litany of excuses," she said, following Brian's advice to keep him talking by pretending not to care. "We told you what we're going to do. Nothing you've said has changed my mind."

Brian turned to her. "Can you believe the self-delusion of this guy?" he said mockingly. "'I was good to them.' I'm sure that's what he said to you." He bent over to direct this at Klein, one last try at getting him to react. "Isn't that what you said to young Sam here? How you rescued and loved Sam, the poor little orphan boy."

Klein looked at Brian, but he was too interested in the invisible thing flying near his right eye to give him more than a glance. He returned to it, right hand grabbing at air.

"I'm not like him," Rydel said to Brian, then shouted, "Dick was cruel! I'm not cruel. You don't know what it was like with him . . . You think you do, but it was worse, much worse. I'm the victim."

"Yeah, yeah, you had your reasons for what you did," Jeff said, sneering. "Well, as Renoir said, 'The real hell of life is that everyone has their reasons.'"

"You didn't have to become who you are," Julie said, fighting off an emerging feeling of pity for this man. This prince who had become a toad wasn't a cold monster; he was an angry, bitter, and pathetic man. Sympathy for this devil vibrated inside her, along with the relief of having released her rage at Klein and seeing for herself that he no longer knew his victims. The true villain was forever beyond her reach. Disappointment, relief, and pity mixed into a strange combustion. With its ignition, her legs trembled, chest quaking, erupting into a fireball of sympathy for Rydel, for herself, for all the ruined children of the world. "I know Klein was horrible to you. I'm sorry for that boy you were, the boy he used. But what you became, that's you. You didn't have to become him. You weren't strong enough to fight for yourself, your real self. I know. I wasn't strong enough . . ." She was shaking too much to go on and Brian took her in his arms. Her mouth was pressed against his chest, silencing her with affection.

Sam Rydel's gray eyes faded into a colorless fury. He glared at her while working his jaw. "I was strong," he said. His mouth looked like it was chewing on something hard and bitter. "You don't know how strong." He was breathing hard through his nose. "I was strong," he insisted.

"Then stop covering up for him!" Jeff shouted, pointing at Klein who was the calmest of the four, slowly waving a hand in the air as if he were a politician in a parade greeting his supporters. "Confess and tell the world about Dick," Jeff said. "You probably won't go to real prison—they'll put you in a psychiatric hospital. Give the millions you squeezed out of the school to the boys you raped—"

"I didn't rape them. I loved them. I took care of them. Everything I did was out of love. I understand my boys better than anyone because I was one of them."

"Okay," Jeff said. "You love them. So give them your money. Do that and we'll shut up about what you did to me and to Julie. You can frame your life story so it sounds like you were just a victim of Cousin Richard, that he made you sick. But stop the bullshit that you're innocent and your accusers are liars."

"You self-righteous creep," Rydel said, self-pity boiling into rage. He abandoned the wheelchair and moved threateningly at Jeff. Brian eased out of Julie's arms and got between Jeff and Rydel. Julie flashed back to them as boys, remembering that the polite Brian was always ready to back up loud-mouth Jeff.

Brian said softly, "Our press conference is scheduled for five. If we don't hear you've made a deal by then, we'll go public."

Rydel looked deliberately at each of them, an enraged inventory. Then, without a word, he returned to the wheelchair. He slapped Klein's raised right hand, hard. "It's a floater! It's *in* your eye!" he yelled, slapping the hand again, although Klein was lowering it. Klein whimpered and cowered, hands shielding his face. Rydel jerked the handicapped chair up, spun it on the rear wheels to do a one eighty so they were facing the hallway. He dropped the front wheels down hard, again shaking Klein violently, then rapidly rolled Klein, wheelchair and himself into the hallway, disappearing.

"Did they really go?" Jeff asked after several seconds of not hearing the door shut.

Brian went to investigate. Julie felt woozy. She fell into a deep leather club chair, shut her eyes, and wished she could go to sleep on the spot. Brian reappeared, confirmed Rydel and Klein were gone.

Jeff was unscrewing the bottom of a Maltese Falcon prototype. "We didn't get anything, did we?"

"No," Brian said. Julie thought, *Good. Now Jeff can't back out.*

Jeff was still squirming for an exit. "What about when he talked about how what Klein did to him was worse than what he did?"

Brian shook his head. "Implication is not confession." He sighed. "There's no way out, Jeff. We don't have a lot of time to arrange the press conference. Who are you going to use to manage it?"

Jeff removed a small black piece of plastic—Brian later explained to Julie it was a flash drive—from the Falcon statue. "I'll talk to Sugarman first. He'll get us a crisis manager."

"Right. Everything starts and finishes with a lawyer. Can we piggyback on your legal and PR?"

"Yeah, yeah." Jeff tossed the flash drive across the room. It landed noiselessly on the thick carpet. "My people will arrange everything. Take care of you," he mumbled.

"You'd better call. It's eleven thirty already."

"I'll call," Jeff said. He took out his iPhone. He paused. "The old fuck really is senile," he announced. "Right?" he checked with Brian.

Brian nodded. "You should have stuck by your fake medical report."

Jeff grunted. "And you said it was bad storytelling."

"God's a hack," Brian said. "Only thing I wondered about . . ." He let that hang.

Julie and Jeff looked at him. "What?" Julie said.

"I think Rydel's abusing him. I don't mean sexually. I mean I think he's hitting him."

There was a silence. Julie sighed.

"I hope so." Jeff set his iPhone down on the couch, shut his eyes, and put his retro Converse sneakers up on the coffee table. He didn't starting dialing until Brian walked over and kicked their soles.

The Truth

—— February 2008 ——

BRIAN ORDERED TEA, coffee, bagels, and two vegan banana muffins while Jeff made a series of calls. He was famished. He ate both muffins in minutes. After a few sips of Earl Grey, Julie recovered from the fatigue and nausea she'd felt in the aftermath of being in Klein's and Rydel's presence.

When Jeff reported that Grace and a "handler" were coming over to brief them on the press conference, Julie said she'd better go home and change. "How do you dress," she asked Brian, her black eyes glistening, "for a sex abuse confession?"

"You're not confessing," he reminded her. "You weren't the abuser."

"Good point. But I'm serious. What should I wear? Not jeans. Not an evening gown. Slacks and a demure blouse?"

"Do you have a simple black dress?" he asked.

"Two." She smiled. "I live in Manhattan." By the time she left for home, he felt sure the shock was past, that she wouldn't require his company. He wanted to stay with Jeff, make sure of his resolve.

After Julie's departure, the suite filled up with Jeff's people. Grace appeared first. Then two assistants: one from the production of the film, the other his year round personal assistant. They were followed by two young lawyers from Sugarman's New York office, male and female, oddly resembling each other in their matching pin-striped suits, short haircuts, and solemn, subdued voices. They asked to hear in detail what Jeff and Brian intended to say.

Brian reached underneath his black cashmere sweater and produced two sheets of paper from his shirt pocket. "Here's my statement."

"You wrote it down!?" Jeff asked, startled.

"I'm a writer," Brian said.

The lawyers looked pleased. The male removed a device as wide as a sheet of paper, but only an inch long, and asked if he could scan and e-mail Brian's statement to Sugarman in LA. "Sure," Brian said. "But tell him not to give me notes."

"Excuse me?" the female lawyer said.

Jeff explained in a grumble, "He means he's saying what's in the statement no matter what."

"You don't want legal advice?" the male asked. "We understood that the firm is representing you."

"I'm sure Mr. Sugarman will have something useful to say," said his twin.

"I hate advice," Brian said. "Especially when it's useful."

Jeff extended a hand. "May I read it first?" Brian handed his pages over to the director, a letting-go he had never enjoyed.

Only Jeff's eyes moved while he read. "I didn't know that," he said when he was done. "Believe me, I didn't know about the Horror's calling your mom to have you come up while I was at Hebrew school." He gave the pages to the scanner bearer. He glanced shyly at Brian. "I'm sorry."

This was the grievance Brian had been fretting about since Jeff admitted his mother had known about Klein, that Jeff had conspired with Harriet to use him as a shield. He had told himself to let it go, but he hadn't. His heart zoomed from calm to rage. "You had me over two more times—"

"I know!" Jeff said. "But I was there those times and figured I could stop him from doing the really bad stuff."

"What the fuck is the really bad stuff? It was all really bad."

"Let's stay calm," the preternaturally calm woman lawyer said.

"Why don't you stay calm by keeping your fucking mouth shut!" Brian yelled, instantly regretting it. He rolled his lips inward, folded his hands in his lap.

"You're right," Jeff said. "I'm glad you fought him off." He sighed. "I'm sorry," he said. "I should've known."

"You were nine, for chrissakes," Brian said. "It wasn't your responsibility."

Jeff looked right at him and demanded, "But you thought it was my fault."

"Yeah," Brian admitted to Jeff. But that had to be wrong. "It wasn't," he told his old friend and, as he did, at last truly forgave him. "You were a child. Just a child. What happened to me wasn't your fault."

A bald man with severe black glasses, introduced by Grace as "a genius crisis manager," and two young women who worked for him at his PR company appeared with a video team, a camera operator, a lighting supervisor, and their gofer. The crisis manager put his glasses atop his hairless skull, explained they should make their own record of the conference in case the press did a poor job but, more important, to provide their own cut to local television stations around the country to "control the story." Grace then suggested they rehearse Brian's statement first and that's when he got to his feet, walked to the second bedroom in the vast suite, and locked the door.

In a moment, Jeff followed him and knocked. "You don't have to do a run-through, okay? That was a terrible idea. Sorry."

"I need to take a nap," Brian said. "I didn't get any sleep either."

"Okay, I'll come get you in a hour."

Brian used his cell to call home. The nurse answered, said his father was doing well, and put Danny on. "So?" His father huffed and puffed into the phone as if he had jogged five miles to the receiver. "You're going through with this fiasco?"

Brian explained what would happen, that it might hit the news as early as six, but probably cable first. "Try CNN if you're curious. Don't worry about what they say about me, Dad, if they bother with me at all. Jeff is the real show."

"They'll talk about everyone and everything. That's what they do. You aren't going to go into all the gory details of what that awful man did to you, I hope?"

"Yes, Dad. The details are important. The details are everything."

"Oh sweet Jesus. Why didn't you at least time this to the opening of your next play and do it on *Oprah*?"

"Never was good at self-promotion, Dad. Didn't have your genius for it."

"No need to bite me," Danny said breathlessly. "I'm not the child molester."

But you were, he thought bitterly as he hung up. Lying fully clothed on the made bed with his shoes on, like a corpse awaiting the undertaker, he admitted that he blamed Danny as much as anyone. He listened in a fury to the increasingly loud hubbub coming from the suite's living room. Sounded as if a thousand people were in there. He covered his eyes with the crook of his elbow and in that blindness thought, *I blame Jeff, I blame his mother, I blame his father, I blame my mother, I blame my father, I blame Klein, I blame Rydel, I blame me.*

He felt again the shock, the naive and stupid shock, of arriving at Jeff's door, having been ordered by his own red-eyed mother after yet another long phone call with the "dying" Harriet, to go up and play Jeff's brand-new board game, Risk. In fact, Jeff was at Hebrew school. Klein greeted him, pulled him close, putting his lips on Brian's, sticking his tongue between his teeth and down his throat. He had pulled away, revolted, retreated (again, stupidly) into the living room, thinking it too public for Klein to follow him there, as Klein then did, too public for Klein to dare, as Klein then did, to push him down on the sofa. The perfumed man opened his gray slacks—they must have been unbuttoned and unzipped already, his ridiculously big Thing growing out of a slit in his boxers. "It's nice to touch, isn't it? So hard and smooth . . ." His hand encircled Brian's skull and pushed him toward it. "Give it a little kiss . . ."

He had acted, for once, the real Brian at last, punching Klein as hard as he could in his bulbous stomach, and ran, out the door, down the stairs, onto the street, knowing he couldn't go home without explaining . . .

I should have told. Julie's right: I would have saved dozens of others. Jeff, Julie, Sam, the academy kids, the Huck Finn boys, everyone else was ignorant or greedy or scared or confused or overwhelmed by bullies, but I was strong enough—I could've pushed him away. I did push him away. I saved myself and let everyone else suffer. Me and the god of creation—we're the villains of this story.

BRIAN WAS RIGHT, of course. Simple black. And her mother's pearls to go with its mournful elegance. To have Ma for company, courageous and right-thinking, was a comfort.

"You look beautiful," Gary said in the unnaturally gentle voice he'd been using since she had told him about her past. She was heading for the front closet. He had been home unexpectedly, had forgone the weekly meeting at *American Justice* over developing stories. His eye had cleared up. There was a dashing bruise underneath, but otherwise eager neediness had returned to his chubby face. "When do we have to be at the news conference?"

She was irritated by his faux-innocent helpfulness. "*I* have to go back to the hotel now," she said. "I'm not sure if Jeff has scheduled the conference for five or six."

"I'll go with you," he said.

She shook her head.

"Honey, I know these people, the legal beat reporters. I can be helpful. Believe me, there are ways I can make sure they're civilized about this."

"Gary, I appreciate everything you've done, but I have to do this on my own."

His eager-to-please manner vanished. He breathed hard through his nose. "Are you coming home tonight?"

She shook her head. "I'll stay with Amelia. And I'll ask around, start looking for a place. We'll figure out about what to do about Zack when things calm down."

"What?" His startled reaction was genuine.

"It's not fair for you to have to move." She looked away from the astonished hurt contorting his features.

"You gotta be kidding. Right? You're kidding."

"This isn't the time to talk about it. I've already said it and I feel this way more than ever—I can't stay in our marriage. I can't be with you and be an honest person. I've been lying too long about every feeling. It's . . ." She paused, unable to figure out a way to make any kinder what she was doing to poor, needy Gary. "Nothing I do is going to be fair to you, so the sooner I get out of your way, the sooner I let you move on. That's the best I can do."

His eyes narrowed. His jaw set. He clenched his fists. He glared. He said, "I love you."

She nodded. "I have to go." She moved toward the closet.

Gary stepped in her way. He sneered. "You're not even going to have the decency to say a merciful 'I love you too'?"

"I do love you, Gary. I've lived my life with you. But that's not relevant to whether we can go on living together."

"Just tell me what you want in bed and I'll do it!" He laughed mordantly. "I might even like it, for chrissakes."

"Gary, this isn't something you can fix. You haven't done anything wrong. I was wrong. I'll tell Zack it's my fault. You can tell everybody I was very damaged, that I'm having a terrible crisis, a breakdown. All that's true and I won't contradict you. I'm the bad guy, no question about it. I have to go..." She tried to step around him.

He grabbed her arm and squeezed hard. He was flabby everywhere but in his arms; they had always been strong. "Ow," she complained, trying to tug away, but he clamped down, pulled her flush to him. His eyes were horrible in their honesty: shot through with hurt and fury, pain and loathing so complete she felt justly condemned. She surrendered. "Go ahead," she said. "Hit me. I deserve it."

"Is that what you like?" He grimaced saying each word, as if spitting up stones.

"Of course not." Her arm was going numb.

"I never stopped cheating on you." He pulled her closer, until their noses touched. "She wasn't the first and she wasn't the last. You wouldn't put out so I got laid whenever I felt like it." His breath was stale from coffee and, yes, cigarettes. "It was better, a lot better than fucking you."

"I'm sure," she said, waiting for him to finish this contest, because that's what he needed—to be the winner. "I'm broken, Gary. I don't work. Of course I can't satisfy you in bed. I can't satisfy you anywhere."

A dimming overcame his enraged eyes, hatred going out, a waning, like death. "Okay." He released the compression of her arm, although he held on. He let her move a step away from the stench of his angry fear, the odor of defeat. *Poor man. The lie of our marriage was good enough for him. I've spoiled his victory over love.*

"I'm sorry, Gary. I really am."

"I don't give a fuck you're sorry. If you can't see I'm doing everything for you, I'm bending over backward for you, that I've been patient for twenty-four years and you don't appreciate that I'm willing to be patient for the rest of my life . . ." His voice warbled. He released her with contempt. "Fuck you. Go to hell, you frigid bitch."

She was angry enough, then, to tell him she believed he was incapable of true sympathy, too selfish to feel as another feels, to defer his desires even for a few seconds. But she said nothing. She left mute and ashamed of her timidity. Any truth, even a mean one, she couldn't speak to the man she had wasted so much of her life on.

JEFF COAXED BRIAN out of hiding in the bedroom into the center of a three-ring circus, consisting of the PR people, their camera crew, the original two young lawyers, and a pair of dour, middle-aged lawyers who had joined them, Grace, her personal assistant, Jeff's pair of assistants, and several others in casual clothes, new to Brian, whom he couldn't immediately assign a role to. The hubbub of parallel conversations died down when he and Jeff entered, a Broadway audience readying itself for the show. They stared at Brian and Jeff, some with open curiosity, others with rueful looks that Brian supposed were meant to be sympathetic. *It's no big deal,* he wanted to shout. *I'm okay. It didn't do anything to me.*

He realized then his shallow, opportunistic, desperate-for-attention father was right—from now on all anyone would see was a little boy who had been diddled. And to make sure that's all they thought, since they'd soon forget his statement, he'd probably have to figure out a graceful way of slipping into every getting-acquainted conversation that he had merely been diddled, no cock shoved down his throat or up his ass, just masturbated, one disgusting kiss, his little penis put in Klein's mouth one time, his hand and lips refusing to touch Klein's one-eyed monster. *He only played with my penis!* Brian wanted to shout. Maybe he should have that printed on his business cards, right above his e-mail address.

"Could you show Brian the video?" Jeff asked. The hubbub resumed. Jeff had lured Brian out by saying he wanted to show him a recording of the statement he planned on making. Grace ushered Brian to a club chair opposite an enormous flat-screen TV, which the video crew had hooked up to the output of their camera. Brian noticed that three of the new people in the room, dressed in jeans and rumpled sweaters, were huddled around their laptops, consulting each other about something on their screens. He leaned over and saw that they all had the same file of prose up. So they were writers. Jeff had brought in three writers to tell his deepest secret.

"Am I supposed to give you notes?" Brian asked of Jeff, who was sipping a Diet Coke, pacing behind him, surrounded by employees who kept whispering questions, as if he were on a set between takes.

"Yeah, you bet. I like notes. Unlike you. If they're good, I use them. If not, I ignore them. I've never understood why writers get so upset about notes." He came to a halt and stared provocatively at Brian as if this were a long-standing quarrel he wanted settled. As far as Brian knew, they had never discussed the value of notes.

"This is your life story, Jeff. I don't see how I can give you notes on your life. What you feel is what you feel, what you say happened is what you say happened. It's not a plot point that's up for a vote."

The room had fallen silent again, Jeff's entourage watching them with fearful expectancy, as if they were about to draw six guns. Jeff threw up his hands. "Just watch and tell me what you think, okay?"

Grace started the video. Brian did his best to concentrate while feeling everyone's eyes on him. Jeff's brisk, brash tone and manner distracted him at first. It was hard to believe Jeff could speak so blandly and efficiently about it. First Jeff explained the family relationships, said that his mother was a very neurotic and troubled woman who today would probably be diagnosed as chronically depressed, that his father worked a hundred hours a week trying to make his failing stationery store a success, and that Richard Klein pretended to be a caring relative, loaning Jeff's father money and offering to take Jeff and his friends out to ball games, museums, Broadways shows, and the like while taking advantage of those occasions to sexually abuse Jeff and later his best friend, Brian, and eventually his cousin Julie. Jeff buried and whitewashed the depth of his mother's complicity, Brian believed, by briefly mentioning that when his mother found out, she stopped Klein from bothering him but didn't go to the authorities because by then the family was completely dependent on Klein financially. Jeff went on to explain about Klein's "adopting" Sam Rydel. Without other specifics, he said that Klein raped him in front of Rydel and ordered him to sexually service Rydel. He raised his voice when he said rape, fairly shouting it. Afterward, Klein threatened Jeff that he would bankrupt his father's store if he told anyone. Jeff said being raped had happened only once because he was injured by the experience and Klein became frightened that he would be discovered. Once he reached puberty, Klein seemed to lose all interest in him and his friends and left him alone. Jeff said his shame and concern for his parents' feelings, especially his mentally unstable mother, prevented him, while he was a child, from believing he could safely tell the world about what had happened, and after the sexual abuse stopped, he went into a state of complete denial that he was still struggling to overcome. He said he convinced himself that Klein had stopped bothering everyone, that he was ashamed to admit that he had agreed initially to be on the board of Klein's broadcasting school as part of his severe and crippling state of denial and also to mollify his mother who was still living at the time. He said he had had no dealings with Klein after Harriet died in 1988 and that he had not seen Sam Rydel since then, other than a recent face-to-face urging him to confess to his crimes. Jeff explained that as part of his condition of living in severe denial he had convinced himself Rydel was solely a victim of Klein's and never suspected that Rydel was a danger to anyone. He regretted his silence, but it was part of his nearly total repression about what had happened to him as a child. He said his own trauma had made relationships difficult, saddled him with anxiety attacks that required medication, had ruined two marriages, and left him, to this day, with nightmares and insomnia. He went on to explain that although the statute of limitations had run out on what Klein and Rydel had done to him, he believed he needed to speak up now that it had become clear Rydel was a continuing danger to society. He concluded by saying he would be going into therapy to fully explore his memories, some of which he assumed he was still suppressing, and that he hoped this public statement was the first step toward healing.

His loud, irritable tone of voice as he hurried through the painful words combined with a blank expression throughout, as if he were giving a weather forecast, made his unemotional, pop-psychology statement profoundly moving.

Jeff, Brian saw out of the corner of his eye, was watching him. He wasn't sure he could talk without yawning into tears, so he cleared his throat a few times. Still, he couldn't speak.

"Well?" Jeff asked. "What do you think? Sugarman hasn't cleared the legal language. But how do you think it plays?"

"Could I talk to you alone?" Brian managed to speak without his voice quavering.

"Give us the room, please," Jeff said.

Most of the assembled left as from a burning building. The quartet of lawyers lingered, slowly packing up their laptops and scanner. Grace got them to hustle out by saying, "Just leave everything where it is. Jeff and Brian won't steal your stuff."

Once they were completely alone, Brian said, "You say Klein raped you, but you don't go into any detail."

"Jesus Christ, isn't saying 'rape' enough? Anyway, what's the point of itemizing? Everyone's going to hear whatever the hell they can stand to disgust themselves with. They won't hear what I'm actually saying. The only thing that's going to matter to anyone today is that Klein and Rydel are sick fucks. Besides, you're giving all those details about Cousin Richard and how he involved Rydel into his sick games. And Julie's gonna talk about that stuff too. It's just repetitive. Less is more, right?"

"No. Less is less and more is more. If more is tedious, you don't say more, but if more is new information, you do. What things did Klein force you to do with Rydel? Did Sam do things to you? Klein tried to force me to give him a blow job. We heard Julie say he made her do it to both of them. Did he make Rydel do that to you? Or was Rydel a willing participant? I mean, set the scene. Say what the fuck happened."

"I can't." Jeff strode two steps toward the window, then back to the couch, then toward the door, then stopped where he had started. "I can't even think about it. I know you're able to remember every fucking detail, but I can't." He folded his arms over his chest as if ready to be buried. "Every time I try to remember, I can't breathe . . ." He dropped to his knees and rocked back onto his ass, propped against the wall, a hand clutching his throat. "I feel like I'm going to pass out."

Brian searched for a crack in this facade of panic. Jeff's face was flushed. His chest was heaving. His eyes were wild with fear. He gasped, breathing faster and faster, gulping air. Still Brian wasn't convinced. But what was he going to do, keep pressing Jeff until he had a persuasive heart attack? "Okay," Brian conceded. "You don't have to."

That didn't stop Jeff's distress. "I'm hyperventilating," he said. He doubled over. "Get Grace," he gasped.

Brian was persuaded. He ran down the hall, opened the door, almost laughed at the sight of the mob standing in the hallway like school children being punished for talking in class. "Grace. You. Just you," he said, and let her in.

She came prepared. She produced an airplane sick bag from her purse. Jeff breathed into it, slower and slower as he calmed. Grace rested a hand on Jeff's head and stroked, a maternal gesture. She grinned at Brian. "Sometimes I'm asked to talk to film students about what a producer does exactly. I tell them to be ready for anything."

Jeff lowered the bag. "I'm okay," he said hoarsely.

"Sure?" Grace asked. Jeff nodded. "Okay, boys," she said, adopting them as her children. "Sugarman wants to talk to both of you."

"He's not going to try to talk us out of it, is he?" Brian asked.

"Yes," Grace said. She raised a hand defensively. "I told him that was useless. But it's his job to advise you about the law. So you have to listen. You don't have to agree, but you have to listen." She looked at Brian. "If you get on the extension in the bedroom, we won't have to use a speaker."

Brian was glad to be alone again in the bedroom, but he soon regretted that he couldn't keep an eye on Jeff's reaction to what Sugarman had to say. The lawyer got right to the point: "These statements leave you both vulnerable for being sued for slander and defamation of character and they don't qualify as evidence of anything to do with the charges the state AG might bring against Rydel. Or Klein. But if Klein's senile, then it's really just Rydel we're talking about. All you're doing is handing Rydel a court case he can actually win. He can divert all the bad PR about what he allegedly did to those disadvantaged boys to make the conversation about the senile Klein, who isn't going to be able to contradict anything Rydel says, so Rydel can turn what you can testify to into how Rydel was a victim and keep the press focused on Jeff's childhood. This is a win for him, in my opinion. If I were representing Rydel, I'd tell him this was a blessing in disguise."

Brian had thought he was prepared to hear any legalistic discouragement, but Sugarman's take was far more disheartening than anything he had imagined. He hoped Jeff would respond, but there was only silence from his end. Brian took on the lawyer himself: "You haven't seen a statement from Julie, correct? She's also going to say Sam Rydel molested her, specifically that he put his penis in her mouth."

"I don't have any paper from her, but I've been briefed by Jeff about her story. This is your cousin, Jeff, whom you were talking about earlier, is that correct?"

"Uh-huh." Jeff's response was barely audible.

"And what Rydel did to her, as with what he did to you Jeff, was at the instigation of Richard Klein, correct?"

"Uh-huh," Jeff mumbled.

Brian said, "Yes, but Julie will say that Rydel was a willing participant and that corroborates Jeff's account that he was molested by Rydel. I know my statement isn't that on point when it comes to Rydel, so I thought hers would make a difference."

"Well, you're certainly right, Brian, that your statement is completely irrelevant," Sugarman said. "In fact, I think you are the most vulnerable to a lawsuit for slander, invasion of privacy, and defamation of character. My advice to you is that you drop out of this altogether, whether or not Jeff and his cousin go forward."

Brian was staggered by this dismissal, hurt and shamed to hear that the deep wound of his life, the distorting event that had colored every relationship, was irrelevant and inconsequential. He had struggled for forty years to have the courage to talk about what Klein had done to him, and now he was told that if he insisted on telling his story he would be sued into penury or humiliated into conceding that his precious truth was slander. Like a child, all he wanted to do was cry and go home.

It was Jeff who answered Sugarman. "I think we need Brian. He confirms our stories about Cousin Richard and also he backs up that Rydel was part of it all."

"Frankly, I don't think it's prudent for any of you to go public. But especially not Brian. You asked me to act as his attorney as well, and my best advice is that what he's got to say, in the context of your statements, defames Rydel without proffering an account of any wrongdoing on Rydel's part. So, in effect, Brian is slandering him through guilt by association. I believe Brian's statement plays into Rydel's hand. If I were Rydel's attorney, I'd pursue a separate suit against Brian for slander and invasion of privacy, making it as expensive and embarrassing as possible for Brian to go through the process. Meanwhile I'd privately offer to drop the lawsuit in exchange for Brian's retracting his public statement, in effect recanting. And as Brian's attorney, I'd have to advise him to grab that offer. That would take Brian's statement out of evidence in the lawsuits against you and Julie and also look bad for your PR. Classic divide and conquer."

"I'll pay Brian's legal bills," Jeff said.

"He'd still get dragged through the courts, having to repeat again and again that Rydel did nothing to him and making his private life subject to investigation."

Brian interrupted. "I'm making my . . ." He had to swallow down whatever it was that wanted to erupt. Tears? Rage? He cleared his throat. Still couldn't talk. He cleared it again. "Excuse me. I'm making my statement, all alone if I have to. And I won't settle if Rydel sues me. Jeff doesn't have to pay a nickel. I'll go bankrupt, live on the streets. I won't settle. Hear me? I'm not fucking settling!" Rage, that's what had come out of him.

"I'm just giving legal advice," Sugarman said, maddeningly free of emotion. "It's my responsibility to provide you and Jeff the best counsel I can. What you do with it is your decision, of course."

"Listen, Ed." All of a sudden Jeff sounded relaxed and confident. "We can't do nothing, okay? It's out there. We've told enough people so that it's sure to leak out. I have no illusions about that. So we have to go forward with some kind of statement. My question is, what can we do to lessen our exposure?"

"Don't hold a press conference. That's over the top, anyway, in my view. Maybe go on a talk show like *Oprah*. Better yet, have Brian write an article about what happened to him. Let Rydel come into the story gradually, as a bystander. In Brian's piece, he wouldn't be accused of anything other than being used by Klein. It might even read as an apologia for him. That would insulate Brian from being accused of defamation of character. Then we let Rydel's attorneys know that you and Julie are about to come forward, as if Brian's article encouraged you and your cousin to tell your stories. In the interval, I could start talking with Rydel's lawyers, coax them into his making a deal with the attorney general. If you haven't gone public, I can turn a lawsuit threat from him around, that if they respond by suing, we will countersue him, and then we can call witnesses, including his alleged victims, and basically try him in civil court, the way the families nailed O. J. In other words, doing a slow rollout allows Rydel time to see he's doomed eventually, and so he might as well make as favorable a deal as possible with the attorney general. After all, what you all have to say is a mitigating circumstance for him. He was a vulnerable, orphaned boy who was abused. But if you start out with a full-blown news conference, damning him as a sex abuser forty years ago, before he can negotiate with the AG, then he's got no choice but to fight you to the last dollar. And he's got thirty million of 'em."

"Julie won't agree to that," Brian said. He was hiding behind her skirts, but he had to; he wasn't impressing this lawyer at all.

"Yeah, she won't agree to that, Ed," Jeff said. "She thinks every day we don't say anything, we're responsible for every bad thing Rydel does."

"And she's right," Brian said.

"That's another point I want to raise," Sugarman said. "You have to be very careful here, Jeff, you in particular. You were on the board of the American Broadcasting Academy."

"I wasn't paid!" Jeff said, voice rising with outrage. "In fact, my crazy mother made me give Cousin Richard money to start the fucking thing and I never took a penny. I was long gone when he took it public."

Sugarman chuckled. "I'm not talking about who gave what to whom, Jeff. Your name on the board makes it conceivable that Klein's or Rydel's victims could sue you for failing to do your due diligence—"

"Oh, for fuck's sake!" Brian's temper took over. Words rasped out of him recklessly. "Even for a lawyer, this is chickenshit bullshit. Jeff cut off all communication with Klein and Rydel twenty-five years ago, right, Jeff? Are you telling the truth about that? 'Cause if you're not, then fuck you. I hope they all sue you. I hope you fucking lose everything."

"Okay, let's settle down," the high-handed lawyer said.

Nothing came from Jeff's end. Brian soon discovered why.

The bedroom door flew open. Jeff, red-faced, screamed at Brian: "FUCK YOU!" He slammed the door behind him. "HOW DARE YOU FUCKING ACCUSE ME. NOTHING HAPPENED TO YOU, YOU FUCKING WHINER. HE TOUCHED YOU A FEW TIMES, SO THE FUCK WHAT! HE SHOVED HIS COCK IN MY MOUTH OVER AND OVER. HE MADE ME—" He stopped as if shot. He was tilted forward, arms akimbo, a teetering statue.

"Jeff?" Brian said.

Jeff straightened, face blank. He backed up into a chair by a small desk, facing the bed. He sat erect, avoiding eye contact, a passenger in a crowded subway car. There was a long silence. A fan buried somewhere in the ceiling turned on. Brian felt hot air drift down to them. He was sweating. He thought about lowering the thermostat but didn't want to disturb whatever was happening inside Jeff. His mind drifted, wondering how Julie was doing.

Eventually someone knocked timidly.

Jeff didn't move, fixed on a inner landscape.

He hoped it was Julie. "Come in?" Brian said.

Grace entered. She looked at Jeff. He didn't acknowledge her presence. "Should I tell Ed you're done talking?" she asked his profile.

Jeff blinked, his nose twitched; otherwise he didn't move.

"Yeah," Brian said.

Grace nodded. She seemed hesitant to go. She looked at Brian. "Are you going to write a play about this?"

Startled, Brian laughed. "What?"

"I think you should write about this. I know it'll be very painful, unimaginably painful, but it'll be your best work." She opened the door and added as she left, "Make a great movie too."

Brian asked Jeff, "Can you believe that shit? Child molesters—producers. Is there really a difference?"

No laugh from the grim Jeff, agape at nothing. Was he catatonic?

Eventually Jeff crossed his legs, took a deep breath, and fixed on Brian. "We're gonna do this, right?"

"Yep."

"All of us, just like we agreed before?"

"Julie's not gonna back out. And I'm not."

"My mother loved me," Jeff said. "Lots of people say they love me. Maybe they do. But I know, I fucking know, my mother loved me. She was the only person I can be sure really, really loved me."

Brian nodded. "I loved you, Jeff."

"As long as I was a good friend. But Ma loved me no matter what."

Brian nodded. The buried fan shut off. The funnel of heat stopped. From the other room, Brian smelled fresh coffee. More room service? He supposed he had to say the obvious, but he took no pleasure in telling Jeff, "But your mother was a monster."

"Yeah," Jeff agreed. "But she was *my* monster."

"I understand," Brian said, and he did.

Jeff released a long sigh. He leaned forward, engaged again, solemnly resolved. "So . . . one question."

"Just one?" Brian smiled.

"You really think it'll help? I mean, after I tell my story, and go into intensive therapy, real therapy, not the whining I've been doing, but really try to call up all the memories, learn yoga, cry on *Oprah,* whatever. You really think, Bri, after all that . . ." He stopped, staring, stiffening again into paralysis.

"Yeah?" Brian prompted.

Jeff was solemn, reverent: "You really think this'll help me win an Oscar?"

Last Chance

—— February 2008 ——

JULIE WAS SURPRISED to find glamorous Grace waiting for her as she stepped off the elevator onto the penthouse floor. As the producer hooked her arm, she announced with glee that Ann Barnes and Gil Fleider, "genius hair and makeup," had set up shop in the suite's cavernous master bathroom and were waiting "to make you beautiful."

Julie was thrilled. She pretended to be offended: "Jeff thinks I need a makeover?"

"Honey, I didn't mean just you. They're here to do Jeff and Brian. I'm even having them do me and I won't be on camera." Grace led the way into the suite.

While Julie was downtown, the place had been transformed, crowded with people and high-tech equipment, as well as littered with half-eaten room-service trays.

"Wow," she said.

Brian appeared. "You okay? You were gone three hours. Something happen?"

"Gary was there. I told him we're done," she said. Brian blanched.

That was irritating. "Don't look so scared," she said. "It's got nothing to do with you."

Brian glanced pointedly at Grace, who was openly eavesdropping.

"So," Julie asked the producer, "when are they going to make me beautiful?"

Gil, a young black man with a completely shaved head, wearing black jeans so tight they could be subcutaneous, spoke in an English accent from the master bedroom doorway. "With your lovely bone structure, I won't have to do very much." He extended a beckoning hand, offering more compliments as an incentive. "Look at those cheeks. Just a shading here and there"—he waved his hand, illustrating—"to highlight what God has given you." He led her into the bathroom, put her in an armless leather chair borrowed from the suite's dining room, facing a floor-to-ceiling mirror. With every touch of his brush, Gil covered her with praise. She wasn't sure what made her feel more lovely, the makeup or his flattery.

Meanwhile Ann, whose own hair was pulled back into an efficient ponytail, studied Julie's shapeless gray helmet. When she took over from Gil, she quickly shaped the sides and back into an elegant cap, mysteriously managing with a blow-dryer to give it body. While snipping here and there, Ann made a hair color suggestion. "I love this dramatic silver—frank aging—but I think some contrast would be really nice. Salt and pepper. Nothing punk. Distinguished. And you have thick, lustrous hair; you should let it grow out, all the way, down your straight back to emphasize your great posture." Ann turned to Gil. "She has great posture, doesn't she?"

"Fabulous," Gil said.

"Be a woman warrior," Ann whispered as she removed the smock.

Julie laughed. "A warrior? Me?" But she knew she looked confident and younger, the best she had in years.

They brought in Jeff to approve, as if she were the leading lady. Brian, glum and pale, appeared at the door. "You better do something about that pale face." She nodded at Brian's reflection.

"I'll get color onto that Irish pallor," Gil said, tugging Brian into the chair.

Jeff teased, "You'd better trim him around the ears. He's looking like a scruffy old man."

Brian balked, trying to rise. "I don't need this. I'll just keep my head down and read my statement. They won't see my face."

Gil pushed him back down. "Writers. Scared of the camera."

"Yeah," Jeff said. "That's always been Bri's problem. He's too shy."

"I'm not shy," Brian complained.

"You've always been too shy. Didn't you know that?"

Brian frowned, became thoughtful, passively accepting Gil and Ann's ministrations. Julie stood behind him, smiling encouragement into the mirror while Gil erased the shadows under his eyes, filled in the scar of worry marring his high forehead. Then Ann snipped a few hairs atop but mostly trimmed his nose hairs and ears. "Don't watch me. This is humiliating," he said to Julie's reflection in the glass.

"I like looking at you," she said. "It's comforting."

He stared at her. A mischievous glint appeared. He stood up before Ann was done. "It's fine," he said impatiently, pulling off the smock. "I have to talk to you." He took Julie's hand, towing her through the rush-hour mob into the living room. She noticed Jeff was looking at a video of himself on TV, huddled with Grace and three young men in jeans and sweaters, all of them talking over each other. Brian pulled her into a second bedroom and shut the door.

"What's Jeff doing?" she asked as Brian moved close.

"They're fussing over his statement. Tone, bullshit, whether to add anything about Halley and his wonderful children. PR crap." Brian stared into her eyes while he somberly laid a hand below her mother's pearls, on the bare skin above her scoop neck. His fingers skimmed down beneath the black fabric, two fingers insinuating under her strapless bra cup until he found and framed her nipple. He sighed with relief. "Watching you all dressed up in a room of people. It was making me crazy." He pinched once, hard, and released. She was immediately deboned, loose everywhere. "Again please," she said.

He stepped away, hand departing roughly, jangling her pearls. "Can't do this now," he said in a husky voice.

"We'll ask Jeff to get us a room after the conference."

He didn't care for her joke. He frowned. She reached for him, but he stepped back. "I'm teasing," she said.

"I wish you'd stayed with Gary," he mumbled at the carpet.

She thought about getting angry, decided not to. "Why?" she asked.

He didn't answer.

"You don't have to marry me," she said. "You don't even have to live with me. I think you'd be happier, I know I would be, but you don't have to."

"You don't understand. Sex has always been a dirty thing, a shameful secret I cherished, something that was all my own, the only thing that truly belonged to me. I don't know if I can enjoy it if it's okay . . . just a fun game I share. I don't think so. It will have lost its purpose."

"Why are you trying to figure everything out in advance?" She sat on the bed, smoothed her dress, picking off white lint here and there, hoping her casualness would soothe him. "We'll see what happens. I'm not going to stay with Gary. Period. Doesn't have anything to do with what happens with us."

"Then marry someone else so we can cheat."

She smiled at his joke. He looked grim. "You're . . . serious?" she asked, for the first time unsettled by his attitude. "You won't just let us be whatever kind of couple we can be? It has to be secret . . . ?" She groped for another word, something else that it was: "It has to be perverted?"

"It *is* perverted," Brian said. "What we have together is born out of perversion. We can't make it into something healthy."

"Why not?" she argued. She was, for the first time in her life, confident of her desires, assured of their rightness. "What we can't do is try to bury it, pretend it never happened, that we're normal. But we can make it ours. All ours."

He covered his face with his hands, to get away from her, it seemed. When he lowered them, he looked very sad. "You know what Jeff's lawyer advised me?"

"Not to go public, right? Jeff called me while I was on my way here. He said that's what his lawyer advised all of us."

"But especially me. You know why? 'Cause I'm irrelevant." Half of a sob escaped Brian. He choked it off and said bitterly, "My fucking life is irrelevant. My work is crippled, I have no children, I'm scared to fall in love, and my story is fucking irrelevant." His makeup-smoothed face shattered.

She hurried over, gathering him as he keened, laying his wet cheek on her scoop collar, temple resting on her mother's pearls. She held him while he wept without restraint, squeezed him tight and kissed the top of his trembling head. He was whispering something through his tears, and when she shifted, to bring her ear closer, to her amazement she heard something from a man she loved that she had never heard before. "Thank you," he whispered. "Thank you."

WHILE GIL FIXED him up again for the cameras, Brian listened to the excitement building in the suite. Even Jeff and Julie seemed to be vaguely happy about this humiliating act of public revelation. He wondered if Jeff had understood his life better than his shrinks, better than himself. He was shy. That was all. Shy of fighting for what he wants. Yes, he had pushed Klein away, but he had never embraced himself.

When they transferred to a small room adjoining the Four Seasons' banquet space where the press was gathering, Julie became unhappily nervous, asking Grace for a bottle of water, saying that her mouth was dry. Jeff too got edgy, after his second phone call from what sounded like a very agitated Halley. Brian listened more to Jeff's tone than to what he said to his third wife. He was reassuring and soothing in an unnaturally patient way, as if he were dealing with someone who was slightly mad and certainly someone he feared at least a little. *He's handling his mother,* Brian thought, and then dismissed that explanation as being too easy.

Grace left the trio alone to make sure everything was ready. Jeff turned into an eight-year-old, teasing Brian that Ann spent more time removing hair from his nose than his bald head. Brian replied that Jeff should have asked Gil to give him a chin. After Julie finished an entire pint of water in three slugs, he took her hand and she moved into his arms. Jeff was silenced by that sight. Brian shot him a warning look.

"I'm not saying anything," Jeff said, and then, behind Julie's back, fucked his left palm with the right hand's index finger.

Grace reappeared to warn them, "Five minutes."

"I need to pee," Julie said, and went off with Grace.

Jeff sighed, tried to rub his face off but stopped when Brian said, "Makeup."

"Fuck," Jeff said. "Do I need a touch-up?"

Brian shook his head.

"Bri," Jeff asked in a sweet tone, the innocent wonder of a child, "you think Rydel had a choice?"

"Doesn't matter," he said. "We still have to say what we know."

"Yeah, yeah. But. I just want your opinion. As a fucking expert in character. Do you think he had any real choice about what he became?"

"No," Brian admitted. "I don't. Klein took that away from him. But we have to make sure Rydel doesn't rob another child of that choice."

They were silent, Jeff pacing, breathing faster, Brian watching him anxiously until Grace returned with Julie and said it was time. The producer couldn't suppress her excitement, as if this were the release of a movie. She breathlessly reported they had a great crowd of all the entertainment and crime-beat reporters, including the *Times* and all the networks.

"Did we get them something to nosh?" Jeff asked as they gathered at the banquet door.

"You kidding? Of course I put out a big spread," Grace said. "You have to feed the press or they'll eat *you*."

The growls coming from the banquet room sounded as if they were still famished.

"Ready?" Grace asked, a hand ready to open the double doors.

Jeff was breathing shallowly and rapidly. Julie wobbled. Brian caught her elbow. He told himself, *I'm here for them. That's my relevance.* "You've got your statement, right?" he asked her.

Julie nodded, opening a black purse, taking out a folded page of yellow legal-pad paper. The lines were filled to the bottom in a meticulous hand.

"Jesus." Jeff swallowed hard. "Listen to them. They're fucking animals."

"You took something, right?" Brian asked. "Beta-blocker, something?"

"Yeah, old school. A Valium. I'm okay," he said. He nodded at Grace and she opened the doors.

The sounds and lights of the press washed over them like a wave breaking. They drowned in the flashes, whirring cameras, predatory microphones. He looked at Jeff. What he saw was alarming. In the last few days, Brian thought he had been exposed to the full spectrum of his childhood friend's emotions: anger, defensiveness, fatigue, amusement, sadness, superiority, defeat, and that old friend, anxiety. But now there was pure fear in those bugged-out eyes, the frantic terror of a cornered animal—he was ready to bolt. "Come on." He took Jeff's elbow. With his other arm, he hooked Julie's. He led them forward.

Either Jeff wasn't up to resisting or he was too frightened to. He allowed Brian to tow him. The plan was for Jeff to sit in the center with Brian and Julie on either side, but Jeff took the chair on the right, leaving Brian in the middle.

Facing the mass of people and equipment overwhelmed him. He dropped his eyes to his lap, down from the blossoms of microphones and three dozen rows of chairs filled with journalists ranging from heavily made-up perky television personalities to the gloomy, pale faces of cynical beat reporters. Brian looked to Jeff. He was supposed to speak first. Jeff's panicked eyes raked across Brain, seeking the door. *He's going to run. It's too late and it makes no sense, but he's going to run anyway.*

Grace, at one side of the table, announced to the crowd, "This is Jeff Mark, Brian Moran, and Julie Rosen. They're each going to make a statement and then you can ask questions." She cued them, then ducked away.

Brian looked up. Peering into the flares of camera lights, he could only make out a row of legs, a woman's stockings, a man's gray slacks. Jeff was staring at the microphones as if they were going to eat him alive. A line of sweat ran down the side of his cheek, through the pancake, a fine streak of dust appearing at its edges. *Poor man, what have I done to him?* He turned to Julie and whispered, "You ready?"

She nodded. "You start," she said. She stared boldly at the crowd, chin up, black eyes glittering with curiosity, and she abruptly smiled with joy. *Was she crazy to look forward with happiness?*

Brian turned to the terrified man beside him. "You ready?" he whispered. Jeff bowed his head and leaned his temple, very slightly, on Brian's forehead. To the press, they must have look like conspirators. Jeff whispered, "I can't, Bri. I can't do this. I'm sorry. I gotta get out of here." Jeff straightened his back. His right hand came up, beneath the tablecloth, grabbing the wooden edge as if to propel him away.

Brian reached for Jeff's other hand, out of sight from the crowd, before it could rise to help him escape. Brian pressed his flesh into another's harder than he could remember ever doing before, although that was a trick of memory. He must have held his mother's hand like that, or his father's, when he was scared or lonely or in need of comfort. And he would hold Julie's hand that way when he needed her and she needed him, at least he felt sure of that. He squeezed his old friend's hand fiercely for a moment, then relaxed his grip enough so Jeff could escape if he wanted to. This time Brian would not let himself be shy. He would lead the way, after all.

"My name is Brian Moran." His voice strengthened. "When I was eight years old . . ." Jeff's hand slipped out partway. Brian continued talking, willing to let him go, but Jeff did not depart. He held on while Brian told their secrets, and thus comforting each other, hand in hand, they faced the future of their past.

ACKNOWLEDGMENTS

I am eager to thank Donna Redel, Tamar Cole, Henry Bean, Susan Bolotin, Ben Cheever, Nicholas Kazan, Alison Petrocelli, Brian Platzer, John Mc-Namara, Gene Stone, Ayelet Waldman, and Liza Zeidner for reading earlier drafts of *The Wisdom of Perversity.* They all provided valuable guidance and advice, as well as encouragement when it was most needed. I owe much more than a well-served client's debt to Lynn Nesbit. This novel would never have been published without her loyalty, persistence and intelligence. That is also true of Chuck Adams, a kind and brilliant editor, who rescued this story from its literary flaws and from the timidity of the marketplace.